THE OLD
CAPE HOUSE

BARBARA EPPICH STRUNA

Cover Design by Loretta Matson
and Timothy Jon Struna

Edited by Nicola Burnell

*This is a work of fiction. Names, characters, places, brands, media, and
incidents are either the product of the author's imagination or are used
fictitiously. Any resemblance to similarly named places or to persons living or
deceased is unintentional.*

2nd Edition

PRINT ISBN: 978-0-9976566-0-2

Library of Congress Control Number: 2014902200

"Artfully weaving together historical and contemporary narratives, *The Old Cape House* conjures up the magic and mystery of Cape Cod legends, past and present. A delightful read for lovers of history and storytelling."

—James Lang, Author of *Learning Sickness: A Year with Crohn's Disease* (Capital Books, 2004) and *Cheating Lessons: Learning from Academic Dishonesty* (Harvard University Press, 2013).

"Struna's novel is a beautifully written story that grabs the reader from the beginning and doesn't let go."

—Saralee Perel, Award Winning Columnist and Author of *Cracked Nuts & Sentimental Journeys: Stories From a Life Out of Balance.*

I dedicate this book
to all women of the past
who sought freedom to be themselves
and dance under the moon.

December 1715
EASTHAM – CAPE COD

THE DAMP WALLS OF EASTHAM'S JAIL felt cold to the touch. Maria Hallett was grateful that her dear friend Abigail had insisted she dress in layers. The extra clothes were warm to her back during the night as she lay on a small, narrow bench against the wall. The rough, uneven cobbles were slippery underfoot as Maria pushed her crude bed toward the opposite wall and under a high slender window. If she climbed atop the bench, grabbed the iron bars, and pulled herself up on her toes, she could catch sight of the sky. The crisp air chilled her body more than she could stand, but the sight of the soaring gulls and billowy clouds gave her a glimpse of freedom and hope for mercy.

Two days had passed with no comforting word from anyone. The third morning's sunrise brought with it the arrival of Abigail. Relieved to see a familiar face, Maria reached out through the tall iron bars of the door and pleaded with her, "What's going to happen to me?"

"Be calm, my dear. I'll tell you what I know." Abigail held the young girl's trembling hands. "Your trial is tomorrow. The weather is too treacherous for the magistrate of courts to come from Plymouth. Reverend Treat and the elders of the church will preside."

"Please don't leave me," Maria begged.

"I'll remain at the proceedings until a verdict is reached." Abigail touched Maria's cheek. "Pray, Maria! If asked, I'll speak in favor of you as much as I can. I must go now; they have given me only minutes with you. Pray!"

Maria stretched her fingers through the bars and into the frigid air. She begged again, "Abigail, don't leave me!" As her friend disappeared behind the heavy wooden door that led to the outside, she screamed in desperation, "ABIGAIL!"

Maria sat on the rigid bench and fixed an empty stare at the toes of her tattered leather shoes. She leaned her body over to one side and slowly dropped down onto the thin cushion of skirts that served as mattress and pillow. Her legs curled into a fetal position and as Maria's eyes closed, she remembered when she first met Sam.

1

Nine Months Earlier – April 1715
EASTHAM – CAPE COD

MARIA HALLETT FEARED THE WRATH OF HER FATHER. Afraid to disturb his sleep, she silently dropped the latch on the weathered door. The grasses, damp with dew from the cool night, wet the leather shoes of the fifteen-year-old girl as she walked to work. She hummed a childhood lullaby through the pine grove; the gentle song was her only comfort since her mother's death. As she stepped forward onto the dirt path that led to Smith's Tavern, questions about her future filtered into Maria's head like the sunlight through the trees across the foggy cart way.

"Good morrow, Mr. Smith."

"Good morrow to you, Maria," the tavern owner echoed back. Descending the cellar stairs to take count of his supplies, Smith called over his shoulder, "There's plenty for you to do. We've new faces in the village and my rooms are full. Start with those dirty tankards and platters on the sideboard."

Maria went to work cleaning the tables. She moved quietly among the local townsfolk and travelers, all mingling about the tavern, each tending to his individual business. Maria wished she was one of them.

At the noon hour, she asked Smith, "May I stop for a short while, sir?"

The tavern owner agreed, but cautioned the girl. "Remember I don't pay for sitting."

Outside the warm spring air smelled fresh and salty to Maria as she settled under a beautiful blossomed apple tree. She pulled her coarse linen skirting around her legs and down to the grass. Beside her was a tied canvas cloth holding her midday meal. She opened the thick material and flattened it across her lap. Clouds drifted above her head as she took small bites of a greasy strip of beef, then a dried apple and finally a nibble of biscuit.

In the distance, a man approached. As he came nearer, Maria noticed he was older than she was, tall in height and very pleasing. His long black hair fell loose around his broad shoulders.

Maria straightened her back and hoped he would notice her.

The stranger's face became more animated as he walked nearer. "Good day, Miss."

Maria lowered her eyes.

He picked a blossom from a branch above her head and offered it to her.

She slowly looked up at him.

With a bow, he said, "Your beauty brings wonder to my eyes and far surpasses this delicate blossom."

His words sounded gentle to Maria. She blushed as she reached out for his gift.

He laughed, and in one bold movement, sat next to her under the tree. Leaning close to her shoulder, he said, "Don't be afraid of me, I'm on my way to seek fortune from the sea. But finding you under this splendid tree is a happy distraction—one, which I'm eager to keep enjoying."

Maria thought him very well mannered.

"May I introduce myself?" he asked.

Maria nodded in approval and this time did not lower her eyes.

"I'm Sam Bellamy. With whom do I have the pleasure of meeting?"

She nervously adjusted her cap and in a whisper replied, "Maria Hallett."

"May I call you Maria?"

"Yes." She felt a smile grow across her face.

"Are you traveling or do you live nearby?"

"I live a short distance from here and work at the tavern."

He glanced over to where she pointed.

His scent of rum and tobacco drifted towards Maria. She took a deep breath and watched him, noticing his clothes, his hair, and his blue eyes. For a moment, Maria's words seemed to be trapped inside of her. She just smiled and studied him even more. He was interesting. He made her laugh. Within a short time, Maria found her voice and began to chat back and forth with him in idle conversation. He seemed as if he were listening to her, and Maria found his attention irresistible. She felt special. She twirled her hair around her finger; he leaned back on his elbow.

As the hour passed, the two grew friendlier and Sam inched his body closer to Maria. He placed his hand on her knee and asked, "Shall we meet again?"

Maria knew a girl of her age should not be alone with strange men, but Sam intrigued her. Uncertain, but curious to discover more about this mysterious man, she couldn't help herself and dismissed her concerns. "There's the old abandoned McKeon house, not too far from here."

Sam smiled. "Where is it?"

Maria gave him directions and they set the time for noon the next day. He helped her up from under the tree and kissed her delicate hand. She felt her cheeks turn red as the charming stranger whispered, "Until we meet again, Miss Maria Hallett."

He looked pleased as he stepped backward, turned and walked away. She watched him disappear around a bend in the road. Maria gathered her things and wondered if this could be a chance for happiness. Could it be a way to leave her father and the loveless life that she was accustomed to? Unafraid, she would go to meet him, against everything she knew to be right, and find out more about this Sam Bellamy.

2

Present Day – Early June
CAPE COD

CARS AND SEMI-TRAILER TRUCKS WHIZZED BY the blue van as I reached for a bottle of water. I took a drink, glanced at the number of miles that had passed and decided to tell everyone behind me how far we'd travelled, even if they didn't want to hear. "We've driven 456 miles and we've got 350 more to go before we reach Cape Cod." No response from all four kids, as usual. Even Paul, my dear sweet husband, was quiet, dozing next to me, his arms crossed in front of his chest, his head bobbing up and down. As the odometer on the van clicked off another 50 miles, my precocious four-year-old, Molly, started singing and woke Paul from his nap.

"Did you get a chance to sleep honey?" I asked.

Paul rubbed his eyes. "A little. How far to the next exit?"

"About 15 miles. Hey, do you remember the day we told the kids about buying a house on Cape Cod?"

Paul looked over to me. His hand gently stroked my hair and the nape of my neck. "How could I ever forget, Nancy Caldwell? You were like a little kid about to do something you knew you shouldn't."

"I remember my heart went through the roof the day we walked into the old farmhouse." I stared ahead at the road. "If you recall, we fired ideas at each other all the way back to the cottage about how to fix up the antique house, and how its location could help sell more of your art." I laughed out loud. "We tried so hard to justify buying it. We absolutely had no extra money."

Paul was gazing out the side window. He turned back to me and said, "You know, I sensed even then that we were all beginning a new chapter in our lives."

Glimpses of the children popped in and out of the rearview mirror. I called out to them, "After we get settled into the house, who's going to be my assistant researching the legends of Cape Cod?"

Brian looked disgusted as he played a game on his phone. At sixteen, our unhappy son was headed to a new high school on the Cape for his junior year. Thirteen-year-old Casey always ignored me. She continued to look at the trees flying by, keeping a beat with her head to the music coming from her headphones.

Persistence was my strong suit so I tried to get the family talking. "Remember the house that we saw on Goody Hallett Drive in Eastham, before we bought the farmhouse?"

"Oh yeah," Paul answered. "The realtor scared the kids that morning with her recap of the Maria Hallett and Sam Bellamy legend."

I took a deep breath and dramatically chanted, "Maria Goody Hallett haunts the bluffs in Eastham, for nigh' 300 years, forever looking for Sam Bellamy, the lover who abandoned her."

Brian leaned over and poked Casey. She turned on him with a prickly voice. "Stop it!"

I yelled over my shoulder. "You could be a little nicer to one another. I know we've been on the road a long time, but we all need to co-operate." At last, everyone was paying attention to me and I couldn't resist throwing out another tease. "It's funny how all of you got so scared when you heard the Bellamy-Hallett legend."

Casey shouted above a loud truck that was passing and tried to defend herself with, "Yeah, but it was creepy, Mom! Sure glad we didn't buy a house on THAT street. And Brian, you're such a jerk."

Brian just smirked at his sister, pleased to get a response.

I gave up. Maybe some different music would help the miles go faster. As I waited to hear my favorite new age instrumental come through the speakers, the van began to pass through Eastern Pennsylvania and New York on Interstate 90.

Rolling hills and lush farmland blended with the modern smooth sounds that now filled the van. The music in the background made me feel like I was in a movie. Imagining a camera filming from above, I drove down the highway hopeful for a new adventure.

As soon as cruise control steadied the van to a good speed, my feet and legs began to move to the rhythm of the music. Leaning back, I felt happy. Memories flooded my mind from all the vacations on Cape Cod, and the years of our dreaming about moving there. How during last summer's visit, the van had broken down in the small town of Orleans, and needed repair before we could leave. How we'd decided to visit a real estate office and found four property listings for quick drive-bys. How the last one we saw in Brewster had caught our eyes as well as our hearts.

I could hear Molly's little voice singing over my music.

Jim called out, "Mom, we better stop soon!"

I pulled into the next rest stop and the family began to straighten themselves, unplugging earphones and turning off iPods. I tossed the keys to Paul as I got out of the car. "Come on. Let's power-walk!"

Over my shoulder I told Jim, "Grab Molly's hand!"

*   *   *

Hamburgers, French fries and soft drinks were spread over the table inside the rest stop in a jumble of papers and napkins. Hungry hands reached for ketchup and straws as all of us enjoyed our feast. I tried to catch Molly's attention. "Are you going to come with me to see the Provincetown Pirate Museum?"

"Yeah," Molly answered with a giggle.

I lowered my head to get close to her and spoke in my best pirate voice. "Arrrrrrgggg! We're goin' to have some mighty fine adventures livin' on ol' Cape Cod. What say ye, my little lass?"

Casey, embarrassed, said, "Shhhh, Mom. Don't do that. Everyone can hear you."

I didn't care. My coffee tasted good, and I was keyed up about moving. After all, we were on an adventure. "I can't wait to discover who lived in our old Greek Revival house." Paul simply placed his hand over mine in agreement.

*   *   *

Crossing over the Sagamore Bridge, we had less than an hour before we would reach Brewster, located on the bayside of the Cape. Incorporated in 1803, this Sea Captain's Town was quiet and, like most New England villages, was steeped in folklore and a few ghostly tales. The local historians would refer to its location in the 1700s as North Harwich.

*   *   *

As we pulled into the driveway, the darkness hid the beauty of the house, with its white clapboard siding and classic lines. Set back and up a slight rise on the Old King's Highway, its two acres had a bonus of a nice old barn and an attached cranberry shed. Abandoned for years and labeled a 'handyman's special', it had looked friendly when we purchased it, but now, in the dark of night, it almost seemed ominous.

As the dome light lit up the van, Paul said, "I'll go in first and make sure everything's okay."

I was thankful we'd already made several trips to the Cape, prior to our final arrival, with the essentials that would make our first night bearable. By the time Paul returned, everyone was ready to get out and find their beds.

"Be careful where you step when you get inside," Paul warned. "The contractor and his crew didn't finish everything."

Once the complaints and grumbles ceased, and the kids were settled, Paul and I were too tired to set up our new bed frame. We crawled onto the mattress, which, for now, lay on the floor. I couldn't sleep. Random thoughts flew around my head. Who else had stared at these ceilings and passed through these doorways? Were they sad or happy people? Had anyone died within these walls?

3

Eastham 1715
CAPE COD

WHEN MARIA'S CHORES WERE FINISHED the next day, she quickly flew behind her father sitting at the table and called over her shoulder, "I'll be late tonight. The tavern will be busy."

"Foolish girl, close the door," he growled, stuffing his mouth with food.

Tom Hallett's nasty demeanor didn't bother Maria today. She simply ignored his cruel words and thought of the coming afternoon with Sam Bellamy. Her dreary days and nights may soon be over, if this new man was agreeable to her and she to him. Eastham and its people offer nothing to her for the future.

She hurried along the path to Smith's Tavern rehearsing the words she would say to Mr. Smith. "I shall have to leave early today as Father needs my help...no, that won't do." She walked a little further. "I'm sorry, but I don't feel well today. May I go home early if I promise to work all the harder tomorrow?" That sounded just right to her.

Once at the tavern, she hung her woolen shawl on a wooden peg just inside the door and went over to Mr. Smith to repeat her rehearsed words.

The tavern owner answered back, "It's agreeable, you may leave early."

"Thank you," Maria said, turning to hide her smile.

After rushing through her chores, Maria gathered her shawl and placed the back of her hand against her forehead. She spoke as if weak, "Goodbye, Mr. Smith, I hope I'm better tomorrow. Sorry for the trouble."

She only had to walk a short distance to be out of sight of the tavern owner, upon which she gathered her skirts and ran.

At this time of day her father should be gone, collecting hides for his tanning. This gave her an opportunity to stop at the house to fill a basket with cider, bread and beef strips for her and Sam. When she had gathered all that was needed, she adjusted her cap in a small mirror that had belonged to her mother, pinched her cheeks for color, then splashed some lavender water on her wrists and in between her breasts. As she hastened out the door she saw Matthew, her childhood friend, across the field. She decided to go the other way to the deserted McKeon house, knowing no one must see her or people would talk. Maria was so excited she could feel her heart racing, and had to stop several times as she rushed through the grove of pines on her way to meet this new interest in her life.

Sam was sitting on a wooden bench next to the doorway of the old house, waiting for her. As soon as he spotted Maria, he walked towards her. Reaching for her basket he said, "Here, let me help you with that. A delicate flower such as you shouldn't be carrying so heavy a weight."

Maria blushed.

They fell into step together. He asked, "What did the innkeeper say? Did he suspect anything?"

"No," Maria replied. "I pretended to be ill."

Sam stopped and placed his free hand on her shoulder. "Well, you look beautiful to me, and I don't see any sign of sickness in your soft brown eyes." They stood nearer to each other. "Here, let me look closer at them."

His gentle touch stirred her. She tried to hold her breath, to stop the quickness in her heart as he stood in front of her. They both stood frozen, lost in each other's eyes. It was over in a moment and they continued walking toward the old house.

"I hope you're hungry," Maria asked, still feeling shy.

"That I am, and I've a surprise for you."

As they approached the door, Sam bowed and with a sway of his arm said, "After you, Mademoiselle."

Maria curtsied, joining him in the fun. "Thank you."

The wooden table in the empty house was set with a small linen cloth, a candle and a jar filled with wild sea lavender that Sam had gathered as he'd walked across the marsh grass to meet her. Maria smiled, but at the same time, she trembled. She began to feel nervous and doubted her decision to meet with this stranger.

"Are you all right?" Sam asked gently.

"No one has ever given me flowers, or treated me as you do," she said, sitting down in the chair Sam had pulled out for her. "I'll be fine. Thank you, Sam."

She watched him move around the table to the chair opposite her. Maria emptied the contents of her basket onto the cloth that covered the rough, splintered board. The food's pungent smells covered the staleness of the old musty house. From the corner of her eye, she caught sight of what was around her. The house was empty, except for cobwebs, some broken pieces of wood in one corner, and night bedding crumpled on the floor. Feeling cautious again, she kept her eyes on Sam and her task at hand of presenting their meal.

As they ate and talked, they became focused on each other, paying no attention to the food they were eating.

"You said you were from Devonshire, in England. Is this so?" Maria asked.

"Yes, I was the youngest of four children. My mother died soon after I was born and my father raised us poorly." Sam reached for his cider. "When I was old enough, I left for the sea, joined the Royal Navy and never returned home. It's been almost ten years."

"I'm so sorry...." She placed her slender fingers over his strong hand. She felt truly saddened about his childhood, with both losing their mothers.

This small gesture from Maria gave rise to questions for Sam about his intentions towards this beautiful girl. He kept his stare on her. Slowly, he put his cup down, then removed his hand from under hers. The sun shone on Maria's hair in such a way that it cast a heavenly glow around her. She is so lovely, he thought...so innocent.

The young girl leaned over the table. "Tell me of the things that you've seen and the people you've met."

"There's not much to tell, except that I'm finished with being told what to do by pompous men who use their wealth to keep people like me living in forced poverty." Sam rose from his chair. He walked to the door and looked out across the marshes toward the sea. "I want to find my fortune, and then someone to share it with. When that happens I'll settle in one place."

"Where will you go? How will you find your fortune?" Maria admired his square cut jaw and black hair tied behind his head.

He turned and moved closer to the table, took her hand and tenderly stroked it. "I've heard of a great treasure in the Caribbean. There are stories of two thousand chests of newly minted silver coins from a sunken Spanish fleet. Treasure beyond any man's wildest dreams! There, in the waters, all for the taking by anyone who can get to it."

As Maria listened, he held on to her hand. She considered how strange it was that she felt so comfortable with Sam. She dismissed her earlier doubts. She liked him. His rough tapered fingers were gentle but strong; she did not want him to let go. Hoping to prolong his touch, she quickly asked another question, "How will you get the treasure from the water?"

"I was told there are divers who know how to bring the treasure up to the surface." His deep blue eyes lit up with excitement. "I'm in contact with a goldsmith from Rhode Island, a man known as Paulsgrave Williams. We're meeting at the tavern tomorrow to discuss the details of sailing to the Caribbean and finding a crew and divers. Maria, this is what I want."

"It sounds dangerous, Sam. I'm worried for your safety."

"Do I detect a tone of affection in your voice? I hope so, because I like you very much, Maria." He knelt on one knee. "May we meet again?"

Maria wanted to, but knew she couldn't. Her cheeks flushed red as her heart fluttered. She looked at him, trying to form the right words, "I...cannot come tomorrow, I promised to work at the tavern."

Sam was persistent. "Then shall we meet the next day?"

She hesitated again, but couldn't say no to him. "Yes! But I must be going now."

She gathered the remaining food into her basket and cautioned him, "We must leave separately, so no one will notice."

Maria stopped at the door's entrance, then turned to face Sam. "This seems to be a good place to meet. Yes?"

He moved between her and the outside. Touching a piece of hair that had fallen out of her cap, he held it in his hand and stroked her cheek with the back of his fingertips. "Yes, I think this is a wonderful place." He kept his ground in front of her and moved his free hand across the opening, blocking her way even more. "I would like to thank you for such an enjoyable afternoon, Miss Maria Hallett, and I look forward to seeing you again, upon which I hope there'll be good news concerning my meeting with Williams."

Maria appreciated his politeness and was becoming fonder of Sam by the minute. She spoke without any wavering in her voice, "I do hope so, Mr. Sam Bellamy."

His face was close to hers. She wanted to touch his cheek, but stopped herself. She didn't want to leave, but knew she must. "If you would be so kind as to let me pass, I can see the sun is beginning to set." He didn't move. "Please Sam, I must be on my way," she whispered

"Of course, my lady, until we meet again." He let go of her hair, lowered his arm and stepped aside.

As Sam watched Maria walk down the path and disappear beyond the crest of the road, he thought about how different she was from the others, and that she needed to be carefully pursued. He closed the door behind him and walked away from the McKeon house with one thought: Maria Hallett must be his.

4

Present Day – June 9
BREWSTER – CAPE COD

ONE WEEK HAD PASSED SINCE THE BIG MOVE from Ohio of kids, furniture, garden tools, Paul's artwork, and even an old 1947 Farmall tractor. Life felt better, less complicated. I looked around at the quaint glass cabinets, which lined the west wall, and marveled at how all the china and glassware filled the shelves, as if they were always meant to be there. The sound of the van as it rumbled over the gravel driveway signaled that Paul was home from the hardware store. As soon as he stepped across the damaged floorboards of the unfinished foyer, I had to ask, "Did you finally find the right color of stain?"

He grinned. "Yeah, it's pretty close to the shade I wanted, a nice warm brown."

I pecked him on his bearded cheek. "Let's sit a minute out on the front porch."

Paul looked relieved. He'd been to the store several times in search of the certain color that would satisfy his inner artistic yearnings. He gladly walked outside while I went the other way, stepping over boxes still stacked in the dining room. As I maneuvered my way into the original kitchen, I couldn't help but notice how bizarre the old room looked today; a coffee pot sat on the washing machine, and the microwave rested on the clothes dryer. Stacked beneath the 1950s speckled yellow counter were bowls, pans, magazines and newspapers. I thankfully found my favorite flavored tea in the bottom of a small basket. When the microwave sounded a 'bing', I plopped the teabag into my cup, retrieved Paul's iced tea from the refrigerator, and grabbed a few gingersnaps. After eying the progress of the new kitchen across from the old one, I thought 'Hope springs eternal' and assured myself it wouldn't be much longer.

The afternoon sun felt warm as I pushed the old screen door open to the porch with an elbow and my backside.

"It's so nice out here," Paul said.

I settled next to him on a twin oak rocker. "Who would have thought that in less than a year we'd be living by the sea in an old historic home?" I held my drink in the air. "Here's to you selling your paintings and living a dream that we've both had for years."

Paul grinned in agreement as we clinked our drinks together.

I studied the lines of the exposed rafters across the ceiling of the old porch. "Next week I'd like to trace the history of this ancient house."

"Good idea. By then we should have all the rubbish cleaned out of the carriage house so we can turn it into an art gallery," he said, glancing across the grass to a small garden "But first, we have to tear down that old three-seater outhouse that's attached to the back of it."

"I wonder what's at the bottom of the holes?"

"It looked like they're just filled with dirt." Paul winked at me. "But we might find some treasure down there."

My curiosity rose. "It would be very cool to find something mysterious about the people who once lived here. You know, years ago, that's where people threw all their trash."

"Nancy, you would be the one to uncover any secrets. Based on your Hungarian-Gypsy ancestry, you know how to sense things, good or bad about a place." Paul rubbed the back of his neck. "Remember when we brought the kids to look at this house for the first time?"

"Yeah, and when we walked around the property outside, I sensed only good feelings."

"Sure you did, but not poor Brian; he didn't like it at all. I can see him now, with his arms outstretched and swinging on an old clothesline that connected the barn to a big maple tree. His face was pale white, not wanting anything to do with our plans of leaving Ohio for Cape Cod." Paul rocked a little faster.

I collected the cups, placed them back on the tray, and wondered: why is he still questioning our decision to move? "Brian's young.

He'll be all right. I think everything will work out." I bent over to kiss Paul on the little bald circle on top of his head. "I'm convinced that someone, or something, is very happy that this old house will be taken care of. This house is different. It feels right, and if there are any spirits, they're friendly."

Paul looked up at me. I knew he would usually laugh off my words of spirits and ghosts as nonsense, but this time I sensed that he thought the house was different, too, but in a good way.

That night, after the kids had gone to bed early, Paul and I were on the couch listening to the nightly news as he rubbed my feet. "I don't know if I'll be able to sleep tonight, I'm just so excited about this whole new adventure we're on. How about you?" I asked.

"I'll probably fall asleep; you know me. How long are you staying up?"

I coyly smiled at him. "Well, that depends on how tired you are."

Paul looked over at me with a twinkle in his eye.

I didn't need to hear his answer; I knew what 'that look' meant. I sat up, grabbed my socks and encouraged him with, "You turn everything off, lock the doors, and I'll see you under the covers." After closing down the house, he double-stepped up the stairs.

I stood in the dining room. "I need to find something first; I'll be right there." Cardboard boxes were still stacked to the side of the room; I started rummaging through a few of them. "I know it's in one of these. Where's the box labeled bathroom?" Paul was out of sight and didn't hear me. "Damn it. Where is it?"

I tried to remember when I'd got my last period and figured we would be safe without any protection, just this one time. When I arrived in the bedroom, Paul was already in bed waiting for me. The air was warm that evening and a soft breeze from the trees ruffled the curtains. I ached to feel his arms around me. We may have been broke from all our moving expenses, but tonight our pleasure was absolutely free. As the two of us made sweet love, we eventually fell asleep to the calming sounds of the summer night.

* * *

The following week was spent working on the carriage house so it could be renovated into Paul's gallery. Two truckloads of debris were taken to the dump. Once the building was empty, the walls began to talk. Up in the hayloft, hooks were found on the rafters with dark stains on the floor beneath them. Our contractor, Henry, an elderly red-plaid shirted Yankee craftsman, surmised some butchering of animals had been done years ago and this was where the meat had hung.

Down on the main floor, an old diary of an occupant from the early '40s was nailed on the door with a carpenter's pencil hung from a piece of rope. Inside were notes that read: '...gone fishing back at noon', or '...caught a big cod today.'

Evidence of children who had once lived in the house, probably relegated to outside play in the barn on rainy days, could be seen throughout. Childish pictures decorated the old weathered barn walls. A skull and crossbones painted across the rough-cut planks caught my attention and I whispered to myself, "They must've been some fierce pirates."

When the electric wiring was upgraded in the soon-to-be-gallery, Paul and the boys finished the interior décor. Track lighting lit the wide-plank wooden floors that now were clean, except for traces of grease stains from car repairs of previous owners. When I'd finished hanging all the framed pieces of art, my last job of the day was to arrange fresh flowers in the center of the gallery.

Paul whistled a sigh of relief. "Remember when Henry's crew laughed at us about finishing our project in one week? Well, we finished by our deadline and beat them working on the addition to the house."

I gave Paul a big hug. "It's official: Tomorrow we'll be open! And I'm going to make the first sale for you."

"I hope so. We could certainly use the money." No smile on Paul's face this time.

I have to remember to be positive for him. We stepped back to admire our work and then closed the sliding barn door to the old carriage house, now a country gallery.

5

April 1715
EASTHAM – CAPE COD

TWO DAYS LATER, after the morning sun broke the early dawn, Maria and Sam hurried through their separate daily routines.

* * *

Maria woke early, as usual, and saw the door was shut on her father's room. She knew her father enjoyed his Friday nights at the tavern, so he'd be sleeping through the morning hours. A stew had been simmering all night and was just what she needed to impress this Sam Bellamy, a new opportunity in her life. Into her waiting basket she put a covered kettle filled with the meat and vegetables; it rested next to biscuits, dried apples and a small jar of cider. Making sure all was right, she left with basket in hand to her secret meeting.

As she approached the McKeon house, Maria saw that Sam was not there. Cautiously, she pushed in the weathered door. As it opened it revealed the table still holding the cloth on its topside, with candle and flowers, but no Sam. Not to worry, she told herself, he would come.

Inside the abandoned house, Maria spotted a shabby bed linen on the floor in the corner. She took it outside to shake it clean. Still not seeing Sam, she went back in the house and placed the bedding on top of a wooden frame near the back of the room. After adjusting her bodice, she went to look out the door once more to see if he was coming. Not seeing him, she positioned herself outside on the bench, beside the door where Sam was sitting the last time...and waited.

* * *

That same morning, Sam was waking up. He'd slept well even though his mind was clouded from the previous night's ale. He was eager to see Maria to tell her about his meeting with Williams. He donned a loose shirt and hurried down the stairs to the main tavern where he saw Mr. Smith. Sam walked up to the sideboard and reached for a tankard of cider. "Good morrow! What a fine morning it is today."

"It is, Mr. Bellamy. How fares your friend Williams? It seems that you two will be going on an adventure soon." The tavern owner wiped the sidebar and questioned Sam again. "The word around here is 'treasure' and how much you two will find. What say you?"

"I can't say for sure how much, Mr. Smith, but I believe the fates will be kind to us."

Sam heard a loud voice coming from outside. He turned his head and saw a well-dressed gentleman in the doorway with his cane raised in the air. He was angry and yelling at a dark rumpled figure near his feet. "I told you before not to be in my way when I enter!"

Just as the man was about to lower his stick, Sam jumped between the two of them and caught the wooden rod before it hit its target. He wrestled the weapon away and shouted, "Is there a problem here that can't be solved by talking?"

Remaining steadfast and separating the two, he blocked any more conflict. Within seconds, he saw the object of the man's anger. An old drunkard was sprawled on the ground by the door of the tavern with his legs halfway onto the threshold. Sam turned back to the rude gentleman. "Have you no compassion for those who are so unfortunate in this world?"

The man, clearly upset with Sam said, "I don't intend to waste my time with such foul-smelling humans. And who are you to tell me what to do?"

"I go by the name of Sam Bellamy." Sam loosened his grip on the man's cane. "You must know that no human being is a waste of time."

He remained guarded in case another blow would find its way toward the old man. "It seems that respect doesn't come easy for you, sir."

The man grabbed at his cane. "I've not heard of you, and I don't care about you." He seemed poised to strike, but kept his stick at his side. "Let me pass!" With one long step, he abruptly rounded his victim, gave Sam a threatening look, and entered the tavern.

Sam reached down. "Come, old timer. Let me help you."

He pulled the scruffy man up and sat him on a bench against the outside of the tavern. His smell of dirt and ale made Sam wince. His clothes were piss-burnt and torn. "Oh, you sad creature of God's, where do you live?"

The toothless grin mumbled a few words.

"I don't understand you," said Sam. He called into the tavern. "I say, Smith, do you know where he lives, so I may take him home?"

"Up the hill and past two houses," Mr. Smith called back. "You're a good man, Mr. Bellamy."

Sam knew he was going to be late for Maria, but felt certain that he would still be able to meet with her. "Let's go," he said and helped his charge up by his elbow. "I'm sure you would be much better at home in your own bed."

The old man was able to walk if Sam steadied him along the path. When they reached the house, the old-timer was still muddled in his demeanor. Sam asked his name.

He slurred his words. "Hallett! And what name do you go by?"

The sound of Hallett surprised Sam. He hesitated. "Sam...Sam Bellamy."

Once inside the tidy little house Sam saw no fire in the hearth, but noticed a woman's touch about. "Where is your wife?"

"I ain't got no wife, only a wretched daughter who never listens to me." He landed hard on a chair by the table. "MARIA," he yelled out, "MARIA HALLETT! That girl is never around when you need her."

Shocked, Sam looked around. Here I am, he thought, in Maria's house.

Hallett stumbled toward his bedroom. The door was latched and closed. It wouldn't open. He began to curse.

Sam hurried over. "Mind your tongue and let me help you."

Finally, the door opened and Hallett flung himself on top of the bed. Saliva sprayed from his lips as he said, "I'll be fine. I thank you, kind sir, and...." his voice trailed off as he passed out.

Afraid that he might be late for his meeting with Maria, Sam turned and bolted outside. He recognized a few familiar landmarks and recalled that she said one could get to the McKeon's from behind her house and then through the pines.

Towards the back he spotted the pine grove and followed the narrow dirt way. He hurried along the path until he came to the crest of a hill where he saw Maria sitting on a bench. His heart began to race. His shirt billowed around his waist as he ran. He waved and called out, "MARIA!" The closer he came, the happier he felt.

Out of breath and grinning, Sam slid across the bench towards Maria. She laughed at him. She noticed his blue eyes again; they were the same color as the crystal-clear sky above their heads. His unfastened shirt revealed a muscular chest that rose and fell with each of his deep breaths. She couldn't stop looking at his strong body.

Sam teased her. "An old man crossed my path today."

Maria looked at him with a quizzical expression.

"Does your father enjoy his drink?"

"Yes, on occasion. Why do you ask?"

"I think I met him this morning."

"What do you mean?" she asked.

"Evidently he's not well liked by a certain wealthy tavern patron whose walking stick tried to teach him a lesson this morning."

"My father was asleep in his bed when I left, I think you're not correct about this matter. His bedroom door was closed."

"Is it possible that the wind blew it shut? The poor man I saw in front of the tavern said his name was Hallett and he had a daughter named Maria. He also had some very unflattering words about you."

"What are you trying to say?" Maria seemed agitated with his questions. She rose from the bench as if she would leave him.

Sam stood, took hold of her arm and placed his other hand around her slim waist. "Don't be angry with me. Don't go. I was teasing you. I think that you must live with a great burden of taking care of your father. If the man I saw this morning is he, you must be an angel from heaven." He lifted her chin with his finger. "My sweet Maria, I want to take you away from all this harshness." He stood close to her, let go of her waist and cupped her delicate face in his hands. "Someone as beautiful as you should be surrounded by elegance and the finest of things. You deserve better, and to be loved by someone like me. Stay with me this day."

He kissed her gently on the cheek, then lightly on the lips. Maria opened her mouth to speak, but he kissed her again. She did not pull away; circling her arms around him, she kissed him in return. He lifted her up and carried her into the house.

As he walked, he held her near his heart. His comforting arms felt secure to Maria; her body stirred and she shivered deep within. Her heart told her that she could trust him; he was sensitive and caring. It seemed dizzying to her, but this man could be someone she might spend her life with. Her life with Father was so unbearable...something must be done. She would take a chance.

* * *

The spring sounds of tiny frogs from the nearby marshes woke Maria. Sam was sleeping next to her. She turned and leaned on her elbow, tracing his face with the back of her fingers. How handsome he was to her young eyes. She never realized a man could be strong and exciting and at the same time gentle and kind. He opened his eyes and smiled at her. She closed them with her fingertips, kissing him on each eyelid, then on the tip of his nose, and finally caressing his lips with hers. "Sam, I don't want to leave you."

"Then don't. Stay with me longer."

"Father will be wondering where I am."

He leaned on his elbow and faced her. "I think I should officially meet your father. We could go now. What do you think?"

She lay back onto the rumpled bedding and thought about his question. "I think it's a very good idea."

He laughed and kissed her, "Your father is probably just getting out of his bed."

Maria smiled and sealed her decision with another kiss.

6

April 1715
EASTHAM – CAPE COD

HANDS TOGETHER, THEY WALKED, and every step brought them closer in their feelings toward each other.

"Are you sure you want to meet my father today?"

"Why do you ask? I think it's as good a time as ever." He stopped and reassured her with a quick kiss on the cheek.

His touch was soothing to her. She could not disagree with him. They saw the top of Hallett's chimney as they went over the crest of the hill. When they entered the pine grove, Maria began to feel anxious about him meeting her father; she held Sam's hand tighter. "I shall have to go next door to Matthew Ellis's to borrow some starter for the fire."

"Don't worry; I'll tend to the hearth."

As they crossed the threshold of the house they heard no sound. The door of her father's room was closed. Sam whispered, "I told you he would be sleeping it off."

Maria grabbed a small covered pan for the starter and rushed out the door.

"Be careful," he called after her.

Sam went outside to bring logs in for the hearth and noticed that the log pile was low. It's still spring, he thought to himself, there ought to be enough time for the old man to replenish the wood throughout the summer. Maria should be fine while he's away at sea. But he still decided that he would leave money with Mr. Smith at the tavern, just in case Maria needed anything.

Once back inside the house, Sam began to prepare the hearth. He leaned his head into the wide stone opening with his back to the door. The sound of dirt crunched behind him. He turned to see the end of a rifle pointing at his face.

"Stand slow, whoever you are," the disheveled old man commanded Sam.

As the rifle's barrel followed his every movement, Sam stood straight with hands outstretched at his sides. He glared into the face of his attacker. "Hold on now, I'm not an intruder; I'm a friend. Are you not Hallett?"

"What's that you say? Who are you?" Hallett wiped his dripping nose with a fast swipe of his hand.

"I'm Sam Bellamy. You don't remember me?"

"I know no Sam Bellamy and I don't think I want to." He flicked the end of the rifle to show Sam where to move and ordered, "Get over to the other side of the room."

"Take it easy, I know your daughter Maria. She's gone to the Ellis's to fetch some starter. Here she comes now."

As Hallett turned to look, Sam lunged for the rifle, knocking him off balance. The rifle fell into Sam's hand and the dazed father hit the floor. Sam yelled as he helped him up. "What's wrong with you? Don't you remember who brought you home this morning?"

Hallett fell into a chair by the table. He squinted his eyes to see who stood before him. "Well, I recollect walking with someone this morning, from the tavern, but I don't remember anything else." The confused old man looked around. "Where's that Maria? Where is she?"

"Father!" Maria called out as she hurried into the house. "What's happening here?" She quickly deposited her starter into the hearth under the logs and turned to face him. "I pray that you've not caused a problem. I see your gun is in Sam's hand. Can you explain this to me?"

Her father said nothing. Angered, he rose from his chair, knocking it over, and went outside.

Maria took the gun from Sam, placed it behind the open door and waited for an explanation.

"It seems that your father thought I was going to steal from you." Sam picked up the overturned chair. "As I was setting the hearth, he came upon me, so I took his weapon, and he didn't like it."

"Oh Sam, his drinking brings me such sadness, I'm sorry and embarrassed for my father's actions." Maria failed to hold back her tears. They wet her face as she busied herself preparing something to eat for the three of them.

Sam took her hand and wiped her cheek. "I'll go out and talk to him. Don't worry yourself."

"Wait," Maria called after him. "Take some ale to him, and you have one too." She passed Sam two tankards from the shelf on the wall, and as he held them, she filled them halfway.

"This will appease him for a while."

Hallett didn't move a muscle when Sam sat down next to him on the bench. He took the cup that was offered to him and drank, but still said nothing.

"If I may refresh your memory a little, Mr. Hallett? It seems that you had a bit too much to drink last night and encountered a very angry gentleman and his stick this morning. Any recollection, yet?"

"Possibly." The old man looked at Sam a little closer now. "You do look familiar." He scratched his unshaven chin, seemingly lost in his thoughts.

Sam took a drink of his ale and looked straight ahead. "Well, it doesn't matter anymore. I have come to your house not for your company, but for your daughter's."

"Wait a gol'darned minute," Hallett called out. "I know you. You're that privateer who's goin' to find treasure. What a bunch of hogwash all those rumors are about finding gold and such. You stay away from my daughter."

Sam stood, towering over the old man. "I'm not what you think. I'm going on a salvaging expedition and you will not prevent me from seeing Maria...."

Hallett stood, reached for a broom leaning by the door and cut off Sam's words. "Get away from here. I don't want to see you near my daughter. She might be worthless, but she's still my property."

Maria appeared in the doorway. "Father, now what's the problem?"

Sam remained in his stance, all the while glancing back and forth between father and daughter. "I'm not welcome here, according to your father."

Hallett waved the broomstick in circles, lunging its end at Sam as if it was a sword. "Get off my land!"

Maria cried out, "Stop this!" and jumped between them.

"Get out of the way, stupid girl." Hallett hit Maria on her shoulder with the wooden handle of the broom, pushing her to the ground. Before he could strike her again, Sam caught the broom and broke it in half. He threw the broken pieces to the side and grabbed Hallett by the scruff of his neck. "Listen to me, old man, if I ever find out that you've harmed your daughter, in any way, I'll make sure that you never lift anything again." He let go. Hallett crumpled to the bench.

Maria lay on the dirt. Sam picked her up in his arms. A bruise began to swell on the nape of her neck as he carried her into the house and to her bed. He found a clean cloth, wet it with cool water, and placed it on her neck. "I'm sorry that I've caused such pain for you. I can't stand to see you hurt."

"Sam, I'll be fine. It's not your fault. My father has a nasty temper. It's his drink and when he has no drink, he's just plain ornery."

He sat next to her on the bed. "I best be going. Your father doesn't want me here. But I must see you again."

She sat up slowly. "Tomorrow is the Sabbath, but Monday we'll meet."

Sam agreed. He cautioned her, "I'm fearful for you in this house."

"Go," Maria whispered. "Monday we meet. I'll be fine."

He kissed her and left.

As Sam passed through the doorway to leave, he noticed the old man had finished his drink.

Under his breath, Hallett slurred, "And stay away."

7

April 1715
EASTHAM – CAPE COD

MARIA CHOSE HER CLOTHES CAREFULLY as she readied herself
to go to meeting on Sunday Sabbath. She picked out a large plain
handkerchief to conceal the bruise on her neck and a thick shawl to
go over her shoulders. She wanted no one to notice her today. Her
father was asleep as the young girl left the house.

On her walk to the church, she joined with other neighbors fulfilling
their obligatory honoring of the Sabbath. As Maria came closer to the
meetinghouse, she encountered nods from a few elderly ladies, but
nothing welcoming.

She found her seat in the upper balcony, where the poorer members
of the community were relegated. As Reverend Treat began to speak,
his words mingled with the thick, warm air that drifted upwards
toward Maria. It made her sleepy. Within seconds, the face of her
mother, Sarah Hallett, appeared in her thoughts. Maria missed her
so much and longed for the soft touch of her mother's hand, her
laughter, the lullabies and rhymes they would sing in secret as they
did their daily work. She never understood how a song could be evil,
but her church forbade such singing and dancing. Mother Sarah
would always caution her daughter, "Remember, Maria, when out
amongst the others, keep these melodies in your heart, so no ill will
comes your way."

She recalled the day her mother had told Maria of how she'd met her father, Thomas Hallett, and how sad she'd felt, knowing she would face an arranged marriage to an older man.

It had broken Maria's heart to hear the story. She knew her mother had always desired love and companionship, but had settled for the promise of security through a husband. The notion of a marital match for convenience was an evil Maria promised herself would never happen to her. She smiled as she thought of Sam and how their children would be happy and cared for within a marriage of love.

She sat up, straightened her shawl and looked around at the people below her. She noticed a man sitting in the far corner of the crowded church with similar mannerisms and a strong resemblance to her father; her smile fell off her face. Why did her father hate her so? He made her life so unbearable. How happy she had been with her mother. She winced as pain shot through her shoulder and neck, wishing she had rubbed salve across her bruise.

Glimpses of her past came to life in her thoughts. She pictured herself helping her sick mother at only seven years of age. As young as she was, she never forgot what was needed for her mother, yet she forgot her own medicine this morning.

Maria had always tried her best to care for her mother, but it wasn't enough. When she had needed help she called on Minda, the Indian midwife. Her mother believed in the old Indian, and accepted her comfort, both in words and medicines. While they both loved Minda, Thomas Hallett hated everything about her. Even now, Maria must still hide Minda's herbs and potions from her father. He despised them, calling her Indian ways 'abracadabra'.

Lately, Maria missed the *Pow Wah's* visits and the little gifts she brought her. The bouquets of flowers, beautiful shells from the sea, and scented waters meant so much to Maria. She wondered if Minda would come soon.

"...and the Lord hath said, 'Work is blessed, and idleness is the work of the devil'...." Reverend Treat's loud preaching startled Maria and she snapped open her eyes. Quickly glancing from side to side, she tried to see if anyone had seen her daydreaming. Thankfully, the congregation seemed to be lost in their own worlds. Once again her gaze settled upon those meeting below her. She saw where the Hallett family had sat for services before her mother had died. She gently massaged her throbbing shoulder and thought very quietly: Why does father blame me for everything? I'm his daughter, not his servant! Mother always said I was a gift from God. Why can't he think of me like that?

Reverend Treat's words became distorted and she was sure she heard him scolding her, "Obey your father!" She shook her head, but the words then twisted into her father's accusing voice. He growled that Maria's birth had made his wife weak and caused her to spiral into bouts of sickness, and eventually death. His condemnations echoed in her head; "What am I to do? You're nothing but a burden."

Maria began to feel sick in her stomach at the image of how he always soothed his rage with his drink. When he was drunk, she oftentimes feared for her life. Maria furrowed her brow and searched deep inside her heart for pleasant memories. She recalled her mother humming while baking at the broad table, flour swirling around in the sunlight; her mother's wispy hair feathering out from under her linen cap. She'd always felt so safe with her mother.

"Maria, wake up." Matthew, who was sitting beside her, gently shook her shoulder.

"Ohhh," Maria winced at his touch.

Alarmed, her young friend asked, "What's wrong? Are you all right?"

"Oh.... Yes," she answered. As she leaned down to readjust her stocking, her handkerchief puffed away from her neck and revealed the bluish mark on her skin.

"Maria, what happened to you? Did your father do this?"

"It's nothing," she whispered, moving the cloth over to hide the bruise. "I hit my shoulder on the lug pole when I was cleaning the ashes from the hearth."

"Do be more careful, Maria. May I walk home with you today?"

"Of course, I would enjoy that." Matthew's presence always reminded her of how happy they had been as childhood friends and when her mother was still alive. Now older, they didn't see each other as regularly as Maria would have liked. Matthew was usually away fishing with his father; he only stayed home during inclement weather.

As the two friends walked over the crest of a hill and towards their houses, Matthew surprised Maria when he asked, "When I was home the other day, I saw you sitting on the bench outside the door of the old McKeon house. What were you doing there?"

Maria stammered, "Oh...I...just went for a walk and was feeling a little tired. That's all." She quickly changed the subject. "How are your parents?"

Matthew was oblivious to her words; he was lost in the details of Maria's delicate lips as she spoke. They opened and closed in soft movements, touching each other the way he longed to feel them against his own lips. He wanted to hold her arm as they walked, but thought he should not. It wouldn't be right.

Maria turned her head towards Matthew and asked again, "Matthew, how are your parents?"

"Oh...they're fine."

Embarrassed at his inattention to her question, he took a deep breath and blurted out, "Father is having a good year on the boat, and Mother's gout is much better."

Maria returned a smile to Matthew, unaware of his secret thoughts. She was only thinking of Sam holding her...kissing her...anticipating her meeting with him again.

As they came to Maria's house, she turned and said, "Goodbye, Matthew. It was nice to see you."

He tipped his hat in silence; placed one hand in his pocket and waved goodbye with the other.

Maria hurried into the house to gather the items she was going to bring to her next meeting with Sam. She never noticed Matthew as he walked away, because if she had, she would have seen him looking back for glimpses of her as he loudly berated himself for not saying what he felt in his heart.

8

April 1715
EASTHAM – CAPE COD

THE MORNING FOLLOWING THE SABBATH, Maria waited for her father to leave for the landing dock to get his supplies from Barnstable. After he'd gone, she rushed out the door, carrying her basket close to her, being careful not to drop anything as she hurried toward the pine grove to meet Sam.

Maria found him waiting by the McKeon house. When Sam saw her, he ran down the path to meet her halfway. He plucked the basket from her hand, grabbed her around the waist, twirled her once in the air and then kissed her. "I missed you, my Maria."

"I, too, missed you." She kissed him back with equal passion.

Arms entwined, they walked the short path to the old house.

As Sam closed the door behind them, the dust and shabbiness of the deserted house seemed to disappear for both of them. Their eyes could only see each other, and their bodies filled with a yearning that flowed quickly between them. Few words needed to be spoken. Sam and Maria understood each other. Lustful passion took control of their bodies and as the hours lingered for the lovers, they each satisfied their deep desires.

* * *

Sam spoke just as the sun began to set for the day. "Maria, tomorrow I must leave."

Her eyes moistened. "Oh, Sam, can't it be another day?"

"I'm sorry. The winds are in our favor, and my men await me." He gently assured her, "Don't worry."

He rolled his strong body over hers. Looking into her eyes, he continued, "I may only need to be away from you a short time, but if not, you must remember I will return for you with my ship filled with riches." He leaned closer and whispered in her ear, "I will carry a wedding ring next to my heart to give to you upon my return," and then in her other ear, "I promise to take you as my wife." He moved next to Maria and traced the outline of her lips with his fingertip as he murmured, "Stay the night with me."

She softly kissed his finger and then his lips. Stroking his long black hair she wrapped her arms around his strong back, pulling her body closer to his as he entered her again.

Maria fell asleep in Sam's arms.

He wanted to hold her forever. As the night grew darker, the song of the whippoorwill and the gentle breezes of the spring night accompanied the two eager lovers as they surrendered to a night of contented slumber.

*   *   *

Early dawn came too quickly. Sam had held Maria as long as he could, but knew it was time for him to take his leave. He pulled his arm from underneath the nape of her neck, kissed her on the cheek and prepared to leave, hoping not to wake his beloved. Goodbyes were difficult for Sam and it took all of his courage to step quietly into the early-misted morning without waking her. He paused in the doorway, looked back once more, and whispered, "Be safe, my Maria...I will love you forever and will return to you."

He then ran with all his strength towards the harbor for fear that his feelings for Maria would make him turn around and go back. His face and body were wet with perspiration that mingled with his tears, concealing his overwhelming sadness. He hoped others would not sense his heartbreak. The pounding of his body against the dirt path and the rapid beat of his heart kept him focused on what he must do. Once at the landing, he caught a packet to Provincetown where, later that night, he would set sail with Williams.

* * *

Maria woke with the memory of their last night in her heart and thoughts. She stretched her arms lazily above her head. When her hand fell to the side she realized Sam was gone. She sat up calling his name, "SAM!" Her heart sank.

Grabbing her shawl, she ran out of the old house and down to the sea, hoping to catch a glimpse of Sam as he sailed along the coast. As she ran, she knew that she had slept too long. He was nowhere in sight. Angry with herself that she had missed him, she ran up a high bluff to see the coastline. Breathless, she reached the top of the bluff and screamed over and over, "Sam! Sam!"

Her futile calls exhausted her and she collapsed to her knees. She reached deep inside her thoughts, trying to encourage herself to believe: He WILL be back…he had promised. I must not be sad. He WILL return.

Maria scrambled to her feet and stood tall. The spring air blew her hair back behind her head like ribbons in the wind. As she turned away from the coast, she noticed the bright green grass of the sand dunes and smelled the fresh salty air. She was sad, but began to feel light and excited too, as if she were beginning her own journey of waiting that would be filled with hope. Her course now would be different from her previous life. It would require planning for Sam's return. She knew he would come back. He loved her. He would rescue her from her dismal life. She would wait for him.

Soon a smile began to grow across her face as thoughts of Sam circled in her head. With each step she took toward home she imagined the two of them together, working side by side, as husband and wife. She became intrigued with what they would say to each other. She pictured Sam waking her up in the morning with a kiss before they would start their day. She felt good about their future together.

By mid-morning, her father's house came into view. She conjured another image of Sam standing in the door. As she reached out to grab its latch, her father's loud voice jolted her from her day-dreaming with, "MARIA!" It yelled again, "MARIA, where you bin? Where's my food?"

"Coming...." She hurried over to the hearth to stoke the fire. She didn't care that he was angry with her.

"Where you bin?" he yelled as he hunched over the table.

"Just walking," she sweetly replied. "Sorry, Father." Maria was thankful he had kindled the fire and did not question her whereabouts during the prior night. She ran to her room, promising, "I'll be right back Father," and closed the door.

Maria relieved herself in the nightjar and changed into a clean shift and skirt. A pile of soiled clothes lay in the corner by her bed, a grim reminder of laundry and her ongoing ordinary life. Today, it didn't bother her; she was in love.

As she prepared breakfast for her father, Maria pretended it was for Sam. She placed the Dutch oven with biscuit dough on the hot embers, poured strong cider into a tankard and opened a jar of beach plum jam for the table. She liked the idea of Sam as her husband and imagined how this fine meal would satisfy him. Checking the biscuits in the hearth, she reassured herself that her future would be with Sam. She knew it.

Suddenly the angry voice interrupted her thoughts again, "Hurry up, you worthless girl."

"Yes, Father."

She was accustomed to hearing her father's fury in so many ways; his actions and words were always sharp towards her. This time she turned away from him. With her back to the old man, she held his plate of biscuits and closed her eyes. Whispering a pledge to herself, she mouthed, "I promise to keep my hopes and dreams in my heart right next to Sam's promise of returning to me, and no one will take that from me!"

Her father yelled over his shoulder, "What's that you're saying, girl?"

"Nothing, Father."

Hallett banged his fist against the table. "God has cursed me with an irritating and useless female. Where's my drink?"

From that day forward, Sam's face and touch stayed with Maria. She worked hard and tried to do as she was told, even when her father's harshness interfered with her secret daydreams. Her solution was to pay little to no attention to his words. By ignoring his rudeness she could weave her dreams of happiness throughout the day, making life with her father easier to endure. Sadly, her lack of attention aggravated the old man to such an extent the tension between them grew stronger. Each night, exhausted in her bed from the day's work, her hopes felt shattered into tiny pieces of broken glass across the sandy floor. But knowing that Sam was coming home to her, and remembering his promises, she was able to patch them back together so she could sleep and dream of her future with him.

9

Present Day – June 23
BREWSTER – CAPE COD

AS I LOOKED OUT OF THE FRONT BAY WINDOW, I couldn't believe that three weeks had passed. On this gorgeous morning I felt a light ocean breeze caress my face. Leaning closer into the middle window, I touched my forehead against the old screen. What a great idea it was to move close to the sea. A deep breath of salty air dispelled any doubts I'd had about our uprooting the family. I sensed a perfect day was ahead of me. If I had one more cup of coffee and then secluded myself into the downstairs bedroom, alias office, I could polish off those pesky bills.

Within a few minutes, Jim quietly knocked on the bedroom door. "Mom?"

"Hi, honey." He looked handsome in his white shorts and shirt. "Will you be late tonight?"

"Yeah, I have the late shift."

"How's work at the restaurant?"

"It's okay. Everyone's pretty nice." Then with a quick kiss on my forehead, he was off. As he shut the door he said, "I'll see you tomorrow morning. Have a good night."

I was sorting through the mail as I watched him back out of the driveway. I marveled at how much Jim had matured. I wished Mom and Dad could have lived a little longer to see everyone's accomplishments and how our decision to move east was turning into such a good idea. A wave of inspiration for some gardening blew over me from the open window—physical work that I didn't have to think about. I hid the bills under the roll-top desk and looked for Paul. I found him in the garage working on a carpentry project. "Paul, I'm going to do some digging out back."

"Okay."

I grabbed a shovel, trowel and kneepads. Near the rear of the barn a sunny spot beckoned me to choose it for a vegetable garden. I placed the shovel's blade over the grass. Its sharp edge hit the ground and sliced into the green grass. I set the sod aside for planting in a bare spot on the lawn. My foot hit the top of the shovel again, pushing eight inches into the black dirt. This is easy, I thought.

Moving to the right, I repeated my movements, slicing the grass and hitting the ground. But this time my foot stopped with such a force that it vibrated through my whole body, sending a sharp pain into my hand. I shook my fingers, then massaged my palm. One more try, but I reminded myself to go slower this time. As I dug down, the shovel stopped again. Lifting the dirt, I could see the edge of what looked like a red brick. A brick? That's odd. Of course, my curiosity pushed me farther in my digging. The more I dug the more bricks I found. They began to make a flat pattern that covered an area of about four to five square feet.

I dropped the shovel to tell Paul, who was still in the garage. Before I even reached the side door, I was yelling his name, "PAUL!" Out of breath with excitement, I called out again, "You've got to see this. Come on."

Paul has always loved me for my adventuresome spirit and this time was no exception. He stopped sanding the old cabinet door from the dining room and attentively followed me out to the back of the barn. I thought I heard him mumble, "Never a dull moment with you."

"What did you say?" I asked as I hurried ahead of him.

"Nothing." He was laughing.

It didn't matter; I was too keyed up to care. I pointed to the uncovered bricks. "Take a look at what I found." I watched him walk around the red bricks. "What do you think?"

He looked intrigued. "You want me to dig them up?"

"I don't know. I guess we could use them in another garden area. Wait! Let's take a picture of this for our scrapbook. I'll get the camera."

Paul grabbed a shovel. By the time I returned he'd uncovered another layer under the bricks that consisted of old gray stones. He stopped and stared. "Look at this."

We stood in silence, gazing upon the multi-layered mystery. I handed him the camera. "Take some pictures of it just the way we found it."

Paul took two close-up shots and one to show the position of the find in the yard.

"Should we keep digging?" I asked.

Paul didn't wait to answer me; he started to pry up the red bricks, one by one. I quickly put them in a wheelbarrow. Slowly, the gray stones were uncovered. They formed a circle beneath the red bricks. Its center was filled in with dirt, but was broken on one side, with an opening of about three feet. Paul dug within the open space. His first shovel went down several inches before hitting another flat stone. He lifted more dirt away.

I couldn't resist getting closer and knelt down on the grass, scraping away the black topsoil. "Look, it's a step." I leaned in farther and brushed more dirt from the top of it. I pointed to the other side. "Dig over there, on the inside of the circle. See if the dirt goes down below this step."

Paul dug down twice more with his shovel on the opposite side, to reveal only dirt. That confirmed my idea of steps on only one side. Now I was excited. I stood up to get a better look. "What do you think?"

"I'm not sure, but it looks like a stairway down into some kind of a small room?"

"Maybe it's a root cellar?" I asked thinking of where people, centuries ago, used to store their winter foods.

"You may be right; it's too small for anything else," Paul said as he stood up.

I could smell the freshly dug dirt. It reminded me of spring, but within a few seconds, my thoughts slowly turned dark. I wondered if there was anything dead—animal or human—underneath the soil.

10

Present Day – July 1
BREWSTER – CAPE COD

THE SOUND OF RUMBLING GRAVEL on the driveway distracted the two of us as we stood over the mysterious stone circle. What time was it? I brushed the dirt from my hands. "That must be Molly."

I left Paul in deep thought, staring at the circle. He called over his shoulder, "I'll stay here."

Molly was smiling from inside the big SUV's rear seat. She waved with one hand and flattened her drawn picture up against the window with the other. "Mom, look what I made," she said as she scrambled out of the car.

As we walked to the backyard, I waved goodbye to my new carpooling partner for day camp and asked Molly, "Do you want to show Daddy your beautiful picture? He's in the backyard and...we have something to show you."

"What? Is it for me? Can I play with it?" she said, happily skipping, holding fast to me with her tiny fingers and gripping her artwork in her free hand. We rounded the garage and saw Paul leaning on his shovel. Molly ran over to him, circling his legs in a big hug.

"Hi, Daddy!" She pointed to the round patch of dirt. "What's that?"

"Well, it's something that your Mommy and I found. We're not sure what it is."

"Can I dig in it?"

"Yes, but only if you stay on the grass. Go get your digging stuff."

In a second she was back and squatting on the edge of the stones with eager anticipation of finding something important.

The crunch of gravel echoed again into the air. "I'll go see who it is. You keep your eye on Molly. I'll be right back." I headed towards the back of the gallery. My head ducked under the low doorframe that was once the entrance to the old outhouse. As I passed our antique cash register, I could see potential customers already browsing the artwork.

Paul looked at his little girl, "Molly, Daddy will be in the garage painting a cabinet. I can see you through the garage window. Be careful to stay on the grass, and no eating dirt!"

Molly smiled with satisfaction. She loved to get dirty and this giant hole pleased her. As she dug, she found several broken clamshells and laid them carefully on the grass in a row. She pulled out an old spoon, which she conveniently made into a shovel, and scooped out more dirt from inside the circle. Something small and round embedded in the dirt caught her eye so she knelt down to get closer. Cautious not to go into the circle, she reached in as far as she could and dug around the tubular shape. Her old rusted spoon quickly uncovered what looked like a pipe, almost two inches long, with a flat handle attached to its end.

She whispered to herself, "What's that?" She spat on her fingers and rubbed them over the handle to reveal markings. Pleased, she pushed her hair behind her ears to get a better view, leaving long black smudges across her cheeks. With a big smile on her face, she looked around to see if her Daddy could see her, then she stepped into the circle to pull the treasure out of the dirt.

I returned from the gallery to find Paul in the garage. "They were just browsing; here for the week. They said they'd be back before they head home to Connecticut." I sat down in the lounge chair next to the drawing table. "They seemed interested in your full sheet watercolor, *Cape Cod Bay*." I looked over to Paul. "It would be great to sell a big painting. We could really use the money…where's Molly?"

"I let her dig in the dirt. She's fine. She was getting pretty dirty a few seconds ago."

I peered out the window of the garage and saw Molly standing up, covered in dirt, examining something in her hands.

"What did she find now?" She was holding an object straight out with her hands. "Oh my God, what is that?" Fear gripped me as I ran outside, Paul following close behind me.

"Molly!"

The little girl turned, pointed the object at me and said, "Bang!"

11

Present Day – July 1
BREWSTER – CAPE COD

I TRIED TO REMAIN CALM and gently coaxed Molly, "Give it to me, honey."

Molly kept her hands on its handle. The gun was covered with dirt, but its identity was obvious and Molly knew exactly what it was.

Coming a little closer, I asked again, "Molly give it to me so we can look at it together." I had hoped she would just drop it on the ground. Lunging forward, I latched onto it as fast as I could and whisked it away from her little fingers. Up close I could tell, with a sigh of relief, that the gun was only a toy. "Do you know what this is?" I demanded from her.

"It's a gun, Mommy," she answered timidly.

"Yes it is, and thank goodness it's only a toy." The gun fit into the palm of my hand. I turned it over and brushed more dirt off it.

Tears began to wet Molly's eyes, and her bottom lip quivered.

Paul asked, "Can I see that?" He reached to take it from me.

"Here," I said, eager to be rid of it. Even though I was angry with Molly, thinking about what might have happened, I couldn't stop myself from imagining what else was in that hole.

Paul immediately examined the old toy, then turned back to look at the freshly dug dirt. "We better be careful if we're going to dig any deeper."

"Yeah, I guess we better watch our step," I agreed.

Molly started to bawl.

Paul scooped her up in a big hug. "I told you not to go inside the circle, didn't I?"

She nodded.

"All right, now don't cry. Let's go inside and wash your hands and face." He gave the gun back to me and walked into the house with Molly nestled in his arms.

I called after him, "I'll be right in. There's a snack in the refrigerator for Molly."

I laid the small toy on the edge of the grass by the hole. Afraid someone might trip on the exposed bricks and stones, I decided to find something to cover the open circle. I found two sawhorses leaning against the back wall of the garage. It only took two trips to carry them outside and arrange them in the front and back of the circle, with enough room for me to continue digging. "That should do it." I put my hands on my hips, feeling confident about my well-constructed barricade.

Casey appeared at the back door of the house. "Hey, Mom."

I motioned to Casey. "Come and see what your Dad and I found."

She came nearer as I grabbed a trowel and plunged it into the dirt. My heart was racing so fast with what already had been discovered, I didn't even make eye contact with my own daughter. Finally I looked up. "Sorry, honey, I'm so curious about what's buried in here." I tossed the toy gun across the grass to her. "Look at what your sister found!

Casey bent down to look at the gun, then started to push the dirt around with the old spoon that Molly had used. "Dad told me. How did you know it wasn't real?"

I pointed to a small stamped image on the gun. "When I brushed off some of the dirt I could see a little circled star printed on the handle. My brother and I had one just like it when we were kids."

Casey examined both sides of the toy. I was just about to tell her that it was too rusty to be dangerous when she casually dropped it on the ground and asked, "What's for dinner?"

"I don't know. I guess I got too engrossed in all this digging to think about food. I completely lost track of time." Dinner was not a high priority on my list of things to do. Too bad she's not interested, I thought, this is such fun.

"Okay, I'm goin' in." Casey stood up and sulked back to the house in one of her teen moods.

Intent to keep digging, I hoped to uncover more buried items and possibly even a little treasure. Maybe I'd find something worth a lot of money. I scooped more dirt out. With each shovelful I kept pushing myself to dig deeper, hoping that the next shovelful might be the one that revealed something out of the ordinary.

One hour later, after finding only a few pieces of shells, colored glass, and an old, navy blue button, my quest for riches began to lose its luster and disappointment took over. I looked at the huge mound of dirt to the side of me that was growing by the minute. I needed to find a place to put all this extra dirt. Frustrated, I leaned back against my heels. It was getting dark, and I convinced myself that I could always work on this tomorrow. Reluctantly, I gathered my found treasures: the spoon, the button and the gun. I tossed the shells onto the graveled driveway.

The items cradled in my hands didn't look that great to me. I wished that I'd found something...anything unique. Grudgingly I walked into the house to face five starving people.

*   *   *

That night, I couldn't sleep. I kept thinking of buried treasure, gold coins and pirates. I moved closer towards Paul under the sheets. A flapping noise, somewhere close, began to prey on my nerves. I tried to dismiss it as something outside blowing in the wind, but with every little creak or groan from the old house I slid even nearer to Paul. By the time I found a good position, Paul had already begun to breathe deeply. When he was snoring an even rhythm, my eyes finally closed and I fell asleep, nestled up against his back.

It must have been an hour later when I felt someone shaking me. I sat up, half asleep and covered with sweat. I felt more shaking. I screamed, "No, I can't stay here. I want to get out! I can't get out!" I heard someone talking, but their words weren't clear. I was panicked.

Paul had his hands on my shoulders. "Nancy, wake up! You're dreaming. You're having a nightmare." His voice softened, "Honey, are you all right?"

I rubbed my eyes and arms. Running my fingers through my hair, I finally recognized Paul. "Oh, my God, what a terrible dream. I felt all this shaking. I'm so glad it was you just trying to wake me." I sat on the edge of the bed. "I need to eat something before I tell you my dream."

Paul was half asleep as he grinned at my silly superstition; I always ate before sharing my dreams. If I didn't eat, I believed they might come true. We walked down the steps in silence to the kitchen for some gingersnaps and milk.

"Okay, spill your guts," Paul said to me as I sat down at the table.

"It was so scary. I was floating in the air and looking down into a small round room. I could see a dark figure in the corner, bending over a box or something. There was dirt all over the floor. It was a woman in a long dress and she was digging. Then all of a sudden she turned and looked up at me. I tried to leave the room, but I couldn't get out. Her face was covered in grime, and she had red lines on her cheeks that looked like blood."

Paul calmly leaned against the counter, munching a cookie. "I bet the room was the cellar that we found yesterday. You know how your subconscious pulls things together that you see during the day into random images, then mixes them up so that your dreams are just plain weird."

"I guess so. But it all seemed so real."

"Did you see any old movies or unusual commercials yesterday?"

"No, but I've been thinking a lot about pirates and treasure. Come to think of it, after supper I showed Molly an ad for the Pirate Museum in Provincetown. It had a discount on tickets for Tuesday mornings before 10:30." I reached for the ad in the newspaper that was ready to be recycled come morning, and pointed to the colorful figures in the ad. "See, it shows pictures of Sam Bellamy—they call him the Prince of Pirates—and his supposed lover, Maria Hallett."

"Well, that solves the mysterious long dress. Don't worry about it. Let's get to bed." He gave me a hug and followed right behind me, turning off the lights as we went back upstairs.

July 2

The following morning I could tell Paul was already up. The coffee smelled delicious. I lay in bed trying to figure out if the nightmare and the late night snack actually happened. I shook them off as silly and began planning my day. With eyes half open I ticked off the things that needed to be done. First, get Molly off to day camp, look through yesterday's mail and then get back to my digging. I should have plenty of time to explore in that old root cellar. I hoped it wasn't the same one in my nightmare.

No shower now, I'll take it later. Jogging pants, a Beatles t-shirt and old sneakers would make a fine outfit for digging. After tucking the bottom of my pants into socks to ward off ticks, I glanced out the bedroom window to look at the barricaded hole. Thoughts of buried treasure flooded my head again. Calm down. Remember, whatever I find will be a treasure, even if it's nothing valuable. Walking down the stairs and into the kitchen, I still hoped to find money.

I gave Paul a big kiss. "I had such a terrible dream last night. Did we eat cookies in the kitchen, or did I dream that, too?"

He laughed, "No, we ate cookies, and then you told me about your dream."

"Well, I'm glad the creepy lady wasn't real."

A Carolina wren's song echoed into the house from the open back porch. I grabbed a cup of coffee to calm my fears. "Is everyone still sleeping? I better go and get them up."

After I dropped Molly at camp and everyone had left for their summer jobs, I decided to tackle the bills before doing any more digging. As I picked through the letters, I came across a thin envelope from the bank. This was never a good sign; it usually meant an overdraft or some other problem. I ripped it open. It was a notice of overdraft. What? In small black type, information for four checks was listed and noted that they were not paid due to insufficient funds. I felt irritated as I pulled the checkbook out and reread the notice, comparing the numbers. It couldn't be. I read it again. That's when I saw it. In my checkbook ledger I had recorded a check for $60.36. The bank's amount read $6036.00. Someone had typed the decimal point in the wrong place!

I picked up the phone. Thank God this isn't my fault, I thought. After a few seconds of waiting to be connected to a real person who could help me, I imagined my future life. Living on the edge, with an up and down income, could become tiresome real fast.

A polite woman on the other end of the phone eventually answered and listened to my explanation; then she put me on hold again. I started to doubt our decision to move. We had been doing okay where we were.

A gentleman answered and quickly resolved the situation by waiving the fees, but I still had to call the four people that didn't get paid to tell them to resubmit their checks. Such a waste of energy; I could have been outside in that old cellar, looking for treasure. When I explained the whole scenario to Paul, he looked relieved. I rounded up my gardening tools, along with a wheelbarrow, and headed straight to the back to the barricaded hole. Paul was at his drawing table again, and with a quick wave I yelled, "I'm going digging."

I removed the barricades faster than I'd set them up. After repeatedly sinking my shovel into the center of the dirt, lifting it out and heaving it into the waiting wheelbarrow, I could finally stand knee-deep in the center of the hole with dirt walls encircling my legs.

Paul watched from his studio. Inquisitive, he wandered outside. "How's it going?"

Wiping my forehead, I said, "Well, it's a lot of work, but not too bad."

"Want some help?" he asked.

"Sure. Do you think we'll hear a customer pull in from back here?"

"Maybe. Anyway, the sun is so hot today, it seems like a beach day, not a shopping day."

"Could you empty the dirt for me?" I pointed to where the grass met the woods. "Dump it over there."

"Okay," he said.

Still determined to find something, I crouched down in the hole and picked at the dirt with my trowel. The point of the shovel hit some wood. "Paul, look here."

Clambering out of the hole to get my thermos of water, I let Paul get in for a closer view of the wood. He dug a little harder and wooden splinters began to fall away. All of a sudden, he hit a solid wall of stone. He looked up at me. "I think this wood was part of some shelving."

He chipped away at the narrow piece of wood. "I'm betting this was definitely a root cellar." It fell to the ground; he picked it up and placed it on the grass by my feet.

"Is that a square-headed nail in it?" I asked.

"It sure is."

"I want to get back in, Paul. Come on out."

Casey, home from her baby-sitting job, came out the back door of the house. "Are you two still digging?"

We felt like treasure hunters and called out in unison, "Yup!"

I added, "Casey, when Molly comes home, get her to wash up and give her a snack. Your father and I may be out here for a while. And tell me if any customers pull in."

"Do I have to?" Casey asked.

"Yes, you have to." I turned to Paul. "Let's do take-out tonight. That way we can work here till it gets dark, or at least till we get to the bottom of this mystery."

We looked at each other and smiled in agreement. With our backs together, the hole continued to widen. Over the next two hours we were able to dig to a depth of three feet. Three steep steps could be seen on one side and were now used to climb in and out of the hole. My fingernails were thick with dirt as more clamshells, broken pottery and wood were found and laid flat on the grass around the opening.

As the other kids began to arrive home, each one came outside to see what we were doing. We sent Jim to get pizza for supper. When he returned with the food, we took a break and explained to the kids about the root cellar and what we had found so far.

Everyone sat at the picnic table and crowded close together to see the items that were uncovered.

After supper Brian asked, "Do you need any help?"

Paul answered, "I think we can handle it. We want to go slow, being very careful with anything we find, but thanks anyway. Just help Casey watch Molly."

There was only one more hour of daylight left for digging. Our method was simple. Paul did the grunt work by filling a five gallon white pail with dirt, then lifting it up onto the grass so I could dump it in the wheelbarrow and search for any artifacts.

"I bet we don't have much farther to go to reach the bottom. This kind of cellar was not very deep," said Paul.

Within a short time, Paul's head, shoulders and the top portion of his chest could only be seen above the ground. As he dug deeper, his shovel hit something with a loud thunk. I stopped in mid-sift and looked at him.

"What was that?"

"I don't know," he said.

He dug again. It was definitely something hard. He dropped the shovel and knelt on one knee. His hands moved quickly to remove more dirt, finally revealing the top of a wooden chest.

12

Early Summer 1715
EASTHAM – CAPE COD

IT WAS A COOL MORNING IN JUNE, and Sam had been gone two months. Maria lay within the safety of her bed. She wondered when Sam would come back. She scratched the tip of her nose, pulled the quilt up towards her chin and opened her eyes. Above her head, planks of wood held the stairs in place that led to the long room where she spun and wove her cloth. Her father's snoring pleased her. She whispered, "Please don't wake yet."

The sun pouring through the window cast blocks of light on the floor. Specks of dust floated across the room and into the kitchen towards the hearth. For the past several mornings, Maria had struggled to get out of bed. Tired and nauseous, she had slept late again, and lay silently dreading her day's chores. The sky outside her window was a cloudless brilliant blue; she wished Sam were lying next to her. Flickers of Sam's image holding her in his arms drifted in and out of her thoughts. Even on this beautiful day, she had no desire to get out of her bed.

A great wave of nausea suddenly flooded her body, and she sat upright. Confused, she looked around her room, searching for any item out of place, but everything was as it should be. Anxiety stirred her mind as if it were a pot of stew. Am I with child? She placed her hands on her stomach and then covered her mouth. She wanted to vomit, but pursed her lips together, trying to hold it back. Her hands perspired as a rush of warmth flushed her neck and face. Maria pulled at her shift to loosen its hold on her clammy body. What have I done?

Fear fell upon her whole being. If I am with child, she thought, no one must know, not even Father. She swiveled her body around and clambered out of bed. Her bare feet felt the grit of the sandy floor, but she felt as if she were in a nightmare. She needed help. She needed Minda, the old *Pow Wah*. Quickly dressing, before her father awoke, Maria slipped in silence out the door.

She followed the path away from her house towards the coast, repeating over and over in her head, I am with Sam's child... I need Minda. She'll know what to do.

Minda

Minda pulled back the brown, supple leather that was the door to her *wetu*. She took a deep breath to draw the fresh morning air into her body, then she prayed aloud, "Good Morning, *Kiehtan*, my Creator. You are good to us; you give us another young season to start life again. Thank you." The old *Poh Wah* squaw smiled.

Looking around with love at the other *wetus*, the medicine woman continued in her heart. My people are still quiet in their beds. It is time for me to go and gather roots and herbs. Quietly closing the flap behind her, she turned inside and walked to the back of her small dwelling.

Her feet followed familiar steps on the soft dirt floor to her bed, made from a raised platform of sewn reeds. She reached up to touch the primitive arched wall of her *wetu* that she had built many seasons ago. The sapling poles, tied with strips of cedar and layered with bark, made her dwelling round and secure. These pieces of bark still protect me well, she thought, tracing the rough edges with her fingers, as a mother would follow the lines of her child's face. Minda shook her head back and forth as she noticed daylight coming through some of the reed mats that covered the bark roof. It will soon be time for me to sew new reeds. But she hid this reminder of extra work behind her thoughts so that she could focus on her task of gathering what she needed for her potions.

Before she took her leave on this peaceful early morning, she gazed upon a piece of smooth tan leather, tied by its four corners to the *wetu* poles above her primitive bed. Decorated with fanciful drawings in colors of red from the cranberry, yellow from the jewelweed, and blue from the wild berry, this natural wall hanging kept her warm from chilly drafts and reminded her of pleasant summers and plentiful autumn harvests.

Minda indulged herself with a passion for painting. She reveled in it when the winds blew in early winter and the village was quiet. She cherished her solitude during this short time, when she could steal away to paint alone, before her people were forced by deep snow to move into the six-fire *wetu*.

Throughout the other seasons, she loved to see her drawings by the light of the fire as she lay in her own bed. A contented sigh came from within her; she had a good life, and a sense of pride surged inside her. She pulled a large bag from under her bed and placed its strap over her head and onto her shoulder. Made out of brown deerskin, it was soft and smooth, decorated with beautiful painted symbols of the sun, moon and stars. She stopped to adjust its fit on her hip, then softly stepped outside, leaving her sanctuary.

Minda could see in the eastern sky, *Mishanok*, the morning star. The soft coo of mourning doves echoed through the forest's canopy, and in the early sunlight, drops of dew from the night reflected in trees like jewels. Leaving the clearing on which her village was built, Minda entered the deep woods.

She was never fearful when she walked in these woods. The tall trees were like warriors who stood close as brothers, their dense branches becoming shields protecting the Nausets. Only Minda and her people knew the path she followed through this natural barrier. There were signs and signals from fallen or twisted trees that would tell a Nauset which way to turn, or warn them not to go further. Dangerous places were identified by secret markings. Passing an ancient tree with lines in its wood from the termite, Minda knew to be careful. To a Nauset it said, 'Do not pass beyond this point'. To a white man it said nothing more than just old insect trails.

As she approached the last of the great cedars, she could hear the distant sound of the ocean waves making their tidal rush onto the beach. Minda knew she was near the end of the woods. She felt happy in her heart as she made her way among the trees toward the sea. At an age of fifty years, her moccasin-covered feet flew along the path like a young maiden's.

13

Early Summer 1715
EASTHAM – CAPE COD

THE MEDICINE WOMAN EMERGED from the protection of the forest and stared at the white man's wooden meetinghouse built high on a hill that looked out to sea. Its location was a vantage point for the Eastham settlers; it enabled them to spot unfriendly foreign ships and served as a gathering place for religious services.

As the old *Poh Wah* stepped around the timbered house, she kept her distance by staying close to the edge of the woods. She passed the stone where an engraved T marked the property of Rev. Samuel Treat. Minda could see the tall green grasses and cattails of the marsh as she walked.

Following the narrow path around his land, she felt proud that the reverend had always shown respect and kindness to her. When she offered words of advice to him on healing, he listened. He even spoke the Nauset language. In turn, she felt the reverend's words would do no harm to her people and welcomed those Nausets who had turned to his God. She nodded her head up and down in agreement with herself. Reverend Treat had made progress in quieting the tension between the white settlers and the Indians.

A large grey rock appeared before Minda, where her people honed their arrows and tools. She slid her fingers along its surface, feeling the long narrow grooves of many years of sharpening. In the distance, a young woman sat on the trunk of a dead tree that had washed onto the shore. The dark-haired girl turned her head back and forth as if looking for someone. As soon as she spotted the old woman, she stood and waved, beckoning her to come closer. Minda recognized Maria and quickened her pace toward her. As she climbed down the high dune, she remembered her promise to Sara Hallett that she would watch over the girl and teach her ways that would help her grow into a happy and strong woman. She was pleased at how quickly Maria took to the secrets of healing and the intricacies of the loom.

Minda understood how the young girl felt without a mother because she too was motherless. She always held onto the heartbreaking day, at eight years of age, when her parents and most of the Narraganset people in her village had been killed. The survivors of that massacre, 102 children including herself, were taken to Boston and sold into the homes of white people to become 'civilized'. The Widow Jackson, of Cambridge, had bought Minda and taken her into her home. Kind at first, she'd given Minda opportunities to learn the ways of the white man, especially the craft of weaving, but had always kept the girl at a distance. She had offered no affection to the orphaned Indian child.

As she walked closer to Maria, Minda recalled her few pleasant memories during captivity. There were travels with the widow, when they would visit friends during the summer in Eastham, and the North Parish of Harwich, near the village of the Nauset Indians. She'd always enjoyed these journeys away from Cambridge. They took her to familiar places like dense forests and the beautiful seaside. They reminded Minda of her childhood in Narraganset, when she would scavenge for herbs and roots with her mother, and gather favorites like sea lettuce, marsh mallow root for candy, and sweet grass for fragrant bracelets.

When, at age eighteen, the law finally allowed Minda her freedom, she left the Jackson House, but remained ever grateful for the widow's benevolence. She took whatever money was saved from selling her weaving and traveled as far east as she could go, to the land of the Praying Indians. There, she was welcomed for her knowledge in the traditions of the spirits and gifts of healing. Her magical ways, passed down by her mother, had assured her status among the Nausets.

Minda shielded her eyes with her hand from the morning glare as she descended to the shoreline. She felt Maria's fear as soon as they embraced. With a tender touch she pushed away strands of hair from the frightened girl's face and asked, "What is troubling you?"

Maria pulled back. "I'm not sure what's wrong with me." She folded her arms across her breasts and draped her shawl over her stomach, as if to conceal something.

Minda reached forward again to hold her. "Sit down, so we can talk."

The two figures sat on the blackened tree trunk. Maria revealed her symptoms that sparked the notion of carrying Sam's child.

Minda patiently listened. "It is possible that you are with child," she concluded.

Maria stared at the old Indian as she explained who the father was.

"Maria, the laws of your church are very strict."

Maria nodded her head, knowing what was expected of a young girl in her condition. Naming the father of the unborn child made everything acceptable while a girl carried the child, and upon its birth she would marry the named father. But if she did not know who the father was, or did not want to name him, she was branded a fornicator, treated as a whore, and eventually punished or banished.

The *Pow Wah* fondled a small loop of twined flowers on her wrist and looked at Maria. "Tell me more."

The young girl's voice trembled. "Few people in the area know who Sam Bellamy is; he only stayed a short time. What should I do? No one knows him. I'm so frightened!"

Very fond of Maria, and never having had children herself, Minda cherished her as one of her own. Any advice that she would now speak would have to be given carefully. She cradled Maria's face in her hands and spoke from the heart. "You must reach deep inside yourself and listen to the voice that speaks to you. You will hear it telling you what to do." She took Maria's hands into hers and continued, "If you choose not to carry this child, you must know that I have ways to help you."

Maria stared out to sea.

Minda offered more words. "If you believe that Sam will return to you, and you have a true love for him, keeping his child will be right. If you choose life, then let this little one inside you grow and blossom."

Maria stood and placed her hands on her stomach. The old *Pow Wah* held Maria's shoulders once more and caught Maria's gaze. "Let this be a sign of love. Remember, you are a strong woman. I will help you and our great Creator will watch over you."

14

Early summer 1715
EASTHAM – CAPE COD

MARIA'S SLENDER FINGERS TRACED PATTERNS through the sand as she sat near the water's edge. She watched Minda gather sea lettuce and clams along the tidal flats. As the water slowly made its return along the shoreline, Maria thought about her options. She knew a healthy child was the common outcome, but was also aware of the dangers of childbirth. Assisting Minda in several births, Maria had witnessed the pain and anguish of a little one's death, either prematurely, by the woman's choice, or by the order of an angry father.

She sifted the tiny particles of ground stone through her toes and told herself that Sam would marry her. A decision must be made.

When Minda finished her work, she placed the found treasures into her shoulder bag and sat down next to Maria. "Today I am going to the North Parish to see Abigail. As of late, she has not felt well. Have you finished her cloth?"

"Yes, I have.... Why?"

"Then you must come with me." Minda hoped she would say yes.

Maria weighed the Indian's words for only seconds before she answered, "I'll go. My father is going to Barnstable for business, so he'll be gone for several days."

Happy that they were both going to visit Abigail Doane, Minda fondly recalled when she had first met Abigail. As a child, she had taken trips from Cambridge to North Harwich with Widow Jackson to visit Abigail's mother. Being similar in age, the two young girls, Minda and Abigail, had become fast friends and kept their friendship over the years. Maria had developed a strong bond with the two women, who both appreciated her beautiful weaving talents.

As they stood on the beach, Maria hugged Minda goodbye, suggesting they meet at the house when the sun was high above their heads, after her father had left for Barnstable. Matthew Ellis, from the neighboring farm, would help her get the horse and wagon ready for their trip west to Abigail's. Maria knew Matthew would never say no to her.

Maria hurried along the path. Mindful that she was only wearing her shift and shawl, she ran faster, not wanting to be seen by anyone. As the sun heated her skin, she began to perspire. By the time she arrived home, she was dripping wet.

She placed a clean shift and skirt into a small sack and prayerfully thanked her mother that her father was already gone. He would have been angry with her for not fixing his breakfast.

She went outside to raise the green flag on a pole that topped the roofline of her house. It signaled to Matthew that she needed him to get the wagon ready. This was a game they had played when they were younger, pretending to be sea captains on the high seas, using colored pieces of material to send messages back and forth. Now that they were older, they occasionally played the signal game, even though their elders frowned upon this silliness, expecting them to be more mature. She trusted that he would see her signal.

Surprised to see the flag, Matthew was more than pleased to accept Maria's request. He stopped splitting wood, set aside his axe and walked towards the Hallett home.

Meanwhile, Maria brought water from the well into the house and set it down on top of her bureau. After dropping her soiled garment onto the bed, she withdrew a bottle of Minda's lavender water from inside a drawer. Into the cool water, she sprinkled two drops. Then, she took a deep breath, letting the wonderful scent calm her.

After bathing, Maria patted herself dry and reached for a fresh shift hanging on a peg under the stairs. It slipped over her head with ease. She pulled a corset from the bottom drawer of the bureau, placed it over her cotton shift and laced up the front, being careful not to pull it too tight across her stomach. Next came her drawstring petticoat. As she tied the strings that held her skirt she realized that she would be able to adjust her skirts to accommodate the child as it grew. Her thoughts surprised her; she sat down on the bed. She closed her eyes and tried to listen to the voice inside her that Minda spoke of. Maria squeezed her eyelids together, trying to listen to her thoughts and feelings. Her hands moved over her stomach. Her next words almost sounded like a prayer. "I think I will keep this child. I know that Sam loves me. I trust him. When he returns, he'll take care of me, and this little one inside me too."

Her decision made, she felt better. With determination to move forward with her choice, Maria continued dressing, pinning a pocket to her petticoat and then smoothing it flat. She felt joyful at the thought of bearing Sam's child.

A second petticoat was laid over the first and fastened in the front with long pins. It had a large slit to its side for access to the pocket, hiding it from view. She hid a shilling for an emergency. Chanting her words now, she repeated, "I'm going to have Sam's child."

Maria moved with lighthearted steps to the bureau and chose one of her better handkerchiefs to go around her neckline, tucking it in across the top of the corset. She felt confident Sam would return before the birth. She folded her apron into the carrying basket, in case she needed it when they arrived at Abigail's house.

She could hear Matthew in the barn preparing the wagon. As he brought the wagon closer to the house, Maria relieved herself in the jar under her bed instead of going outside one more time before they left. Lifting her skirts, she looked down and noticed she wore no shoes or stockings. She giggled to herself and thought that being with child must make women do silly things. She scooped up the basket that held her apron and placed Abigail's new woven cloth inside, along with biscuits wrapped in a piece of cotton plus her shoes and stockings. As she grabbed her cap hanging by the door, Maria glanced over at her unmade bed and promised herself that she would empty the bed jar when she got home.

15

Early summer 1715
NORTH HARWICH – CAPE COD

MATTHEW HELPED MARIA INTO THE WAGON. As he touched her hand, he looked at her face and thought how beautiful she was, there was such a glow about her. "Be careful now," he said.

Maria joined Minda on the wagon's worn wooden seat and placed her basket in the back. "We will. And thank you, Matthew, for hitching up Old Brother. See you in a few days."

He stepped away from the wagon as Minda gave a clicking sound and flipped the leather reins up and across the horse's back. Old Brother trotted off down the path that led to the dirt cart-way.

The rough old wagon cradled them as they passed through familiar landscapes. When they approached the deforested land of the King's Highway, Minda pulled back on the reins to stop Old Brother. "So many fine-looking trees are gone Maria. I cannot understand why your people take not only our lands, but our forests too. We are left with so little. My heart weeps for what will become of us and your children yet to be."

Maria had no words of consolation. There was nothing either one of them could do.

The landscape looked so barren to Minda, she closed her thoughts about something she could not change and looked over at the young Maria. "You seem better, not so nervous. I think that you have decided to become a mother."

Maria held her head down, looked sideways towards Minda, smiled and nodded yes. The old woman covered Maria's hands with her own, gently squeezing them as a comfortable silence fell over the two friends.

They traveled for hours before they came to the Namaskaket lands and finally to the North Parish of Harwich. They could see Abigail from the road as they came over the crest of the hill; she was sitting under a large oak tree next to the house. Her new home was nearly finished with only trim remaining. Abigail spotted the wagon and waved at them with a weak sway of her hand.

Minda took notice of Abigail's demeanor and hoped she was feeling better.

A widow from Yarmouth, Abigail was forty-two years old and enjoyed being the second wife of fifty-three-year old Nathanial Doane. When Nathanial surprised his bride with plans for a new dwelling farther east, she didn't mind the move. She looked contentedly around her property and thought it was advantageous that Nathanial had inherited this land in the Namaskaket area from his father, one of the Purchasers or Old Comers. The happy bride felt comforted with the thought of how endearing Nathanial was because he was so worried about her health. Yes, it was bothersome to her that her stamina and well-being was causing some concern, but Nathanial reassured Abigail that his wedding gift of a new dwelling would cheer her up and be good for her. She sat in front of her promised new house, enjoying the shade from the lone tree above her head, waiting for her guests to arrive.

The two travelers pulled alongside the large tree. Minda called out, "I am glad you are getting fresh air, Abigail, my friend."

Maria jumped out of the wagon, straightened her skirts and greeted Abigail with a hug. "Wait till you see what I've brought you. I know you'll like it." She lifted her things out of the wagon just as Jacob took Old Brother into the barn for oats, water and a night of rest.

Abigail looked tired, but eager to visit with her friends, and reached out to both of them. Laughing, with arms around one another, they walked into the house.

The raised threshold of the simple full cape house greeted them; it led to a narrow staircase that ascended upstairs. Abigail, being first inside, moved to the right and into the kitchen. Maria looked at the two windows that faced front and then glanced back at the large center chimney fireplace. She ran her hand over the thick smooth wood of the long table and placed her basket next to a small jar of spring flowers. Two long benches ran along each side of the table, and shelves opposite the hearth held cooking utensils, bowls, spices and various condiments. When Sam returned with the riches he had promised, this was the kind of house that she would like.

Minda peered into the borning room in the rear of the kitchen. It was small, but adequate for birthing and for anyone who might become sick. She nodded her approval, thinking it was good to be so close to the kitchen in times of tending.

Abigail gestured to the two travelers. "Come, let me show you the rest of my house."

Minda placed her arm around Abigail and rubbed her back. "Your house is good."

On the other side of Abigail's kitchen was the parlor, where the single center chimney opened to another large hearth. Maria admired two winged chairs and a small folding table, where guests would be entertained. To the rear of the parlor was the master bedroom for Abigail and Nathanial. Following Abigail into the room, she stared at a large four-poster bed with soft, green velvet curtains tied back around each post. "What beautiful fabric, Abigail." Maria stroked the luxurious curtains.

"Aren't they wonderful?" Abigail asked. "They keep Nathanial and I warm from drafts." Abigail smiled as she touched the green material. "I chose them for their color; when I wake up in the morning I feel as if I'm sleeping outside under the trees."

As the two friends trailed behind their gracious hostess, Abigail apologized for the sparse furnishings in the other rooms. Maria didn't mind; she thought the house was cozy. She liked the simple jars of water holding little flowers that Abigail had placed around the rooms; it was so welcoming.

"Most of my treasures have not yet arrived from Boston," Abigail added, beaming with pride. She walked over to the stairway and pointed upstairs, "That's where you will be spending the night. Go on up, don't mind me."

Abigail settled herself on the bench in the kitchen to catch her breath. Smelling the little bouquet of flowers on the table she called out to her friends, "I'm a little tired. Hestor will soon be here to fix dinner for us."

There were two small rooms upstairs; one on the right was washed a soft green and the room on the left had a light blue tint on its walls. Maria favored the blue room with its little bed covered in a matching blue and white coverlet. Before sitting, she checked under the bedding and noticed how it was tied. "Very strong and tight," she said, giving her approval. She sat down and placed her hands on either side of her body. Bouncing up and down, she called out, "Oh, this will do." She jumped up and walked across to the other room. "Minda, how's your bed?"

The green room was in disarray.

"Minda! "Where are you?"

Over by the window, she saw that Minda had placed blankets on the floor between the bed and the wall under the window. She was lying on top of them.

"I am making sure it is right, so I can sleep tonight." Minda smoothed the pretty green quilt with her hand, shaping it into a nest. Then, as if this was normal behavior for her to be on the floor, she looked at Maria and asked, "Shall we go find Abigail? I am sure she needs help."

Maria agreed, ignoring her dear friend's strange Indian ways, following her down the steep steps into the kitchen.

Hestor had already arrived with a simple stew she'd cooked overnight at her house and was stirring it over the fire in the kitchen hearth. Nathanial had hired Hestor, a local woman whose family had encountered difficult times recently. He knew she needed extra money and would help Abigail with the cooking and various chores around the house. A portly, round faced woman, Hestor spoke few words, but always did what she was told. Although the housekeeper was not much of a companion to Abigail, Nathanial thought it useful to have someone look after his wife while he was away at sea. As the two women entered the kitchen, Abigail introduced them.

Hestor looked up from her stirring, gave them a look up and down, rolled her eyes and muttered under her breath, "Yes, ma'am. She returned to her chores without any other acknowledgment of the guests.

Minda felt uneasy with this cold reception and took the blame to herself. It had happened before, many times, as she traveled to places outside her Nauset home. The memories of King Phillip's War, four decades ago, still echoed with anger and distrust of the Indians who lived within the colonies.

Abigail sensed the tension. She thanked Hestor and instructed her to leave. "We'll be fine for tonight. See you tomorrow."

Hestor answered, "Yes, ma'am." Gathering her things together, she muttered something about 'those savages' and slammed the rear door of the house.

Maria got up from the bench and looked out the window to see Hestor's large behind, covered with layers of skirts, swaying from side to side as she walked away. "Good riddance. How can you stand her, Abigail? Doesn't she ever smile? I hope her stew is better than her manners." Maria gave the steaming kettle a quick stir and the hearty smells drifted into her nose. "Well, I must admit, it smells good."

*   *   *

Within the hour, the three friends sat down to a satisfying dinner of meat stew laced with carrots, potatoes and onions. They cleaned their bowls with fresh bread. As it was getting dark, apple cider was heated over the fire and the women enjoyed their beverages along with sweet treats of maple sugar candy. Abigail had made them from the syrup that was harvested, several months prior, on their property. A warm rosy color glowed on Abigail's face from the potent cider and warm hearth. She wiped her brow with a handkerchief and asked, "Now, Maria, where is my cloth?"

Maria blushed next. "I'm so sorry, I forgot to show you." She stood to get her basket from the floor where she had placed it before dinner. All eyes were focused on Maria as she unfolded the beautiful cloth. Its intricate woven patterns of blues and yellows were magnificent.

Abigail touched the soft linen, "I love it, Maria. When my new tea table arrives this will complement its surface. I'll be the envy of the whole Massachusetts Bay Colony."

As Maria's teacher of weaving, Minda was very proud of her student and the well-made cloth.

Pleased with it herself, Maria put her basket back on the floor. "Now I have news to tell you. But you must hear me out until I'm finished and then tell no one." She sat down opposite Abigail and looked over at Minda for approval.

Minda agreed with a silent nod of her head.

Maria took a sip of cider, then a deep breath, and began telling Abigail about Sam, her talk with Minda on the beach, her questions, and finally her decision to have Sam's child.

Abigail sat quiet and listened. "You've delivered me news that is almost too much to grasp tonight." She folded her hands on the table and looked straight at Maria. "Do you trust this Sam to come back for you?"

Maria replied with a sparkle in her eyes, "Yes, I trust him. I trusted him right away. There was something about him and I knew he was sincere."

Abigail cupped Maria's hand with hers, searching for the right words. After several seconds, she spoke. "It seems that you love this Sam."

"Yes, I do," Maria replied.

"What if he does not return to you? Are you prepared to live with the consequences of your decision? You must realize many people like Hestor live within the colony. They are narrow-minded and blindly follow the laws of the church."

"What do you mean?" Maria asked.

"Sometimes the good people of our community forget that we are all trying to survive as God's family in this new land," Abigail explained. "They become unforgiving towards people who don't follow the rules, even if they are unfair rules. They often forget they need to keep love in their hearts for one another."

Abigail took a sip of the strong cider. "Many times, because people's own lives become difficult to live, they blame bad things that happen to them on the evil of the devil. Anyone they do not approve of or dislike, becomes, in their minds, a servant of the devil." Abigail shook her head in disgust. "I've often thought this misguided reasoning takes the blame away from their own mistakes and problems." She touched Maria's cheek. "You must remain strong and take very good care of yourself until your Sam returns. Attend church as usual and do not call attention to yourself. Remember that Minda and I will be here for you."

The old *Pow Wah* placed her fingers over Maria and Abigail's joined hands. The three friends were different in age, race, and social stature, but it did not matter, for they found that another bond was forming among them.

*   *   *

When Maria retired, the bed felt softer than hers at home, and the room smelled fresh. Happy that Abigail knew about the child, and pleased that she had some extra shillings to take home from the sale of her cloth, sleep came quickly to Maria that night. She dreamt of Sam holding her in his arms and speaking words of promise to her, "I will return for you, I love you!"

As dawn came, she could still feel Sam's kisses and heard a sweet, delightful song being sung close by. She felt warm and safe as the melodic sounds lulled her; she kept her eyes closed, not wanting to wake up. Warm tender feelings filled her thoughts, shifting between visions of Sam, to her room, and then back to Sam again. In a dream-like state she called out his name, but there was no answer.

Looking around the empty room she realized it was just a dream, but she could still hear the sweet sounds surrounding her. Peering through the window, Maria saw a tree rustle in the wind with little birds swaying on its branches, singing their morning song. It sounded like the music from her dream; everything had seemed so real, Sam's touch, his words. Disappointed, she rubbed her eyes, surrendering to reality. Turning back the covers, Maria rose from her bed and walked over to the window. Old Brother was tied to the fence and the wagon was ready for the trip back to Eastham.

It is another day closer to when Sam comes home to me, she thought. Then with a deep sigh...it's also time to return to Father.

Gathering up her few possessions that lay around the room, Maria went down the stairs and into the kitchen just in time to see Hestor's cap disappear beneath the kitchen floor. Maria looked up to see Abigail entering from the back door. "Good morrow, Abigail." She pointed to the cavernous hole in the floor. "What's that? I didn't notice that opening before."

"My new root cellar," Abigail replied. "Nathanial thought it would be convenient for storing our supplies in the house. When the weather is cold, I will have no need to go outside for anything. I keep the rug over it to hide the hinges, lest I trip."

Maria peered down into the hole and saw flat stone steps leading into a small room. She couldn't see anything else from up above because Hestor's behind filled up the whole space. She caught glimpses of wooden shelves that had been built on the sides of the round cellar as Hestor ascended the steps.

"Out of my way, girl," Hestor called out from below.

Maria stepped back as Hestor lumbered up the flat steps carrying last season's peaches into the kitchen. Maria twisted her head, trying to look further into the underground room.

Hestor turned to face the young girl. "If you ask me, it was mighty wasteful to build those steps with such fancy stone pieces when wood is better and more practical." She muttered loud enough for Abigail to hear her opinion.

Abigail, who usually ignored Hestor's comments, shrugged her shoulders. She looked at Maria and smiled in resignation at the fact that Hestor always complained about something and felt she knew everything. Abigail motioned to Maria. "Let's sit outside with our cider while breakfast is prepared. Minda is already awake and wandering in my yard for any interesting herbs."

Trying to stay out of Hestor's way, Maria did as she was told and joined Abigail on the bench in the back of the house. "It has been so pleasant here, visiting with you."

"Well, it's too short of a visit for me." Abigail smiled at Maria. "I will count the days to the next time my two friends visit me from Eastham." She drank her cider and watched the early morning breeze ruffle through the high oak leaves above her head.

Maria, also enjoying the fine morning, could not stop daydreaming of Sam and the new life growing inside her.

*   *   *

They arrived in Eastham a little after sunset, when it was still in twilight. Maria's father was not yet home from Barnstable. Matthew was waiting on the bench.

Maria waved and called out, "Hello there, Matthew."

He placed his tankard on the bench and rose to meet the wagon. While tying Old Brother to the post, he watched Maria's every move. "Did you have a pleasant trip?"

"Wonderful," she answered. "Abigail's new house is splendid, except for her housekeeper."

Matthew helped her out of the wagon, eager just to touch her.

Maria laughed. "The woman never speaks a kind word, but surely delivers a fine stew."

He held her waist and looked straight into her eyes. "It's good that you had an agreeable visit." When he unloaded the weary traveler's bags, Matthew looked back at Maria. "I'll take care of Old Brother. Go on in and get some rest. We'll talk another day."

Minda watched Matthew from across the other side of the wagon and thought what a good man Matthew is...too bad that Maria does not see him as he sees her.

16

Present Day – July 2 & 3
BREWSTER – CAPE COD

IT WAS GETTING DARK, BUT PAUL KEPT DIGGING. I went to find a flashlight.

He called over his shoulder. "Bring one of my old paintbrushes?"

I was too excited to walk and found myself running to get the brushes from Paul's studio and grabbing a lantern off a shelf in the barn. By the time I returned, Paul was down on both knees inside the cellar, digging around the wooden box.

I scrambled in next to him. "What is it?"

He brushed the dirt from his hands and leaned back. "It's a box, all right, a wooden box with writing carved on top." Without looking up, he asked, "Did you bring the brushes?" He held his hand out like a surgeon in the operating room.

With light from the lantern, I quickly picked the biggest brush to hand to him, then coaxed him on with, "Do the top first."

Gently sweeping away the black dirt Paul whispered, "It looks like a letter D."

I looked closer. "You're right. I think I see something else."

Careful not to damage the rotted wood, Paul's gentle movements revealed two iron strap hinges across the wooden lid. "This is awesome," he said.

In less than a millisecond, the top caved in. "Damn it!" he shouted.

"Crap," I whispered. A cloud of crumbling wood and dirt descended down upon the contents. Whatever was inside the chest was hidden once again. I leaned in to touch the sides of the box. "It must have been beautiful at one time. I wonder how old it is?"

Paul ran his hands over the exposed sides. "I'm not sure— maybe a hundred years."

The chest measured about 16 x 20 inches. "How far does it go down into the dirt?" I bent my head over, trying to get a better idea of its depth. Neither one of us said anything for a few seconds, lost in our own curious thoughts. Standing up, I rubbed my hands clean. "Paul it's really getting dark. Maybe we better go in…. Should we cover it with something?"

He looked down at the find. "Go get a piece of plastic and a couple of bricks to hold it down for the night."

I left in search of what was needed.

After covering the chest and pushing the sawhorses close together to guard the hole, we walked towards the garage. Paul carried the lantern, and I held the brushes. I could sense the restlessness between us as we hurried across the yard. I knew we both wanted to keep digging, but it just wasn't going to happen anymore tonight. Anxious to tell the kids what we'd discovered, I wasted no time in getting to the house.

I dropped the brushes on the worktable in the garage, kicked off my muddy shoes then ran up the steps and into the living room. Paul stayed behind to clean up, as usual. I called out to the kids, "Guess what we found?"

They were all sitting in a line on the couch watching TV. I recited in one breath, "We found an old chest at the bottom of the cellar, but it's so dark we had to stop digging. It even had a big letter D on it and it was about this big," I showed its size with my hands. Then I took another breath and continued, "It could be over a hundred years old, but the lid broke, so we're not sure what else we'll find, if anything. We're going to try to dig it out tomorrow."

"Cool Mom," Brian said, keeping his eyes on the screen.

Jim chimed in. "Maybe you'll find treasure!" He tickled Molly, who was sitting next to him. "And then we'll be rich!" She laughed and flung her legs up into the air, hitting Jim in the mouth with her tennis shoes.

"Molly, be careful," I yelled out. "And don't forget," pointing at Molly, "it's almost time for your bed."

July 3

When morning came, Paul was up first. I stayed in bed a little longer, sleeping. As I stretched my arms above my head to wake up, Molly came running in next to the bed, "Mommy, come on. Let's go! Let's dig up treasure."

"Okay. Okay. I'm coming!" I sat up on the edge of the bed, dangling my feet. "Did you already eat your breakfast?"

Molly looked at me with wide eyes. "Yup, Daddy said I could watch and MAYBE dig a little." She leaned close to the bed and fidgeted with her foot, then pulled it up against her back in a stretch, "…IF I was careful."

Within the hour, the three of us were marching to the backyard armed with brushes, trowels and garden shovels, intent on resuming our dig in the old cellar.

"Molly! Until your brothers get home from work you'll have to stay with us," said Paul.

That was just fine with her.

After removing the sawhorse barricade, Paul pulled the tarp away to reveal the top of the chest and stepped down into the cellar. He began slowly to cut away at one side of the box. Molly sat on the edge of the hole with a pile of dirt, a pail and a shovel. I jumped in next to Paul.

We first worked at trying to clear away some of the wood and dirt that had caved in on top of the box, but before long, it was evident that the contents inside the chest had disintegrated. Disappointed, I pulled my finger back and forth through the dust, trying to find anything. As I took one last swirl through the dirt, my fingertips brushed against two tiny pieces of paper. "Paul! I found something."

Carefully I pulled them out of the dirt and rested them on my thigh. They looked like parchment or vellum. I picked one piece up. "I see some letters." Reading out loud, I said, "…here's an M, and there are two t's. Look, right above the two t's there," I pointed at the paper, "there's another letter that looks like an S…and there's an m-y."

Paul reached for the other piece. The second vellum was smaller and had numbers written on it. He brought it closer to his face. "I can make out a 1, a 7, and another 1, but not the last number. Wait, I think the last number could be a 5!"

"Oh my God, this is so exciting!" I leaned closer to inspect the piece that Paul was holding. "The numbers look like they could be a year. Like 1715 or 1775? Is it possible? Do you think this box has been down here that long?"

"I don't know. Let's see what else we can find," Paul said.

Molly was quiet and had stopped digging to see what we were looking at. She crawled closer to the hole. "Mommy, what's that over there?" she asked, pointing to the side of the chest nearest her view.

"Where?" I asked.

She leaned farther into the root cellar; her outstretched finger pointed to a dirty beige object. "There."

We stopped and scanned the dirt. I spotted what Molly had found and picked it up. "I wonder what it is?" I sifted through the area that it came from. "There are a few other white fragments, but that's all. They could be bones, but I really doubt it."

Paul said, "If the chest and its contents were buried hundreds of years ago, it would be safe to presume that whatever was buried here, would not have survived." He reached over and took the piece from my hand. "You know, maybe it is a bone, it looks like the top of a skull."

"Mommy, what's a skull?" Molly asked.

Unsure of how to explain to our five year old that we might have found the remains of a body, we looked at each other for answers.

Paul tried to find the right words. "Uhhh, a skull is what's under your skin on your head…." Before he got the next word out, Molly took off, running towards the back of the house.

"Oh, crap!" I climbed out of the hole to try and comfort her. "Molly, don't be afraid, it's all right. Come on back." She shook her head in a no. I picked her up and started to open the back door. "Come on honey. We can go inside if you want to."

Paul put the bone fragment back in the dirt, picked up the two pieces of parchment and followed us inside. Before sitting down next to Molly at the kitchen table, he put the small pieces of vellum on top of a newspaper by the counter, washed his hands, and asked her, "You okay honey? It's just some old bones. Remember when we lost Bernie? We buried the old pooch in the back of our barn in Ohio. You helped me bury him, remember?"

Molly nodded her head up and down.

"Don't be afraid. It surprised your Mom and me too." He humored her as he tried to steal a bite of her cookie.

She wiped her eyes, smiled and sipped her milk.

"Molly, you want to watch some Sesame Street for a while?" I asked.

"Sure."

"Okay, finish up and I'll turn it on for you."

I could see Molly calming down as she settled herself into a big chair to watch her favorite show. I whispered to Paul, "Should we call the police?"

"I guess we could."

Grabbing an old towel from the counter, I told Paul, "Why don't you cover up the area where we found the bone for now and I'll give them a call."

"Okay, make sure you tell them that we don't know what it is," Paul said as he went out the back door.

With my back to Molly, I picked up the phone and dialed the non-emergency number of the Brewster police station.

"Brewster Police," the lady dispatcher answered.

"Hello, this is Nancy Caldwell, and I have a non-emergency. We just moved to Brewster a few months ago and we were digging in the back of our house and discovered an old root cellar. As we dug down into it, we found a chest containing, we think, a small skull. We weren't sure if we should call you or not."

The dispatcher took the address and put me on hold. While I waited for a response from the other end, I kept studying the old parchment fragments on the counter.

17

August 1715
EASTHAM – CAPE COD

THE WARM SUMMER MONTHS WERE FILLED with hard work for Maria. The everyday chores that had to be done, along with gardens that needed tending, and her father who became more demanding, all plagued her daily. By mid-August, Maria had begun to grow fuller under her skirts. To her relief, no one noticed her changing body as she observed the Sabbath on Sundays, or on the rare occasion she needed to enter the village for supplies.

She tried to maintain a good diet and rested as much as she could, knowing that she needed most of her strength to harvest not only her vegetables and fruits, but the flax that she had planted for spinning and weaving. The flax beds were the most difficult to care for, but very important because her weaving had become the only source of income which was hers alone.

One morning, while standing among the flax plants, Maria looked down at her bare feet and smiled at how fortunate she was that her feet were small enough to walk and weed between the rows of flax. She knew to be careful among the delicate plants. Stroking her round belly, she thought, I have no children to help me now, but soon enough...there will be.

Bending over to weed, she recalled Minda's words to her when she was small, "Dig the plant, do not pull it out...as you weed, step carefully down the rows of flax."

Maria learned everything about weaving from Minda: how to soak the harvested plants in streams or ponds to loosen the flax fiber from the woody core of the plant; how to dry and break it apart by skutching or hitting the hard stalks with a wooden skutching knife to scrape off the hard pieces and reveal the fibers. Maria became skilled at hackling and combing the strands into coarse, short, and long fibers. She needed more of the long fibers to spin into fine twisted threads, carding the short for coarser, everyday woven cloths. As the morning sun warmed her back, she felt good, and the memory of Minda's encouraging words stayed in her heart, "Maria, you are a smart child, and you learn fast. You will make a fine weaver. Your mother would have been proud of you."

As September neared its end, Maria had grown too large under her skirts to hide her secret from those around her so she was forced to stop working at the inn and attending church services. Almost daily, her lack of energy became a burden for her; she took to napping. One afternoon, a knock on the door of the Hallett house roused Maria from her rest. She cracked open the door and pulled her shawl close, hoping to hide her protruding stomach from whoever was outside. It was a woman from church. Maria's voice trembled with fear, "Good afternoon...Widow Baker."

"Miss Hallett, I have come to call on you...on behalf of Reverend Treat."

The thin elderly widow, dressed in a black dress and hat, cocked her head to look past the young girl to see what was inside. Maria stood large, blocking the widow's view into the house.

The inquisitive woman stretched her neck high above Maria's head, but saw nothing unusual. She stepped back and focused her attention onto Maria. "I am here to inquire as to why you have not been honoring the Sabbath."

"I have not been feeling well," Maria replied. "I'm tired from the harvesting."

"I see." She pushed on the door and stepped a little closer into the house to take a better look at Maria's body. "You don't look tired. In fact, you look very healthy indeed." Then she noticed the bulge under Maria's shawl. "Very healthy!"

Eager for the woman to leave, Maria spoke quickly, "My father will be home soon, I must get back to my work. Thank you for your concern." Frightened of this mean and meddlesome old woman, Maria wanted her to go. In a panic, she pushed her outside and slammed the door shut behind her.

The Widow Baker quickly turned on her heel, only to stand face to face with the weathered and splintered door. "Well, of all the rudeness. I never...." She left in a rage. "The ladies and the Reverend will be very interested in this little encounter."

18

September 1715
EASTHAM – CAPE COD

AS MARIA CLOSED THE DOOR she knew her life would never be the same; the Widow Baker would see to that. She leaned her back against the wooden door and let her head fall forward, her emotions exploding in cries and fits of piercing screams. She slid to the floor, her arms cradling her distended body. "Sam, where are you?" Her shawl caught on the rough edges of the old door and trailed in a pattern of grotesque shapes above her head. With her legs outstretched on the dirt floor before her, and her face wet from tears, she called out to her mother for help, and then she screamed, "SAM! WHERE ARE YOU?"

With her energy depleted, both physically and emotionally, she remained motionless on the dirt floor—quiet, desperate and alone.

The Sunday Social

The gathering after Sunday meeting was held at the house of Widow Baker, a tragedy for Maria, but a social coup for the widow. Of modest means, the Widow owned a simple house: smallish, yet large enough to accommodate the men and women who wanted to meet socially and hear about the activities of their neighbors. As some of the ladies gathered in the corner by the sideboard, the Widow Baker came over to them and spoke, "I am so glad to see all of you here at my house." She sat down and folded her hands against her black skirts. Smugly, she smiled. "I have some interesting news, but I am not sure I should be telling you."

Mrs. Eldridge leaned closer. "What is it?"

Mrs. Paine urged her on, "Yes dear, you must tell us." She took a large bite from her sweet bread.

Reaching for her teacup, Widow Baker took a sip, clinked her cup back onto its saucer and continued with pursed lips, "Well, if you insist. I was passing by the Hallett house the other day and thought I would stop in to see how the girl, Maria, was doing."

With her mouth full, Mrs. Paine sputtered, "Go on. Go on."

The widow paused in mid sip. "When she opened the door to me, I knew immediately something was wrong."

Mrs. Eldridge leaned in so close that she almost fell from her seat.

The Widow Baker continued, "After a few impolite words from the young girl, I could see that there was something different about her."

The women stopped eating and grew quiet.

She whispered to them, "I do believe she is with child!"

A collective gasp echoed from the small group of women.

"What?" Mrs. Eldridge yelped.

"I said, 'I think she is with child!' "

The women all leaned back in their chairs, resumed their nibbling, and shook their heads back and forth in disapproval.

Reverend Treat noticed the commotion coming from the corner and walked over to them. "Well, how are we today, good women?"

Mrs. Eldridge spoke, "Fine.... Thank you, Reverend." She snatched up her piece of the bread.

Mrs. Stone set down her teacup and braced herself to share the news. "You see, my dear Reverend, the Widow Baker was telling us that she thinks the girl, Maria Hallett, might be..." she empathized her words with a bravado, "...with child."

Reverend Treat responded slowly, "I see...." He furrowed his brow. The Widow Baker was quick to finish her news. "I saw her, months back, walking with a stranger. And my hired hand said he saw the same man at the tavern, talking of finding treasure. Well, what would you expect? The poor girl has no mother and her father is, you know...."

Reverend Treat interrupted her. He was not going to tolerate the sin of gossip. "Ladies, please let us not pass judgment on the girl. Until evidence is brought before the church, we must not make assumptions. Should such evidence of sin become apparent, then the proper punishment will be administered. Now, let us continue with our repast and enjoy our afternoon."

The ladies were silent as the reverend walked away to join the other men. Whispers of 'whore' and 'shun' were soon floating into the air from the women's little circle amidst the clanging of teacups against saucers.

19

October 1715
EASTHAM – CAPE COD

MARIA WAS TOO AFRAID TO LEAVE THE HOUSE after the Widow Baker's visit. The prying eyes and judgmental behavior of the church's good ladies were unbearable for her. Over the past month of Maria's self-inflicted seclusion, she was miserable. She did her chores as well as her swollen body would allow her to do, but it was never enough for her father. Oblivious to her physical limitations of carrying a child, he demanded food and labor from her with no relenting. On one exceptionally cold morning, gentle puffs of steam billowed from Maria's mouth into the chilly bedroom air as she lay under the coarse, prickly blankets, not wanting to get up. Approaching her seventh month with child, her body temperature usually kept her warm during the frosty mornings of late October, but not today. She finally rose from her nest, dragging her bedcover like a large cape behind her.

Grabbing the long iron stick from its hook in the kitchen hearth, she poked at the fire's embers and waited until a spark ignited, then fed it some kindling and a log. Maria walked back to bed and lay down. Her eyes closed, she stroked her large belly, moving her hands in circles over her bloated stomach. She felt the need to relieve herself and groaned in irritation. This bothersome task plagued her morning, noon and night and usually she accepted it. Today she felt annoyed.

Pulling herself from her bed once more, she squatted on the necessary jar. As she reached for a clean shift, she heard her father stir. Worried that he would notice her condition, she dressed quickly, then went into the kitchen to begin her day.

Her father was as ornery as ever. He'd continued drinking his liquors, rendering him irrational in his demeanor. During the day he remained in the barn, tanning hides that he'd caught himself, or from others who'd brought skins to him. Maria took note that his longtime customers were keeping their distance. His reputation as a craftsman, able to make superb vellum and soft leather, was slowly being replaced with an image of an unreliable village buffoon. He seemed to Maria a man who cared little for anything except his drink. He never even noticed the physical changes in his own daughter's body.

Supplies were low in the pantry and today Maria barely had enough flour to make breakfast. The low staples meant that she must face the scrutiny of her neighbors. She hoped to wait one more day before having to enter town. Perhaps she could stretch her supplies if she didn't eat as much, then she could save her portion for her father and stay home.

Old man Hallett finished his morning biscuits and pushed his empty plate away. He ordered, "You need to deliver my hides to Mr. Eldridge today."

Maria had forgotten that she had to go into town for him. More frightening than facing the wrath of her father was the possibility of meeting church ladies with their scornful glances aimed at her and her "sinful" condition. She did not want to go. She grew defiant. "I'm sorry, Father. I simply can't go today, I must finish my cloth. You said you needed my weaving money for your debt."

Hallett knew she was right. His debt required more money than he had. Reaching for his jacket, he spoke, "Mind your chores today, girl. I expect you to finish that cloth. I'll be back late."

"Fine," Maria answered, pleased with herself for the rare time that she got her way. She watched him close the door, then moved to the small window, where she saw him enter the barn. Let him make the delivery, she thought. He'd get his money, get drunk and not return till late.

Within minutes, he had the bundle of hides under his arm and was walking into town.

Maria rubbed her belly in soothing circles. In her isolation, she had become accustomed to talking to her unborn child. She spoke in a soft voice. "At least we'll have the day to ourselves. Now what song would you like me to sing to you?"

20

Tuesday Morning – October 29, 1715
EASTHAM – CAPE COD

THOMAS HALLETT EAGERLY ANTICIPATED his payment as he walked to the house of Jacob Eldridge. He had hoped that Jacob's wife, Mrs. Eldridge, was not at home so he could drop off the tanned leather, get his money, and leave quickly. He knocked on the door.

A shrill voice called from inside the house, "Just a minute!"

He cursed under his breath at the whiny sound of the irritating Mrs. Eldridge. The door opened, and the elderly woman greeted him.

Tom Hallett gave no greeting in return. "This package is for your husband. He said the money would be waitin' for me."

The puzzled lady looked him up and down and then instructed him: "You will have to wait until I speak with my husband. He's busy right now. Wait here, please." She took the package and shut the door in the old man's face.

Hallett cursed again, wiping his nose on his sleeve as he stood his ground.

Several minutes went by before Mrs. Eldridge opened the door once more. "Here's your money, sir. And if I may ask, how is your daughter, Maria?"

He answered, "She be well."

The woman was persistent. "I hope that the state she's in will not bring shame on our community."

Hallett did not wait to hear her comment. He turned and walked away, counting his coins.

* * *

The tavern was empty except for a few travelers eating their midday meal. Hallett slammed a coin on the table and instructed Mr. Smith to give him a drink. Ale was set upon the dark wooden sideboard. Hallett finished it with a single lift of his hand. As several coins spilled out of his bony fingers, his tankard crashed down once more and he yelled, "MORE!"

Mr. Smith was happy to have the old man's money, but was prepared to cut him off when necessary. It wasn't good for business. The tavern keeper drained ale from the tap as he tried to engage Hallett in idle conversation. "How's the tanning business these days?"

"As good as it should be." Leaning closer, he took another long swig from the tankard.

The stout proprietor began to wipe the spilled ale from Hallett's sloppiness. "How's Maria? I haven't seen her for several months."

The old man snarled back at him. "She's fine, and it's none of your business."

"I was just wondering when she was coming back to the tavern for work. She, no doubt, is a pretty little thing."

"Pretty? It's nothing but a curse for her and me. Why, some scalawag by the name of Sam Bellamy tried to get his hands on her a while back, but I wouldn't let him. I showed him my fist." He raised his gnarled hand in a ball. "Then I told him to get off my property!"

Mr. Smith leaned closer. "My missus told me that some of the ladies think something did happen with him and your Maria."

"What?"

"I said that some of the good ladies of the church are concerned that your Maria might be with child."

Hallett stood straight. Ale dripped from his lips as he asked again, "What's that you say?"

Before Mr. Smith could speak another word, his first words sank into Hallett's brain. The old man slammed his tankard on the table and stormed out of the tavern, pushing chairs over in his path.

21

Tuesday Afternoon – October 29, 1715
EASTHAM – CAPE COD

LAUNDRY DAY WAS A TIRESOME CHORE for Maria. The extra weight of her unborn child made any physical movement difficult for her, especially the moving of heavy, wet clothes. While the sun rose above Maria's head, she draped the clean clothes to dry across boulders, low branches, bushes, a fence and the rock wall. When she finished, she sat on the wooden bench against the outside of the house for a rest and nibbled on some dried fruit.

The autumn sun grew warm on her face. She decided a little more weaving on a promised cloth for Mrs. Ellis, Matthew's mother, could be accomplished before her nap. Weaving was so enjoyable to Maria. It was a skill that she was proud to have conquered and, to her surprise, it brought a welcome profit.

She climbed the stairs to the long room above the first floor. In the eaves, she lifted a twelve-inch wooden square up and away from its frame, and tied its anchor rope to a nail on the center beam. The fresh air blew cool; it felt good. Her hands rested across her stomach. Outside, she noticed something strange on the path leading to their house. Her eyes focused on a figure approaching. She thought it looked like Father walking, but it couldn't be, he never came home this time of day after he got his pay. Maria whispered under her breath. "It IS Father!" She quickly walked over to the stairs and began to descend into the kitchen. As she neared the bottom, she heard her name. "MARIA!"

Startled, her foot slid on the edge of the last step and she fell backwards. Swiftly she righted herself.

Her father threw open the door. He sounded furious. "MARIA! Where are you?"

"Here, Father! What's wrong?"

He came closer to her. She backed towards the wall under the stairs. As she clutched one hand to her shawl, the other rose slightly, ready to defend herself.

Hallett yelled, "Show me yourself, or I'll show you the back of my hand! Drop your hands so I can see!"

Maria let go of her covering and waited for the pain of his hand.

But it did not come.

Hallett stood with his hand raised as if to hit, but instead his wide eyes settled on Maria's protruding stomach. The back of his hand moved to cover his own mouth.

Silence passed between them.

"You little whore...did you think you could fool me and everyone else in Eastham?"

"Please, let me explain...." Maria begged.

Hallett glared at her. "I want nothing to do with you and your bastard child! You've brought shame upon me." He reached for the iron poker hanging by the hearth. "I want you out of my house. Go find whoever did this to you." He held the iron stick in the air above his head and roared, "Let him take care of you; I'm done with you. You've been nothing but a burden since your mother passed."

Maria closed her shawl to cover herself. Her hands trembled as she pleaded again, "Father, please... I'll work hard and listen to everything you tell me to do. I have nowhere to go."

Behind Hallett, Maria caught a glimpse of a man coming into the house. It was the tavern owner, Mr. Smith. Hallett remained poised to hit Maria. Within seconds, Smith took the poker from the angry man's hand and led him out of the house. He spoke as a friend and implored, "Come, Thomas...outside...before you do something you'll regret."

Maria stood with body shaking, thoughts paralyzed. Confused, afraid and fearful, she didn't know what to do or where to go.

Mr. Smith came back into the house to find her crying on the stairs. "Are you all right?" he asked. He took a seat at the table and swiveled his head from side to side in despair. "You must realize that your father will never come around to this. His pride has been hurt, and he's stubborn as an old mule. You should have told him, and not let him find out from others."

Maria stayed close to the wall, and with tears answered him, "I was afraid to tell him."

He gently scolded her. "The damage has been done. I presume you know that your condition will not be agreeable with the ladies and Reverend Treat?"

She moved away from the shadow of the stairs and into the light of the hearth. "Yes, I'm aware of this."

"Your father wants you to leave. Do you have somewhere that you'll be safe?"

"No.... I do not."

Smith added, "I was able to get him to agree to you staying till tomorrow morning, but then you must go. He does not want to set eyes upon you, ever again. He chooses to sleep in the barn tonight. I'm sorry, Maria. I have done all I can. I'm afraid that most people will not be sympathetic to you; in their minds you have committed a grave sin." He pulled a small pouch from the inside of his waistcoat and placed it on the table. "Here's something to help you on your way."

Maria stepped forward to examine its contents. She opened it, and several coins fell into her hand. "Mr. Smith, I could not accept this from you."

"It's not from me. Sam Bellamy left this for you in my safekeeping, in case you had need of it in his absence. I questioned at the time, but he spoke no reason to me." Looking at Maria, he added, "I understand now."

Maria returned the coins to the pouch.

"I must go...may the Lord be with you." He left a heavy silence hanging over the room.

22

Tuesday Evening – October 29, 1715
EASTHAM – CAPE COD

THE SILENCE IN THE SMALL HOUSE was deafening to Maria's ears and her knees would not stop shaking. She cradled the small pouch from Sam in her lap, nestled into the folds of her skirts. The anxious trembling of her legs caused the coins to strike one another. Their clinking became the only sound in the empty house. At last, she was still, but then she felt movement under her skirts. A tightening formed a point on one side of her stomach. "Oh, I'm sorry little one. I've upset you." Maria looked down. "Yes, I need to think. We must have a plan, but what?" Abigail's face appeared in her thoughts. "We could go to Abigail's house."

She began talking to herself, working through her options, "Abigail said she would help me. But how do we get there?" She walked over to the window and looked to the barn. "I can't use Old Brother. What can I carry my things in? The pushcart will have to do. I shall take only what I need and walk there. I know this will work."

Maria remembered her mother's travel bag. Pleased, she began looking in the storage space above the main floor. The top of the bag peeked out above baskets of wool and threads against the far wall. After carefully pulling the cumbersome bag to the middle of the floor to inspect it, she wiped the dust away with her hand. Her mother's initials were stamped on the outside: S.A.M. for Sarah Anne McNeill.

Maria thought it odd that it spelled "Sam" and took it as a good omen. Fearful that she might slip again, she shoved the bag down the stairs. Dust flew into the air as it tumbled to the bottom.

Maria stuffed four skirts, three shifts, two corsets, several hand-kerchiefs, two pockets, straight pins, one apron, two shawls, two pairs of stockings and her mother's looking glass into the old bag. She looked around her tiny room. "Now where's Minda's lavender water?" She stopped. "Minda! How will Minda know where I am?" Frantically, she secured the latch on her mother's bag. "I can't think about the *Pow Wah*, I must keep going."

Her legs began to ache, warning her that she needed rest. Grudgingly, she lay down, but kept thinking of other things to bring: food for the trip, her spinning wheel, tools for carding and spinning. Restless, she soon got up and continued her packing.

After her last meal of the day, Maria eventually retired to bed. Still worried about what to pack, she accepted that she had enough items, but doubts plagued her dreams throughout the night. She awoke after only a few hours, concerned about the bumpy and rutted roads she must walk on, and the distance she needed to travel.

23

Wednesday – October 30, 1715
EASTHAM – CAPE COD

BY EARLY DAWN, Maria had already brought the pushcart around to the front of the house. Her mother's case was placed in first. To her disappointment its bulkiness nearly filled the whole cart. She pushed her weaving supplies in tight around the outsides of the bag, using their thickness as a cushion. Wrapping her scutching knife in a handkerchief, she pocketed it for easy access, if needed for protection. She was barely able to squeeze her food across the top of her pile of belongings. Lastly, she covered everything with a shawl and a blanket, then tied them down with rope. Having hurried back into the house to check if anything was forgotten, Maria paused to look around.

"My spinning wheel!" she cried out. "I can't leave it behind; I need it." She paced back and forth in front of the hearth, holding her head in her hands. "How foolish of me to think that I could take it with me. There's no room in the cart." Her head shook in despair. The wheel meant so much to her; it was her freedom from being dependent on others. It was the one thing that she needed the most.

Maria climbed the stairs to the loft. She spun the wheel and held her hand over its movement as it whirred on its axle. The other hand caressed her belly. "The spinner must stay. We need to leave now, before Father wakes."

Returning to the kitchen, she looked once more around the tiny house. Nothing else would be missed; memories of her dear mother were stored in her heart. After adjusting her heavy cape, she put on her cap, closed the door and never looked back.

As Maria pushed the two-wheeled cart through the sleepy village and onto the open road toward Abigail's house, the misty morning sunlight illuminated her way. The damp air felt cool on her exposed face and hands.

During the first few miles, Maria rested against the side of the cart as needed. Once outside the village, near a small grove of pines, she finally stopped to remove stones that had found their way into her shoes. She decided this was a good place to eat her biscuit and relieve herself in the trees. Feeling refreshed, she noticed the sun was now high in the eastern sky and the air warm enough that she could remove her heavy cape. She laid it over the ropes on the cart and took hold of the handles to resume her journey. She pushed off with a shove, but a loud crack echoed into the air and she fell forward onto her knees.

The cart had broken an axle, spilling her weaving supplies across the road. Her mother's bag lay half in the cart and half on the dirt. She knelt as if praying, but instead began to curse and scream, saying things that she had heard her father say time and again. Taken aback at her cursing, she covered her mouth to quiet the angry words and slumped back on her haunches. Unaware of a figure approaching in the distance, she began to pick up her few possessions from the dirt.

* * *

The lone traveler slowed his walking to get a better view of what was before him. He looked closer and saw a woman who seemed to need help. He decided he was in no hurry and didn't mind lending a hand. As he got nearer he called out, "Good morrow...do you need assistance?"

The woman straightened and turned towards him.

Stunned at her face, he called out to her, "Maria? Is that you?"

Maria could not believe her eyes. "Matthew?"

He dropped his bag on the road and ran to her. It was not the custom to show affection to a single woman in public, but he couldn't help himself. He hugged her. As he held her in his arms, he felt Maria's swollen stomach against his waist. Leaning back, he looked into her eyes, avoiding the sight of her bulk. "Maria, I've missed you. How are you?"

She stepped away from him and covered herself with the shawl. Embarrassed at her situation, she ignored his question. "Matthew, it's good to see you. Where have you been?"

"Looking for adventure at sea, although I realized I might find a safer way to seek my fortune right here on land."

"What do you mean?"

He began to collect some of her things, "Let's not talk of it now, perhaps another time."

Maria looked at the broken wheel. "I don't know what I'm going to do!" She began putting some of her belongings into the pushcart.

Matthew stood and caught her by the shoulders. "Maria, we have been friends a long time. Please tell me what you're doing out here, by yourself."

Ashamed by everything and overwhelmed with despair, she began to cry on his waistcoat.

He cradled her in his arms and gently rubbed her back. "Maria, don't cry. I'll help you." His love for her filled his heart again. His head swirled with words of...I love you...I love you, Maria. But the words stayed within. Like two lovers, they stood swaying in a locked embrace.

It had been an eternity since anyone had hugged Maria, and she didn't want to let go of Matthew. She felt so safe in her dear friend's arms.

Matthew missed her touch and wanted her close to him. "Maria, where are you going with this old cart?"

She wiped tears from her eyes. "I'm trying to get to Abigail's."

"Abigail's? Do you realize how far that is?"

"I do!" she answered with a slight stubbornness in her voice. "I can't go back to my house. Father wants nothing to do with me and my...child."

"Where's the father of this child?" Matthew asked, trying to get more information from her.

"He's not here, but.... He'll be back to take care of me. I just need to get to Abigail's house. Will you help me?" She hoped that he would not refuse her, thinking of the many times Matthew had fulfilled her every request.

He looked at Maria, and then at the broken cart, and back to Maria. "Of course I'll help you." He smiled. "Go wait on that rock, and I'll fetch my wagon and horse. Then I'll take you to Abigail's." He picked up the rest of Maria's things, along with his own bag, and carried them over to the edge of the pine grove. Then he dragged the broken cart from the pathway.

"Matthew, would you do me another favor?" Maria asked.

"What is it?"

"Would you please bring my spinning wheel from the attic? Father will still be asleep. I'm sure that he'll not hear nor see you."

"Yes, I'll get it."

"Matthew, could you find one more thing?"

He stopped and turned towards her. "Yes?"

"In the bottom of my chest of drawers is a box with a rose painted on it. Will you bring that too?"

He walked over to her, held her hand in his and reassured her. "I'm at your service!"

*   *   *

Matthew felt exhilarated as he ran. He had been eager to come home to see Maria and finally make his feelings known to her. He knew a life at sea was not for him, and right now, land beneath his feet was satisfying. He picked up his pace. His true feelings would have to wait, he decided. My Maria is in trouble and needs my help.

Many questions raced through his head as he sprinted home. Who is the father? I need to know why this man left her. I would never have left Maria, knowing she was with child. Maybe he didn't know! He shook his head to clear his thoughts and concentrate on his footing as he pushed himself along the path. I'll be there soon. I'm almost there. I love her.

24

Thursday Afternoon – October 31, 1715
EASTHAM – CAPE COD

IT WAS THE BEGINNING OF THE COLD MONTHS in the colonies. The air carried a chill, but the sun felt warm on Maria's shoulders as she waited on her stone seat for Matthew. She busied herself with folding and refolding the clothes in her bag. She cleaned her weaving tools. She straightened threads, yarns, and pieces of unfinished cloth. As she walked back and forth along the tree line, her thoughts turned to Abigail. She knew her friend would be surprised to see her, but it didn't matter. There would be a warm welcome for her and Matthew; that was Abigail's way.

The sun's path in the sky marked mid-afternoon. Maria grew nervous about the lateness in the day, but remained hopeful that Matthew would come back for her before dark. She traced the initials on her mother's bag: S.A.M. *Sam, how I wish you were here.*

A jingling horse bridle broke the quiet. Maria jumped up from her stone seat and breathed a sigh of relief. It was Matthew. He waved to her and she waved back, watching him guide the wagon closer.

After tying the reins to a handle on the wagon, he paused to look at her. *She was so beautiful. Her face was glowing. How could anyone leave her?*

"Matthew! You're staring at me."

"Forgive me. Shall we load everything into the wagon? I found the spinning wheel and the box." He added with a laugh, "You were right about your father; he was still sleeping in the barn."

Maria found her small box in the wagon. It was decorated with a beautiful rose painted on its top, near the right corner. "Thank you, Matthew." She turned away from him and opened it a crack to check its contents, then pushed the decorative box under her clothes in the travel bag. "Shall we get started?"

Matthew helped her onto the wagon's seat. He had placed a large blanket across the bench for warmth. As they rode, he noticed Maria holding her stomach. They had already traveled over eight miles and he wondered if she was all right. "Are you well?"

"I'm fine. The child is moving."

As they got closer to Abigail's, the sun disappeared behind grey clouds forming above them. Maria felt chilled and covered herself with part of the blanket. When they pulled away from a wooded area of dense trees, tiny snowflakes began to drift through the cold air.

Matthew looked over to his silent passenger. "Don't worry. We'll be at Abigail's shortly." He wanted to hold her hand, but instead he held steady on the reins, keeping the wagon straight on the old cart-way.

By the time they reached Abigail's house, the sun had set; it was dusk and lightly snowing. Matthew had hoped to talk to Maria about what took place while he was at sea, but Maria seemed preoccupied.

*   *   *

Abigail was sitting down to her evening meal when she thought she heard the sound of a wagon approaching. She wondered who would be out this time of night. She peeked through the small window on the door, but darkness clouded her view. The unexpected arrival of a stranger frightened her, so she backed away, ready to grab the iron rod hanging in the hearth.

Maria stood next to Matthew as he knocked on the door.

Abigail called out, "Who is it?"

"Maria Hallett."

"Come closer to the window so I can see your face," Abigail ordered.

Maria positioned her face as close as she could to the little opening on the door. Abigail grabbed the Betty lamp. "Maria, it IS you." She lifted the heavy latch to let in her friend. "What are you doing here?"

As soon as Maria saw Abigail, she began to cry in relief and leaned into the comfort of her arms. "Father has forbidden me to stay in the house and wants nothing more to do with me."

Matthew entered the house behind Maria.

"And who might you be?" Abigail took a stern look towards Matthew.

Maria pulled away from Abigail and wiped her tears. "This is Matthew Ellis, the dearest friend that anyone could have, besides you and Minda. He lives with his family next to our house."

"Well, come in and close the door or all the warmth will be lost."

"Yes, ma'am." Matthew closed the door and took off his hat.

"Let me look at you, my dear," Abigail said noticing the sizable stomach on Maria. "You are coming along as expected. Sit down, both of you. Please join me in dinner so we may talk."

Matthew inquired if he would be allowed to bed his horse down in the barn for the night. Abigail agreed and he left, informing them that he would be back presently. The two women decided they should wait for Matthew before eating. During their short wait, Maria confided to Abigail that she had not told Matthew about Sam and she asked her not to speak of him to Matthew. Abigail agreed. And as Maria hoped, the kind woman invited her to stay in the house for as long as was needed.

All three were hungry when Matthew joined the two women at the table. Maria spoke of how her father had discovered she was with child and then explained how angry he'd become.

Matthew listened in silence.

She relayed her futile attempt to walk the roads, pushing the old cart, and then her rescue by Matthew.

Finishing the last of the biscuits, the young man complimented Abigail. "Everything tasted wonderful, Abigail...thank you so much."

"It's my pleasure to serve such a kind man as you."

She poured him more ale, usually reserved for her husband Nathanial, and asked, "Tell me about how you came to be walking on the road this morning."

Matthew settled himself into his chair. "After being at sea for nigh six months I was heading home to Eastham. Our ship had landed at Boston Harbor, so my shipmate, Jonathan Quidley, and I caught a packet to Barnstable, where he makes his home. We had the stench of the sea on us, but we didn't care; it was home that mattered most to us." He smiled at Maria and placed his open hand down on the table, nearer to hers. "As the boat traveled along the bay, I bought food for the two of us, for a few shillings, and we sat outside in the sea air. It was the least I could do for my friend, who was going to put me up for the night."

Maria inched her hand closer to his across the smooth wood.

"Upon arriving at his home, Jonathan's mother washed my clothes and let me clean myself up. In exchange, I helped Jonathan fell a tree that had its roots exposed. We cut and stacked the wood, and added it to his family's woodpile for winter. When my things were in order, I said my goodbyes and caught the packet out of Barnstable Harbor to Breakwater Landing, in the North Parish. From there I started walking home. It was a long journey, but I didn't mind. He looked at Maria, then to Abigail. "It became a fortunate event that I saw Maria and was able to help her." He reached out and gently held Maria's hand.

Abigail asked him, "Tell me, did you happen to sail near the West Indies on your route?"

"Yes, we did, and I'm glad we made it home safe from there." Matthew looked up towards the heavens in gratitude to the Lord.

"Did you come across a vessel commanded by my husband, Nathanial Doane? His ship is named the *Voyager*."

"No, I don't remember seeing that ship; but we did see pirates."

"Pirates!" explained Abigail. "Tell us more."

Matthew wiped his mouth, straightened his back and began his story. "It started out a fine day on our voyage home; the wind was at our backs. We had just loaded our cargo of indigo, rice, sugar, and 500 pounds sterling when we spotted them off our bow."

Maria held her tightening belly and began to massage it with both hands.

Matthew continued, "Our Captain began yelling orders as he came up from his cabin. 'Break out the weapons. Be quick lads. We have no time!' " Matthew took a drink. "It was my first encounter with real danger, and I was quite nervous, but steadfast in my actions. I stood by the rail and watched them fast approaching. I stayed there far too long, so one of my mates hit me on the back by my shoulder and ordered me, 'Get below, if you're not ready to fight!' "

"What did you do?" Maria asked, her heart racing, fearful of the outcome.

"Fortunately, he knocked me out of my daze, upon which I grabbed a pistol from the arsenal." Matthew leaned close over the table. "After all were ready, we stood our ground, poised with cannons facing the pirates, waiting, hoping they would not bother us. But before we could breathe easy, they were upon us. They came alongside and swung over to board us. We managed to get one shot of the cannon off, but it did little damage to their craft."

Matthew motioned for more ale. "A hard fight ensued but they were too much for us. They overpowered the crew and gathered us together, to one side of the deck, and made us kneel while the two captains talked below."

He took a drink and leaned even further into the center of the sideboard. "It was strange. While I was kneeling and praying that they would have mercy on us, I overheard one pirate call another by the name of Bellamy! I thought to myself, I know that name. I'd heard it around Eastham before I left."

Maria stared with wide eyes.

He looked over to Maria. "Remember, Maria, there was a Sam Bellamy staying at Smith's Tavern? He said he was going off with Williams to salvage treasure."

Maria was stunned. Her face turned pale and she felt sick. Sam was not a pirate. He couldn't be!

Matthew saw Maria's reaction and was pleased that his encounter with pirates seemed so interesting to her. "One poor soul, a Dutchman hired in the West Indies, tried to reach for a pistol that had been dropped and was hidden under a sail. Before he was able to get his hand on it, he was run through by one of them foul pirates standing near me." The young storyteller took a deep breath. "After that, we all closed our eyes, prayed, and waited for our turn."

Abigail could see that Maria was visibly upset. She took Maria's hand and held it tight under the table.

Matthew asked, "Are you feeling well enough to hear the end of my story, Maria?"

She moved her free hand over her belly. "Go on, Matthew."

"After a short time, I could hear footsteps on the deck," he continued. "Opening my eyes just a crack, I saw the two captains together. The pirate captain by the name of Henry Jennings ordered the tall, black-haired Bellamy to go with two other fellows and fetch the spoils. They took the 500 pounds sterling, most of our food supplies, and all of our weapons. With a wink in his eye, Jennings told Bellamy he could take anything else that he fancied. It seemed that Bellamy was the favorite of his captain. When all was loaded onto the pirate ship, to our amazement, they left us."

Maria stood up from the bench and excused herself. She thanked Abigail for her hospitality, and Matthew for all his efforts to take care of her, and went up the stairs to her bed.

Matthew watched her exit, then asked Abigail, "I hope I didn't frighten her with my tale? She looks quite ill."

Abigail stood to clean the sideboard. "Don't worry about Maria; she's a very strong woman. She'll be fine now that she's here with me." As she carried the dishes to the dry sink, Abigail turned to Matthew. "I must ask you, Matthew. What did your Captain do or say to that pirate Jennings?"

"From what the crew could figure, he convinced the old pirate that his ship was too small to be of any value and he would gladly give him anything he wanted as long as he spared him and his men. Jennings must have been in good favor that day, or he was just practical in his thinking. It was too much work to kill everyone and destroy the ship. The gods smiled upon us that day." Matthew stood to stoke the fire in the hearth. "If it is agreeable to you, Abigail, may I bring in some wood for the night and check my horse in the barn?"

Abigail was grateful. "Of course, thank you, Matthew. I'm afraid that by the time you return I'll be sound asleep, so I must say goodnight now. You may sleep in the borning room here off the kitchen."

"Much obliged. Goodnight, Abigail. Thank you for being such a wonderful friend to Maria."

"And thank you, Matthew. I'm not sure what would have happened to her if you hadn't come along when you did."

He grabbed his hat and opened the door. "I'll make sure the doors are latched. Good night."

Friday, November 1, 1715

Matthew was up early, anxious to go home. By the time Abigail awoke, he already had the hearth warm and was preparing to leave.

"Please wait, Matthew, so I may fix you something to eat before your journey home," she coaxed.

He smiled as he grabbed his coat and hat. "I must be on my way. My mother will be worried. I told her nothing of what I was doing when I fetched the wagon, except to trust me and that I would be back shortly."

"Maria is still sleeping; she'll surely be sorry to have missed you." Abigail insisted. "At least let me give you some bread and beef strips so you may eat them on your way."

25

Friday, November 1, 1715
NORTH HARWICH – CAPE COD

MARIA SAW MATTHEW THROUGH THE WHITE FROST that circled the small windowpanes in the upstairs bedroom. As his wagon pulled away she felt regret at not saying goodbye to him. Matthew was such a good friend. She knew she would not have been able to refrain from asking more questions about Sam; the thought of Sam as a pirate was frightening to her. Her child—and the fact that Sam would return to her someday—was more important than any other notions assaulting her mind.

Abigail called up the stairs. "Maria, are you awake?"

"I'll be right down." Abigail's house was so comforting to her. She straightened the lovely blue coverlet across the cozy bed and threw a shawl over her shoulders. As she entered the warm kitchen, Maria feigned innocence. "Did Matthew leave?"

"Yes, I'm afraid he did."

"Oh, that's too bad." She sat down to a bowl of hot porridge. "I do hope that he's careful on his trip home." She fell silent.

Abigail could not help but notice that Maria appeared unsettled. She sat down at the sideboard across from her and extended her hand over the young girl's arm. "Maria, are you all right?"

"Why yes, I'm fine, Abigail."

"Do you want to talk about last night and the terrifying news of Sam?"

"Oh, that? I'm sure that Matthew was mistaken about Sam. If you remember, he was quite afraid when he met those dreadful pirates and he probably heard the wrong name being called out." She continued eating her breakfast, "I know that when people get frightened their minds play tricks on them. I'm not worried about my Sam."

Abigail added, "When Nathanial comes home from his voyage in a few days I will ask him if he's heard any truth to Matthew's words about Sam Bellamy being a pirate."

Maria's face paled again at the idea of Sam as a pirate, and she suddenly felt nauseous. She felt her stomach tighten as it had throughout the previous night. It felt so tight that she dropped her spoon.

Abigail jumped up and held her around the shoulders. "Maria, what's wrong?"

"I'm not sure. It's too early for the child to come, but it feels like I'm in my travail."

"Do the pains stop and then repeat?"

"No, I don't think so. I just feel this tightening every so often."

Abigail went over to a small box high on a shelf in the corner of the kitchen. "Here is something Minda gave to me when I was feeling unwell and had great pain in my back."

Maria watched from the corner of her eye as Abigail opened the box on the table. "What is that?"

Abigail opened a leather pouch from inside the box. "Minda told me to be very careful with this medicine. It's a special mix of herbs and roots. It worked to calm me down and it took some of my pain away."

"Do you think that I'll have need of it?"

Abigail cautioned her, "You may not need it, but if it be, then you only need a pinch boiled in a small amount of water. After a few minutes, sip only the liquid." Abigail closed the small box. "You must be sure to tell me when you have another tightening and we'll note the times with the hourglass." She put the box back on the shelf and took the hourglass down, placing the timepiece near the hearth.

Maria saw Hestor walk into the house through the back door. She greeted her with, "Good morrow, Hestor."

Mumbling under her breath, she responded, "Good morn, Miss."

Maria watched Hestor work in the kitchen until she'd finished her breakfast. She then went upstairs to sort through her weaving supplies.

When Maria was out of sight, Hestor spoke to Abigail, "Mind you, ma'am, I don't think it be a good idea to have that girl with you. Given her condition and all."

"Oh, Hestor, don't worry about me. Things will prove fine."

Hestor added, "I heard her singin' and talkin' to no one when she was here last. Don't it seem strange to you?"

"No, it's just her way."

"Well, I don't like it. I think she's tetched in the head and ripe for evil to take over."

Abigail answered Hestor's rude words with firm politeness, "I must ask you to stop talking about that poor sweet girl. You will keep your opinions to yourself. She has enough problems for now."

To Abigail's relief, Hestor left early with no further comments.

For Maria the morning hours passed with no recurring pain. She was happy to spend time with Abigail, helping her with whatever was needed.

EASTHAM

When Matthew arrived home his mother was laying out the clothes to dry in the sunny but cool autumn air. He gave a loud call, "Mother!"

Mrs. Ellis turned to wave back.

As the wagon pulled past her, she coyly said, "So I see you finally came home. This time I hope you'll stay a little longer?"

Matthew smiled and drove on into the barn.

She shook her head and whispered to herself, "That boy has a mind of his own. When he sets to do something, he certainly does it." She smiled with pride for her only son. Oh, how she'd missed his boyish presence while he was gone to sea. Today she was happy to see him again. She turned towards the barn and watched him walk closer to her.

After hugging his mother, Matthew picked up the laundry basket and escorted her into the house. "I have so much to tell you, Mother, I don't know where to begin."

She patted her son's back and said, "It's good to have you home again. We can talk forever if you like. But first, you must eat."

Mr. Ellis returned home within the hour of Matthew's arrival. Over a hearty late breakfast, the young man told his parents of his adventures with the pirates, and his rescue of Maria.

His mother finally asked, "And how is your friend, Maria Hallett? I have not seen her in almost a month. I was wondering if she ever finished the linen cloth that I asked her to weave for me."

"I'm afraid, Mother, that Maria has gone and landed herself in a difficult set of circumstances."

Mr. Ellis looked curious. "What do you mean? Come to mind, I haven't seen that drunken old father of hers for a while either."

Mrs. Ellis began to clean away the trencher from the middle of the table. "I hope it has nothing to do with the gossip about her being with child."

Matthew grew silent.

Mrs. Ellis sat down. "Is it true, Matthew? Is it?"

"I'm afraid the rumors are correct, Mother, and I fear for her very survival. She seems to be close to birth and has no one but an older woman from the North Parish of Harwich, the old Indian midwife Minda, and me to help her."

His mother wanted to help the poor girl and offered some information. "A few days ago, Minda came here to ask if we had seen Maria. I told her I didn't know where she was."

Matthew, unwavering in his tone, said, "Thank you, Mother. Tomorrow I'll to try to find Minda and tell her about Maria. She needs to know."

His mother cautioned him. "You must be careful when you travel through the Indian territory."

"Don't worry, I have been on their trails with Maria when we were small. Minda showed the two of us the secrets of their forest. She's my friend."

NORTH HARWICH

Throughout the day, Abigail kept reassuring her young friend that her birthing would be normal. She knew several women who would come to be with her when her travail began. And after the child was born, Maria would also enjoy the usual 'lying in' for several weeks; during which time she would be taken care of, as was the custom.

By midday, the two sat for a cider and dried fruit. When near finished, Abigail presented Maria with the gift of a small chest filled with the child linens from Nathanial's children. The oak chest was lined with cedar.

"It's beautiful," Maria said, as she ran her slim fingers over the decorative scrolls that were carved onto the surfaces of the wood. She paused over a large letter D that flowed in script across its lid.

With a twinkle in her eye, Abigail replied, "Let me show you something very interesting."

Maria watched in amazement as Abigail lifted the chest to the table, took out the linens and placed her fingertips on a half-moon shape that was carved into the floor of the chest. She carefully pulled back on the wood and the floor of the chest slid away and out the front of the chest, revealing a two-inch space beneath it. "For secret items." Abigail smiled.

"Thank you so much, Abigail. I will treasure it forever. You're my best friend."

Abigail went over to her desk in the parlor. "I have one more gift for you."

She returned with three coins and handed them to Maria. "Here, take these and keep them in this secret compartment. You may need something extra one day."

"You are a true friend, Abigail." Maria gave her a hug.

Finding an old receipt from Nathanial's affairs in the firebox, Abigail folded the paper around the coins and tied it with string. "This will keep the coins quiet so no one but you will ever know they are in there."

Maria placed the little package at the bottom, slid the thin piece of wood back into place and replaced the linens. Closing the chest, she thought of how fortunate she was today.

* * *

Settling into their evening meal the two women heard a knock on the door.

"Well, my stars, who could that be?" The older woman stood and peered out the window. "People seem to visit me at such late hours."

Ezra, the town constable, was standing outside.

She opened the door. "Come in, Ezra."

"Sorry to trouble you, Abigail, at such a late hour, but I have news of Nathanial."

"What is your news? Tell me now."

The constable greeted Maria with a nod and continued, "It seems that Nathanial took sick on board his ship traveling from Antigua. They put into harbor at Barnstable and he has taken up residence at the home of Captain J. Hicks, where he will remain until he is able to travel home."

Abigail sat down on the bench next to Maria. "I must go to him. Ezra, I know of this Captain Hicks. I'll be on the first packet to Barnstable in the morning."

"Yes, ma'am. I'll come by and take you to the landing, if you would like," offered Ezra.

"Thank you. Now get on with you so I can ready myself to leave," she said, pushing him out the door.

Abigail looked straight at Maria. "My child, I'll have to leave you for a while, but I know you'll be fine. I'll leave word with Hestor to come by and check on you. There are plenty of supplies to keep you warm, fed, and comfortable. You know where the medicine is, if you need it...although I do not think you will."

"Of course, Abigail, don't worry about me, I'll be able to take care of things. You need to go to Nathanial."

Abigail hustled towards her bedroom. "I have so many things to get together; I seem to have lost my appetite. I might be out later for a cup of cider to warm myself before bed."

Left alone in the kitchen, Maria stored what food was left from their dinner and cleaned up as well as she could. She thought it best that she retire early, to leave Abigail alone to pack her things.

As she lay upstairs in bed, waiting for sleep to come, she could hear Abigail moving about downstairs late into the night. Early the next morning, Saturday, November 2, the temperature dropped to near freezing. The women said their goodbyes. As Maria watched Abigail leave, she prayed that she would not feel any tightening pains in her stomach—at least not until her friend returned.

26

November 4, 1715
NORTH HARWICH – CAPE COD

MARIA STRUGGLED TO KEEP HERSELF WARM. She longed for Sam as November's chill tightened its icy grip over Cape Cod. Still alone on the third day of Abigail's absence, Maria waited for her friend's return. The young girl pulled her shawl around her shoulders and hummed a lullaby for comfort. She prayed to her mother…how she missed her and her gentle words.

Her taut skin, stretched to its limit across her stomach, could not be eased, even after massaging it with circular patterns. Maria swept the floor and scattered new sand on top of the rough-cut planks.

Wood was needed for the evening fire, so she ventured outdoors, only to be pummeled by sleet that beat against the wooden shingles, and a bitter wind that slapped its fury across her face. It reminded her of her father's harsh words. She hurried back inside.

Desperate for a distraction, Maria carefully climbed the narrow enclosed steps to the bedroom, steadying herself by holding onto its sidewalls. In the gray light she sorted through the childbed linens Abigail had found in the attic. She wished Sam could hold these tiny cloths now meant for their coming newborn.

A white linen bunting fell to the floor. As she bent over to pick it up, Maria's stomach stiffened. "Be calm," she cautioned herself. "It's not time. It's only my eighth month."

Her face grew pale and she felt faint. A quick breath cleared her head as she returned to the warm kitchen to stoke the fire in the hearth. With the heft of a length of firewood, the pain returned with the same force as before. She reached for the hourglass above the hearth and set it on the table. After the sand fell three quarters of the way through the hour, her stomach grew tight again.

She thought it best to stay near the hearth and hope the cramps would stop. The wind and icy rain from the storm were the only sounds filling the chilly house as the glass bulb sifted its sand twice more. Another tightening repeated, but Maria decided it was still too irregular for a pattern. When her stomach relaxed, she began her evening meal and whispered a thank you to Hestor for the stew that had been prepared the prior day.

As the night grew darker, Maria finished her supper. Another log was added to the fire; its yellow flames soon lit the small room. She yearned for Sam to be by her side.

Gathering her skirts and the hourglass, she climbed the stairs to retire for the evening. The cold air hung heavy throughout the upper room. Maria's kneecaps shook as the chilly air penetrated her body. She left her skirts on and tied a shawl around her head and shoulders. With the hourglass on the floor beside the bed, she nestled her swollen body inside the blankets. Closing her eyes, thoughts of Sam's embrace slowly warmed her.

*   *   *

The pains came back after midnight, Maria rolled onto her side, trying to comfort herself. Unsuccessful, she decided to look for Minda's medicinal potion downstairs. Heavy with child and clumsy in manner, she slowly rose from her bed and crept down the steep stairs to find the Indian's potent leaves. She knew it was too early for the birth; maybe the herbs would ease her anxiety.

She reached for the medicine box on the high shelf. Opening the small pouch inside, Maria measured two pinches of herbs into the bottom of a large tankard to make her brew. The fire burned hot as it boiled the watery contents of the black kettle that hung on an iron pole inside the hearth. Swiftly, she poured the steamy liquid on top of the strange smelling mix, waited a few minutes, then strained it through a piece of linen and into a bottle with a glass stopper.

After taking two sips of the pungent liquid, she resolutely climbed back up the stairs, with potion in hand, confident that she would now sleep.

Restless, Maria tossed and turned. She dreamt of horrible images; creatures clawing at her body; her hands and feet frozen in ice; her back and legs covered in a sticky liquid. As she slowly began to waken from her nightmare, she held her eyes closed for fear that her dream was real. Finally, she cautiously pushed her hand over the bed linens. They felt cold and wet. Her fingers moved up and down, sliding across the icy bedding.

A deep, searing pain rippled across her stomach, and her eyes flashed open. The murky morning light that filtered into the freezing room revealed that the warm nest she had been lying upon had indeed become wet and frozen. She threw the bedcovers aside and looked down between her legs. Her body shook in horror as she realized her water had broken during the night. Her travail had begun.

Maria lay in the damp, clammy bed trying to capture her thoughts. The low temperatures had hardened her skirts and shift, making each movement almost impossible. She scrambled to get off the bed, all the while fighting to rid her body of the frozen clothes. At last, she stood naked, clutching her stomach. She leaned against the wall shaking, "Please, no...not now," she cried. "I can't do this by myself."

As she pulled two dry shifts on for warmth, her body contracted again. When she was able to breathe normally, Maria glanced towards her bed and saw the glass bottle filled with the dark liquid on the floor. Abigail's warnings of its power cautioned her against drinking from it. Ignoring her misgivings, she took the glass bottle, along with the hourglass, and wrapped them in a shift. After tying the material into a sling around her neck to keep her hands free, she returned to the kitchen to be closer to the fire.

Midway down the steps, a sharp spasm knocked her off balance, and she landed hard on the fourth plank. Her hands gripped the wooden board while she waited for the pain to pass. While the wind roared outside, a piercing draft of air dropped from the upstairs against her back, sending her body into more violent shivers.

Maria stood and dragged her weakening body down the remaining stairs to finally the fire that she so desperately needed. After placing the hourglass on the table and the medicine bottle on the bureau, she leaned into the hearth and pleaded, "Please, where is Hestor? Where are you Sam? I'm so frightened to be alone!"

Her hands shook as she worked the bellows to engage the fire. She waited for the next tightening but it did not come. Relieved, Maria leaned her head over the table and began to whimper like a small child, realizing no one was coming to help her. Sam was so far away; no amount of praying or wishing was going to help her this night.

Maria raised her head and decided that she must prepare to face her travail alone. With determination, she gathered old cloths, her knife, a pillow, extra blankets, pieces of string and the child linens. She placed them on the bureau in the borning room and rested on the small bed. Her travail returned with a savage force. She screamed, "Stop pushing. Stop it! Be strong."

Her screams changed into cries for help. "I can't stand the pain! Please, someone help me!"

She looked over to the glass bottle on the small chest of drawers. Dragging her body into the borning room, she lunged for the bottle. No longer caring about Minda's cautions, Maria took a sip from it, then another and another. Soon she felt drowsy. Collapsing onto the small bed near the wall, she finally closed her eyes.

Within a short time her labor returned with even stronger urges to push. Maria tried to stand but the contractions folded her body forward and she fell back onto the bed. She fought to right herself, then tried to stimulate the child to come faster. She pulled her body around the room by holding onto the walls with her hands. Her heart pounded and her body grew heavy with sweat. Her stomach felt as if it would explode and her lower body split open. She forced her legs to keep walking. With each turn around the enclosed space, Maria stopped and sipped more of the potent drug until it was all gone.

When the pains became stronger and closer together, the natural processes of childbirth took control of her body and mind. Her screams of agony mingled with the screeching wind and icy rain smashing into the window. As the storm swirled around Abigail's house and the tiny village's deserted cart-ways, Maria's cries went unheard.

27

Present Day – July 3
BREWSTER – CAPE COD

FROM INSIDE THE HOUSE, I could see Paul staring down into the hole. After a while, he went in. I wondered if he had found anything else. I decided to join him, leaving Molly in the house watching TV.

The dirt cellar was about 4 feet deep and 4 wide. I climbed down the narrow steps into the hole next to Paul. It easily accommodated both of us. He picked some of the bigger pieces of wood from the box and carefully moved the dirt from under the iron straps that now extended out into thin air. He looked desperate for anything that might catch his eye. I didn't want to miss anything either, or be left out of any new discoveries, so I also started to sift through the dirt.

"Did you call the police?" he asked.

"Yes. They're sending an officer over to take a look."

"Good. It sure is exciting, but also kind of weird," he said as he leaned back to study the black dirt surrounding us.

I touched his arm. "You know, standing here makes me think of the nightmare I had the other night. I don't know what I was expecting to find when we started digging, but I didn't think we'd find part of a dead body." Shivers rippled up and down my back.

Paul leaned over to make sure the towel covered the bone fragment.

Molly stood by the back door watching us. "Mommy, someone is…."

I cut her off. "Just a minute honey. We'll be right there."

We both climbed out of the hole.

Casey, home early from her summer job, walked around the garage to the back. "Why is a police car in the yard?" She looked a little nervous.

"It's okay; nobody's hurt. We think we found a small skull in the old box," I explained, walking over to her. I put my arm around her back and asked her, "Is the officer coming back here?"

Casey nodded, then peered into the hole with a squeamish look on her face. "Is it in there?" she asked, wrinkling up her nose.

"Yeah, it's under the towel."

"I don't want to see it." She rolled her eyes and walked backwards toward the house. "I'm going in. You can tell me all about it later."

"Would you keep an eye on Molly?"

"No problem," she smiled.

Paul and I walked around the barn to meet the police officer halfway. Paul shook his hand.

The young man introduced himself as Officer Gomes.

"Sorry to be a bother, but we think we've discovered something unusual in our back yard."

"Not to worry, sir," Officer Gomes replied, his eyes scanning the house. "Why don't you show me what you found."

The policeman swaggered as he walked, holding one hand on his holstered gun and the other loose by his side.

Paul explained what had happened. "We accidentally discovered this root cellar," he said, leading the officer closer to the hole. "As we dug deeper, we found a wooden box, but when we tried to dig it out the top collapsed. We found pieces of parchment and a bone that looks like a skull in the dirt."

Paul climbed into the hole and lifted the towel off the skull.

The officer crouched by the edge of the cellar. "Interesting."

Paul held up the bone piece so Gomes could see it, pointing to small indentations where the eyes would have been. The bottom half was completely missing.

"I'm going to give my sergeant a call. I'll be right back."

I watched the officer round the barn toward the front of the house. Kneeling down by the edge of the cellar, I asked Paul, "What do you think they'll do?"

"I don't know," he sighed, resting the skull fragment on top of one of the iron straps.

When Officer Gomes returned, he took a wide stance and looked straight at us. "My sergeant is contacting the State Police." He stood a little taller. "Until then, we should not disturb the site. I'm going to have to ask you to please vacate the so-called root cellar, sir."

As I watched Paul and the officer reset the sawhorses to barricade the opening, I couldn't help but wonder, "What's next? What have we gotten ourselves into now?"

Officer Gomes continued his instructions. "You may go back into the house." He waited for us to reach the back door before he strode to the front of the house, pausing to make sure we entered the kitchen. "I'll be by my car."

I closed the screen door behind us. "This is so weird. We might have a real crime scene in our backyard."

Paul looked at me. "Should I open the gallery?"

"Probably not a great idea," I said. "No one is going to come in with a police car out front."

We both agreed to remain closed for the day and kept ourselves busy preparing lunch. After putting the dishes into the dishwasher, I glanced over to the driveway just as a black car pulled up alongside the police cruiser. A man dressed in a navy blue suit got out and shook hands with Officer Gomes. They headed for the backyard.

"Paul," I whispered. "Someone else is here."

We hurried out the back door and approached the two men. The suited man turned to show us his badge. "Hello. You must be Mr. and Mrs. Caldwell?"

"Yes," we responded in unison.

"I'm Detective Jacobs from the state police. I was over at the Orleans Courthouse when I got the call, so I thought I'd stop by to see what you found."

"Nice to meet you." We shook hands with the detective and told him all about the discovery of the cellar, then the chest, the parchment, and finally the skull.

I hurried back to the house to get the parchment pieces, which we'd placed in a small zip lock bag. By the time I returned, the detective was already sifting through the dirt with the end of his pen. I handed him the little bag.

After examining its contents, Detective Jacobs said, "I might have to call the medical examiner." Climbing out of the cellar, he added, "I'll be right back."

We stood quietly around the edge of the opening.

"Is this the first time you've ever encountered human remains?" Paul asked Officer Gomes.

"Yes, sir," he nodded.

I attempted to make small talk with him but he seemed very serious. We waited in silence for the detective to come back into sight.

"Well, it looks like one of the State Archaeologists will be coming instead. We only have one Medical Examiner for this whole area, including Boston. You know, state budget cuts and all."

"Oh, I see." I caught Paul's eye.

The detective explained. "Procedures call for the medical examiner to be summoned whenever human remains are found. But in this case, when the bones are obviously over a hundred years old based on the parchment that you found in the box, we can call in the archaeologist. He's coming from Orleans so he won't be long. Officer Gomes will stay here until then."

He extended his hand to say goodbye. "It was nice meeting you, Mr. and Mrs. Caldwell. Have a nice day."

History and mystery...my favorite subjects. Even if it was an inconvenience for us, I could hardly wait to see what would happen next, and shot Paul a big smile. He returned my look with a sly grin and left for his studio.

"Would you like a cup of coffee or a glass of water?" I asked the remaining officer.

"No, thank you, ma'am."

A few minutes of awkward silence passed before I decided to go back into the house, leaving the officer by himself. Within the hour, a big pickup truck pulled in next to the police car.

Casey yelled from the front parlor, "Mom, now someone else is here."

I went out back and saw Paul watching from his studio door as an older man with long gray hair approached the officer. I watched him gesture back and forth from the cellar to the woods and back to the hole. Setting down his brown briefcase he climbed into the cellar to examine the skull piece. He spent several minutes evaluating the dirt around the chest. He snapped on white plastic gloves then picked up the plastic bag containing the parchment paper.

Paul motioned for me to move in closer. The archaeologist appeared oblivious to us. When he'd finished his analysis he climbed out of the cellar. "My name is Salinger," he said, "I represent the State Historical Commission."

In his gloved hand was the small skull fragment that had been left near the iron bars by Detective Jacobs.

"How old is your house?" he asked, walking over to the picnic table to put the evidence down.

I proudly answered, "We think it was built around 1880."

Opening the plastic bag, he gently removed the two pieces of parchment and laid them out on the wooden table. "This piece with the numbers is very interesting." He pulled a small magnifying glass out of his breast pocket. "Can you see the numbers here? I believe they read 1715."

I leaned over the table and was elated that we were right about the dates. "So you think there might have been another house here before this one was built?"

"It was not uncommon for land to be handed down from one generation to another, with different houses existing on the same lot at different times."

"What do you think of the bone, or skull, or whatever it is?" Paul asked him.

Salinger ran his fingers over the smooth part of the top. "Not sure yet."

"Is it a baby's skull?" I asked.

"Possibly, but again, I'm not sure," he repeated.

Silence. I heard the sound of someone's lawnmower as Paul and I stood around the picnic table, anxious for any information from Salinger.

"May I take this with me?" Salinger pointed to the parchment.

"Of course, but we'd like to make a copy of it first," I told him.

He found no problem with that request, so Paul took it to his studio to copy it.

"I'm amazed that anything survived this long down there," I commented, glancing over to the cellar.

"Well, given the right conditions...." Salinger surveyed the backyard, then asked, "How far are you from the bay? A mile?"

"Exactly nine-tenths of a mile," I answered, pleased with myself. "It was on the appraisal when we bought the house."

Salinger continued, "That distance would explain a lot. There's more clay here, and you seem to be on higher ground."

Paul walked towards us with the photocopy and the little bag. "What did I miss?"

Salinger repeated, "I was just telling your wife that based on the location of where you found the chest, and the dryness of the area, it's possible that something could have survived from the 1700s." He squinted into the setting sun. "Centuries ago, people would bury their loved ones on their own property or in very small out-of-the-way cemeteries. But I must say, this one is unusual. If it is human remains, burying them in a cellar would happen only under strange circumstances."

"Can you make anything out of the letters here on this other piece?" I asked trying to pick his brain.

"Not sure," he said looking at the faded letters.

"I'll see if I can run some tests on the paper and the bone." Salinger routed in his briefcase for a larger plastic bag and a small camera. "If you don't mind, I'm going to take some photos of the area in question for my report."

"Of course," I agreed. "Will you let us know what you've discovered? If anything?"

"No problem."

"What happens now?" Paul asked.

"Once we determine what we have, we can proceed with the proper disposal of the remains."

I questioned the word, 'remains' in my head, given the fact that there wasn't anything left of the body but one bone. I could see the expression on Paul's face, which told me that he thought the same.

"Are you going to do any more digging?" I asked Salinger.

"Not sure," he said, clicking away with his camera.

Paul cautioned the archaeologist, "If we try to remove the rest of the chest it will surely crumble into nothing. But if we're very careful, could we see if there's anything else down there?"

"You should hold off on any more digging so as not to disturb whatever might still be buried in that dirt." Salinger looked adamant.

28

Present Day – July 11
BREWSTER – CAPE COD

WE'D BEEN HEARING ABOUT an approaching hurricane all week, and everyone was anxious. Paul and I were especially so, as we waited to hear what Mr. Salinger would tell us about the items we'd found in the root cellar.

The attractive blonde forecaster on the weather channel repeated, "...a good possibility of a strike along the East Coast, especially for Cape Cod and the Islands."

By Friday, the predictions turned into when and where it would hit the Cape. This was my first encounter with a hurricane, and it sent me into survival mode. I shopped for batteries, water, canned meat, instant coffee, pop tarts and anything that would keep without refrigeration.

Paul and the boys took care of the outdoors, securing any large unattached objects and bringing smaller items into the garage. Paul removed the sawhorses, which barricaded the old cellar and drove two spikes into the tarp covering the area where we'd been digging.

By early evening, the winds were gusting to over 50mph. The night proved restless for both of us, each wondering what we were going to wake up to in the morning. At 7 a.m. the howling wind was smacking branches against our bedroom windows and rattling the glass.

Paul jumped out of bed. "Okay. Tell everyone to get themselves washed and dressed before we lose power."

I scurried to rouse the children. "Let's go. Everyone up and get downstairs. Molly, come with me."

The family all pitched in, gathering blankets, pillows, a radio and a large plastic clothesbasket filled with books, crayons, playing cards and a few board games. As the sky blackened and the rain traveled sideways, the power suddenly went out.

We watched the trees whip themselves into circles from the wind, shedding most of their leaves in a swirling mass of green. Jim filmed the spectacle outside through the windows of the front parlor.

Paul looked nervous. "I've never seen anything like this. We'd better get into the kitchen; it's the newest construction and has the least number of windows."

Paul hollered out orders. "Everyone into the kitchen! Brian, go and get some duct tape and big sheets of cardboard from my studio. Jim, make sure the radio is working and all the flashlights are usable."

A wave of nausea drifted over me, I rushed to the bathroom thinking I was going to vomit, but my stomach held strong. Back in the kitchen, I quickly recovered. I watched the boys cover up the windows to protect us from the possibility of shattering glass. I felt bad for Paul. I knew he wanted shutters on the outside of the house, so that he could close them over the glass, but for now, the cardboard would have to do.

We listened to the latest news on the radio; the wind had reached over 75 mph, so the two bridges—our only access on or off of Cape Cod—were now closed.

Paul shut the door as all of us crowded into the new kitchen to ride out the storm.

The kids busied themselves trying to find something to occupy their minds. The room began to get stuffy, and no one seemed to notice me turning paler by the minute. I thought I was going to lose my breakfast. As the winds blew at 75 mph, with gusts to 120 mph according to the radio, I whispered to Paul, "I don't feel well. I'll be right back." He looked at me, but I don't think he really heard what I was saying.

I literally burst out the pocket door of the kitchen and ran into the downstairs bathroom. With a flashlight in one hand, I slammed the door behind me, just in time to throw up in the toilet. I prayed quietly, "Dear God, please don't let this be the flu!"

When I returned to the kitchen I took my seat in the rocking chair that Brian had brought in from the living room.

"Everything all right?" Paul asked.

"Must be all the excitement," I said with a half-hearted smile, trying to cover up how miserable I felt.

Everyone looked bored from being cooped up in the small room. I closed my eyes, inhaled deep breaths and tried to soothe my wretched body as the wind pounded against the house. I looked at Paul. He didn't seem aware that I was still feeling sick. I couldn't blame him; he was worried about the storm. I tried to gain a bit more sympathy from him. "I'll be better; just let me relax a minute."

He looked at me and smiled.

I felt a little selfish wanting more attention, but darn it, I really felt sick! I could hear Molly giggling as she played Chutes and Ladders with Casey. Jim fiddled with the radio, searching for music. Brian lay on the floor with his eyes closed. I was determined to feel better.

As the sounds and sights of the storm began to blur inside my conscious mind, I thought of my mom. How I wished I could call her about the hurricane…and tell her that our family was safe. I remembered the day of her funeral. At the viewing, one of my peculiar aunts had told my older sister, Barbara, that my moving away is what killed Mom because I was the baby of the family. The crazy lady's stupid words had hurt when I heard them back then, and they still hurt today. After all, I was not an only child; I had five brothers and sisters. My moving away did not kill our mother. My eyes began to tear. I really missed her. I forced myself to think of other things: my wonderful family, the fact that everyone was healthy—that Paul is in love with me.

After only three hours the storm was over. The sky lightened, and the rain stopped. We ventured outside to see the devastation surrounding the house. Leaves covered the ground, and branches were sticking up and out of the strangest places. Trees lay across Route 6A blocking access east and west. It was strange to walk down the middle of the road and not meet a car. I warned the kids to get back indoors when I saw that power lines were strewn across the road. They were humming and sparking, sending little bursts of light into the rubble of tree limbs in all directions.

Over the next few days, trying to live without electricity became uppermost in our minds. Our interest in the cellar was pushed back behind the immediate care of the family. We never noticed that the tarp had blown away from the cellar; revealing at its bottom the shiny edge of a small gold coin now peeking through the dark, wet dirt.

29

November 5, 1715
NORTH HARWICH – CAPE COD

NO SOUND CAME FROM THE CHILD who lay between Maria's legs. It was covered with blood and thick body fluids that had protected the babe in the womb. When the afterbirth brought the last agonizing screams of pain and the birthing process was complete, the infant struggled to breathe as Maria slipped deeper into unconsciousness.

The presence of someone alongside Maria would have seen the trauma of the child whose umbilical cord had wedged itself next to the head. As it had moved through the birth canal, precious air had been blocked from entering the small body.

Eerie shadows flickered on the walls from the glow of the kitchen hearth. Maria lay unconscious in the dimly lit borning room. It was now mid-morning and the storm continued to rage its fury outside. A clap of snow thunder awoke Maria from her stupor, but Minda's potent herbs still lay deep inside her exhausted body.

Her blurry eyes fell upon the newborn child. The bed-covers, crumpled under and around her, had absorbed most of the blood that was still dripping from her body. She pushed away the soiled sheets, lifted her legs over the child, and rolled onto the floor. Struggling to stand, she pulled her shift through her legs and fastened it over the waistband of one of her skirts.

Maria stared at the red-stained bedding that surrounded the body of her son. She placed her hand on his small chest and felt no heartbeat. Dazed and grief-stricken, she blocked the reality of what lay before her and calmly went into the kitchen to get a cloth and a bowl of water.

She cleaned her child with slow and gentle motions. A lullaby drifted from her lips as she swaddled her beautiful son in the bloodied blankets. Cradling the little body in her arms, she carried him to the kitchen and sat by the hearth to rock him in a slow, even rhythm.

Time seemed to stop on this cold winter day for the young girl. Hours passed and by afternoon, Maria had not moved, nor had she let go of the dead child. She chanted her somber song, her face expressionless. Soon the hearth grew cold. She carried the infant back to the borning room and placed the lifeless body onto the soiled bed. She kissed him softly on his head and returned to the kitchen to tend the fire.

Upstairs, Maria found the Doane's family chest in the corner of her bedroom and ran her fingers over the carved 'D' on its top. Wind lashed at the windows as she looked inside the wooden box at a small white linen shift. She carried both down the steep stairs.

Reverently placing the inscribed chest next to her child on the bed, she opened its lid and removed the shift. With loving hands, Maria pulled away the stained bedcovers, revealing the naked body of her newborn. Her fingers traced his perfect face. She whispered, "You're so beautiful, my son."

After dressing him in the clean shift, she held him close to her face. She then placed the infant inside the chest, gathered a piece of the linen and covered his head in one last attempt to protect him.

At the sideboard, she opened the decorated box that her dear friend Matthew had brought her from Eastham. She spread its contents out on the table before her. There were pieces of vellum that had been salvaged from her father's tanning, a quill pen, a small piece of carbon stick and a jar of gum arabic. Using her knife, she scraped powder from the stick and funneled it into the empty ink well. She added water and a pinch of gum arabic to complete her ink.

She dipped her pen into the black liquid and wrote:

Here lies the son of Sam Bellamy, Devonshire, England
And Maria Hallett, Eastham, Massachusetts
May this sweet child sing with the angels of the Lord.
Born & Died Nov 4, 1715

Her crooked letters were primitive but legible. When the ink dried, Maria placed the vellum on top of the child's body, marking him for eternity. She caressed the sides of the wooden box as if to leave her scent across them, then she slowly closed the lid. She was sure that if no one could find this precious gift then no harm would come to her or to Sam.

Maria realized the storm had ceased its fury as light rain now fell around the house. He must be hidden, she thought.

The setting sun reflected crimson in the sky, but the troubled girl paid no attention to its beauty as she ventured outside, staring at the earth before her feet. Opening the door to the barn, she reached for a shovel and returned to the house. No one must know, she repeated.

Maria noticed drips of her own blood were trailing her. She pushed another old cloth between her legs and secured it into her soiled shift. Lifting the rug that revealed the root cellar door, she carried the shovel down the steep stairs. The child would be safe down here.

A basket of apples lay near the corner of the darkened room. Maria moved it aside and began to dig with purpose. Impatient to complete her task she scratched at the black dirt with her fingers. No one would call her fornicator! More blood dripped onto the dirt floor but went unnoticed as she pressed forward. When the hole was finally dug deep and wide enough, Maria buried the wooden chest that held her son.

30

November 6, 1715
NORTH HARWICH – CAPE COD

AS HESTOR ROSE FROM HER BED, a deep dread hovered over her. Leaning toward her husband, she shouted into his ear, "It's too cold to do anything today." Then she poked him, so he, too, would share in her misery of getting out of bed.

He growled, "Go away and leave me alone, old woman."

"I shall be off to check on that girl, Maria Hallett, at Miss Abigail's," she snarled, "but I ain't staying too long. The girl spooks me." She turned once more towards the lump in her bed. "I'll return shortly. Tend to yourself."

He pulled the covers over his head.

At that, Hestor donned her heavy cape to empty the necessary in the woods. Upon her return, she readied herself to leave for the Doane's, grabbing several beef strips to eat on her way. She slammed the door behind her.

The grumpy housemaid nibbled on the greasy meat as she walked, all the while, mumbling to herself, "Such a terrible day to be outside!" She looked around to see that the previous night's storm had knocked down several fences, scattered tools and uprooted the cover from their well. As she came closer to Abigail Doane's house, the absence of smoke from the chimney only added to her misery. She grumbled, "Oh, if I didn't have enough work to do already, now I've got to find kindling for their fire." She wiped her mouth with an angry swipe of her hand.

Hestor opened the door of the Doane house without a greeting, eager to give an earful to Maria for sleeping late and not tending to the fire, but she never crossed its entrance. The smell of bodily fluids tainted the air. She spotted blood dotted across the kitchen floorboards and immediately stepped backwards. She whispered the young girl's name, "Maria?"

The hearth was dark, and a shovel leaned against the stones with fresh dirt on its blade. Hestor cautiously walked over to the center stairway and saw more drips of blood. She called up the stairs, "Maria?"

Hestor's superstitions began to fuel her fears. There was an empty bottle on the sideboard. As she lifted it to her nose, the distinct odor of opium made her wince. Then she glanced over to the borning room; creeping closer, she peered in.

Hestor's wide eyes circled the small room. She could see blood randomly staining the floor and walls. Terror took control of her and as she leaned against the doorframe to steady herself, the glass container slipped from her grasp and fell to the floor. As it rolled towards the corner, the bottle's repetitive rumble led Hestor's eyes across the wooden boards to the pile of blood soaked bedcovers and the apparently lifeless body of Maria. She leaned in closer and could see the girl's pale left arm dangling over the side of the bed; her delicate fingertips touching the thick blood-streaked mass of afterbirth congealing on the floor.

Hestor whispered a silent prayer. Her white skin turned ashen gray, and her body quivered with fear. She covered her mouth and turned away from the horrifying sight.

As her curiosity peaked, she looked one more time and then shouted, "Satan is here!" Her words rose to a mind-piercing screech as she ran out the door and down the path towards Constable Ezra's house. "Be gone from me, Evil One. Be gone!" she repeated, stopping only once to hold onto a tree to vomit.

* * *

Ezra Smalley enjoyed the respect he received from the North Harwich community after he'd accepted the appointment to be their constable. He was their guardian of peace. Among his many duties were collecting taxes and checking each house to confirm they had enough buckets for water in case of fire. One specific chore he complained about was arresting those who were found loitering outside during the Sabbath meeting. Since he was not akin to religious doings, this was distasteful to him.

On this November morning, he sat in the privy with a small lamp for light, going over a notice from Barnstable County concerning whom he should be watchful for in his district. Cold air drifted up the deep hole under his bare bottom. It did not bother him; his routine of regularity pleased him no matter what the weather was around him. He could hear someone yelling his name in the distance. Ezra grumbled to himself. "Gol'darn it, now who could that be?"

His arthritic fingers fumbled to button up his breeches. "If it isn't one thing or another...it better be important...interrupting my morning habit!"

The noise came closer to his ears. "Ezra!!!! Constable Ezra!!!" The excited voice called again, clearer this time.

Stepping into the chilly air, he heard, "Ezra, come quick!"

He entered his house from the rear, stuffing the official papers from his superiors into his side pocket.

Hestor, finding an inner strength after heaving by the tree, ran up the path toward Ezra's main door, desperate to report the terrible scene she had discovered. Her fist beat against the wooden entrance. "There's trouble at Abigail Doane's house."

Ezra muttered as he hurried through the kitchen, "Yes, yes, I'm coming."

As he opened the door, Hestor stood before him, the handkerchief around her neck stained with drips of vomit. Her face and body were wet with sweat.

"Ezra! You must go to Abigail Doane's house." She sat down on a chair just inside the door. Gasping for air, she finally spoke, "I warned everyone...about that girl...living with Abigail." She hissed, "She's ...evil!"

Ezra did not like this woman in his house. She had a reputation for a loose tongue, and today she emanated a dreadful stench. Irritated but calm, the constable said, "Now, my good woman, please control yourself. Would you not be more comfortable outside on the bench?"

Ignoring his question, Hestor continued, "I think the girl is dead and her newborn is missing." She shook her head back and forth in disbelief. "There is so much blood. I fear the worst has happened. I fear that wickedness is upon this village."

"Madam, you must leave and go home. I will investigate this so-called evil and will not have need of your service." He took hold of her large upper arm and led her to the door. Ushering her out, he added, "I will inform you later of what I discover."

Hestor turned to face Ezra. "Well, if you ask me...."

"No one is asking you anything, woman. I will see for myself what has happened," and with those words he closed the door behind her.

The simple housemaid, growling under her breath, straightened her corset and smoothed her skirts. Mumbling with indignation, she stepped away from the constable's house, eager to find the ear of someone else.

31

Present Day – July 12
CAPE COD

LOUIS SALINGER HAD BEEN AT HIS OFFICE in Boston for most of the week and had missed the hurricane on the Cape. His mailbox contained the results of various tests he'd ordered on the fragments that were found in the Caldwell's backyard. He ripped open the envelope and impatiently unfolded the official document. It read that the bone fragment was indeed part of a human skull, most likely an infant, and along with the two vellum pieces, it dated back to the 1700s. A smile broadened across his face as he returned to his desk to call an old friend.

* * *

Neil Hallett, according to those who knew him, had every right to his quirkiness. After all, he was connected by a thin stretch of the imagination to a famous local legend about a woman named Maria Hallett. He was known around town for his continuous bragging that he was related to the 'Witch of Billingsgate'. His house was a small Cape on Goody Hallett Drive, in Eastham, and across the front of his garage was a quarter board that read, *Whydah*. He spent hours hovering over his computer, searching eBay for anything about her legend.

He was placing his final bid in an online auction, with only sixty seconds left to post his price, when the call from Salinger interrupted him. The phone rang four times before he finally picked it up. He answered with a quick, "Hello? Oh, hey, Salinger, what can I do for you?" He frowned as someone else placed a higher bid and his time ran out. Rubbing his bald head in frustration, he leaned back into his swivel chair. "Who found what? Where?" he grumbled into the receiver.

Turning away from the computer screen, he gazed out the window behind his desk. "You don't say! Why yes, I'd be very interested in taking a look at them." He spun back to his desk and wrote down the Caldwells' address.

* * *

On the third day after the storm, our power returned. The sun shone bright against a deep blue sky. I had just finished raking the last of the shredded leaves and branches from the backyard when I heard Brian call out, "Mom, Mr. Salinger is on the phone."

It's about time, I thought, dropping the rake. I casually glanced down into the cellar as I walked past it. That's when I saw it—the top half of a shiny small disk. I stopped and stared. It beckoned me to pick it up. Impulsively I climbed in to retrieve it.

"Mom! Telephone!" Brian yelled again.

I clutched the circular object in my hand. "I'll be right there." Climbing up the stone steps of the cellar, I couldn't take my eyes off what looked like a gold coin. As I hurried into the house I wiped it clean on my shirt and thought about what I'd tell Salinger, or if I should even tell him about the coin. I slipped the disc into my jeans pocket as I answered the phone.

"Mr. Salinger, nice to finally hear from you. What did you find out?" I fiddled with the coin in my pocket. The information coming through the other end of the phone was good news. "I see. Yes, you can come by tomorrow. We'll be home. See you then. Goodbye."

As soon as I hung up the phone, I raced to look for Paul. I found him at his drawing table. "Hey, what's up?" he asked.

"That was Salinger on the phone, he said he's coming over tomorrow." I plopped down into the lounge chair by the glass doors. "He said the skull and vellum were definitely from the 1700s." I glanced over to the dirt surrounding the cellar and then held the coin up for Paul to see. "Look what I found."

"Where did you find that?" He walked over to me, took the gold coin and gave a little whistle. "This looks real."

"It sure does. I was just walking past the hole, and it shouted at me to come and get it." I touched his arm. "I know we weren't supposed to disturb anything, but I couldn't help myself. Do you think we should tell anyone? What if there's more down there?"

Paul examined the coin. "I wonder what the laws are about found treasure. Do we get to keep it?" He went over to his drawing board to look at the coin under a brighter light.

*   *   *

By 9:00 a.m. the next morning, Neil Hallett and Louis Salinger were drinking coffee over the tailgate of Salinger's truck in the back parking lot of the local donut shop. Other commercial vans and trucks were parked alongside them. Hallett was looking at the two pieces of vellum inside the plastic baggie.

"What do you make of the letters?" Salinger asked.

"Well, I'm kind of partial to the Hallett/Bellamy story, and these letters could definitely fit their names. I just don't understand why they were found in Brewster, and not around Eastham or Wellfleet, where Maria was supposed to have lived." Neil shook his head. "Did they find anything else besides this and the skull?"

"I noticed there were two iron bars. Probably from the old box."

Hallett sipped his black coffee. "There's never been any physical proof that there even was a Maria Hallett, just speculation and stories that were passed down from generation to generation. But I know she was real. My grandfather told me about her when I was a kid." He stood taller and looked Salinger right in the eye. "I know her story is true, and I've got the name to prove it."

"I've only heard about it in the *Cape Cod Gazette*," Salinger picked up the baggie, and added, "...and that pirate museum in Provincetown. So what did your grandfather tell you?"

Hallett grabbed the vellum. "He said Bellamy was coming home to Maria the night of a terrible nor'easter. His ship wrecked near Marconi Beach, and everyone died, except for a dozen survivors. Two pirates were found innocent, but the rest were hanged in Boston." Hallett leaned against the tailgate of his truck. "All the old salts of Cape Cod say Sam Bellamy was never found."

He handed the vellum back to Salinger. "The rest of the legend is about Maria. She was distraught when Bellamy failed to return to her, as he'd promised he would. When her baby died, she felt abandoned and then cursed all sailors who sailed by the Cape Cod coast."

"Nothing like a woman scorned," Salinger muttered.

Hallett twisted his mustache. "I want to believe those letters could stand for Maria Hallett and Sam Bellamy, but I just don't know for sure. The location isn't right."

* * *

Meanwhile, two cars down from Salinger's truck, a bespectacled young man was sitting in his car with the windows open. He stopped eating his powdered donut when he overheard the conversation about the Hallett legend. Brushing the white powder from his dark shirt, he got out of his car and casually walked over to the two men.

"Excuse me," he said. Extending his hand out, he introduced himself, "I'm Andrew McNutt, a reporter for the *Cape Cod Gazette*. My editor would be very interested in what you've been discussing. Legends around the Cape are always newsworthy."

Hallett and Salinger exchanged quick glances.

McNutt asked, "Do you think I could interview you for a story?"

Salinger looked at the reporter. "Sure, I'll talk to you, but you'd have to get permission from the property owners before you print anything."

Hallett looked worried. He'd had bad experiences with neighborhood newspapers. A while back, a reporter had written a human-interest story about the local characters and had poked fun of him and his lineage.

Salinger continued, "I guess a little publicity would boost my reputation, but as I said, the Caldwells would have to approve any news articles."

McNutt thanked him and followed them to the Caldwell house. Neil Hallett did not look happy.

* * *

Three vehicles pulled into our driveway. "He's here," I yelled out to Paul. "Remember, we're not going to say anything about the coin. Let's research the law regarding found treasure on private property first."

"Okay," he agreed.

"Who's in the other cars?" I asked.

"I don't know."

We walked out back, and Salinger introduced us to his friend Hallett, and a reporter from the local newspaper. Salinger explained the results and quietly added, "Do you know about the legend of the pirate Sam Bellamy?"

I glanced at Paul. "Wasn't he the pirate captain of the *Whydah*?"

The archaeologist grinned. "Yes, that's him. The Provincetown museum at the end of Macmillan Wharf is all about Sam Bellamy and his ship. It features an incredible exhibit of the pirate booty he'd stolen to bring home to a girl named Maria 'Goody' Hallett."

My hands started to perspire, and my heart beat faster as thoughts of gold coins, treasure and everything pirate tumbled into my head. Suddenly I connected the letters on the vellum to Maria Hallett and Sam Bellamy. Everyone's voices distorted into mumblings as the men talked to Paul about the parchment and the skull. I was concentrating so much on my own thoughts that I could barely hear their conversation.

"Nancy," Paul looked at me.

I was standing still as a statue, peering downward into the cellar.

"Nancy, are you okay?"

"Huh? I'm sorry. I was just wondering about something." I shook my head, trying to come up with a nonchalant way to ask Salinger about the laws regarding found treasure on someone's property.

As if hearing my thoughts, he also peered into the cellar. "Whatever you find down there belongs to you as the rightful owners of the land."

Hallett walked closer to the edge of the root cellar. "Yup, that's a real old Cape Cod root cellar. Small, round and built out of big stones. Do you mind if I go down and look around?"

Paul nodded.

"Go ahead," I agreed.

Hallett climbed down into the cellar. Paul and I watched him sift through the dirt with his fingers. He examined the iron bars of the wooden box that were still suspended in thin air and picked up a few pieces of the decayed wood.

I approached Salinger. "I wasn't sure about showing you this," I held the coin out in the palm of my hand. "I found it in the cellar."

His eyes widened as he reached for it.

Hallett yelled out from below, "Well, I'll be darned. Look what I found!"

Together we turned to see him holding up another dirty gold coin.

"Whoa, you're kidding!" Paul strode toward him.

"Look!" Hallett held it higher in the air.

Finding the second coin made me giddy with excitement—I could see the same expression on Paul's face. The thought of real treasure buried on our land made me anxious for everyone to leave so we could keep digging.

The reporter began to scribble in his notebook. "How did you come upon the cellar?"

I ignored his question and joined Paul at the edge of the hole.

Hallett crouched down to dig with his hands while Salinger just stared into the bottom of the cellar.

Using his most polite voice, Paul asked, "Would you please come out of there, Mr. Hallett?"

Hallett ignored Paul's request and dug even deeper.

Paul yelled at him. "Mr. Hallett!!"

This time Hallett stopped digging and reluctantly climbed out of the hole.

"I'm sure you can understand the private nature of this whole situation," Paul explained. "If word gets out there might be buried pirate treasure on our property, no matter how small it is, we're going to be in for some rough days ahead." He looked directly at the reporter. "Mr. McNutt, your article could make my land and home a dangerous place for my family. Every weirdo will want to come here and dig for treasure, even if it is private property."

My excitement now turned to concern.

Salinger also looked distressed.

McNutt was not convinced by Paul's request for confidentiality. "This is a real scoop for me; I have to write the story. I promise not to reveal the exact location, or print your names, but I have a professional duty to share this with my readers."

I wondered why Salinger had to invite this reporter to join him. We didn't need any other problems.

"Okay, just a small piece—nothing sensational," Paul replied. "But if you mention our names or this address, I'll sue you and your newspaper."

"Thank you! Your privacy will be protected," said the young reporter. "Don't you worry about a thing."

* * *

McNutt said his hasty goodbyes and left. As he drove away, he felt elated. The paper was struggling to survive the online competition, and the publisher was trimming their budget with a cleaver. This story might guarantee he'd not be one of the reporters on the chopping block. Folklore, treasure, and mystery would surely entice readers to buy the newspaper. He raced back to his office to share the good news with his editor. His job would be to keep this story going for as long as possible.

* * *

Everyone stood around the opening of the cellar for several minutes before Salinger broke the awkward silence. "Mr. and Mrs. Caldwell, it has been interesting working with you." He sealed the skull fragment in a small plastic bag. "I trust that, if you find any more human remains, you'll notify me immediately?"

"Of course we will," I said.

"These vellum pieces are yours to keep, Mrs. Caldwell, along with the coins. Good luck."

Paul extended his hand to Salinger, "It was nice meeting you." He turned to Hallett. "Now if you don't mind, could I please have the coin?"

"Oh, I'm sorry." Hallett handed the coin to Paul.

I noticed it had already found its way into Neil Hallett's pocket. I decided I'd think twice about alerting them to more discoveries in the cellar.

* * *

At the end of the Caldwell's driveway Hallett paused and wound down the window of his truck. "Hey, Salinger, I have a gut feeling there's more to this story."

Salinger leaned through his opened window. "Go on."

"I just feel there's a real connection here—the Bellamy/Hallett legend has so many twists and turns—and by God, one of those stories about buried treasure has got to be true."

Salinger laughed. "You be careful."

Hallett turned his truck left. "Oh, I will. See you around."

Salinger drove off in the opposite direction.

* * *

By the time the men left it was almost high noon. I felt queasy again. "Paul, I don't feel well," I said, holding my stomach as I turned to go into the house.

He followed, cradling the second coin in his hand. When he found me in the bathroom, I was throwing up. He put the coin into his pocket and asked, "Honey, is everything all right?"

I grabbed a tissue and wiped my lips. "I think I'm fine."

"Maybe you should go to the doctor?" He held me in his arms and rubbed my back.

"I guess so." I snuggled into his shoulder. "Paul, what if I'm pregnant?"

"What?" He drew back, surprised at my comment.

I looked straight into his eyes and repeated. "What if I'm pregnant?"

"How could you be? When was your last period?"

"I lost track of the days with all the excitement about the hurricane and buried treasure. I think I might be late." A few tears ran down my cheeks.

Paul gently wiped them away. "Don't worry. Sit down for a minute. Let me make you some tea."

I felt vulnerable and did as I was told. At the table, I rubbed my forehead. "We can't afford another kid, we have no extra money! Besides, forty is too old to have a baby."

"It'll be fine." He filled the teakettle with water.

"Paul, I'm serious. All kinds of birth defects can happen to a baby born to a woman my age."

I tried to distract myself and took the first coin out of my jeans pocket and ran my fingers across its shiny face. It didn't work; my head switched gears, and I wondered out loud, "If I'm pregnant and I choose to have this baby, what's going to happen in twenty years or so, if there's something wrong with it? I don't want any of my children to be institutionalized because no one will be around to manage their care."

The teakettle whistled. "Let's stop talking about it. We don't even know if you're pregnant yet."

I held my mug of cinnamon tea and stared at the gold coin on the kitchen table.

"Feeling better?"

"A little. It's hard to explain how I feel." Unconsciously, I traced the edges of the coin around and around. "Are you going back out to the cellar?"

"I thought I would. Come with me. I'll bring you a chair so you can sit down if you need to." He smiled and kissed me. "Let's go and find some pirate treasure."

*   *   *

Brian arrived home early from work. He came around to the back garden. "Need help?"

"Sure," I said. "Get the wheelbarrow and another shovel." Paul's idea of a chair was a good one. I was tired. I watched them dig deeper into the cellar's floor. I enjoyed seeing my once sad boy join his father in an adventure. He looked happy again.

They separated the two metal bars from the rotted chest. Brian handed them over to me. "This is so cool, Mom."

Another thirty minutes passed before Brian stopped his digging and shouted, "Mom, Dad, I think I found something!" His hand held a third coin. A big grin spread across his face.

I got up to get a better look. "It looks like the one I found yesterday." I fumbled in my pocket, eager to show Brian my coin.

Paul chimed in, "Here's the other one Hallett found today."

"You already dug up two gold coins? Holy shit, Mom! Why didn't you tell us?"

"Watch your language, young man," his father cautioned him.

"Sorry. When you said you found a chest at the bottom of this cellar, we thought you guys were just fooling around. But man, this is awesome. What else is down here?"

"We're not sure, Brian. We do know that the coins probably have something to do with whatever is written on these old pieces of paper here." I handed him the plastic baggie.

Brian examined the vellum. "What do the letters mean?"

Paul continued to dig. "That's what we're hoping to find out."

32

November 6, 1715
CAPE COD

ABIGAIL DOANE'S FACE PALED as she boarded the packet-boat *Osprey* in the early morning hours of Wednesday, the same day Hestor made her gruesome discovery. Whenever she sailed, Abigail's comfort gave way to seasickness, forcing her to stay topside. There were few people on deck, so there was to be no talking, which suited Abigail.

As the waves assaulted her fragile stomach, a cold wind blew its sting across her cheeks. Not one for the outdoors, she carefully stepped her stout frame across the deck as they sailed from the town of Barnstable to Ellis Landing. She felt confident that she'd survive her journey and set her eyes on the horizon to steady herself. Nathanial had insisted he would be fine after taking ill during his recent sailing as captain of his ship, the *Voyager*. Abigail knew he was feeling guilty for abandoning his duties and agreed that he should stay behind a few more days to check on his cargo. With the knowledge that he remained in capable hands, recuperating at the Hicks' home in Barnstable, Abigail had left early so she could return to North Harwich to be with Maria.

She took a solid grip on the railing by the cargo hold and focused her thoughts on the young unmarried girl that she had taken under her wing. With a deep breath of ocean air, Abigail stood her ground and worried about Maria. She wanted to contact Minda, who was needed now, as Maria might be beginning her travail, or God forbid, had already begun it.

As the packet drew closer to the landing, she saw her neighbor George Eldridge waiting to pick up supplies from the hold of the *Osprey*. She waved, trying to get his attention, in hopes that she could enlist him to take her home in his cart. It was far too cold to walk. "George! Can you spare a ride for your neighbor?"

Seeing Abigail, he said, "Of course. You shall have to wait while I load my supplies."

With relief, she pulled her hat closer to her face as the boat finished docking.

George packed the last bundle into the back of his cart. "How does Nathanial fare?"

"Just fine, just fine," Abigail answered, climbing onto the seat next to him.

"That's good to hear; he's a fine man. Things have been quiet here except for the terrible storm that we had a few days past. Why, we had rain, sleet, and such strong winds."

Abigail squeezed her hands together on her lap and wondered how Maria had fared in the storm. As the cart rumbled closer to her house, she spotted several men standing outside, near the open main door. She saw no smoke coming from atop her roof.

George also saw the men. "I wonder what's going on? I recognize that man; he's employed by the Constable."

Abigail rose from her seat for a better view, startling George.

"Whoahhh!" he called out.

She fell backward onto the bench as he pulled the horse to a complete stop.

"Abigail, are you alright?" he asked, worried that she might have hurt herself.

"I'm fine. I need to see what is happening at my house."

Not waiting for assistance, she quickly grabbed her travel bag and scrambled out of the wagon. Thanking her neighbor, she hurried past two somber men standing by her fence and made her way into the house.

Constable Ezra was near the hearth. Between anxious breaths, she implored him, "Ezra...please...explain."

She dropped her bag just inside the door and sat down at the sideboard, all the while patting her racing heart. Her eyes glanced down to the sandy floor and to the dark drops that stained its rough surface. She looked up, her head spinning with questions. Where was Maria? Why was the constable standing in her kitchen? Where WAS Maria? Her hands trembled.

Ezra faced her and was about to speak when the door of the borning room slowly opened. The local midwife, Mehitable Cole, stepped out and closed the door behind her. She acknowledged Abigail's presence with only a nod of her head, then walked directly to the constable. The two spoke in hushed tones.

Impatient, Abigail buoyed herself with a new strength and voiced her feelings aloud. "This is my house and I intend to hear your words. Mehitable, please speak to the both of us. Where is the young girl, Maria?"

She needed Minda.

The midwife looked at Ezra for approval to speak. He nodded his head yes.

Abigail was furious as she stared at the woman. Of all the nerve...I want answers, she thought.

Mehitable shared her interpretation. "The girl is alive, but her heart is weak. She's been delivered of a child, for there's proof of afterbirth. We found her in the borning room but the child is missing. When asked questions, she is mute, as if possessed."

"How long will she be in this state?" Ezra asked.

"One cannot tell," the midwife shook her head with concern. Mehitable directed her next words to Abigail in a show of respect between women. "Her bleeding has stopped but she's very ill. When her trauma is over we must help her regain strength. Then we'll find the truth."

Abigail sat listening but remained puzzled. Where was the infant?

Ezra thanked the midwife for examining the girl, paid her a small fee and dismissed her.

He then asked Abigail, "Will you be able to nurse the girl back to health so that she can be questioned?"

Abigail looked dazed.

"Abigail?"

She glanced up at Ezra. "It all seems peculiar to me. I'm not sure of anything right now. But I'll try my best to do as you ask."

"Thank you. I will be speaking to the Reverend and the church elders concerning this grave situation. There are many unanswered questions and some that seem to be criminal in nature. I do not think I need to elaborate with you the seriousness of this matter." When he reached the open door, he turned around. "Mind you, there's something very odd here, I feel I need to warn you that evil may have infiltrated our community and your home."

"Thank you, Ezra. No need to concern yourself about me." Abigail waved him away.

She closed the door and waited for the men to leave her property. Her hand shook as she held onto the latch of the borning room door hesitating for several seconds before opening it. She was afraid, but she knew she would be able to do as asked. Maria needed her. Still lightheaded from the boat, Abigail managed to find another deep breath and entered the room.

Two Days Later

The wind seemed to clear Nathanial Doane's head as he inhaled the fresh salty air. He stood upright, his feet planted strong on the deck, the sense of "Captain" emanating from his presence.

Nathanial had captained his *Voyager* for over twenty years, transporting goods from Cape Cod to the West Indies and back. He was happiest when at sea, and his trip from Barnstable to his home in the North Parish of Harwich had been pleasant. Coming closer to land he looked for his hired hand, Jacob. As the packet boat, *Osprey*, approached the landing he could finally see his employee. He was curious also to see his old friend Constable Ezra standing next to Jacob.

Once on land, the Captain greeted him. "How are you, my friend?"

With a serious tone, Ezra answered, "Fine, Nathanial, but I have news for you. May I ride with you and explain?"

As he listened to Ezra's words, Nathanial fidgeted with his waistcoat and chewed on the stem of his clay pipe. He knew the young Hallett girl had sought help from Abigail for her unfortunate circumstances. While he'd never been pleased with the fact that she was staying in his house, Nathanial had accepted Abigail's kind intentions towards her as being part of his wife's nature. The idea that now his house might be host to witchery, according to Ezra, strained his affection for Abigail and her so-called friends.

"Thank you for your information," Nathanial politely said. "I'll be sure to take it to heart and decide what must be done."

Ezra warned him, "I must caution you that there will be a trial, as soon as the girl is of sound mind, which may also involve the missus."

Nathanial drew deep puffs on his pipe as silence between the two men ensued for the final mile. After the Constable was delivered to his own residence, the wagon finally reached the Doane's. Nathanial seemed irritated, even more so, because now his pipe was empty. He yelled his orders. "Jacob! Take care of the horse. Then you may leave."

The hearth was ablaze as he entered his home; the borning room door was ajar. He placed his bag on the floor and walked closer to see for himself who was in his house. Minda had already settled into the downstairs room next to Maria. She had brought her healing medicines and enough supplies so that she could stay as long as was needed. Nathanial noticed Minda and Abigail sitting in separate chairs close to the bed where Maria lay. Abigail looked up. She quickly rose and pushed him back out of the room and into the kitchen.

"Nathanial, I know this does not look well in your eyes. Please understand, it's all under control," she whispered. "Minda will help me in the care of Maria. It's all a horrible state of affairs. We're trying to persuade the girl to talk to us about what happened, but she has not even acknowledged our presence."

Nathanial was quiet. He turned away from his wife and retired to the bedroom.

Abigail watched him show his back to her. At that moment her compassion and motherly love for the young girl surpassed the love for her husband, convincing her even more that her duties were with Maria.

This had not been a normal homecoming. When Nathanial was at home, he liked the order of the house to run smoothly, just like his ship. He was stern, but there was always a kiss and a smile for her. Abigail tried her best to please him during those few times a year when he was on land and was always quite successful in making him happy. Her efforts toward his comfort were a small price to pay in her older years, and along with a small income from her family, she lived the lifestyle she desired. In fact, Abigail believed that Nathanial truly loved her.

Suddenly, Abigail felt dizzy as her heart accelerated. The tension in her body, which had passed between her and her husband minutes earlier, was bothersome but tolerable. She returned to her bedside vigil near the pale girl.

Minda leaned over and touched Abigail's arm. "Nathanial is angry?"

Abigail nodded.

"I will not stay long if my presence is not welcomed."

Abigail looked to her friend. "Please stay at least a fortnight. Maria's color seems to be coming back with your medicines."

"Let us see what Nathanial wants."

*   *   *

Nathanial was in the middle of removing his waistcoat when he spotted Jacob by the carriage house through the bedroom window. He had an idea. He thought it would be far better if he didn't stay home at this time, and Jacob might be the answer to his problem of the Indian living in his house. He buttoned up his coat and hurried outside.

*   *   *

Meanwhile, Abigail thought it wise to have something to eat. She stirred a soup on the hearth that had been cooking since early morning. As she prepared three bowls, she glanced through the window and noticed Nathanial talking to Jacob. What's he doing now? she wondered. Ignoring her thoughts, she turned away and asked Minda, "Would you like to join Nathanial and I for a small repast?"

"I think not; I will wait till you are both finished."

Abigail smiled a grateful thank you, knowing that her husband would prefer not to share a meal with an Indian. When Nathanial came back into the house, Abigail implored him to eat something after his long trip home.

He accepted her invitation and sat down at the sideboard in front of a steaming bowl of chowder. "I can't refuse you, my good wife. You've always had a special touch when it comes to cooking."

His compliment relieved Abigail, and she hoped it was the end of their tension. Closing the borning room door, she sat opposite him at the table. "I want to apologize again for my actions. The young girl means so much to me."

Swallowing a mouthful of clam, he replied, "I have come to a decision."

Abigail looked up from her bowl.

While wagging his spoon at her, he said, "It would be far better if I went back to Barnstable Harbor and stayed on the *Voyager*. There's nothing I can do here and it seems that you would not be very much company for me, seeing that you'll be occupied with the girl." Another spoonful found its way into his mouth, and he continued, "I've spoken with Jacob, and everything is arranged. His daughter Hopeful, being terminated at her last employer, is looking for work; she'll come here and live with you in my absence."

Aggravated with the dominant tone of her husband, Abigail tried to remain calm and hold her feelings in.

Dunking his bread into the creamy broth, he gave his last word to her, "That way you have no need of the Indian *Pow Wah* anymore. I want her to leave my house."

At long last Abigail was ready to speak her mind; she opened her mouth but stopped when she saw the borning room door open.

Minda called out, "Abigail, come quickly. Maria is asking for you."

She pushed aside her bowl and rushed into the room. Nathanial smiled, pleased that this perplexing situation was ended, according to him.

* * *

The sight of Maria sitting on the edge of the bed filled Abigail with hope, only to be disappointed when the young woman asked, "Where's my child?"

Pain was evident across Maria's face. She held her forehead as she asked again, "Abigail, where is my child?"

Abigail sat down beside her. In her calmest voice, she spoke, "Maria, you're finally awake. We've been worried about you."

Agitated about her unanswered questions, Maria began to rub the pain that wrinkled her face. "What do you mean?"

Abigail responded with another question, "Do you remember anything of what happened when you were in your travail?"

Maria looked to her friend and then searched her own thoughts, trying to make sense of it all. She whispered, "It's hard...it all seems like a blur...like a nightmare."

Maria looked to Minda sitting opposite her. "I took some of your medicine when the pain came. I felt so alone and frightened. I saw my child. Where is he?"

Minda quickly asked, "How much did you drink of my medicine?"

"I'm not sure. I poured it into a small bottle and kept it by my bed."

"We found no such bottle," Abigail added.

She began to coax the girl into lying back down again.

Maria was determined to stand and tried to shove Abigail away. "I don't want to lie down." She threw off her covers. "I want my child!" she screamed.

"Now, dear, put your head down; you're safe now. We'll stay with you." She gently pushed the girl back by her shoulders. "Please, you need to get better."

Maria accepted her friend's pleas and settled back on the small feather pillow. While she rested, the two women talked in the corner.

Minda cautioned Abigail, "We must find the bottle, so no one will connect me to what occurred here." Fears of being branded a witch ran through her head.

"The amount of herbs in her body would explain many of the strange things that have happened," said Abigail. "Tomorrow, when Maria is awake and she leaves her room, I'll look for the bottle."

*   *   *

The last meal of the day was quiet between Abigail and Nathanial. Minda ate alongside Maria as the girl dozed in and out of consciousness throughout the evening.

Minda retired on a mat in the corner of the borning room with a small Betty lamp on the floor beside her. Its glow reflected something shiny under Maria's bed. Minda reached her arm far under the bed's roping until her fingertips felt the smooth shape of a bottle. When placed near her face, she immediately recognized the odors that came from within. Thankful that she'd found the medicine she'd given to Maria, she wrapped it in one of her winter leggings and pushed it to the bottom of her leather bag.

As Nathanial retired to bed, Abigail was still making things right in the kitchen. She peeked into the borning room and whispered to Minda, "Thank you for your stay with me and for all your understanding. You're a good friend."

Minda smiled and motioned at her to come closer. "I found the bottle and will take it with me when I leave."

"Good," said Abigail.

They exchanged a quiet embrace and whispered good night to each other.

*   *   *

A late November chill remained in the night air as Abigail climbed into bed next to her husband. She had not seen this unattractive side of him in all of their three years together. Nathanial had spoken very little of his past to her during their married life, except for one tragic event that had occurred when he was young. He'd witnessed the murder of his older brother, in 1676, by an Indian during a vicious attack on their homestead as King Phillip's War was waged across the new land. Feelings of prejudice had stayed with him and sullied his complete acceptance of her dearest friend, Minda. Now mixed feelings stirred in her heart about Nathanial. Feeling his warmth next to her, she reached for his hand under the blankets, thinking that, if they held each other, their disagreements and her doubts might be smoothed over.

Nathanial moved his hand away from her grasp and quietly spoke, "My dear wife, I'm not comfortable accepting your advances while certain people are within my house. I'll be leaving early tomorrow morning."

He turned over on his side to face the wall and placed his right hand on a pistol, which, for this night only, lay under his pillow.

*   *   *

The morning came with a light dusting of icy snow that covered the ground. Nathanial had been gone since daybreak. Abigail, waking later than usual, had slept well. The assurance that Maria was beginning her road to recovery had eased her thoughts throughout the nighttime hours, despite the disagreement between her and Nathanial.

Minda was attending to Maria's needs when Abigail saw Jacob's daughter, Hopeful, kneading the flour for the daily bread on the sideboard. Somewhat surprised by the 14-year-old girl's presence, Abigail greeted her. "Good morrow!"

"Mum," Hopeful replied, not missing a step in her working of the dough.

Abigail asked, "Will you join me in some tea so we may talk?"

"No, thank you, I have my work." Hopeful continued pounding the dough with her hands.

Not comfortable with a stranger in her house, Abigail kept an eye on the newly hired girl as she fixed her morning drink.

The serious-faced Hopeful did not favor chit-chat. Unable to bond with her, Abigail finally said, "I best be hurrying along soon. The pots should be emptied, and I know there is mending to be done."

"It's done, ma'am."

Taken aback, Abigail asked, "How long have you been here, Hopeful?"

"Daybreak. I have me orders from the Captain."

The girl's smugness annoyed Abigail. "Excuse me. What did you say?"

Hopeful stopped in mid-pound of the dough and tersely repeated, "I have me orders from the Captain."

Abigail slammed her cup down on the table. "We'll see about that!"

33

1715
CAPE COD

MINDA LEFT NORTH HARWICH as soon as Abigail felt secure enough in her caring for Maria. Abigail hugged her friend goodbye and couldn't wait to dismiss the arrogant Hopeful. That night, Abigail felt truly confident and breathed a sigh of relief as she closed the door for good on the rude girl. Now she and Maria could look forward to sitting by the fire each evening, wherein Abigail could gently coax Maria into remembering.

To Abigail's disappointment, several weeks passed without any new information from Maria. It seemed that as the young girl regained her natural color and increased her stamina, the ordeal that she had experienced still clouded her memory and prevented her from answering the questions that were asked.

One evening, Abigail sat watching Maria stir their dinner. "Maria, we need to have some answers."

"I'm aware of that; I've tried. But it pains me so to remember. Sometimes when I dream at night, I see images of dripping blood and dirt all over my hands. I wake up crying, trying to clean myself. I don't understand and it frightens me." Maria's eyes began to tear. "I know my child is dead." She looked away from Abigail. "I just don't want to think about it."

Abigail gently reminded her, "Constable Ezra will be coming soon and he'll want answers...there will be a trial."

Maria grew silent.
Abigail shook her head in despair.

* * *

The next day Maria rose before Abigail. She felt better, her eyes brighter, her head clearer. She managed to bring forth a smile upon seeing a bright red cardinal in a snow-covered tree. Abigail was so good to her; she thought a surprise of fresh biscuits would surely please her friend this morning.

As the dough began its rise on the hearth Maria reached for a jar of apple butter; finding it empty, she headed to the root cellar to fetch another. Folding back the small braided rug that covered the trapdoor, she lifted the wooden cover with one hand. With a lamp for light, she descended the stone stairs.

As her foot reached the bottom, Maria noticed dark stains across the dirt floor. A chill slid down her back that truly frightened her. Was it the cold of the cellar or something else? She continued her quest, being careful where she stepped. The dirt crunched and the cellar's dank odor made her uncomfortable. An ominous feeling spread over her; she did not want to stay in this underground room.

She spied a row of filled fruit jars on a shelf. As she reached for one, her eye caught a glimpse of rotten black apples in a basket on the floor in the corner. The sight of the moldy fruit sparked Maria's memory. She dropped the jar of butter; it broke and spilled its contents over the dirt floor. Her heart began to race as frightening images of a dead child wrapped in white linen flooded her head with a believable clarity. She remembered kneeling in dirt, covered in blood, her forearms and fingers blackened with the residue of soil. She remembered the chest with a D carved onto its lid.

Maria dropped to her knees and dragged the basket away from the corner. Her fingers scratched frantically at the dirt. Just under inches of loose, cold soil, she could see the wooden top of a chest. Brushing away the soil she uncovered the carved letter D.

Maria leaned back onto her heels and felt nauseous. She closed her eyes and rubbed them as hard as she could before she opened them to make sure her mind had not played a cruel trick on her. The chest was real. Her child was buried here. Maria's fears rushed over her. "I can't tell anyone," she whispered.

Drops of perspiration dripped from under her breasts and from her forehead. Anxiety clouded her thoughts. Telling no one was the only answer. No one must know, no one must find her child. She would carry this burden alone.

Maria knew she must protect herself from the hatred and punishment of those who wished her harm. Before the townspeople would have a chance to bring their evil upon her, she would run away from the safe haven of her friend's house and find Sam.

She covered the box with dirt and patted it flat. Pushing the basket back to its original place, she hoped it would stand guard and protect the secret that lay beneath it. Maria brushed her hands clean, wiped her face of the dirt and sweat, then climbed the steps back into the kitchen.

A knock at the door startled her as she covered the trapdoor with the rug. Maria wondered who would be calling so early in the morning.

The rap grew more intense. Frightened, she ran into the borning room and shut the door behind her. She held her breath, fearful of making any sound, hoping the visitor would go away.

A gruff voice yelled out, "Open up, Abigail, it's Constable Ezra!"

Maria's back stiffened against the door.

She heard Abigail's voice.

"Coming…. Coming…my word, what is the matter?" Dressed only in her nightclothes and a loose shawl, Abigail opened the door. "Ezra! Lower your voice."

Ezra was not alone. A stout man with a constable's patch on his arm stood behind him.

"May I come in?" Not waiting for a reply, Ezra pushed his way past Abigail and strode into the kitchen, followed by Constable Bayer, from Eastham. "We need to speak with the Hallett girl."

"Of course." Realizing that this was not a social visit, Abigail walked in measured steps to the borning room, stalling for time, trying to collect her thoughts.

Once at the door she asked, "Maria, are you awake?"

Afraid to answer, Maria stayed quiet.

Abigail looked to the two men. "Wait here."

With guarded movements, Abigail opened the door and saw

Maria cowering in the corner near her bed. Quickly closing the door, she crouched next to the girl and began to persuade her to cooperate. "Maria, be strong. You knew this time would come. You must talk with them and do exactly as they say."

They stood up together. "Do you understand?"

Maria nodded her head.

Abigail clasped her hand and led the terrified girl into the kitchen to face the constables.

Ezra needed to identify the suspect. "Maria Hallett?"

Maria nodded again.

"Constable Bayer and I, do hereby inform you that you are under arrest on suspicion of attempted murder and fornication. You will please come with us."

Abigail protested that Maria was not well enough to go anywhere but Ezra would not listen.

He replied in sharp tones, "Enough time has passed for her to recover. This heinous matter must be concluded. We will wait for her to gather her things."

Desperate to see a way out of this, Maria looked to her friend.

After several seconds of tense silence, Abigail guided her back to the borning room to collect the things that she might need. She gave the young girl directions. "Layer most of your clothes on your body in case you need them for warmth."

Maria numbly obeyed her friend.

Abigail's hands trembled as she helped her fasten multiple skirts around her waist. "If they take you to Constable Ezra's house, there is a room off the kitchen which is used as a jail cell. There, your care will be adequate. If sent directly to Eastham, with Constable Bayer, your comfort will be less than minimal. The Eastham jail is cold, dirty and damp."

Abigail tried to keep her composure. She knew this day would come, but more time was needed with Maria; after all, the girl was only fifteen years old. Realizing there was nothing she could do or say to help, and against her better judgment, Abigail opened the borning room door.

As the constable grabbed Maria's elbow to escort her outside, she turned to Abigail in one last agonizing plea and cried out, "Abigail, don't let them take me from you. Please!"

Abigail watched Maria climb through the small door on the back of the wagon. Barely able to contain her emotions, she bowed her head and thought she might die as she leaned against the edge of the open front door. Abigail was angry, sad, shamed for not doing more, and felt utterly helpless. With a broken heart, she backed away and closed the door on the only safe home Maria ever had.

*   *   *

Maria's body shook in fear as the enclosed wagon swallowed her up into its darkness. Used for prisoners, the absence of windows gave her no clues as to where she was going. To keep herself from crying, she bit her lower lip and closed her eyes, trying to imagine Sam's face, wishing that he would rip open the door to her prison and take her in his arms, where she could stay forever. But ten minutes into her journey Maria sensed her fate, and as the hour went by, it became apparent that she was going back to Eastham, to the place that she despised—the one place she had hoped never to return to. She rocked back and forth on the wooden floor as she prayed to her mother.

34

THE SOUND OF EARL'S TRUCK WOKE ME around 8 a.m.; I rolled over and hoped that today he would finally finish the chimney in the new kitchen. Paul was already brewing coffee. With a bit of guilty pleasure I recalled that the night before Paul had told me to sleep in, and that it was important, if I really was pregnant, to get a lot of rest. So I did. At 9 a.m., I appeared in the doorway of the kitchen to find Molly eating her breakfast.

"I'm sorry I slept so late. Everything okay?" I took my seat across the table from her.

"Just fine, Mommy." Molly smiled with a mouthful of cereal and milk.

Paul graciously poured me a cup of coffee. "Why don't you take a drive down 6A, to Barnstable Records, and research the house's history?"

"Are you sure? There's so much to do here at home."

"I'm fine. You should go. Besides, I'm really curious about who's owned the house."

"Well, if you insist. I'll drop Molly off at camp on my way."

He kissed my cheek. "Sounds like a plan. Maybe you could stop at the new gallery in Sandwich and deliver my painting?"

"That's a great idea; we can use the trip as a business expense."

I threw Molly a kiss. "Get your backpack ready when you're

finished eating. I'll be dressed by then." I grabbed my coffee and headed for the shower.

In less than thirty minutes I was loading the painting into the car. "Hurry up Molly. We don't want to be late."

I went over my agenda for the day: drop off Molly at day camp, visit the gallery, and on the return trip stop by the county offices in Barnstable. True to my schedule, Molly was delivered and I headed west out of the camp's parking lot.

The drive down Route 6A from Brewster to Sandwich was beautiful. I sipped my coffee to the sounds of new age music, passing ancient trees, stately homes and rock walls that dotted the landscape along the old road. On my return home, I entered the historic town of Barnstable and parked in the courthouse complex.

I quickly walked towards the inner courtyard of two large buildings. "Barnstable County Deeds and Probate" was painted on glass windows and lettered on the brick façade of the building to my left. I felt a little intimidated by the nervous energy created by the police, lawyers, and maybe soon-to-be convicted criminals. Thank goodness, I was only searching for old property records.

After a short wait for the security check archway, the elderly guard finally waved me through with a smile. I passed more suited men, high-heeled ladies, and a few people who, like me, didn't look like they knew what they were doing. A pleasant receptionist directed me across the hall and into the Copy Center room.

Armed with our deed, I stood in front of a big sign that read "Information". A petite female clerk behind the counter asked a few questions about my visit, so I politely answered that I was in search of the history of our house. Once she'd found our Brewster property on the computer, she explained that the certificate number on the deed would lead to the previous certificate number, which in turn would identify successive owners of the property. As the computer searched back into time, the name Doane began to appear around the late 1920s, then kept resurfacing all the way back to 1815, with only the first names changing on the deeds to the land.

After a few minutes, the clerk leaned her pixie-like body around to my right and pointed to a room across the hall. She whispered to me, "You'll have to search deeper into the records by yourself because a line is forming behind you."

It was already 12:30 p.m., and I assumed that only a few more minutes were needed to finish my project; after all, I'd found records dating back to 1815. I carried my deed back across the hall to a large room filled with rows of tall filing cabinets. I went unnoticed by everyone sitting at tables and computers, probably searching for lost deeds or for clear titles to property for real estate attorneys. No one questioned my presence.

The really old records were stored in blue, black, and white bound metal books. Lined up next to each other in rows, their numbered labels ran into the thousands—as high as Book #10543. I was looking for Book #143, page 387. I walked to the very back of the long room and spotted #143 stamped in white letters on a blue plastic binding in the last row by the windows. I opened it to page 387 to see the name Doane in beautiful Old English script.

When I slid my finger to the bottom of the page, the year 1780 popped out at me. Intrigued, I kept searching and was directed to an even older book and page. Finally, the last entry I found was for a property in the name of Nathanial Doane, posted in 1715. I was elated to discover it was the same year on the piece of parchment we'd found in the root cellar.

As I drove home I mulled over the dates of the property. The house we bought was built in 1880, yet the deed to the land went back to the early 1700s. The property seemed to have a long history with the Doane family, so there could have been another house on it in 1715. I stopped at a red light. What happened to the first house? Where was it in relation to the current house? A horn beeped from behind me; the light had turned green. Pay attention I told myself, opening the window for fresh air. The root cellar must have belonged to another house on the property.

When I got back to Brewster, I was eager to talk to Paul. I parked the car and ran into the gallery. "Hi, honey. Everything went fine at the Sandwich gallery, and I have something neat to tell you about our house."

Paul was at his drawing table. He kept painting.

Plopping down into the big, overstuffed chair that faced him, I exploded with the news, "I went as far back as 1780, then searched in the older books to 1715! A family by the name of Doane owned the land all the way forward to 1927."

I turned away from Paul to the cellar. "There must have been two houses on this property."

Paul put his paintbrush down and looked up. "What did you say?"

"I said I think there was another house here besides ours, before 1880, and it probably was owned by a Doane."

* * *

That evening, I found some quiet time and secluded myself by the computer in the spare bedroom. Paul joined me and lay across the twin bed. Leaning on his side, he gently touched the pieces of vellum. "Now I understand the letter 'D' on the chest that we found; it probably stood for the Doane family. But I'm not so sure about the other letters."

Curious, I typed 'Maria Hallett' into the computer. "Remember what the Hallett guy said? He thought the letters stood for Maria Hallett and Sam Bellamy." Clicking to the next page on the computer screen I said, "I think he's right."

"What did you find?"

"Not very much, maybe two pages about her. They all say that she was the lover of the pirate Sam Bellamy, and she was also called 'The Witch of Billingsgate'."

"Is Billingsgate the island off Wellfleet that disappeared?"

"Yes. Here's another name for her, 'Maria "Goody" Hallett'." I selected the next page on the screen. "Apparently, Goody was a name given to women of the day—like Goody Thatch or Goody Jones."

Paul sat up and added, "Salinger referred to her as Goody Hallett."

"Yes, he did, although she still seems to be more of a myth than Sam. There's a lot of proof that HE lived and that he was indeed a pirate, but there's not much about her."

I kept my eyes on the screen. "I wonder how this whole thing is connected to the Doane house? And what about the baby's skull? Whose baby was it?"

Paul moved toward the doorway.

I clicked on the last entries of the page and read out loud, "According to Maria's legend, she was pregnant with Sam's baby, but it died in childbirth. Evidently Bellamy was on the high seas and never knew she was pregnant."

Paul added, "That might explain whose baby it was and why all the secrecy."

"Yeah, when you think of it, she would have been considered an unwed mother and somewhat of a whore. In colonial days they were pretty strict with that kind of thing."

I looked at Paul. "If the letters on the vellum have any connection to all of this, I bet she must have known someone in the Doane house, or maybe she worked for them?"

Paul seemed tired and not as attentive to my every word as usual. Out of the corner of my eye I saw him slowly back out of the room. "Why don't you go to bed?" I told him. "I'm not tired, and I'm really interested in all of this." I mumbled to myself, "…and what about the three gold coins?"

"Good night, honey," Paul said.

I kept my eyes on the glowing monitor. "I'll be in soon."

His head reappeared in the doorway. "Oh, I forgot to tell you, the doctor's office called to confirm your appointment for tomorrow at 2 p.m."

I stopped typing and went from being excited to feeling queasy. "Oh yeah, I forgot." I shut down the computer, turned the light off and imagined myself pregnant again. I caught up with Paul as he was locking the side door off the laundry room. "Paul, I need a hug."

He wrapped his arms around me and rocked me back and forth. "We'll be okay. I'll always be here for you."

I looked up into his eyes. "Whatever we find out tomorrow, I know we'll be fine, as long as we're together."

He walked me into the bedroom with his arm around my shoulders. As I began to turn the covers down on my side of the bed, I said, "I'm so happy to be living in the twenty-first century with a husband that really cares for me and not 300 years ago. It was awful difficult back then for women."

Paul flipped his blankets to the foot of the bed on his side. "Don't worry. I'll never leave you. I love you."

35

Late July – Present Day

MY APPOINTMENT CAME TOO SOON. It's not that I was afraid to find out if I was pregnant; I was just worried. So many things could go wrong. I started out early for my doctor's appointment in Hyannis so I stayed on the slower, scenic Old Route 6A, instead of turning onto the Mid-Cape Highway, or what the locals call "suicide alley." The single lane of the winding bucolic roadway relaxed me, as usual. I began to rationalize that my body was healthy, my weight was good, and I had no major medical problems.

My lightened mood was obliterated when a car accelerated on my left. The passenger's rearview mirror came so close that I could have touched it. Within seconds its rear bumper cut me off as the driver illegally passed me. My purse flew to the floor as I swerved to the right and slammed on the brakes. The car zoomed ahead of me and out of sight.

"Oh my God!" I screamed. My hands stuck to the steering wheel like glue. I wanted to get off the road. A glance in my rear-view mirror revealed no one else was behind me, so I pulled into the first driveway to my right.

When my car finally stopped on the gravel, I was still trembling. I shouted in the direction of the car, "What a jerk!" Then in a whisper, "Take a deep breath."

I leaned over to pick up the contents of my purse that had spilled all over the floor of the car. A brochure from the Provincetown *Whydah* Museum caught my eye. On the front were images of the pirate ship *Whydah* and the infamous Black Sam Bellamy along with his lover, young Maria Hallett. It seemed odd to be thinking about them after such a close call with my own death but I couldn't stop myself. I knew they lived with danger every day, but me…in modern day…on Cape Cod? Unthinkable, and yet, I had almost been killed.

I pulled myself together, backed out of the driveway and continued onto the doctor's. My mind shifted back to Maria Hallett. It must have been terrible for that young girl to be alone and pregnant. Poor Maria. How frightening it must have been for her. Sam Bellamy was thousands of miles away on the *Whydah* and it would have taken months for him to sail home to her. What she must have suffered all by herself. The 1700s were harsh times.

I closed the windows halfway and found an oldies but goodies station on the radio. I wished Paul had come with me, but reminded myself the gallery needed to be open. Besides, Molly had to be picked up early from camp. I knew Paul loved me. He was always there for me, just not today.

* * *

Dr. Thornton, the gynecologist, was new in town, as I was. His office was shared with another surgeon and was plain but comfortable. I noticed two pregnant women in the waiting room with me. I felt self-conscious about my age. Of course, I was hardly showing, unlike the young woman across from me reading the National Enquirer wearing stretch pants that barely covered her protruding stomach. No one could tell if I was pregnant…yet.

I skimmed through a parent magazine and checked out the other girl; she had red streaks in her short-cropped hair. I was the only one with gray hair. But I liked my hair. It was soft, almost pure white, and it looked good on me. The nurse interrupted my pep talk and called me into a back room. After some chitchat and the dreaded weigh-in, the doctor examined me and performed the usual tests. He told me it would be a short wait for the results.

Back in the waiting room I couldn't stop thinking about the bad things that might happen if I was pregnant. My face flushed with a rush of anxiety. Would our medical insurance transfer from one state to another in time for the birth? Did the old coverage stop on a certain date? If there were a gap in the coverage how would we pay for the baby?

A voice called from behind me, "Nancy Caldwell?"

"Yes, here I am."

"The doctor will see you now."

I gathered my things and followed the nurse to Dr. Thornton's office. As I walked, I couldn't dismiss the threat of something going wrong with the baby who might be growing inside of me.

* * *

The doctor sat behind a large oak desk that contained a telephone, nameplate, and a glass paperweight. They were the only items on the glass top besides a manila folder that I assumed contained my personal medical files. With a sweep of his hand, he invited me, "Please sit down. Mrs. Caldwell, your results are in. Congratulations! You're going to have a baby."

My heart stopped this time, not with fear of dying in a car accident, but with excitement. I quickly forgot all about the horrible thoughts from before. I started to tear up. My motherly instincts took control over my emotions as I thought...a baby...a beautiful baby.

"It looks like you're almost five weeks along," Dr. Thornton said and waited for my response.

Energized I asked, "Can you give me a minute? I want to call my husband."

"Of course," the doctor said and left the room.

"Paul?"

"Yes?" he said quietly.

"You're going to be a Daddy again." I smiled into the phone.

"Whew! Okay, now don't worry, honey. We'll figure everything out. Hurry up home so I can hold you and give you a big kiss. And Nancy?"

"Yeah."

"We'll tell the kids tonight, after dinner."

"Sounds good. The doctor still wants to talk with me, I'll call you when I get in the car."

"Okay, I love you."

"I love you too."

I flipped my cell phone closed just as Dr. Thornton returned to his desk. "Now, I'm not going to hide anything from you," he said. "There may be some complications with a woman of forty. Your chances of giving birth to a child with Downs Syndrome are one in a hundred."

I listened but didn't really understand his words. The palms of my hands began to drip with perspiration. I quickly wiped them on my skirt, looked over to him and hoped he would explain more.

"On the other hand," he continued, "your baby could be born perfectly healthy." He placed his pen alongside the open file and folded his hands as he looked over the words and numbers on the papers that held my statistics. "Let's see, you have no significant medical problems."

I sat quiet and tried to listen. I couldn't think of any questions to ask.

"In about three weeks we can do an ultrasound and an amniocentesis test for chromosomes. Then we'll have more information upon which to decide the next steps."

"Next steps?" I asked.

"Yes, it's up to you and your husband to decide if you want to go through with the pregnancy if the tests reveal potential problems." He closed my file. "I can recommend a good doctor, at that time, based on your decision."

Why wouldn't I go through with the pregnancy? I knew there might be problems, but I would never kill my baby. I stood to leave. I was starting to feel angry that he would even suggest an abortion.

"Are you feeling all right, Mrs. Caldwell?"

"Yes, I have a lot of thinking to do. I'll be fine."

He stood and went to open the door for me. "Remember to make your appointment with the receptionist for three weeks from today."

"I will." I felt numb.

* * *

When I got back into the car, I told myself not to be upset. He was only presenting the facts to me. I gave Paul a call to tell him I was doing fine, but I couldn't erase the doctor's words from my mind.

Before I left Hyannis, I pulled into a drive-thru coffee shop and ordered a small coffee with double cream and a shot of raspberry. I quickly changed my order, "Make that a decaf, please." I'm going to do everything right from now on. No more caffeine—it's not good for the baby.

The coffee was too hot to drink so I decided to drive the short distance to Kalmus Beach, near the harbor. I parked the car to see the whole horizon and rolled down the windows on both sides of me. The gusty wind blew in across my face and hair and out the other window. It felt so refreshing and seemed to smooth the rough edges that had been forming all around me. What a strange day. First I had almost died, and now I was pregnant! The blue water was mesmerizing as a catboat sailed by and then faded into the distant horizon. My heart relaxed into a slow rhythm, and my eyes closed.

36

December 1715
EASTHAM – CAPE COD

HESTOR INTENDED TO MAKE HER PRESENCE KNOWN TODAY.
The temperature was near freezing, and the rain had not stopped since early morning as she traveled on the packet to Eastham for Maria's trial. The nasty weather did not sway her in her decision to don her best hat, skirt and cape. Looking favorable within the community was important to her, and today was a special day. After all, she was the one who'd discovered the young Hallett girl and had run to the authorities with her news.

Her timing was perfect; everyone had already arrived at the meetinghouse. As Hestor opened the door, a collective hush swept over the townspeople, and all eyes were focused on her. Constable Bayer escorted the pompous housekeeper, one of the key witnesses, to the first pew, where Abigail Doane and the midwife from the North Parish, Mehitable Cole, were also seated.

Matthew took his place next to his mother in the upper gallery, overlooking the top of Hestor's hat. His nerves were on edge as he awaited the beginning of his beloved's trial.

Minda stood by the door in the rear of the building. She was alone and felt uncomfortable amongst the colonists. She prayed to the great *Kiehtan* for strength.

Maria tried to make sure that she was presentable this morning. She had removed the top soiled skirt from her layers of clothes and placed it underneath the clean ones. Then she'd wiped the dirt from her face and hands using her drinking water. Her cheeks, rosy from the cold prison room, highlighted her dark auburn hair that fell into natural curly ringlets under her cap. With all of the past events that Maria had experienced, she still retained that simple beauty which had attracted Matthew and Sam to her from the beginning.

As Reverend Treat took his place at the head table, people straightened their backs in their seats, then looked to the front of the meetinghouse. He raised his hand to signal Constable Bayer to bring in the accused.

When young Maria entered the room, the only sounds came from the Reverend as he coughed and blew his nose. She kept her eyes downward in a penitent pose, glancing up and down in quick movements to see whom she could recognize.

A parade of witnesses each took their turn providing facts, assumptions, and opinions concerning Maria's pregnancy and the possible whereabouts of the dead child's body. It slowly became evident there could be no conviction of murder due to the missing body and no clear answer about what had happened.

Maria remained silent throughout.

The Reverend requested a small recess so that someone could find him a pint of ale. His throat was dry due to a cold that had been with him for more than a week. Everyone stayed in their seats for fear of missing a single sordid detail when the trial resumed.

Suddenly the door blew in, and with a gust of wind came Thomas Hallett, Maria's father. All turned to see what the commotion was as he entered. Another hush wafted over the crowd, which turned into mumblings, then quiet chatter.

Reverend Treat banged his cup down on the table. "QUIET!" He wiped away his sniffles and ordered, "Let us continue."

Hallett took up his position in the back of the room, opposite Minda. Folding his arms in front of his chest he leaned his back against the wall. He had not set foot under the roof of the meetinghouse for many years and felt uneasy. He did not enjoy being here, but his curiosity and not wanting second-hand information had coaxed him to show his face.

Another cup of ale was found, and Reverend Treat regained his usual demeanor. He turned his head towards Maria. "Maria Hallett, have you anything to say for yourself in regards to these charges?"

She sat silent, her hands folded on her skirts, eyes downcast.

"In that case, I am left with no other recourse but to charge you with the sin of fornication and association with powerful sources of evil. Throughout this trial I have listened to many witnesses and ascertained that you exhibit tendencies common to the devil and all of its evil. Therefore, with the burden of mixed testimony and scarcity of evidence against you, this court will bring punishment upon you, but it will be dealt with mercy."

Maria's head dropped low, her chin almost touching the top of her chest.

"For the protection of our community," he continued, "you will be shunned and banished forthwith. You are to have no contact with the people of Eastham and the surrounding villages. If, in the future, there is brought forth any further evidence of sorcery or misdeeds, you will be sentenced to death at that time."

Some of the ladies from church, including Hestor, smiled at the court's ruling. Others wiped tears from their eyes. Minda solemnly stared at Maria while Thomas Hallett left before anyone noticed his absence.

Abigail felt faint but sat as straight as she could to show Maria she was strong.

Mrs. Ellis reached for Matthew's hand and held it tight as he tried to cover his tears.

The Reverend avoided eye contact with the convicted girl. Distressed in his heart by the whole situation, he consoled himself by reasoning that it was the right decision, and it would satisfy all parties concerned.

Maria felt numb and didn't understand the verdict that was brought upon her. She was returned to her prison, where she awaited the details of her future.

* * *

On the Sunday Sabbath following the trial, Maria sat alone in her cell while the elders and members of the church held a social meeting after service. Reverend Treat was still not feeling well, but his presence was necessary, along with his input, as the elders finalized the details of Maria's sentence. He sat by the hearth inhaling a mixture of herbs that he held in a cloth on his nose, hoping to ease his stuffiness.

Elder Macon began the conversation. "Let us finish this business as soon as possible. What say you, Reverend?"

Reverend Treat waved his hand in agreement as he coughed.

The elder Macon continued, "The Hallett girl must have some punishment in order to set an example for the rest of our community. Her trial proved to be merely circumstantial, so I have some suggestions." He stood with one hand in his vest and stated his thoughts. "We are all compassionate men here," sweeping his hand in a semicircle. "Her age and lack of a decent family should be considered."

The elders nodded their heads in agreement with a few 'ayes' spoken aloud.

"Most of you are aware of the abandoned McKeon house on the bluff, near the outskirts of Eastham. The church has taken over its title. I believe that it would be an appropriate place to send the girl."

Reverend Treat looked up and listened.

Macon added more details. "Give her minimal supplies for the rest of the winter and let our Lord and nature take its course. She shall have no contact with anyone, nor be able to attend meetings or honor the Sabbath. People may shun her in whatever way they wish."

The reverend asked, "Are we all agreed then with Elder Macon's proposal?"

Elder Kitridge remarked, "I, for one, will be happy to have the strange girl gone from my view. The way the housekeeper spoke of her and what she discovered that morning frightened my wife and, I am not ashamed to admit...even me."

The reverend stood and held onto the top board of the hearth for support as he asked, "A hand vote, please. All in favor of Elder Macon's proposal?"

All raised their hands.

"It is done. May God have mercy on her soul."

* * *

Just after the sun began its rise on the Monday morning following the verdict, Maria awoke to find a letter lying on the prison floor. It was from Abigail.

December 9, 1715

My Dearest friend,

I was informed of the council's decision late last night. It grieves me not to be with you as you learn of your fate, but I must leave for home today. Do not be afraid as you venture into solitude. I was given permission to gather the things that you left at my house and deliver them to you as soon as possible. I pray that you find pleasure in the beauties of nature and fill your heart with warm memories of Minda, Matthew and myself.

God Bless you,
Your faithful friend,
Abigail Doane

* * *

Maria read the letter twice, then folded it into the pocket beneath her skirt. She paced the floor of the bleak cell, stopping every other turn to reread Abigail's letter. She listened for any movement outside her window.

At noon, the sound of a wagon broke the quiet of the winter day as it approached the jail.

Constable Bayer opened the door. "Maria Hallett, gather your things and come with me. By order of the elders and Reverend Treat, I will escort you to your place of banishment."

The constable was quiet while he watched her take the soiled clothes from the bench and roll them into a ball. "Hurry girl. There's a storm comin'."

When she was ready, Maria climbed into the waiting wagon that contained one blanket, a bag of flour, lard, beef strips, salt, ale, some candles and one jar of apple butter, in addition to a small amount of wood and kindling Maria took her place on the back of the open wagon's floor and held herself steady by holding onto its sides. The surrounding landscape slowly turned familiar to her as the rumbling wagon rounded a side path and then traveled up onto a bluff. She could see the McKeon house. Is this where she would be going? It looked worse than when she had last seen it with Sam.

Constable Bayer's face softened with concern for the young girl as he pulled the wagon to a stop in front of the abandoned house. It didn't look safe to him. He said, "Take your things. Here is a letter from the elders explaining their terms." He then offered her a piece of advice, "You need to do as they say, Maria Hallett."

"Yes," she responded, her face downcast, as she began to drag her supplies from the wagon's bed.

Constable Bayer helped her with the sack of flour, then returned to his wagon and flicked the reins to leave. He thought there would be no harm done if he went to check on the girl every so often. After all, he was the Constable of Eastham, and he needed to make sure she was obeying orders. Yes, that's what he would do; he would make sure she remained safe and thought his wife might have an extra jar of summer fruit in the cellar that he could bring to her.

Maria stood amongst her meager supplies and read the decree of loneliness from the elders. Now she understood Abigail's letter. The gravity of her circumstances frightened her to trembling. She sat down on the outside bench that had given pleasure to her and Sam so many months ago. As snow began to fall, covering the ground white, Maria reread the words before her once more. "Shun"; "no contact": what nasty words, she thought. But their meaning became easier to accept as she recalled other punishments that could have been brought upon her. She mulled them over in her thoughts: the embarrassment of being whipped at the post, or listening to people taunt her if she was tethered to the stocks; both would have been unbearable. Then she remembered, as a little girl, seeing a man with his ear nailed to the pillory. Maria squeezed her earlobe tight to see how painful it could be. She shivered as she tried to free her mind of this terrible image and busied herself with picking up supplies from the ground. Under her breath she mumbled, "I will make do. I'll show them that I'm strong."

Determined in her steps, she slipped only once on the wet snow as she carried several items into the house. She saw the worn table and the dusty cloth that Sam had brought to their first meeting. After placing some provisions on the dirt floor, she sat by the table and remembered the sweet times of being with Sam.

Gently running her fingers across the faded cloth, she touched the jar containing the dried black sticks that were once beautiful flowers.

Tears blurred her eyes. Confused, she tried to sort through her feelings. I know he's coming back for me. When he discovers what happened, he'll hold me and keep me safe. Then she recalled Matthew's accusations of Sam being a pirate. Could it be true? What if he never returns to me?

No matter what she thought or did, Maria found no satisfaction. She looked around at the wretched condition of the old house and reality began to show its horrors. She became angry and smacked the little jar off the table. It flew to the corner of the room and shattered. She hit her fist on the table and screamed, "He promised he would be back. I can't believe that he would desert me. Not Sam!" She crumpled the cloth with her hands. Her head fell to the table as tears streamed down her cheeks.

Maria cried until dusk had cast its shadow on the frigid daylight. When she at last wiped her eyes, she noticed the door was open, and snow had blown onto the floor. How stupid of me, she thought.

She struggled in the chilly air to bring in the other supplies. She pushed the snow out with her boot so the door could close. Not able to find the kindling box to light a candle or start a fire, Maria grabbed the lone clean blanket that had been given to her and a beef strip to nibble on. She lay down on the old bedcovers for the night and wrapped herself as if in a cocoon.

Sleep was stingy to her until the realization that she could survive with or without Sam settled into her head. Then, and only then, did she fall asleep.

37

Present Day – July 18
HYANNIS – CAPE COD

A SHRILL SCREAM WOKE ME, and my body shot straight up in the driver's seat. Dazed, I looked around to find the tide was much higher on the beach than before. The wind felt cooler, and the sky was gray. A little girl was screaming at the top of her lungs and rolling around in the sand in front of my car. A woman stood watching her. How long had I been here? My cell phone started ringing. I quickly answered, "Hello?"

"Nancy! Are you all right?" Paul sounded irritated. "I've been trying to reach you for over an hour."

"I'm fine. I'm at the beach. I must have dozed off."

"You had me worried sick."

"Sorry, I'll be home soon. I can't believe I fell asleep."

"Drive carefully, please."

I glanced over to the little girl, who was in a full-blown tantrum. I said a prayer for both of them, started the car and hoped that my new baby never did that to me. As I drove away, Maria Hallett drifted once more into my thoughts. Dear God, how could she have faced being pregnant alone? I love Paul so much.

BREWSTER – CAPE COD

Everyone was home for dinner that evening. Paul had already heated the leftovers from the previous night. We were going to announce the news as soon as we finished eating.

Just as Brian was about to leave the table, Paul spoke up, "Your mother and I would like to tell you something important."

"But I have to meet Tom on the bike trail by 6 p.m.," Brian insisted.

"It won't take long," I said, "trust me." I smiled at everyone. "You're going to be surprised!"

All four kids were quiet while they waited.

Paul held my hand as he told the news. "We're going to have a new addition to our family."

I felt nervous and a little embarrassed, thinking again of my age. I quietly said, "I'm pregnant."

"What's that mean, Mommy?" Molly asked.

Jim leaned over into Molly's face. "It means that you're going to have a new brother or sister."

Casey sat wide-eyed, like a deer in headlights.

Brian looked at me. "What do you mean, a baby?"

Jim smiled and said, "That's great news, Mom."

Molly got up from the table without saying a word and started dancing as if she were in Riverdance on Broadway. "I'm gonna have someone to play with. I'm gonna have someone to play with." Then she sat down and finished her potatoes, pleased that she got her opinion across.

Questions flew through the air: Where is it going to sleep? Will I lose my room? When is it coming? What will the name be?

Paul laughed. "In good time. We just found out today and haven't even answered those questions ourselves yet."

I kept a smile on my face, gently holding my stomach. How lucky I am to have such a wonderful family.

38

Present Day – July 19 & 20
BREWSTER – CAPE COD

PAUL WAS ALWAYS THE FIRST ONE UP, and today was no different. As I walked into the kitchen, I watched him slip the daily paper out of its protective plastic bag. As he was unfolding it, something at the bottom of the front page immediately caught his eye. He looked stunned. "Oh my God!" He sat down to read more.

"What's the matter?" I stood next to him as he slid the paper between us. I reached for my glasses, then zeroed in on the article, illustrated with photographs of our back yard and the exposed cellar. The article's headline read, *"Brewster Couple Digs in Backyard, Solves Mystery."* The subheading shouted: *"Evidence may prove existence of Maria Hallett!"*

I glared at Paul, disgusted by this blatant breach of trust. "McNutt promised he was not going to reveal the location, and he even published photographs of our home! I can't believe it. No mention of our names, thank goodness, but he does state that we just moved in."

Paul stood to refill his cup with more coffee. "I hope nothing bad comes from this whole thing."

"What do you mean?"

"I get a funny feeling about it."

"Maybe it'll be good for business, you know, bring more people into the gallery?" I took off my glasses. "Did you make some decaf?"

"Yeah," Paul said rereading the article.

The kids wandered into the kitchen one by one and all read the news, except Molly, who just pointed to the picture. "Is that the hole in our backyard?"

"Yes it is," I said.

"Cool." Molly took her seat at the table to wait for cereal.

Casey, who had the day off work, poured herself some juice then went back to her bedroom to sleep. A few minutes later, the boys left for their summer jobs. At 9 a.m. the phone rang.

"Hello, The Caldwell Gallery," I answered.

There was nothing but silence on the other end.

"Hello?" I repeated. The line went dead. "That was strange."

Paul looked serious. "Here we go! I knew there would be trouble."

"It's probably just a wrong number. Sometimes the name of a business throws people off, and they just hang up."

"I hope so." Paul left for his studio to begin his day.

I looked at Molly, still eating her Cheerios. "Are you almost done?"

"Yup." She drank the last of the milk in her bowl and jumped up. "I'm going to see what Casey's doing, okay?"

"Fine, I'll be in the shower."

* * *

Paul hung the gallery OPEN sign at 11 a.m., right on time, just as a car pulled into the driveway. I watched through the kitchen window, my decaf in hand, as a casually dressed man got out of his car and entered the gallery behind Paul.

I heard talking, then the man returned to his car as if to leave, but he hesitated and looked around for a few minutes. He walked a little closer to the garage and peered down the hill into our backyard. Without another word to Paul, he got into his car and drove away.

I quickly dressed and joined Paul in the studio. "Who was that?"

"Just some strange guy snooping around."

"Yeah, I saw him checking out the backyard. It's probably nothing."

Paul grabbed a few tubes of watercolor to add to his palette. "Nancy? Don't forget to call the paper about that reporter. Tell them we're not happy with the article."

"Okay. I need some breakfast first." I left Paul to his painting.

I found the orange juice carton empty. "Crap," I sighed. A check in the freezer for a spare can of juice also led to nothing. The grocery store was the last place I wanted to go to today. I hated the crowded supermarket in the summer—too many tourists.

After scanning the pantry and food shelves for items to add to my shopping list, I called up the stairs, "Anyone want to go to the store with me?"

"We're busy," Casey called back.

Molly added, "Yeah, we're real busy."

"Okay, see you in about an hour."

*   *   *

I entered the Super Shopper only to be hit with a blast of cold air from the air-conditioning. It made me shiver. It was easy to spot the tourists. They were the shoppers wearing flip-flops and wet bathing suits hidden under terry cloth covers, pushing their shopping carts aimlessly up and down the food aisles, as if in a trance. I overheard their conversations as I passed them in the aisles.

"We only need three ears of corn but plenty of ice cream, Mom!"

"Do you want to eat out, or should we have a BBQ tonight?"

"...but the refrigerator won't hold all of the food. We better get more ice."

I smiled to myself and remembered when I was a tourist, and having the same discussions with the family before we moved permanently to the Cape.

Rounding the corner to the baking section, I noticed an elderly woman struggling to reach for a can of baking soda high on the shelf in front of her.

A short, stocky man let go of the cart handle. "Let me get it, Momma."

"Why thank you, honey," she replied.

I stepped to one side to make room for them to pass me. They both smiled at each other as the son resumed pushing the cart for his mom. I could tell from the young man's facial features that he was born with Down syndrome. I felt frozen. Placing my hand on my stomach I wondered if my baby could have Down syndrome too. What was I going to do? I wanted to go home.

I wandered through the aisles, my mind far away from my shopping list. How would I care for this child as I grew older? Would I have enough patience and strength to raise a special needs child?

I paid for the groceries and hoped I hadn't forgotten anything. I really just wanted to get home. After loading my bags into the car, I shut the car door and broke down in tears. It was a godsend that the van had tinted windows and no one could see me sobbing.

Taking the highway home, I prayed to my mom, as tears streamed down my face. *Please help me. I don't know what to do!*

* * *

Paul didn't notice me pull into the driveway, so I carried the groceries into the house by myself. I put them away as fast as I could, anxious to be alone. I needed to lie down. I grabbed a cold washcloth for my eyes and headed for the bedroom, repeating over and over in my head that everything would be fine.

After a few minutes, I went into the kitchen. It was getting close to dinnertime, but I couldn't decide what to cook. A simple meal of hot dogs, chips and fruit sounded perfect. It was everyone's favorite and easy to prepare.

Paul came in from the gallery. Right away, he noticed my red eyes and knew something was wrong. "What's the matter?"

"It's a long story," I mumbled. "Just something I saw in the supermarket."

"What was it?" He gave me a hug.

"I saw a woman—she must have been in her late seventies, shopping with her son. He had Down syndrome." I put my head on his shoulder and began to cry all over again.

"Come on, Nancy. You're the one who's always positive," Paul said, holding me tighter.

"I know, I know."

"Why don't you go and lie down? I'll start the grill, the kids and I can handle supper."

"Are you sure?" He's such a good man, I thought, I don't know what I'd do without him.

"Go on. Everything will be okay." He kissed me on the forehead, turned me around and pushed me toward the front parlor. "Get in there and relax."

I lay on the couch under the open porch window listening to the kids eating at the picnic table. They asked Paul what was wrong with me. "Mom's just worried about the baby," he explained.

I started to cry again. How could I ask the children to take on the responsibility for their new brother or sister if Paul and I weren't around, or were just too old to cope? I rolled over and faced the back of the couch with tears wetting my cheeks. I just can't do that to them.

"Mommy? I have something for you."

I turned over, sat up and wiped my eyes. "What is it, honey?"

Molly handed me a piece of paper. "This is for you. I'm happy we're going to have a new baby."

She'd drawn a picture of two stick figures standing under a tree. Molly had cut out a picture of her own face and glued it to the circle that represented her head. The little figure next to her had a question mark on its body, but its face had a big smile. The word "Congratulations" was scrawled across the top.

"Oh, Molly, it's beautiful." I felt new tears again, tears of joy.

"Casey helped me. It was a secret; we did it when you went to the store." She beamed with pride and gave me a big hug and a ketchup kiss.

Casey, Brian, and Jim joined us in the parlor. They lined up in front of the bay windows and stared at me. I felt embarrassed that my kids knew their mother was bawling on the couch.

Jim, the oldest, stepped forward. "Don't ever think of not having this baby, Mom. We'll be there, when the time comes, if we're needed."

Casey and Brian both nodded their heads in agreement.

Paul sat down next to me and took my hand in his. "We're a family. We'll get through this together."

"Okay," I tried to smile as I wiped my tears away.

* * *

I took my time cleaning up the kitchen, assuring everyone I'd feel better working quietly by myself. Through the window I saw rain clouds begin to roll in, making the sky darker than usual for the summer hour of 7 p.m. I stood in the kitchen door to inhale the promise of a salty rain, fresh off the ocean.

As the rain splashed onto the skylights throughout the house, I busied myself with the laundry, straightening up, and thinking. I remembered how angry I'd felt with the doctor for suggesting an abortion, but here I was, actually contemplating the very idea that I despised. Was I being selfish for thinking the choice was really mine and mine alone? Wasn't it up to me to go forward with this pregnancy, or terminate it?

At 10 p.m., I went to bed utterly confused. Paul stayed up to wait for Jim and Brian to come home. Sleep didn't come easily for me. I prayed to my mom again. *I miss you, Mom. I can't believe it's already been a whole year since you've been gone. I really need your help.*

I prayed to my father. I prayed to all those who had passed away: my sister, my aunts, my uncles and grandparents, asking every one of them to help me find the right answers. Finally, I begged God for guidance.

Blocking all of my thoughts, I forced myself to recall the meditation techniques that had helped me with the birth of Molly. Minutes later, I fell asleep.

July 20

Morning brought its usual chaos to the Caldwell household. I sat up and dangled my feet over the side of the bed, my mind still swirling about the decision I'd have to make about the baby. I stretched my arms up and my legs out straight. I felt a little hopeful.

Wrapping a towel around my hair, I stepped onto the white tile of the glass shower enclosure and into my daily routine of bathing. The normalcy was comforting; the shower soothing. I closed my eyes and thought of the baby while water splashed over my naked body. I could hear a little voice inside my head telling me it's okay and the baby will be fine. I closed my eyes tighter so I could hear it. The voice reminded me that God would give me the strength to take care of whatever comes my way. I stood motionless in the pulsating water, listening again to the words that repeated in my head. The harder I listened the louder they became.

I suddenly felt relief wash over me, filling my whole body with a deep sense of peace. I don't know if it was my mom or God talking to me. It didn't matter. I decided right then and there that I would have this baby, no matter what the test results showed. I felt supported and knew I would find whatever was needed to raise this child.

I got dressed feeling calmer and stronger than I had felt in days. I hurried into the kitchen "Good morning! It's a wonderful day; the sun is shining and I'm going to have a baby!"

Molly raised her spoon in the air. "Hooray!"

39

December 1715
EASTHAM – CAPE COD

THE MCKEON HOUSE HAD ONE LARGE ROOM with a hearth and chimney in the middle that warmed both sides of the house. Two small windows in the front and back walls gave Maria a limited view of the outside. Weathered from neglect, holes of daylight pierced the crumbling walls and rotted roof. Maria stuffed pine boughs, needles and oak leaves into as many openings as she could to stop the flow of cold air.

By the second day of her arrival, she was finally able to bring forth a fire to cook with and warm herself. Maria was not a stranger to stretching food when there was little to be had. Living with her father was dreadful, but she'd learned many lessons that could now help her to survive this cruel banishment.

Her furniture consisted of the bed frame to the left of the center chimney, one chair and the small table in the kitchen. The torn and dirty bed covers that had been left in the abandoned house were used as her mattress, and the sole blanket was her cover. She slept in the clothes that she worked in. With youth on her side, Maria managed to make her situation bearable. She gathered water from melting snow on the hearth. Come springtime, she'd hunt for the well that she knew was somewhere beneath the frozen earth.

* * *

Two weeks passed, and on Monday, December 23, Maria heard the sound of a sleigh gliding over the snow. As it came closer, she ran to the kitchen window. The pieces of cloth and leaves stuffed along the perimeter of the panes stopped the penetrating cold air but left only a small opening for viewing. She hurried to the front window to see who it was but didn't recognize the lone figure that was driving the sleigh. He had a scarf over his face, protecting him from the cold wind and hiding his identity. The sleigh stopped just past her view.

The top of a spinning wheel was peeking out from under a large canvas, which was tied down over other items. She could not contain her excitement and ran out the door without her shawl.

"HELLO! HELLO THERE!" she called to the driver.

No greeting was returned. In silence the stranger tied off the reins, jumped down and began to untie the ropes protecting his cargo from the elements.

The young girl stood quietly waiting for a response from her first visitor. Within seconds her body began to shiver from the freezing cold air. She quickly turned away and headed for the house to find her shawl. Once inside, the door blew open. Startled, she stepped back to the hearth. Then saw the mysterious man enter the house and drop a large basket filled with weaving supplies onto the dirt floor.

Maria was stunned. She began to rummage through its contents, ignoring the stranger. To her delight, she recognized her own yarns, strings and threads. As the visitor unwrapped the scarf from around his face she glanced up. "Matthew!!!"

She rushed to his side and threw her arms around him, still holding onto some threads. "It's so good to see you." His coat felt cold and wet. She drew back but stayed close to him. "I can't believe it's you. You scared me so. Why didn't you answer me when I called to you?"

Matthew massaged his jaw as he spoke, "Maria, I'm sorry I frightened you…the journey here was so cold. My lips were stiff; I couldn't speak."

"Take off your wet things and stay for a while." Maria began to unbutton his coat.

He stopped her hand. "Wait. Let me bring in as many things as I can. It looks like the weather may take a turn for the worse." He refastened the top button of his woolen waistcoat. "I've brought your things from the North Parish and some extra items from Abigail and myself."

Embarrassed at her impudence, Maria backed away from her oldest friend. "I apologize for my childishness. I was just happy to see you."

Matthew let a big smile cross his face. "Don't worry yourself. Stand here and open the door for me when I come in; then close it when I go out."

Maria did as she was asked and quickly moved things around to make room for the linens and blankets, along with sacks of flour, cornmeal and oats that Matthew hauled in on his back. In her excitement, she almost tripped over a large narrow bundle that was wrapped and tied with string around both its ends. She wondered what it was but kept her interest on arranging her precious supplies. The last items to be delivered brought tears to her eyes. They were her spinning wheel and the parts to her loom.

As Matthew closed the door with a swing of his foot and placed the loom frame upright in the corner of the kitchen, Maria felt joy fill her heart, something she hadn't felt in a long time.

A Snowy Night

The old house stood in disarray as the two friends sat down to simple fare: a small plate of biscuits, apple butter and warm ale. Maria kept her eyes on Matthew as he ate every last one of the bumpy, odd shaped treats she'd made. When finished, he wiped his mouth with his sleeve in satisfaction. He looked much older to her since she had last seen him. His hair had grown longer and his body stronger.

"Maria, how's your firewood supply? I noticed a fallen tree outside. Would you like me to cut and stack it for you?"

"Oh, yes, please, Matthew, but I have no tools."

He stood up from the table and went over to the long narrow bundle that Maria had questioned earlier. "I do believe I can help you." Untying the strings that held the canvas tight, he continued, "I present to you one used but sharp axe and something else that I think you might need." He unfolded further the weathered covering to reveal a long, slender, and deadly musket. He placed it next to the hearth and then reached for his coat. "I'll go out and cut some wood for you tonight. I have almost an hour or more left of daylight."

The felled tree had been dried of its sap long ago and was ripe for making a good flame in the hearth. The popping of the newly cut wood as it burned warmed and soothed her.

As Maria looked through the supplies that Matthew had brought her, she asked, "Would you consider staying the night? The storm seems stronger now."

Matthew brushed the snow off his boots and looked out the tiny opening in the glass. He could see nothing but snow and darkness. "I think you're right. I'll sleep here by the hearth, if that is to your liking?"

"Yes," Maria said.

"The horse needs tending. I saw a lean-to out back. He'll be fine in there tonight. I already gave him oats."

They sat in silence by the crackling fire while they enjoyed one last drink of warm ale. Maria was the first to rise from the table to find a blanket for Matthew. "I want to thank you for all you've done for me, considering the circumstances that I've gotten myself into."

He stood and placed his hands on her shoulders. As he looked into her eyes, the glow of the fire softened her features, accenting her beauty even more. "Maria, I'll always be here for you and will never put aside our friendship." He wanted to kiss her lips, but instead he held her close.

As the two embraced, something stirred within Maria, something she had not felt since being with Sam. It frightened and delighted her at the same time. She dropped the blanket. Her arms wrapped around him, she felt her whole body accepting his affection and didn't want to leave his arms. She felt as if he could fill a deep void inside of her. Reluctantly she drew back. "Matthew, I must sleep now." She leaned down and picked up his blanket. "Here. Stay warm tonight."

Maria stoked the fire one last time while Matthew settled down near the hearth. "Good night," he whispered.

"Good night, Matthew."

Maria retired to her bed on the other side of the hearth. Exhausted from all the excitement, she fell into a deep sleep as soon as she crawled under her new covers.

* * *

Matthew could not sleep. His thoughts were with Maria and what he was going to say to her. Should I tell her about my feelings for her? And what of our future together? Could there even be a future? He found no answers for his questions but felt comfort in the closeness of her presence.

* * *

A cry came from Maria's room. Matthew jumped up as she began to scream.

"No, No! I can't do this alone. Someone help me, please!"

He hurried to the other side of the room and found Maria sitting up in bed, frantically waving her arms. Sitting next to her on the bed, he held her hands and pleaded, "Maria, wake up! You're dreaming!" He could think of only one thing: to hold her. He pulled her against his chest. "Maria, you're safe with me. Calm yourself. It's only a dream."

Slowly she opened her eyes. Relieved to see her dear friend, she cried, "Oh Matthew, I'm so afraid. Please hold me." She clung to him as he held her tight.

Matthew uttered a soft "Shhhh." Then he gently laid her down on the bed. He moved close to her trembling body and brought the bedcovers over the both of them. As he pressed his body alongside hers, he stroked her hair smooth and pulled her back secure against his chest. He felt content and satisfied to hold his love for as long as the night would allow him. Tenderness prevailed over his deep passion for her, and simple sleep finally came to them as soft snowflakes covered the roof of the old McKeon House.

By the time Matthew was ready to leave, early next morning, the snow had stopped and sunshine sparkled across the snowy fields and marshes. He finished splitting the last of the old tree and readied the sleigh for his trip home.

Neither spoke very much as they ate a small meal of biscuits, both confused by their feelings for each other. Matthew was cautious about going against the law. Maria questioned her affection for Sam, and now Matthew.

"Will I see you again?" She watched him fold the canvas that had covered her things.

He came near to her and, once again, he found it difficult to speak. "My dearest Maria, you know that I will always try to be here for you." He chose his words with care. "Although I'm not sure what I can do."

Maria lowered her face. "I understand."

He turned away, walked to the front of the sleigh, grabbed the reins, and climbed onto the seat. He looked back once more to see her face. Would this be the last time he'd ever see her? Matthew could not bear the thought of it. He must find a way to visit Maria again.

With a crack of leather the horse bolted away from the house and down the path. Maria watched until she could not see him anymore. As she latched the door of the old house, she submitted once again to her world of isolation and loneliness.

40

March 1716
EASTHAM – CAPE COD

THE WINTER HAD BEEN THE SNOWIEST anyone could remember. Freezing temperatures had kept the snow on the ground between snowfalls, making travel difficult and supplies scarce. This inconvenience brought out the ill tempers among neighbors and shortened the patience of many people. Near the end of March, patches of green could finally be seen around the village. People ventured outdoors more and Smith's Tavern became busy again.

No one noticed Timothy Edwards enter the tavern. The new visitor was of average size, dressed in plain clothes, and limped on his left leg. He began asking questions among the people in the tavern. Mr. Smith heard the name 'Maria Hallett' float above the conversation and observed his customers shaking their heads 'No' to the stranger. He caught Edwards's attention by waving his hand, gesturing for him to come closer to the sideboard.

Edwards looked over with an exasperated face. Smith signaled him again. A lack of answers made the stranger annoyed, and he growled at Smith, "Gimme a pint!"

"What seems to be troubling you, sir?" the tavern owner asked, ignoring his rudeness.

"I know I have the right place, but everyone I speak to acts strangely and displays an unusual ignorance to my inquiries."

"I might be able to help you." Smith was curious about the man's interest in Maria Hallett.

"A while back, I travelled with the Bellamy-Williams crew to find treasure off the West Indies coast. Well, it didn't turn out the way we all expected. The treasure was gone before we even got there." The seaman drank half his ale in one lift of his hand. "Not wanting to go home empty handed, most of the men went 'on account'…pirate, I mean. But I decided not to, me having a family in Truro and all."

"So you say that Bellamy went 'on account'?"

"Aye, that's what I said. When we docked in Antigua, I told Bellamy that I wanted nothing to do with pirates. He said that it would be right if I left, but only if I would do one favor for him." He scratched his head. "Bellamy knew I was from Truro and this end of the land. He asked if I would get a message to someone here in Eastham."

"Whom do you seek?" asked Smith, all the while knowing full well it was Maria.

"She goes by the name of Maria Hallett."

"Maria Hallett, you say?"

"Yes, that's her." Edwards looked at Smith with relief. "Do you know her?"

"There's a girl who goes by that name, but no one will agree to it."

The stranger looked puzzled. "What's that you mean?"

"She was accused of murder and witchcraft a while back. Nothing was ever proven, but some people around here still wanted to see her punished." Smith wiped some ale from the sideboard. "They banished her to the bluffs. Poor thing never had a chance against all these supposed God-fearing people. She's dead to most."

Edwards leaned closer to Smith and whispered, "Can you get a message to her?"

Smith looked around before he spoke. "I think I might be able to arrange something. What do you have?"

From the inside pocket of his waistcoat he pulled a small folded parchment, sealed in wax, and handed it to Smith. "Here." The name *Maria Hallett* was written on the outside.

Mr. Smith took the letter and placed it in his cash box. "I will do my best to get it to her."

Timothy Edwards felt at ease. "Thank you, sir. My duty is done." He paid for his pint and walked out of the tavern, heading for his home.

41

April 1716
EASTHAM – CAPE COD

THE SUN FELT PLEASANT ON MARIA'S FACE as she brought in wood for the day. Water dripped from the roof in a steady stream that splashed onto the mud surrounding the perimeter of her solitary confinement. She had counted the days from her arrival with crude markings on a corner wall by her bed, but after Matthew's visit, she used a piece of vellum from her special keepsake box. Winter was near over and the smell of spring drifted through the air. She reached for some oats to prepare her meal but found the sack almost empty. Maria wondered if people's hearts might have softened towards her. Would it be safe to travel to the village store? Unsure of what might happen, she decided to try.

*   *   *

The warmth of the day made the ground soggy, and it proved difficult to walk on. Approaching the first house of Eastham, Maria saw its owner, Mr. Jenkins, staring at her as he walked his horse to the barn.

The Widow Baker's house came next. Maria distrusted her, thinking of the day the widow had pried her way into her life under the pretense of a social visit. She could see Widow Baker's face framed in the little window opening of the door. The old woman's expression quickly changed at the sight of Maria from surprise to disbelief and finally to anger. She opened the door a crack and shouted, "Get away from here. Go back to where you belong!"

Maria hurried past the annoyed woman's house.

She could see the Pierce Stand, where Isaac Pierce sold supplies and served ale on occasion. Mrs. Eldridge was walking towards Maria, approaching the store from the opposite side. When she caught sight of Maria rounding the curve in the road she picked up her pace and reached Pierce's first. She hurried inside and shut the door behind her.

By the time Maria placed her foot on the step of the store, a closed sign appeared, sending a clear message that she was not welcome. When Maria knocked, she found the door locked, and no answer came from within. Sick in her heart, the young girl turned to go home.

* * *

On the muddy road ahead, a group of people watched her as she walked towards them. She pulled her shawl closer around her head, hoping no one would bother her. Suddenly, from one side, she heard a squish of mud, and within seconds a large clump of wet sod hit her on the ear. She twisted around to see a young man laughing. Her feet could not out distance the next mound of filth that he hurled at the back of her skirts. A man, three women and a few small children waited for her to pass by them. They separated and lined up on either side of the dirt road.

Maria had no choice but to walk between them.

"Witch! Be gone!" yelled the man.

One woman warned, "Stay away from our children, you murderer."

The children scooped up black mud and stood poised to hit their easy target. In seconds, thick soggy soil crashed against Maria's body. She stumbled to get away as words were hurled at her from the attackers, but they were muffled by her screams as she ran from them.

By the time Maria came into view of her house her shoes were so caked with mud that she could barely lift her feet. She trudged forward as her breathing became labored in the chilly air, and her body grew covered with sweat. She collapsed onto the bench in front of her house.

After a few seconds she regained her composure and could breathe easily once more.

Discouraged, Maria looked out to the coast; her eyes drifted across the marsh and then to the ground in front of her. Something dark and flat caught her eye among the grasses to the far side of the house, where the snow had melted. She had never noticed it before. Struggling to stand, she stamped her shoes to shake off the mud and walked closer to the object. A two-foot square of wooden slats had been nailed together. She pushed the wood with one foot and it moved. She flipped it over to reveal a black hole. Inside was a rope and bucket attached to a long piece of wood that stretched from side to side. They both dangled above a circle of darkness. She'd found the well.

Hope rippled through Maria's body, and the mud incident was soon forgotten as she lowered the bucket down the well. A loud crack echoed up to her ears as the ice broke. When the bucket filled with water, she pulled up on the rope. To her delight, the container held good clean water. She glanced down at her muddy clothes and shoes with a grateful smile, then carried her liquid treasure back to the house. She knew her winter source of water would be in jeopardy as the snow melted away and the air became warmer. Now Maria was confident that things would be better.

42

April 1716
EASTHAM – CAPE COD

THE HERRING WERE RUNNING; a sure sign of spring for Matthew. The temperature was unusually warm so all he needed was his hat and waistcoat today. His father had recently taken ill and the younger Ellis was given more responsibilities in the household. Even though he was not fond of the sea, he felt obligated to replace his father on several fishing trips. His mother, consumed with taking care of her husband, also needed his help. The sun felt warm on his back as he headed out in the wagon to deliver a barrel of fresh cod to Smith's Tavern.

"Hello, Mr. Smith!" Matthew shouted.

Smith was sweeping the step when he saw Matthew pull up. "Good morrow, Matthew!"

Matthew jumped down and rolled a barrel filled with his fresh catch to the side door.

"We'll have a good bake tonight and plenty of chowder," Smith smiled. The tavern owner inspected his purchase with a long sniff. Satisfied, he accepted his bill and placed it into the drawer next to his cash box. He caught sight of the letter given to him by Timothy Edwards and realized he'd forgotten about it.

"Matthew, you were friends with Maria Hallett, am I not right?"

Matthew paused. "Yes, that's right."

"Are you not close to her house out there? Have you seen her about?"

"Yes, I'm close, but I'm afraid I haven't seen her," Matthew replied.

Smith took the letter out of the box and handed it to Matthew. "I have something for her. Do you think that you could leave it by her door without anyone seeing that you've been there?"

"I don't know if I should."

"It would satisfy a favor, and we could keep it our secret. What say you?"

"I'll try," Matthew agreed. He stuffed the letter into his vest pocket and gave Smith a wave goodbye.

He'd heard what had happened to Maria when she'd tried to buy supplies at Pierce's. Knowing what people were capable of in Eastham, Matthew feared not for himself, but for his parents. They were vulnerable in their poor health, and their stature in the community might be jeopardized. As the wagon rumbled away from the tavern, Matthew noticed his hands perspiring on the reins. Why should he be nervous at this chance to see Maria? He decided nighttime would be the best time to visit her, and if someone saw him, he'd explain that his visit was on behalf of Mr. Smith.

May 1, 1716

EASTHAM – CAPE COD

As Minda approached the Ellis and Hallett homesteads, she heard an axe cracking. She could see Matthew splitting wood in front of his house, but there was no sign of life where Maria once lived. The old *Pow Wah* waved her hand and called out to Matthew.

He recognized the *Pow Wah* and saw that she pulled a black goat tethered on a short rope. He laughed and turned to greet her. "Minda, it's good to see you. I take it you are well after such a hard winter?"

She rested on a large rock and placed the end of the rope under her foot to keep the goat from wandering. "Yes, I am well, even after tending to many women. Spring has brought forth numerous births." Minda gestured to the goat. "What do you think of my payment from the Macon household? The young mistress gave up twins last night." She shook her head while patting the goat's head. "Tis a pity, this poor nanny lost her kid and is in need of milking. I have no need of it. It is a shame because it could provide milk all year long. What say you of giving it to Maria?"

Matthew approved. He thought it would not be dangerous for Minda to contact Maria, but it could be disastrous for him. He knew that Maria's banishment held no sway over the behavior of Indians and Minda's visit presented an opportunity for him to fulfill Mr. Smith's request.

The old *Pow Wah* left with goat and letter in hand.

*   *   *

The clack, rattle and swoosh of Maria's loom echoed across the spring grasses; its sound was lifted by the wind and reverberated into strange noises to an unknowing ear. Minda knew what it was and happily walked towards its rhythms.

"Maria!" she called out, coming closer to the house.

The clacking stopped as Maria waited and listened for what she thought was someone calling her name.

"Maria!" Minda called once more.

The door opened, and Maria stood in its frame, her hair loose around her shoulders. She wore neither cap nor shawl. Her body had become well formed from wielding an axe and being relegated to the duties of a man. The glow of her cheeks testified to her health and beauty.

She ran to Minda, laughing at the sight of her friend and the goat. "I've missed you, Minda!" Pointing to the goat, she asked, "Who does that belong to?"

"You!" Minda smiled as she handed the rope to her friend.

Maria whooped for joy. "For me? Tell me all about how this might be."

After tying the end of the goat's rope around a leg of the bench by the house, Maria grabbed Minda in a friendly embrace.

They entered the simple but tidy house. Minda saw that things were in the right places, a spinning wheel by the hearth and a loom next to Maria's bed. "I am proud of you, my child," she said.

Maria reached for two mugs of ale. "Sit down, sit down."

She pulled an empty barrel close to the table where Minda sat on the lone chair. They satisfied themselves with what little food Maria had, shared recent news and then talked of the coming growing season.

Maria showed Minda the flax and other important seeds gifted from Abigail. When planted, they would provide summer crops for next winter's food.

Minda also had gifts for Maria. She emptied her bag of herbs and medicines onto the table and presented them to Maria. At the bottom of her bag Minda felt Maria's letter. Handing it to Maria she spoke, "Forgive me. I have forgotten a most important item that Matthew gave me for you. He said that a stranger had delivered this to the tavern and Mr. Smith then passed it on to him, hoping you would receive it."

The young girl took the letter in her hands and touched the bumpy wax that sealed it closed. The heavy parchment had been folded twice, making a square. Who would be sending her this and why? She broke the seal and opened it to reveal its message:

My Beloved Maria,

I pray this letter finds you well and not of a sad heart. It has been too long that we have been apart. I dream of you at night and thoughts of you remain with me when I wake. Alas, the treasure that I sought was gone upon our arrival. But soon good fortune came upon me and we now sail with a fleet of ships that transport goods. Hold fast to a faith that I will return to you as soon as I am able.

Keep watch for me...Sam

* * *

Maria held Sam's letter in her hands. She reread its words over and over until Minda finally asked, "Maria, is there bad news?"

"No. No. It's from Sam."

43

Present Day – July 21
CAPE COD

THE SPACIOUS PARKING LOT OF THE LOCAL COFFEE SHOP
was filled with cars. It serviced eight different stores, and at 10 a.m.,
everything bustled with activity. A celebratory coffee and donut
would suffice to honor the coming of our new little one. Paul parked
the car in the back row.

He hesitated before getting out. "Look at those two guys over
there by the black truck. Isn't one of them Neil Hallett?"

I squinted through the windshield. "Yeah, that's him."

Paul took his sunglasses off. "See the guy to his right? He's the
weird man who came into the gallery the other day but spent most
of his time looking around outside."

"Oh yeah, I remember him. What's he doing with Hallett?"

"Do you mind if we sit here for a minute? I want to see what they're
going to do."

"No, I don't mind, but we've got to get home soon and open up
the gallery."

Paul leaned over the steering wheel to get a better view. "They're
shaking hands. Now the weird guy is getting into the same car that
was in our parking lot."

"Maybe I'll give Salinger a call and see if we should be worried
about this Hallett guy," I said. I buckled my seat-belt. "We'd better
get home."

Paul looked over to me. "Sorry honey, no donut today. We'll celebrate tomorrow." He glanced back to the two men. "I'm concerned about those guys."

I agreed. "They look a little sketchy, but I'm sure there's nothing to get upset about. It could be just a coincidence."

That afternoon I made a call to Louis Salinger. His voicemail picked up. I recorded, "Hello, Mr. Salinger, this is Nancy Caldwell from Brewster. I was wondering if you could give me a call concerning Neil Hallett? Thank you."

* * *

Salinger always screened his calls. As he sat at his desk listening to Nancy's message he grumbled under his breath. "What the hell did that jerk do now?"

* * *

Around 4 p.m., the phone rang. I picked it up in the bedroom, hoping it was Salinger. "Hello, The Caldwell Gallery."

"I'm calling from the *Whydah* Museum in Provincetown. I was wondering if I could speak to someone about the discovery that was found in your backyard."

I sat down, taken off guard with the question. "Oh...that...would be me. Yes, we did find some things in our backyard."

"Well, I'm glad I have the right place. Would it be okay if I stopped by to see what you found?"

"I guess so. We're open in the gallery every day from 11 – 5 p.m. We're always here, as our house is attached to the business."

"Fine, I hope to see you soon. Goodbye."

I ran to get the kitchen phone to see who was on the Caller ID. The screen said the last call was 'unavailable'. That's odd, I thought, and went to find Paul.

He was framing his new watercolor. I loved it. The painting captured the shadow of the sun on the roof of the old cottage, just the way I remembered it when we'd walked around Rock Harbor a few weeks earlier. It was stunning. "Honey, it's beautiful."

"Thank you." He stood back to admire it also.

"Oh, I've got something to tell you. We just had a phone call, supposedly from the *Whydah* Museum, in Provincetown. Some guy wants to come and look at what we found. " I glanced outside to see Brian getting dropped off by a co-worker. "The Caller ID said the number was unavailable. I assume it was someone from the Museum."

"They could have been on their cell," Paul suggested.

"I guess so."

"Not to worry. I'm always at home with you."

"I know. Oh, and by the way, the new painting is absolutely gorgeous."

* * *

After dinner, with the kids in bed, Paul and I sat at the kitchen table treating ourselves to ice cream. "Do you think that our lives will ever be calm?" I asked.

"You were the one who wanted adventure." Paul laughed as he ate a spoonful of creamy vanilla bean.

"Yeah, and you came right along for the ride, didn't you?"

I finished up my bowl of chocolate and grabbed the plastic baggie that held the old vellum pieces. I pointed to the old script. "You know, these letters have got to stand for Maria Hallett and Sam Bellamy. And the 1715 date could easily tie in with the Doane people who owned this property."

Paul scraped his bowl. "The cellar had to be connected to another house on our land. Maria could have traveled here from Eastham for any number of reasons. I guess we'll never know."

I stroked the brittle vellum. "Bottom line...I think we have a real connection to an old Cape Cod legend here."

* * *

Paul got a phone call the next morning requesting his attendance at an exhibit in Boston. He'd leave tomorrow but only be gone for a few days.

"I'm sorry, honey. I hadn't planned on going, but they said it would be good for sales if the artist were present. It's very casual; I could take the kids with me. I bet Casey would take care of Molly and Brian could help me load and unload the paintings. What do you think?"

"Sure. I'll be fine. If I need something, Jim will be home at night and in the morning. And I shouldn't need the car for those few days."

"Okay, check your groceries and I'll start packing. If you need anything, we'll go to the store this afternoon." Paul went upstairs to pack and to tell Molly, Casey and Brian, who were still sleeping, about their upcoming trip.

*   *   *

As they all prepared to head out, I stood in the driveway and watched the kids fill the van with their backpacks and snacks. I felt apprehensive about Paul leaving me alone, but I tried to act confident in front of everyone. I knew it was important for Paul to sell as many paintings as he could. Our budget was tight and we were going to have to really save for the winter. I'd be fine, I assured myself, wrapping my arms around my waist. Of course, with the new baby coming, and our insurance coverage still uncertain, this only added to my tension. In fact, we were both turning into two very uptight people.

"I love you," I called out as I waved goodbye to my family. I watched the car as it drove away until I couldn't see it anymore. It was too early to open the gallery, so I went into the house to start the laundry.

44

April 26, 1717
EASTHAM – CAPE COD

MARIA SURVIVED ANOTHER WINTER with Sam's words etched in her heart. She sat in the dimly lit room by her spinning wheel, her eyes closed, not wanting to see her meager belongings scattered around the dismal McKeon house. They were a painful reminder of the deep sadness that consumed her life. With her hands resting in her lap, she slowly breathed in and out.

When she grew tired of sitting, Maria stood to look out the window at the distant evening sky. The last light of day was fading into churning storm clouds. She sighed. Another April had come, but not without a great number of nor'easters that had already wreaked havoc upon the sandy spit of Cape Cod. As the rain began to fall, she could feel the dampness already creeping through her young bones.

It had been a year since Minda had delivered Sam's letter, which Maria kept safe in her keepsake box, now worn smooth from so many readings. She cherished his words as she continued her quest of waiting for him. She knew she had nothing else to hope for and lived for this simple promise from a man who said he loved her. It was a promise that she clung to as she fulfilled her nightly vigil of watching for his ship. The arrival of dusk each night hid Maria from the probing eyes of her neighbors as she walked the bluffs in search of Sam.

Tonight was turning cold and menacing; the approaching storm made her wish in a fleeting moment that she had never met Sam.

Accepting her fate, she gathered a shawl around her head and shoulders and fastened it with a large knot, then reached for a piece of old canvas hanging on a hook. She flung the door open and threw the canvas high in the air over her head; her strong arms like two wooden masts on a tall ship held up her canvas sail.

Maria flew down the path and up the bluffs. The rain blew so hard it blinded her view. As she approached the top of the bluff, her eyes glimpsed something in the churning water. She wiped the seawater's spray from her face, trying to make sense of the object in the sea. The frothing water tossed it back and forth, slowly breaking it apart. She questioned her own eyes before she realized it was a ship.

Her heart pounded as she ran down the side of the bluff. She stumbled onto the beach, where her feet sank into thick wet sand. Struggling to keep her balance, she shielded her eyes from the rain by keeping her head down under the canvas. The swirling sand stung and bit at her cheeks, but she pushed herself toward the shoreline, straining to see the ship in the water.

A gust of wind knocked her over. Maria fell onto a small mound with a dull thump. Her canvas sail was ripped from her grasp. As her fingers moved across the bumpy wet lump, she felt a cold, fishlike object. She screamed and withdrew her hand, pushed herself up and away, too fearful to look down.

The force of the storm raged around her. The dark of the night overwhelmed her senses with fears of the unknown. She held her hands to either side of her face to scan the beach and saw more dark clumps scattered across the sand.

*   *   *

Three men huddled against a sandy cliff and watched the lone figure stagger across the storm tossed beach among the bodies of their fellow shipmates.

"Damn those mooncussers. Can they not leave the dead in peace?" hissed the dark-skinned man.

"Quiet," their captain cautioned them.

*   *   *

Maria turned away from the shadowy beach and searched again across the inky water for the ship. Like an apparition it came into view—it was keeled over to one side. Within seconds the waves had flipped it over; then another crash of the surf tossed it upright again. Maria tried to decipher the letters across the bow of the mangled vessel. She thought she saw, *Whyd*...then remembered what Minda had told her, "There are rumors in town about your Sam. They say he is a pirate who stole the ship *Whydah*."

Her heart swelled in a moment of hope that this could be Sam's ship but instantly fell to despair when she looked at the dark shapes on the beach. *Oh God! Where is he?? Is it possible...? Could he be dead?*

As one monstrous wave crested, it sucked the ship sideways, then rolled it over so its bottom became its top. Cannons from its hull crashed down through the deck and cracked the doomed vessel in half.

"SAM!" Maria screamed into the darkness. "SAM BELLAMY!" She cried above the wind but to no avail; the thundering surf and vicious storm screeched along the beach like a swarm of banshees destroying anything in its path.

Maria forced herself to touch the dark mound nearest to her feet. As she turned it over a lightening flash revealed the corpse of a wretched man, his eyes wide open, frozen in terror. She screamed, slapped her hand up to her mouth and thought she would vomit.

A sudden urgency overwhelmed her fear as she called on her courage to search the dark objects for her beloved Sam—if, God forbid, he was among them. The wind blew stronger, and the force of the rain against her face blinded her. Maria tried to wipe away the water from her eyes, but the darkness further hindered her vision. She needed a lantern. If Sam was here, she must find him.

After only a few steps Maria realized running in the wet sand was impossible. Her feet sank with each step, and her body swayed side to side, back and forth. She was forced to walk with slow, careful steps through the heavy sand. Her mind raced with thoughts of Sam as she climbed back up over the bluff and ran down the path to her house.

*   *   *

Through shivering teeth one of the men said, "We must follow her to shelter."

"Agreed. Let's go." Their captain stood and led his men, keeping a safe distance behind Maria. The three men whispered ideas for their plan as they crept along the sandy path. They needed a wagon and a horse to retrieve whatever valuables had washed up onto the beach. They would raid the nearest houses until they found what they needed... and they'd use whatever means was necessary.

* * *

Breathless, Maria finally reached her door. Once inside, she grabbed the curved wire handle of the glass beacon that hung on a hook by the hearth. As she spun around to close the door to light the lantern in the dry house, she came face-to-face with three dark shapes in her doorway. In the faint glow from the hearth she saw three sets of eyes glaring back at her. Overwhelmed by the terrors of the stormy night, her eyes tricked her into thinking they were demons from the dead men on the beach. The lantern crashed to the floorboards as Maria collapsed and her head slammed against the stones in the hearth.

* * *

John Julian stepped over the girl's body as Thomas Davis slammed the door shut against the storm.

Their captain pushed Julian away from Maria. "Let me see the woman."

Sam Bellamy found himself looking at his beloved Maria. He scooped her up in his arms and carried her to the bed. He knelt down by her side and held her hand.

The other two men watched their captain in silence; fully aware that he had found his love, the young girl he called Maria. They stood by the hearth and waited for their orders.

Sam finally turned to Davis. "Go to the house past the trees where we saw lights. John will stay with me." He knew that John Julian, being an Indian, would have no chance of getting help, as prejudice was still within many a man in New England. He placed his hands on Davis's shoulders. "You are the only one who would be safe. Convince the people that you are not a pirate and in need of their help."

"I'll go," he said.

"Thomas, if you have to, entice them with the promise of a share of whatever we find on the beach." Sam looked at John for agreement.

He nodded.

"Go now and be quick. I'll tend to my Maria while you're gone." He moved towards Maria's bed, where she still lay unconscious from her fall.

*   *   *

The Welshman, Thomas Davis, never imagined himself as a pirate. He originally signed as a carpenter on the ship *St. Michael*, sailing from Cork to Jamaica. Bellamy and his crew, upon capturing his ship, took Davis captive. Badly in need of a carpenter, they'd kept him against his will. Being a God-fearing man, Davis wanted nothing to do with pirating. While at sea he'd stayed quiet, done his work, and always looked for ways to gain his freedom, but that never came. During his captivity, Captain Sam Bellamy had been good to Davis. He'd respected the craftsmanship of the carpenter's work and Davis had returned a mutual respect to him.

Tonight he had survived the shipwreck with minor injuries: cuts, bruises and a possible broken toe, which now made him limp. This was nothing compared to the fate of his fellow shipmates. He wondered if the Lord had a far greater purpose for him yet to come. Convincing himself to do his best to get help, he knew what he had to do. The soon-to-be-salvaged treasure was all he had now, even if it was stolen. After all, he deserved it, considering all that he'd endured.

*   *   *

When Maria woke, she found herself lying in her bed. Lifting her hand, she could feel her coverlet and a dry shift. As she lay still, she remembered there had been a storm. Her clothes had been soaked. She moved only her eyes, trying to catch glimpses of what and who surrounded her. She could see the fire in the hearth and her bare feet stuck out from under a blanket. Two men were sitting at her table.

45

Present Day – July 23
CAPE COD

NEIL HALLETT WAITED FOR HIS BUDDY in Eastham. He needed an accomplice and was stuck with this guy again. The only good trait his partner-in-crime had shown in past schemes was that he could keep his mouth shut. "It's about time you got here," Neil said as he opened his front door to Jack Hennessey.

Jack was smooth and charming, but occasionally exhibited a mean streak, which served Neil's purpose well. He told Jack about an investor he'd met at the donut shop in Orleans. He was willing to provide an advance for whatever they needed to do to find the missing treasure. When Jack questioned him about how he knew the investor, Neil assured him that he had ways of finding people who wanted a piece of the action when it came to a real treasure hunt.

"Well, if you think he's got the money, I'm in," Jack said as he slicked his hair back and straightened the collar on his Hawaiian shirt. He followed Neil to a back office.

Neil turned around. "By the way, thanks for making that phone call for me." He settled back into his swivel chair to explain his plan.

BREWSTER

A Jeep Wrangler pulled onto the driveway the day after Paul had left for Boston. I noticed the bumper sticker on the back read, 'The *Whydah*'. I hurried to the rear of the gallery and tried to look busy sorting bills. When I heard the customer alert buzzer, I walked to the front. "Hello. If I can help you with anything, let me know. My husband is the artist."

The customer had a large handlebar mustache, graying temples against dark hair and a funky Hawaiian shirt; he looked like he was right out of an Indiana Jones movie.

"Mrs. Caldwell? I'm Kevin Kennedy from the Museum," he said with a smile on his face.

"It's nice to meet you," I said. "You know, when I got your call the other day, I wondered how you knew that the discovery in the paper was from our backyard?"

"Oh, I have my sources. I'm quite an explorer, you know." He looked outside towards the woods. After a few seconds of silence, he asked in a polite voice, "May I see where you found the cellar?"

I first craned my neck to see if anyone else had pulled into the yard. After seeing no one, I said, "Of course, follow me." As we walked around the garage I warned him, "If someone comes in, I'll have to leave and take care of them."

"No problem, I won't be long."

"It's right over there." I pointed to the sawhorses that still guarded the cellar.

"Filling the hole in with dirt has not been a high priority for us; making sure the gallery is always open is." And making money, I thought. "Besides, I want to do some more digging."

Kennedy walked around the cellar's edge and then climbed down the stone steps to the bottom. He was quiet as he crouched down to examine the dirt where the rotted pieces of wooden chest still lay. He stood up. "May I see the things that you found?"

"Just a minute, I'll get them." As I spoke, the sound of gravel on the driveway indicated another customer had pulled in. "I'll be right back, Mr. Kennedy."

He quickly climbed out of the cellar. "Mrs. Caldwell, may I use your bathroom?"

I hesitated at first, but then said, "Sure, follow me."

Thank you." He looked satisfied with himself.

I quickly showed him to the bathroom. "You'll have to excuse me. I'm all by myself for a few days because my husband took the kids to Boston on business." As soon as I'd spoken I realized I shouldn't have told a stranger that I was alone.

I found the customers already looking around the gallery. They commented on the weather then asked for directions to where they could find some good ice cream. I offered suggestions to them and said goodbye.

As they slowly walked to their car, I whispered to myself, "Okay, hurry up, get in your car. I need to get out back with that guy from the museum."

When they finally pulled out of the driveway, I hurried to the backyard. "Mr. Kennedy?" He was nowhere to be found. I went through the outside porch and into the back of the house to the living room. I called again, "Mr. Kennedy? Mr. Kennedy?"

I found him in the kitchen, standing over the table holding the three gold coins in his hand. Seeing him there took me off guard. How stupid I was! I should have put the coins away after breakfast. I became angry that he'd taken the liberty of roaming through my house and glared at him through the doorway.

"I hope you'll forgive me. You were busy with your customer, and I saw these on the table as I passed by to the bathroom." He flipped the coins over a few times in his hands. "They're so interesting."

I tried to ignore the rush of irritation welling inside me. With an inner strength, I calmly walked over to him and without a word held out my hand.

"I should be going; thanks for your time," he said, placing the coins in my palm. "I'm sure the museum will be contacting you if they're interested in learning more about your discovery."

I watched him leave through the screen door and thought it strange that he didn't leave through the back porch where he'd come in. I kept my eyes on him, following his every move until he stood by his jeep. He stared back at the house. It gave me the creeps—God, I wished Paul were home.

I remained guarded closing the gallery. Just to be safe, I double-checked all of the doors to make sure they were locked. The wind began to pick up, and it looked like it was going to rain. I closed the windows half way throughout the house. Remembering the baby, I tried to remain calm. *Don't talk yourself into a bundle of nerves.* Massaging my stomach, I took a few deep breaths. *Everything will be fine.* I felt as if my imagination was trying to take over my head, so I busied myself with fixing something to eat. I microwaved a veggie burger and turned on the news to watch during my dinner. The weatherman warned of thunderstorms, especially on the Cape. *Oh great, that's just what I need.* I looked outside—no rain yet, only dark clouds.

46

April 27, 1717
EASTHAM – CAPE COD

HIS DARK, WET HAIR CLUNG TO HIS NECK like the exposed roots holding fast to an eroding cliff. Whispered words floated in the air as the two men sat drinking ale at Maria's table, their damp shoulders hunched over. "The fates have dealt me a bad turn; my fleet, my men and the *Whydah*...all gone." Sam Bellamy hung his head and looked at Julian.

The salty Indian held his forehead and cursed under his breath. He knew their prisoner, Captain Montgomery, of the newly captured vessel Anne, had purposely led Bellamy and all of his shipmates aground on the treacherous sandbars of Cape Cod.

"That damned Montgomery," said Bellamy, slamming the table with his fist. "I said he could have his freedom, and his ship, if he steered us in safely...I gave him my word. But that bastard led us into hell." He hit the table again.

The sound of his angry fist made Maria jump. She took a quick breath in and out as the two men turned towards her.

"Maria?" The dark haired man said her name again. "Maria?"

I know that voice, she thought. She squinted to get a closer look. "Sam...Sam is that you?"

As he approached her, his torn clothes revealed stains of red on the front. Sam took her hand and placed his head on her breast. "I am sorry, so sorry."

Maria stroked his damp hair and lifted his head. "It's you, Sam. You're here...you came back for me! I always knew you would."

He looked into her eyes. "I've come back, but not the way I wanted."

She sat upright and placed her bare feet down onto the cold, sandy floor. She reached for Sam's hand and tried to stand up. The other man looked up from the table and stood to help her. They both took hold of her as she righted herself. The touch of a man's hand was unnerving to Maria after being alone for so long. Even though she knew Sam, she began to tremble and felt afraid in the presence of a stranger.

Sam stepped to the side and quietly introduced his cohort. "Maria, this is John Julian. He is the best pilot that I've ever known. Do not fear him. Rest assured he is trustworthy."

She looked at John; he had the look and face of an Indian. She reached for her shawl, wrapped it around herself, and walked over to the fire to consider all that was going on around her. She wanted to speak, but no words could describe her troubled emotions. She swiveled her head to look at Sam, then faced the hearth again.

Sam's strong hands came to rest on her shoulders. He turned her towards him. "Come over to the table and sit down, Maria...we need to talk."

He looked so pale to her.

He lost his balance and reached out for a chair. "I need to sit down."

Maria caught him before he reached the floor. As his bloodstained shirt came clearer into view she drew back and gasped. "You're hurt, Sam!"

"I'll be fine...just let me rest." He placed his hand inside the shirt, just below his heart, as Maria helped him to a seat by the table.

John looked worried. "Sam, we must hurry. There's not much time. He'll be coming back soon." He stepped outside to look for Davis.

*　*　*

The rattling shutters against the house were normal sounds for Samuel Harding and his wife. They were accustomed to living on the outskirts of the village, never minding their isolation or the constant wind. Given their closeness to the coast, the occasional shipwreck was taken in stride, and they always offered help to those who were unfortunate enough to find themselves in trouble. Tonight, pounding against their door awakened them, and they heard a voice yelling. "Hello! Hello in there!" Davis screamed, "I need help. Please help!"

Samuel sat up in his bed. "Now what?"

His wife turned over. "You better go and see what's the matter."

"Yes, yes, I know," he grudgingly agreed.

By the time Harding reached the entrance, Davis was pounding with both fists. "Help! Help, is anybody in there?"

"I'm coming. Stop the noise," Harding called out.

As he opened the door, the shipwrecked, exhausted sailor stumbled into the house and was caught by Harding. The old man prayed under his breath, "Oh Lord, give me strength tonight."

Harding's wife, Mary, came around the corner of the hearth to see Davis sprawled on a chair by the table and her husband leaning over him. "Who is it?" she asked.

"Not sure," Samuel answered. "What's your name, sir? What has happened?"

Davis looked up into his rescuer's face and chose his words with caution. "My name is Thomas Davis...ship-wrecked...all dead...." He paused for a few moments. "It was a pirate ship. They held me against my will, kept me as their prisoner." He waited for their response and kept his hand on the knife he carried in a small leather sheath strapped to his lower leg.

"Oh my son, don't worry; we'll help you. Tell us more of your plight. Are you hurt?"

Mary moved a little closer. "Young man, would there be any treasure on board?"

Davis released his grip on the knife's handle; that was all he needed to hear.

* * *

"Let me look at your wound, Sam." Maria gently lifted his shirt.

Sam winced with pain and leaned back into the chair. "One of my men has gone for help."

She pulled the stained shirt farther away from his injury. Blood covered his side with splinters of wood embedded in the skin. Her eyes also caught sight of a gold chain with a small ring attached that hung against his chest near his heart. Thinking of Sam's last words to her, she felt encouraged for a moment, but reality pulled her back as she saw the seriousness of his wound.

"My ship went aground…" grabbing onto the table with one hand, "…on the shoals …and the storm was fierce." He swallowed back his pain as Maria began to pull splinters from the reddened open wound.

"Where's your father? What are you doing here?" asked Sam.

"He's gone from me."

"Is he dead?"

"No." Maria hesitated. "Sam…there was a child, a boy child."

"Our child?" He saw no evidence of a young one. "Where is he?"

"I lost him…we lost him, in my travail," lowering her head, she began to tear. "No one was there to help me."

"Oh Maria, we had a son?" He bent forward, resting his elbow on the table and tried to hold her, but the pain of his wound stopped him, and he leaned back once more into the chair. "I am so sorry." He looked into Maria's eyes. "Why are you here in this house, alone?"

"Do you not remember the old McKeon house? They sent me here in banishment because I was accused of…." Maria stopped. She could barely utter the words, "…murder and evil doings."

"What? Because of the child's death? How could they punish an innocent mother for such an unfortunate accident? Ridiculous!"

Not wanting to talk about it anymore, Maria fetched some warm water and a soft cloth. "I'm fine, Sam. You need not worry about me."

Sam desperately wanted to take her from this God-forsaken place.

When she returned, she cautioned him, "This will hurt, but you'll feel better when I'm finished. Now tell me more of what happened to you."

As he reached for her free hand, their eyes met. The love that had brought them together years ago rekindled their passions once more. She kissed him on his forehead and then his hand. "Sam, I knew you would come back to me. Now hold still."

His face softened. He loved her so very much. But his protective instincts quickly surfaced and made him feel ashamed because he was not there when she needed him the most. He willingly accepted his pain as punishment.

Maria cleaned his wound as gently as she could.

Sam steadied his gaze on her face. He wondered in his heart. How do I find the right words to tell her the things that I have done? She needs to know; she is part of me now.

"There are so many splinters in your wound; I can't get them all out," Maria said. "I think I have something that might work." She retrieved a small bag of salves from a shelf on the wall.

As she prepared the drawing salve, Sam talked of the prior night when he lost his ship. "When the three of us found each other on the beach, we saw a figure searching the bodies of the other crewmen. We didn't know it was you."

Even Maria's careful touch to Sam's wound made him cringe. She gave him two wooden spools to grip and a leather strap to bite. "Hold on to these."

As brave a man as Sam was, he felt relieved when she finished wrapping his side with a long strip of linen. The storm had begun to subside as Julian checked outside again for the return of Davis, hopefully bringing help. Feeling better, Sam began to talk more in bits and pieces about why he turned away from the law and the reasons for his choices. "After we found there was no gold to salvage, Paulsgrave and I were desperate. We could not sail home with an empty ship."

He forced himself to stand and went to the window to look for any sign of Davis. He turned back to Maria. "When we decided to go 'on account', it seemed the only answer, and by God, we were good at it."

Maria poured him more cider.

"We first met Henry Jennings, who introduced us to the ways of pirating, and we were able to rob the salvage divers in their camps. It was easy, they were not fighters, and as long as they got paid for their time, they didn't care who got the treasure."

As Maria layered the rest of her clothes over her shift, she wondered who had taken her wet clothes off. "Sam, I trust that it was you who removed my wet clothes?"

He watched her tying the final skirt around her waist and grinned. "Maria, your beauty is for me alone to see." Desperate to hold her in his arms, he walked over to embrace her and whispered into her ear, "I missed you so, but now I'm back I will protect you." Suddenly his body tensed against hers as his pain returned.

She held him around the waist and walked him back to the chair. "Sit here and rest." She offered him a sip of one of Minda's special teas. "Just a little," she said, being very careful and ever mindful of the drug's potency. "Now tell me more."

"Come fall of that same year, we joined up with Captain Thornigold," Sam continued, "A good man, but stubborn when it came time to attack the British ships. He refused to do it. That riled most of the men; they felt those ships were missed opportunities." Sam held his hand against his side. "They made me their captain—we conquered over 100 ships. I had more than 150 men...."

Maria heard the sound of a wagon outside. Sam got up as Julian came in the door.

"Davis is coming, and he brought help," the Indian announced. "My Captain, you don't look well. Are you able?"

"I'll be ready when you need me," he told him.

"Then we must leave, before others get to the wreck." Julian hurried back outside.

Sam faced Maria. "Please stay here. Prepare some food for when we return. The horrors on the beach should not be for your gentle eyes to see."

He followed Julian out the door, pausing to look at his beloved. "I love you."

Maria handed him a blanket to keep warm. "Be safe."

Sam and Julian could see a horse and wagon approaching Maria's house.

*   *   *

"Up ahead a few yards. There...you can barely see the light," Davis pointed in the darkness.

As Harding, a willing accomplice, held onto the reins, he questioned the rescued sailor again, "You say there are two other men? Friendly, I pray?"

"Yes, yes, you can trust them," Davis replied. "We need all the help we can get. Time is of the essence."

"I agree. It will be dawn soon." Harding adjusted the pistol tucked inside his waistcoat. The old man recognized the McKeon house and knew of Maria. He had seen her about the property but never paid attention to her, keeping to himself also. "I know this place; a young girl lives here."

"Yes."

"I have heard rumors of her being a witch. You go and get your friends. I'll wait outside." Adjusting the lantern hanging from a pole on the wagon, he saw Maria standing in the doorway but kept his eye on Davis and his two new partners. Harding scanned the bluff and dunes for any movement or flashes of light as all climbed into the wagon. He greeted them with a nod of his head, and last names only were given.

With a snap of the reins the wagon rolled on into the dark. Harding knew which roads were the fastest, and within a short time, they arrived at the edge of the coast where they could see the remains of the *Whydah*. The sky had turned into the misty gray of dawn and exposed the sheer devastation to all who were alive to see. Mangled bodies and large pieces of the ship with rope and iron still attached were strewn along the wrack line. A few yards away, several chests were being pushed back and forth by the waves crashing onto the beach.

"Look!" Davis yelled, pointing to the floating chests.

Sam jumped down from the wagon and doubled over in pain; his impulsiveness had irritated his throbbing wound. After a few seconds, he regained his strength and ordered his men, "Hurry, lads, we must be quick."

With each chest that was loaded into the back of the wagon, Harding's excitement grew stronger for treasure. By the time they were finished, he was ready to burst with anticipation of what was inside. When all was ready, Davis and Julian looked for Sam. They saw him standing over the dark mass of what once was a man. He turned him over and recognized James Fergursen, the surgeon on board the *Whydah*. His clothes barely covered his body from the fury of the water and waves. Sam covered him with the blanket from his shoulders that Maria had given him for warmth. A few feet to the left lay young John King, whose arm was torn off as he tried to hold onto part of the rigging during the storm. Sam thought John should have listened to his mother and not chosen piracy.

"Sam! We must leave!" Julian called out from the back of the wagon.

Sam didn't listen and walked further down the beach. Finding more of his men, he slowly pushed over another body, that of Joseph Rivers, the oldest pirate he had ever known. His face was bloated and blue but this career pirate died doing what he loved.

He could see the *Whydah*, or what was left of her, floundering amidst the dark, frothy water. All is lost, he thought: my ship, my men and my fortune...did the past years of my life mean nothing?

"Sam! Now!" Davis yelled.

Feeling beaten and in pain, Sam turned and dragged his weary body through the thick, wet sand to the waiting wagon.

Harding pulled the reins back to turn the horse around to leave. He was pleased to be carrying whatever was in the chests to the privacy of his home.

47

Present Day – July 25
BREWSTER – CAPE COD

THE NEXT EVENING, my cell phone rang, and I recognized Paul's number right away. "Hi, honey. How did the exhibit go?"

"Pretty good. I sold four paintings. Not a sell-out but well worth the trip."

"That's wonderful news."

"I'm at the hotel waiting for the kids to come down to the car. I stayed at the gallery till 6 p.m. Now I'm going to take them back with me to load up the unsold paintings."

"Glad they were a help."

Paul's voice softened. "Hey, I really miss you."

"I miss you, too. Everything else okay?"

"Yeah, we're all fine."

"Paul, the guy from the *Whydah* Museum came into the gallery yesterday, a Mr. Kevin Kennedy. Things got a little strange. He really made me feel uncomfortable."

"How so?"

"Well, he wanted to see the cellar, so I showed him. As we were standing in the backyard, a car pulled in. I told him I had to take care of the customer, but before I left him, he asked to use the bathroom."

"Who used the bathroom?" Paul sounded distracted. "Jesus... Casey! Hold Molly's hand!"

"What's wrong?"

"Molly almost tripped down the stairway coming from the second floor. What did you say?"

Exasperated, I repeated again, "The guy from the museum, Kennedy, asked to use the bathroom when some customers came in."

"So...?"

"It was just weird."

"What happened that was so weird?"

"When the customers finally left, I went back to find Kennedy, but he wasn't by the cellar. I found him by the kitchen table looking at the three gold coins. I had them out this morning and forgot to put them away. When he finally handed the coins over, he quickly rushed to leave, saying something like he couldn't resist looking at them. The whole thing just made me uneasy."

"Okay. Just make sure the doors are locked tonight. Is Jim home?"

I could hear the kids bickering in the background as they got into the car. "No, not yet. He's working an extra shift at the restaurant."

Paul yelled out, "Casey, make sure your sister is buckled in."

"What did you say?" I asked.

"Just talking to the kids. I'll be home tomorrow morning, early. Don't worry."

"I'll be fine." I said. "You be careful driving. I love you. Give the kids a hug for me."

"Okay, I love you, too."

*   *   *

Jim came home from work and was showered and dressed so fast that I couldn't tell him my concerns about the stranger.

"Sorry, Mom, I gotta go," he said, buttoning his shirt, "or I'll be late." He went for the door to leave. "See you later. I guess you'll be sleeping when I come home?"

"I think so." I came closer to him for a quick hug. I must have looked a little worried.

He turned around to me and asked, "You alright?"

"Yes, I'm fine. I guess I miss your dad."

"Okay." He kissed me goodbye and ran out the door to his car.

I yelled after him, "Got your key?"
"Yup." He drove away in a hurry.

*   *   *

As the night fell across the Cape, I double-checked the doors of the house and settled in the front parlor to watch one of my favorite movies, 'Goonies'. It always made me laugh, and tonight I needed a distraction; something funny suited me. The couch was close to the television in the middle of the room. White lace curtains on the windows framed the dark night into black holes. Raindrops began hitting the skylight with loud splats.

I got up for a cup of tea and passed the laundry room, opposite the new kitchen, just as flashes of lightening sparked on the driveway side of the house. As the microwave heated the water, another flash of lightening lit up the sky. It was unsettling; I braced myself against the counter, anticipating a loud rumbling of thunder. I counted the seconds for the distance of the storm; by the time I reached ten its booming sound rattled the glass cabinet doors above my head. When it stopped, I turned to look on the other side of the house for another flash. Right on cue, it came and lit up the birdfeeder just beyond the side door. The image of the guy from the museum popped into my head. I shook it off. There's nothing to be afraid of, he's gone, and hopefully won't be back. When the microwave played its little tune to signal my tea was hot, I grabbed the steaming comfort and quickly returned to the safety of the front parlor and my movie.

48

April 27, 1717
EASTHAM – CAPE COD

THERE WERE ONLY A FEW OATS LEFT IN STORAGE; Maria didn't think she would be able to satisfy the hunger of Sam and his two shipmates with such meager rations. Instead, she took some dried corn that had been harvested in the fall from her small garden, ground it into meal and prepared flatbread in the traditional way of the Indians. She had less than a cup of maple syrup remaining with which to sweeten the plain bread. How she wished she could buy from the stores in the village. The winter had been long, and she had become so tired of her miserable life.

The thought of Sam, now home with her, gave her hope. If only she had taken the three gold coins out of the hidden compartment in the chest that held her tiny son. She realized that she had not been capable of normal thinking the day she'd buried her child. She had not been herself. Now the small pouch of Sam's money from Mr. Smith was all she had left—a pittance, but maybe it was enough. Pouring a scant amount of goat's milk into three cups, she understood that whatever was salvaged from the wreck, if anything, would probably still not be enough to allow them to leave. Maria sat at the table crying, waiting for the men to return.

* * *

The horse struggled with the heavy load of men and chests over the rutted cart-way. No one spoke the distance, each man hiding his thoughts of how the treasure should be divided. Harding stopped the horse.

Sam ordered, "We need to hide the chests for fear that someone might see them."

Davis and Julian jumped off the wagon and began to haul each chest into the small shack behind Maria's house. Sam put his hand on the last chest Davis was unloading. "Wait, this one is his," he said, pointing to Harding. Davis turned away.

"Aye. What might be inside?" Harding asked.

"I'm sure you'll be pleased." Sam opened it a few inches for him to see. "I trust that you'll be silent when questioned about this night's events?"

The look on Harding's face told Sam that there would be no problem. "What events?" A smile curled across his lips. He flicked the reins, which made the horse bolt, and Harding, along with the wagon and chest, disappeared over the dune.

As dawn lightened the sky, Sam, Julian and Davis entered the McKeon house, where they planned to stay until they felt it was safe to leave. Soon the men lay exhausted on the dirt floor, grateful for whatever nourishment Maria had provided for them.

While they slept, Maria's curiosity grew stronger as to what was in the chests that had been stored behind the house. Without a sound, she crept through the back door to discover what was inside them.

In the shack, she saw three chests of similar size, the fourth smaller than the rest. Kneeling down, she ran her hands over the sides and top of the lesser one. The latch was held with a nail that slid out when shimmied to one side. She opened it and leaned back. Her hand shot up to her mouth in wonder. "Oh Sam," she whispered. Pieces of beautiful blue flowered china protruded up from gold and silver coins. Long sections of colorful silk material were wrapped around larger pieces of the china, and as she dug deeper into the chest she found red rubies, sparkling diamonds and gold necklaces. Lost in the brilliance of the treasure, a voice startled her from behind.

"I see that you have found your gifts." Sam leaned on the doorway of the old shack.

She dropped the coins from her hand and closed its lid. "Sam, forgive me." She stood and backed towards the wall, fearful for the first time in Sam's presence. "My rudeness is inexcusable." She knew he had become a pirate, and as her back pressed against the wall, she whispered, "I should never have been so bold."

He came closer to her. "Maria, I love you. Don't fear me." He stroked her lips. "We are in this together. What you found is yours, my beloved."

Maria could feel herself relax. "Is it really for me?"

"Yes."

She knelt down again and opened the lid. Pulling out a teacup, she pretended to sip her tea. "Never before have I seen such treasure. I have no words." Her hands sifted through the coins. She looked over to Sam. His black hair was tied back and revealed his handsome face. How she loved him. Her heart filled with joy as she turned back to inspect more of her treasure.

She heard a thump behind her. Spinning around, she saw Sam had crumpled on the floor; fresh blood seeped through the linen.

"Sam!" she screamed and crawled over to him. "Please, don't leave me again!" She cradled him in her arms and lowered him down to the dirt floor then ran to the house.

"Help!" She screamed, waking the two men. "You must help me. Something's wrong with Sam."

When Davis and Julian entered the shack, they were surprised to see Sam lying in the dirt. Then they saw the open chest and could not believe their eyes. Staring at the gold and imagining their share, the two ignored Sam's plight.

Maria pleaded with them again, "Please take Sam into the house."

Julian looked at Davis, and both assumed that they each would do as she asked, for now.

Sam's shipmates laid him on the bed as Maria fetched another clean linen.

Sam grabbed Davis's arm. He was becoming weak with fever. "If I don't survive this night," squeezing his arm tighter, "promise me...."

"What say you?" Davis asked.

"Promise me that no harm will come to Maria."

"You have my word," he said, looking over to Julian who was standing near the edge of the bed.

Julian nodded, "Aye."

"Davis!" Sam whispered again.

"Aye."

"The small chest is Maria's, hers alone."

"You have our word."

"Listen to me: there are three chests, one for each of you, the third is mine. But if I die before the morrow," he rested his head back and breathed heavily, "my share belongs to Maria."

Davis looked at Julian.

Sam held onto Davis's arm one more time. "Do you swear to do this?"

Reluctantly, he answered, "We have an accord!"

Exhausted, Sam lay back and closed his eyes.

Maria pushed the two men aside and began cutting away the bloodied linen. As she attempted to dab the wound clean, the open skin that still held several splinters seeped with yellow puss.

She moved behind Davis and Julian to retrieve more drawing salve from the shelf. They sat at the table eating the last of the flatbreads. When she returned to Sam's side, she pulled him towards her body and removed the soiled linen from his back. Before securing the clean linen once again, she reapplied the drawing paste, hoping the slivers would come away from his infected skin.

Through half closed eyes, the sight of Maria's smile eased Sam's pain. She offered more of Minda's numbing herbal tea. Her soft words soothed him as she stroked his forehead. "Sleep now. Rest is what you need."

He closed his eyes, content in knowing that his responsibilities to her would be honored.

*   *   *

Davis wiped his mouth. "We need to hide the chests and ourselves."

"Aye."

He leaned into Julian. "They'll be searching for us."

Maria tended the hearth, listening to their words.

Davis whispered, "My plan is to leave tonight. I'll pay a visit to Harding and give him another chance at kindness."

Julian tugged on his gold earring, saying nothing. He was a man of few words and his plans were for him alone. He needed no one.

As dusk came, Davis was ready to take his leave and gather his share of the bounty.

Julian followed him into the shack. "It's not that I don't trust you, my friend, but I'm no fool."

Davis grinned and proceeded to inspect his chest.

Julian knelt next to him beside his own riches. They opened their chests together.

Davis's lips parted and stayed apart long enough for saliva to drip onto the mound of shiny gold pieces.

Julian said nothing, as usual, his long black hair falling on either side of his face, concealing his expression. Only his hands showed emotion as they sifted through the jewels, gold pieces and necklaces.

Davis swiveled around, opened Sam's chest and began to take some of its contents.

Julian stopped his hand. "Wait, we pledged to Sam. He ain't dead yet."

"No matter, we've earned it. Where would he be if it weren't for us?" Davis brushed Julian's arm away. "We'll leave him enough."

Julian let go and he too began to take of Sam's share.

Filling their chests to the rim from the third chest, they stuffed even more into their pockets. Davis commiserated as he finally closed it, securing the pin. "I know it ain't right that we're taking some of Sam's booty before he's dead, but he would understand. It's the pirate's way." He looked into Julian's eyes. "Don't you agree, partner?"

Julian's teeth contrasted with his dark skin as he grinned in agreement.

Thomas Davis took off to Harding's house, eventually convincing the old man to hide him and his treasure for payment in more gold.

Davis returned within the hour, along with a wagon to load his share. As he left, he saluted Julian. "Better days ahead, mate." His last look was to Maria sitting beside Sam. "May good fortune attend you and the captain, ma'am."

By the time the sky darkened into black night, Julian was nowhere to be seen, but he was heard. As Maria lay next to her sleeping Sam, she could hear him chopping and cutting. She wondered what he was doing but stayed with Sam, eventually drifting into a light sleep by his side.

Several hours passed before Julian came to Maria. He knelt close and touched her shoulder, trying to rouse her. "Maria," he whispered.

Half asleep, she woke with a start. "What's wrong? Have they come for you?"

"Shhhh. He still sleeps," he said, looking at Sam. "I take my leave of you now." He stood and walked away from her towards the shack.

Maria followed him, but kept a safe distance, interested in his doings.

From the shack's door, she watched him fasten his treasure chest to a short pole stretcher, cover it with a blanket and tie a shovel across the top. He saw Maria in the shadows and looked to her for approval concerning the taking of her tools. She nodded yes.

John Julian struggled to pull his treasure as he disappeared into the night. When the sky had turned to the dark gray of early dawn, Julian had finished burying his chest beneath the largest rock in Eastham. Wasting no time, he piled stones and rocks on top of the freshly dug dirt to hide what was buried. He smashed the rustic stretcher to further elude anyone from his nocturnal secret and heaved the shovel as far away as he could. He took only a small pouch of gold coins with him, leaving the rest buried. Now he needed to hide through the daylight hours and run through the night to safety.

* * *

Maria looked in on Sam and found him quiet. Returning to the shack, she spotted one large chest and hers, the smaller. Opening her chest, she was thankful that the pirates had not emptied it. All was safely secure. Relieved, she turned to the larger chest. Lifting the lid, she could see the yellow color of gold, but it was half empty. Her thoughts ran from disappointment to anger and then to acceptance in knowing that she and Sam would still be able to make a new life. Her treasure alone would be sufficient.

She closed both chests and used a covering of straw and wood from the woodpile to conceal her secret from any intruding eyes of the law, as they assuredly would be searching for survivors and seeking goods from the wreck. Hopefully, when Sam was better, they would leave Eastham forever.

*   *   *

Within two days of the *Whydah*'s demise, the news of the ship's fate spread across Cape Cod. Samuel Harding's brother, Abiah Harding, along with Edward Knowles and Jonathan Cole, were the first to salvage barrels of nails and liquor along with rope, pulleys and wood. Many God-fearing Cape Codders, along with the notorious mooncussers, who tricked ships into sailing closer to the dangerous rocks and shoals with lanterns on moonless nights, salvaged everything. The mangled bodies that had washed ashore did not bother some of these grizzled hardy scavengers as they cut off fingers and ears to retrieve jewelry from the doomed pirates. It was a gruesome business, but Cape Cod was poor, and its inhabitants felt that it was their right to reap whatever floated ashore, and looked upon it as a gift from God.

*   *   *

As Sam drifted in and out of a healing sleep, Maria tended to him and watched for any person coming to search or ask questions. At the same time she began to think of what she could carry with her when they finally were able to leave. Wasting no time, she prepared her mother's travel bag and began to gather her prized things: the painted box that held vellum and inks; the looking glass from her mother; Minda's herbs, salves and the few coins from Sam. The rest would be purchased new.

"Maria," Sam murmured.

"Yes, my darling." Maria sat next to him on the bed.

"What day is it?"

"It is the fifth day since I found you."

"Where are my men?"

"They've gone."

"Did they take anything with them?"

"I'm afraid so." Maria lowered her head.

Sam struggled to sit up. Feeling lightheaded, he pleaded with Maria. "I need to see."

Steadying himself, he walked to the shack to see no sign of the chests. He leaned back against the wall, hung his head in despair and beat his fists against the wood.

Maria hurried to pull back the straw. "Wait, Sam. Look!" She revealed the two remaining chests.

He fell to his knees. The first one he opened proved empty save a small layer at the bottom. "Those bastards, they took more than their fair share."

"What about yours?" He looked up at Maria.

"They took none of mine."

Relieved, he slumped down against the rough wall to the dirt floor. With his elbows on his knees, he held his head. "Maria, I'm sorry for not having more for you."

She knelt in front of him. "Stop, Sam. We have enough, more than enough for us to leave. Do you not understand that we could start again? Go someplace far away from here, far away from the hatred of this god-forsaken land."

He looked at his beloved Maria. "You're right, but we must leave soon. But how?"

With confidence, Maria spoke, "I know someone who can help us, and he can be trusted."

49

May 1, 1717
EASTHAM – CAPE COD

"IT HAS BEEN A PLEASURE DOING BUSINESS WITH YOU,
Mr. Ellis," James Carter said as he shook hands with Matthew.

"The same." Matthew shut the door to the house that he was
born in.

He wanted to forget every minute of the last year. He sat at the
table that had been the focal point for many family meals with his
parents. He knew he should eat something but wasn't hungry. His
father's place at the head of the table was empty; pneumonia had
wreaked its havoc on the poor man's aging body and taken him
early. Poor Mother had followed him in a short time. Matthew wondered
if his mother had just tired, or was her love for her husband so strong
that she lost her will to live? It was hard for him to understand the
sudden loss of his parents.

He despised himself for selling the family property to the Carters of
Rhode Island. He banged his fist on the planks of the sideboard. The
deal was done. There was nothing left for him in Eastham...except
Maria. He stood to fill his cup with ale and realized that now might
be his chance to speak of his feelings for her. She had always seemed
so unattainable to him before. Maybe selling his homestead was a
stroke of luck. With its profit, they would be able to go far away from
any trouble.

Matthew remembered Peter Johnson, a printer and bookbinder
in Barnstable, with whom he had struck a friendship during one of

his journeys at sea. At that time Johnson told Matthew he was looking for an apprentice. Matthew reached for pen and paper from his father's desk. He dipped his pen into the inkwell and began to write a letter, which would craft a new chapter in his life.

Dear Mr. Johnson,

My letter is in regard to your seeking an apprentice in the business of printing. I am eager to answer your request and will be happy to meet with you about our future together. I await your reply as to the date of our meet…

A knock on the door startled him, interrupting his written words. He grabbed his gun, ready to face whomever it was. The knock grew louder. With his ear close to the door, he asked, "Who goes there?"

"It's Maria." The voice was familiar. It repeated, "Maria Hallett."

He opened the door a crack to see if it really was her.

"Matthew, may I come in?"

He stood the gun next to the doorframe and opened the door. "Maria, what brings you here? It's not safe for you to be out."

"I've come to ask a favor. I know I shouldn't be here, but it's important."

Matthew looked out into the dark and side-to-side to see if anyone had seen Maria before he closed the door. She stood by the hearth and loosened the shawl that was wrapped around her shoulders. Matthew could not take his eyes off of her. She was more beautiful than the last time he had seen her. She wore no cap and her brown hair fell around her head and shoulders in large waves and ringlets. Her eyes were bright and her lips looked so soft. He wanted to hold her, to kiss her.

"Matthew, I need to talk with you."

"Of course, Maria, please sit."

He grabbed the letter, folded it in half and hid it in a drawer of the desk.

Maria paid no attention. She was only concerned about what she would say to her friend. She knew he would ask for an explanation as to why she needed help, so she was ready. Her words were difficult for her, but in the end, she told her friend of Sam's return and confessed that he was the man who had left her when she was with child.

As Matthew listened, he clenched his fists under the table and struggled to hold his composure. "What is it that you want me to do?' he asked her. "Now that you have your Sam, what do you need me for?"

"There is treasure!" she whispered.

Matthew looked unfazed by the revelation. "Treasure means nothing to me." In his heart he wanted her and only her. He wanted her to stay with him. He held back his words of passion. "Tell me more," he said.

"We need to travel but Sam is hurt. The salvaged treasure is too heavy to take by foot. We need you and your wagon."

Matthew stayed silent and in these few awkward seconds, Maria noticed the absence of anyone else in the house. Looking around the empty kitchen she asked, "Where are your parents, Matthew?"

"Gone, this past winter." He stood and turned away from her, leaning his arm on the hearth's mantle. "Father took sick and died. Soon after, Mother followed him."

"I'm sorry," she moved next to him and reached for his hand. She held it against her cheek.

As he looked at her, her gentle touch moved him more deeply than ever before. He knew he would do anything for Maria. He loved her with his whole being.

"I'll help you. What do you want me to do?"

50

May 1, 1717
EASTHAM – CAPE COD

MARIA RAN THROUGH THE NIGHT TO HER HOUSE, eager to tell Sam the good news of Matthew's willingness to help them. She was too happy to notice the cold chill of early spring that blew across her face. It was the beginning of a new life with Sam; nothing could stop them now.

She found Sam in the shack making sure the chests were secure for traveling. He had emptied most of her treasure into the larger one. She was pleased to see more color on his face and his bandages showed no new blood.

He sat on the floor making a small pile of coins. "Do you have a pouch for safekeeping?"

"Yes I do," she answered and stepped closer to him.

"What news do you have for our transportation?"

"My friend Matthew Ellis said he would take us to Abigail's, in North Harwich."

"Who is Abigail?" Sam glanced up at her. "Can this woman and Matthew be trusted?"

"Yes, you have my word. We journey tomorrow night."

Maria knelt down next to him and pulled his face to her lips. "My heart is bursting with joy because of you."

Sam grabbed her around the waist and pulled her nearer to him. "I want you...now."

He kissed her and cradled her across his lap. She looked up into his eyes, waiting and hoping that he would touch her. She could barely contain her desires for him. He held her tighter. His kisses escalated from soft and gentle to wild passion. Maria responded with the same intensity.

Suddenly he broke away from her, his heavy breathing pushing his words out in a staccato. "Maria, I have dreamt of this night …for so many days. Indulge me ….so I may enjoy every inch of you."

She smiled in submission as he laid her down on the bed of straw. He loosened the laces of her corset and then followed the lines of her torso with hungry eyes. She was radiant. He could not believe that she was finally his. As he kissed her exposed breasts, he watched her chest rise and fall in deep breaths that increased their depth each time he touched her. His fingers moved slowly across and into her body.

She lay quiet in full sensual arousal as he enjoyed the pleasures of her delicate skin. She wanted more. She grabbed at him. Soon neither of them could control themselves as their sexual desires overpowered them. He entered her, and they became one in body, mind and heart. They both had waited for this moment for so long.

Exhausted, Maria finally spoke, "My darling Sam, it's getting late. I should clean your wound once more before we sleep." Refastening the binding on her corset she smiled, "You perform as if you had no wound."

Sam sat up and took hold of her hand. "We'll have many nights and even days like this, you'll see. I'll make you happy. This I promise," he said, kissing her on the neck.

It tickled Maria and made her laugh. "Come, Sam, we must prepare for our journey." She affectionately pushed his hand away and stood up.

Taking hold of her wrist, he stopped her. "Maria?"

He took a gold chain from his pocket with the ring attached to it. Maria remembered seeing it the night of the *Whydah's* demise. As Sam slipped the ring off of the chain and onto her finger, he knelt before her. "Maria, will you be my wife? I promise to take care of you and love you with all my heart."

With tears in her eyes, she knelt opposite him and whispered into his ear, "Yes!"

It was the only word he wanted to hear. They embraced once more, and she accepted Sam into her life again. Pledging their love to each other, they became husband and wife, blessed only by their will to be together.

That night before sleep came to them, Maria was relieved to discover that the last of the splinters had fallen away from Sam's side. Wrapping his wound with clean linen, she bound it and placed a kiss on the bandage that lay over his heart.

May 2, 1717

The next morning, Maria made flatbreads for their journey. While she gathered her belongings, Sam walked around and through the house, examining its contents. He wanted to see and touch everything connected to his Maria. He admired her weaving and spinning and ran his hands over her woven cloths. Maria was a capable woman: strong, kind, and well skilled in the way of herbs and healing. He asked himself, what more could a man want?

"Sam," Maria called to him. "We must hurry. It's almost dusk, and Matthew will be coming soon."

Sam thought about Matthew, this so-called friend of Maria's. He was very curious to meet him.

* * *

Matthew had just finished his dinner and was getting ready to hitch his horse to the wagon when he heard someone approaching on horseback. A shot of adrenalin raced through his body when he looked outside and saw Constable Ezra. He must not find out about his plans to help Maria.

"Matthew, Matthew Ellis! You in there?"

Matthew opened his door and answered, "Aye, Constable. What brings you out here?"

Dismounting his horse, Ezra said, "Looking for pirates. Have you seen any?"

"Pirates, you say?"

"Yeah, pirates, from the wreck on the coastline a few days back. We're searching everywhere and everyone's house."

Matthew kept calm. "No, I haven't seen any strangers, except Mr. Carter, the man who bought my land."

"Oh yes, Mr. Carter. I heard you sold. I'm going to miss you around here."

Eager to tell what news he had, the constable leaned close to Matthew. "I've heard that as many as fifty-four bodies and five Negroes washed ashore on the first morning after the wreck." He waited for Matthew to react to his interesting news, then continued, "and twenty-two more on the second day. Mark my words: there'll be more of them."

He got no response from the brooding Matthew, who wished the man would leave. Ezra turned and grabbed the reins to his horse, ready to mount. "I'll take my leave now. If you see any pirates, let me know. Boston is hungry for some hangin's."

As Ezra climbed back onto his horse he asked, "Matthew, would you favor me with a look-see by the Hallett girl?"

"Of course."

"Thank you, son. That'll help me; I'm on my way to look in on old Samuel Harding."

As he turned his horse away from Matthew, he glanced back. "Mind you be careful. They found an Indian pirate who'd survived the wreck hiding behind the Widow Baker's house. They say he had some gold coins on him. Thank the Lord that the widow is gone till next week. As we speak, that pirate is on his way to the Barnstable jail."

"Safe ride home, Ezra," Matthew waved him away and retreated into his house till the Constable was out of sight.

* * *

Maria had nestled her new china in the near empty smaller chest among the softest of the cloths, along with her painted trinket box and a pouch filled with the gold coins that Sam had set aside. Her mother's bag contained her clothes and as many threads that she could fit.

Disappointed that she would have to leave many of her belongings behind, including her spinner, she was optimistic that she would be able to replace them with her new-found fortune. Sam, who still wore his clothes from the night of the wreck, had virtually nothing to take but the chest of gold. Maria was pleased that Matthew had offered to find a home for the goat.

The sound of a wagon made Maria and Sam stop what they were doing and listen. She looked out the tiny window. It was dark, but she recognized Matthew in the light of the half moon.

Turning around she whispered, "It's Matthew!"

Sam retreated to where Maria's old gun leaned in the corner.

There was a faint knock on the door. As Maria opened it, she smiled and put her arms around her friend. "Matthew, thank you for coming."

Embarrassed at her show of affection, he took off his hat and greeted her simply with, "Maria."

Sam remained in the shadows, taking a long look at the other man in Maria's life. He saw that he was young and handsome, and Sam decided that there was a good possibility that Matthew was more than a friend to Maria—at least in Matthew's mind.

"Matthew, this is Sam, Sam Bellamy."

Coming forward, Sam released his hold on the gun and extended his hand.

Matthew held back and greeted Sam only with a question, "I hope you are well enough to travel?"

"That I am."

"I have filled the back of the wagon with hay and straw. You'll have to stay low as we travel through the villages.

Maria added, "I have a blanket to cover us. I think it'll do."

The three stood in awkward silence, each looking at the other.

Matthew spoke next, "We best be going. We have a long journey ahead of us."

Sam asked, "If you could be of assistance to me, we have a few heavy chests to load."

He followed Sam to the shack.

Removing the chest's cover of straw and logs, Sam asked Matthew, "How long have you known Maria?"

"Since childhood."

Matthew returned the same question to Sam. "How long have *you* known her?"

"Long enough to know she loves me." He stared at Matthew as he threw a log over to the side.

Matthew threw his log crashing against the wall. He was angry. "Then how could you have left her when she needed you the most?"

Sam stood as straight as he could and grabbed Matthew by the arm. "Do you have a concern about Maria and me?"

Matthew pulled his arm away from Sam's hold and grasped the top of Sam's shirt, bringing him face to face. "No, I do not, sir, but if you ever hurt her, I will hunt you down and...."

Sam shot his hands up between Matthew's forearms and pressed his arm across Mathew's neck, pushing him against the old wall of the shack. "Do not threaten me. Maybe you haven't heard of my reputation, or perhaps you're just ignorant?"

Matthew locked his eyes on Sam as he gasped for air. "I'm not fearful of you. Lest you forget, I'm here for Maria's sake, not yours."

Sam released his pressure on Matthew's throat and stepped back from him. "Forgive me. It seems you also care for Maria very much."

Matthew straightened his jacket and massaged his throat. "I pray you have a plan. They're looking for survivors to take to Boston for trial. I can get you safely to Abigail's, but after that you'll be on your own."

51

Morning May 3, 1717
NORTH HARWICH – CAPE COD

ABIGAIL LANGUISHED IN HER BED. Nathanial had left for sea without a goodbye this time. She mulled over their relationship, now strained as husband and wife. Her involvement with Maria Hallett and the tragedy that befell the young girl seemed to mark the beginning of strife in her life.

Adding to her suffering, Abigail was experiencing stronger heart palpitations daily, and she sensed that her body was under attack from all of the resulting stress. It frightened her. Everything seemed in disarray within her otherwise peaceful existence.

Always an early riser, today she struggled to get out of bed. As the sun ascended higher in the late morning sky, Abigail dressed and opened her bedroom door. She noticed a large barrel by the sideboard. "My stars, what is that doing in my house?"

She walked closer and bent down to examine the wooden barrel that intruded on her lovely sitting room. It had a white skull and crossbones on its side. "Gunpowder! For Lord's sake." What was Nathanial thinking? "I won't stand for this," she muttered.

A recent terse scolding from Nathanial flew through her thoughts. He'd been angry about her buying supplies for Maria last winter. She jabbed at the fire in the hearth with gusto, "Heavens almighty!" Under her breath, she mumbled, "Those items were a gift and bought with funds from my own account."

Nathanial had issued commands and rules to her over the past several weeks, and she thought it so unusual for him to behave this way. Abigail recalled him sitting by the table a few days before he left. He'd spoken in such a patronizing tone: "You should not spend so much money buying things for this house; you have enough! It's for your own good!"

How this reprimand irritated her. She became outraged, and her emotions energized her to want to right the wrongs that surrounded her. She stood by the hearth, straightened her corset and dropped the poker with a clank. A discussion would be entered into with Nathanial over his dislike and low regard for her and her friends. Something would have to be done. But first things first; she went out to find Jacob so he could remove the ugly wooden barrel from her house.

* * *

Matthew guided the horse onto Abigail and Nathanial's pathway. Maria and Sam lay hidden under the blankets in the back of the wagon.

After only a few steps to the barn, Abigail heard someone call out from a distance. She turned and spotted the wagon.

"Greetings!" called Matthew.

Abigail waved and yelled out, recognizing Matthew. "Good morrow!" A broad smile swept across her face. "How is it that I have the pleasure of a visit from you today?"

"You will see," he said as he stopped the wagon on the side of the house. "Are you alone, Abigail?"

"I think so. Jacob might be in the barn."

"I'll go see for you," Matthew said, climbing out of the wagon.

Abigail stood near the horse. She heard a small voice whisper behind her. "Abigail." Turning and seeing no one, she rubbed her ear as if to clear it of a clump of wax.

"Abigail," the tiny voice called again.

This time she heard it but didn't know where it was coming from. "Who's calling my name? Show yourself!"

Maria lifted a section of her cover and whispered, "It's me, Maria Hallett."

Frustrated Abigail asked again, "My eyes and ears deceive me. Show me."

At the same moment, Matthew came from the barn. There was no sign of Jacob. He threw the covers away to reveal the two stowaways.

Surprised at seeing Maria and aghast at the sight of the beggar with her—or possibly he was a criminal—Abigail felt her heart speed up. She managed to say only a few words as she held onto the side of the wagon. "Please come quickly into the house."

She turned, picked up her skirts and hurried inside, followed by the three unexpected visitors.

Abigail sat down to dab perspiration from her forehead with a linen kerchief while Sam, Maria, and Matthew paraded in front of her to their seats. Abigail was wary of the stranger Maria called Sam. She remembered his name and knew he was the beginning of Maria's troubles.

Maria told her story, explaining what had happened over the last several days and the reasons why they'd come to North Harwich. It seemed to satisfy Abigail's curiosity but didn't change her disapproval. Sam and Matthew sat as if they were young boys in trouble with their mother. Abigail's presence commanded respect, and Sam knew that she represented their only hope for safety.

With her hands folded in front of her, Abigail looked directly at Maria. "What do you want from me?"

"A night to stay. That's all I ask." She reached for Abigail's hand across the table.

With hesitation in her voice Abigail finally said, "You may have that, but then you must leave." She squeezed Maria's hand to show that she still felt a kinship with her.

Each one sat involved in their thoughts.

The room was quiet as Maria bowed her head in thankfulness for her friend's kindness.

Abigail felt a slight hint of remorse at not helping more, but she could not add any more stressful events to her life. She'd had enough.

Sam didn't know this elder woman friend of Maria's and did his best to keep to himself, refraining from his usual commanding posturing.

Matthew listened, hoping deep inside that Sam's identity as a pirate would some how be revealed, and then he'd be taken away. In his mind Maria deserved better.

Their host rose from the bench in the kitchen. "Maria, come with me. Let's find some clothes for Sam from Nathanial's things."

"Of course." Maria placed her hand on Sam's shoulder, reassuring him that everything would be fine; then she followed Abigail, leaving the two men alone.

Sam, wanting to keep a watchful eye on his chest of gold in the wagon, left the kitchen while Matthew stayed behind to drink his cider.

Once outside, Sam could see the Doane homestead was situated in an unpopulated part of the North Parish of Harwich. He could stand on the rise of Abigail's property and look out upon the Namaskaket River all the way to the bay. It was filled with grasses, marsh, natural springs and a few pockets of standing timber. He thought of the years that he was 'on account' as a pirate. They were not to be dismissed lightly. He had looted, maimed and even killed to insure his freedom from the tyranny of the rich and powerful. Uncertain if he would be able to safely carry his treasure with him on their journey, he decided that it was too important to be left to chance. A large boulder caught his eye not more than 200 feet from Abigail's house. Checking his distance and surveying where it lay in regards to his position, he thought that it would serve his purpose.

* * *

Abigail was not angry as Maria selected respectful clothes for Sam to travel in, hopefully unnoticed, but she could sense tension between her and her friend. "You look well, my dear. It seems that your dreams are coming true." Abigail straightened the clothes on the bed.

"Yes, almost. We have far to go, and we're not safe yet, but I know Sam will take care of everything."

"You are so trusting. I hope you're correct." Abigail smoothed the green curtains that surrounded her bed. "How does Matthew feel about all of this?"

"Oh, he's been very kind, helping us with the use of his wagon."

"Yes, I know, but how does he feel about you and Sam?"

"What do you mean?"

"Oh my dear, never mind." She sighed and stroked Maria's back with her hand. "It doesn't matter; I love you so much." Abigail sat on the edge of the bed and began to tear. She dabbed her moist eyes. "I have always loved you as if you were my daughter. I'm worried about you, and now Sam, too."

Maria sat next to her. "This is our chance to be together." She held Abigail's hand. "You were there when I needed a mother, and I'm so grateful for everything you've done for me. I love you, also." Maria paused. "I want to tell you something."

"What is it, my dear?" Abigail hoped Maria would finally tell her where she had buried her child.

"It's so hard to say these terrible words."

"Take your time. I'm listening."

As Maria began to speak, Matthew called from outside the door, "Abigail, someone is coming. Quick, we must hide them."

Abigail rushed to the kitchen and threw aside the rug that hid the trapdoor to the root cellar. "Down there, you'll be safe. Now hurry."

Maria turned pale. She stared as Sam lifted the door and began to make his descent down the stone steps that led into the darkness.

He turned. "What's wrong, Maria? Hurry!" He reached out for her hand.

Matthew pushed her towards the opening while Abigail gave Sam a small glass covered candle for light.

The trapdoor shut above them and rained down particles of sand onto their heads and shoulders. Sam and Maria sat quietly on the dimly lit steps as they waited for whomever it was to go away.

"That was close," Sam whispered. "Don't be afraid. I'm with you now." He wrapped his arm around her shoulders as they huddled close together in the flickering light.

Maria moved her eyes back and forth, circling them from one side of the cellar to the other. She inhaled the dampness of the dirt floor. A few dark reddish-brown spots of dried blood on the stone step beneath her feet reminded her of that horrible night. She moved her foot to cover the image and closed her eyes.

"Sam."

"Yes, my beloved?"

She looked at him. "I must tell you something." Her desire to reveal her dreaded secret to someone was surfacing. "When our child died," — she held her fingers to her trembling mouth — "I buried him."

"Where, Maria?"

She extended a shaking finger toward the corner of the cellar. Sam looked in the corner and then turned back to Maria, then back again to the corner. Her secret was finally being released as he began to understand what she was showing him.

Maria knelt down on the dirt floor. She removed the empty apple basket from the corner and pushed several inches of dirt aside to reveal the edge of a wooden chest. Tears welled into her eyes as she buried her head into Sam's lap.

"I'm sorry, Sam. May God forgive me."

"Shhhh, you must be still," he said. "Hold tight to me until the sorrow passes from you."

When Sam could feel her composure return, he got up and replaced the dirt upon the wooden chest that held his son. He turned and whispered to her, "You did nothing wrong." He cradled her face in his hands. "You are young, and we are healthy. We'll have another child. I know this; I can feel it."

They held each other in the silence, hoping their confinement would be over soon.

52

Afternoon May 3, 1717
NORTH HARWICH – CAPE COD

IT WAS NOT LONG before the darkness surrounding Maria and Sam was replaced with slivers of daylight as Matthew opened the trapdoor. "Come up. It's safe. Someone only passed by the house."

Sam let Maria go ahead of him. He held her from behind for fear that she might fall backward. Abigail stopped stirring the meat stew that was warming on the hearth and noticed his concern for her. It pleased her.

Few words were spoken as they ate. Midway through the meal Sam looked over to Abigail. "I would like to thank you for your kindness. I know it is dangerous for you if we were to be discovered in your house. We'll be gone in the morning," he reassured her.

Sam placed his hand over Maria's and spoke on her behalf. "We are eternally grateful."

"You're welcome. I pray that you both will be safe." Abigail smiled at them from across the table. The clatter of spoons upon plates and the chewing of food filled the kitchen. As Abigail took a drink from her cider, she felt warmer than usual and dropped her spoon. Her hand flew against her heart, patting her chest. Everyone stared at her as she tried to catch her breath.

"Abigail!" Maria cried out.

"It's all right, Maria…I'll be fine…give me a minute for my heart to slow." She waved her kerchief at Maria to sit back down. "I think it best I retire for the night, if you'll excuse me. I fear that I may have had too much excitement." She pushed herself away from the table. "Maria, I know you're familiar with my kitchen. Would you be kind enough to take care of things?"

"Yes, of course." Maria felt anxious about her friend's well-being.

Abigail steadied herself by holding onto the walls as she walked.

"Let me help you." Maria rose to hold her around the waist and guide her into the bedroom.

"Now don't fret over me. This will pass as the other ones have." Abigail shooed her away. "Go and take what you need for your journey. Make yourself ready."

Maria stayed with her and as they passed through the sitting room, Abigail remembered the barrel of gunpowder. She stopped and pointed to it. "Maria, would you please have Matthew remove that unsightly barrel of Nathanial's?"

"I will," she said, helping Abigail onto her bed.

Abigail turned to say goodnight. "I will see you in the morrow." She unlaced her corset and immediately felt relief.

Maria returned to Sam and Matthew in the kitchen. They had finished eating their food and both were sipping cider.

"How is she?" Matthew asked as Maria began to scrape the plates.

"I think she could be better. When you arrive in Eastham, Matthew, will you tell Minda of Abigail's health?"

"Yes, I'll see to it right away."

"Thank you. You are such a good friend." She placed her hand on his shoulder.

Sam watched Maria interact with Matthew. He felt jealous and stood up so fast he knocked his chair onto the sandy floor. He left the kitchen without a word.

Maria looked over to Matthew. "Pay no mind to him. He's allowed to be out of sorts, he's been through a lot."

Having the same envious thoughts, Matthew thought it best to leave also. "I will check on my horse and wagon." He grabbed his hat and nodded goodbye.

Once alone, Maria avoided stepping near the rug covering the cellar's trapdoor as she finished her work in the kitchen. She enjoyed seeing all the nice things that Abigail had and marveled at the bountiful supplies stored in the pantry. The thought of having the same items in a new home with Sam made her smile.

She looked out the window but could hardly see through the dark night into which Sam had stormed. She checked on Abigail and found the green curtains had been pulled around the bed, which signaled that her friend was probably asleep.

After closing the door, Maria spied the gunpowder keg and decided to take it outside herself. Since it proved too heavy to lift, she pulled it across the floor, leaving a trail of black powder that leaked under the floorboards and blended with the floor's dirt. She stopped once to tie her shawl around her shoulders then continued to struggle with the heavy keg. At the door, she was finally able to push it outside. Now she would search for Sam.

*   *   *

Matthew was brushing his horse in the barn as Maria entered. "Matthew, where's Sam?"

"I'm not his keeper, and I don't ask questions of him."

"Don't be so short with me. We're still friends, are we not?" she asked sweetly.

"I'm sorry, Maria, but I'm worried about you."

"Oh, Matthew, I'll be fine. Sam loves me and I him." She stroked the horse's back and wondered out loud for the benefit of Matthew's ears. "Still, I'm a little frightened about where we'll be going and how we'll get there. But I do trust him."

Matthew caught her hand as she moved it across the brown softness of the horse. "Maria, I love you." He said the words so quick that they surprised even him.

Maria withdrew her hand and looked at him, frozen in surprise.

He dropped the grooming brush on the floor and reached for her hand again. "I love you, Maria. I always have. I knew it from the very beginning, but was too shy to do anything about it."

"Matthew, I don't know what to say to you."

He held her hand tighter. "Tell me that you love me. Say you'll leave Sam and will stay with me."

Maria pulled her hand from his grasp and backed away from Matthew. Her feelings for Sam and Matthew began to muddle her thoughts.

He walked around the horse toward her.

She caught her breath as she watched him come nearer.

He placed his arms around her waist and brought his face close to hers. "Please, Maria, stay with me." He held her chin and pulled her lips to his.

His kiss triggered a flicker of passion through Maria's body. She stood still, questioning who she was really in love with.

Matthew pleaded with her, "I have money. We can go away from here and start a new life. Please give me a chance; give us a chance for happiness." He pulled her even closer.

Maria's arms hung at her sides, not responding to his advances, until he whispered again, "I love you."

Then he kissed her with such passion that Maria thought she would faint.

She wrapped her arms up around his shoulders. "Hold me, Matthew. My heart is so troubled."

As they stood together, the sound of a shovel slicing into the ground behind them broke the two apart. Turning, they saw Sam standing in the door of the barn. His face and clothes were smudged with dirt.

He charged at them. Sam first pulled Maria away from Matthew and off to the side, where she lost her balance and fell against a pile of straw. With another quick movement his fist hit hard against Matthew's jaw, sending him to the ground.

Stunned, but only for a moment, Matthew stood up and rivaled Sam's hit with as much strength, knocking him to the floor. "Get up, you freebooter. Get up!"

Sam stayed low. As he wiped blood from his mouth, his other hand found the wooden handle of a pitchfork buried in the hay.

Matthew, braver than ever before, stepped closer to Sam and taunted him, "Get up, you coward. We'll see who wins Maria."

Sam quickly grabbed the end of the tool under his fingers and swung it against Matthew's leg with a crack, knocking him down.

This time Matthew couldn't stand, the lower part of his calf felt as if its bone was broken.

Sam took his advantage; he leaned over and pulled Matthew up, then hit him again.

Maria screamed, "Sam, stop it!"

But Sam repeatedly whaled his fists against Matthew's face and head until blood covered every part of his exposed skin.

Maria ran to them, screaming, "Stop! Stop!" She pulled on Sam's shoulders. "It's enough! You'll kill him!" He shoved her away again, and she fell back against a post. Crying, she screamed, "I'm sorry, Sam. I'll never leave you. I love no one else but you. Don't hurt him anymore!"

Hearing these words, Sam ceased his brutal attack. Without a word, he wiped his bloodied hands on his pants, reached for Maria, and dragged her out of the barn and into the house.

Matthew lay unconscious on the floor.

*   *   *

Sam slammed the door of the house behind them. They stood in front of the open hearth. Maria was numb with shock and unsure of this side of Sam that she'd never seen before.

"Go to bed!" he ordered her, forcing her towards the stairway.

Maria's shawl fell away from her shoulders. Unnoticed, its tassels spread over hot embers that lay close to the hearth's edge.

53

Evening May 3, 1717
NORTH HARWICH – CAPE COD

MARIA LAY STILL IN BED as Sam climbed in next to her. "Sam, I'm sorry. It won't happen again."

"Best it not."

"Where were you tonight after our meal?"

"I'm tired and need sleep," was all he said.

But sleep proved difficult for Maria. Her mind kept going over the past events as she tried to understand why everything went so wrong. She wanted to erase the bloody images of Sam's violent temper and squeezed her eyes tight together. Why had Sam been covered with dirt when he'd stood in the doorway of the barn, she wondered. Where had he been?

Maria turned on her side, facing away from Sam, and thought of poor Matthew. His words 'I love you' had surprised her. She recalled Abigail's conversation with her in the bedroom and remembered her question about Matthew and how he felt about her and Sam being together. How foolish she'd been. Maria berated herself at being so ignorant of Matthew's love, when, all around her, even Sam, could see it.

Rolling over on her back, she could hear Sam's heavy breathing. She decided to check on Matthew.

Unable to find her shawl, she took a blanket from the chest at the foot of the bed. The light of the moon lit her way down the stairs and into the kitchen where smoke drifted in the foggy moonlight, nothing unusual for Maria's eyes. Smoke always blew down the chimney when it was windy. Her steps took her across the floor and over the darkened unseen shawl; she closed the door behind her without a sound.

Matthew lay sprawled on the hay where she saw him last, his handsome face cut and mottled with dried blood. She tore the bottom edge from her inner skirt and found a pail of water to clean him.

Maria's first touch to his forehead woke him with a painful start as the cool water dripped down his cheek. He tried to sit up.

"Stay down, Matthew. Let me help you."

He looked into her eyes. It hurt to move his head. He held still while she dabbed his face, being cautious not to move his leg for fear that it was broken. "You should not be with me. It's too dangerous," he whispered.

"Shhhh." Maria continued patting his face.

Matthew held Maria's hand against his cheek and was comforted by her soothing touch. Behind them, through the openings of the boards on the barn walls, flashes of yellow and orange flickered outside.

*   *   *

As Sam turned over to lay the hand bruised from his rage under his pillow, the pain woke him. He smelled smoke. Opening his eyes, he could feel the heat around him. His body was wet from perspiration. Turning around, he saw Maria was gone. "Maria!"

He bolted down the stairs to discover a fire that had already engulfed the whole kitchen. Maria was nowhere to be found, and Sam assumed her to be safe. His next thought was of Abigail. He ran to her bedroom, threw open the door and pushed the green curtains surrounding her aside. "Abigail!" He shook her. "Abigail! Get up!"

Flames quickly spread across the ceiling of the bedroom from the kitchen. As he continued to shake her, the canopy over Abigail's bed caught fire. Smoke filled Sam's lungs. He shoved his arms under Abigail's back, trying to lift her, but she was a dead weight. "Abigail, please! Get up!"

Sam quickly realized it was too late for Abigail but not for him. He needed to find Maria. He spun around just as he heard a loud crack above his head. The main roof rafter had split away from the ceiling, and within seconds the massive timber fell, breaking Sam's back and rendering him unconscious. As flames enveloped everything, Abigail's peaceful green curtains that she'd loved so dearly swallowed her and Sam in fiery death.

* * *

Smoke drifted under the barn walls. Matthew saw it first. "Maria! Fire!"

She turned to see the yellow flames through the cracks. "Oh no…Sam! Abigail!" She ran out the barn door to see the raging fire.

Matthew struggled to stand. He grabbed the pitchfork for support and hobbled out behind her.

Maria ran to the well and grabbed a pail of water. She threw it through the door of the burning house. As she turned to fetch another, Matthew held her back.

With all his strength he held onto her, hoping to prevent her from going any closer in her futile attempt to douse the fire. As they backed away, together, Maria broke from his hold and tried to enter the house again.

"Maria! Stop! It's no use. You can't do anything for them now." His body shook, fearing the worst for Abigail and even Sam. As much as he hated Sam, Matthew felt no human being deserved to die like this. He grabbed Maria's arm and pulled her as far away from the intense heat of the fire as he could.

They huddled together against the barn, staring at the flames that leaped high into the dark sky. The barrel of gunpowder beside the door caught fire and with one final blast destroyed everything, leaving no trace of Abigail, Sam or the house that Nathanial had built. The explosion tossed burning pieces of wood on top of the barn's roof, which began to smolder a few feet above their heads.

Matthew pulled himself up. "Hurry Maria, we must leave, NOW!" He limped into the barn. "Help me hitch the horse to the wagon."

She sat unmoving. Her face blackened by soot, Maria stared through smoke filled eyes at the inferno before her. A deep, blood curdling wail escaped her lips as she realized everyone and everything she had ever loved was now gone. She had no desire to live without them.

"MARIA!" Matthew yelled, his mouth stiff and aching from his beating. He didn't think he could go on. The pain in his shin doubled him over with every step, but he continued his quest. He wanted to save her; he needed to save her.

Matthew struggled to ready the wagon, but as he climbed in, he hit his wounded leg on the side of the bench and let out a scream of pain. This spooked the already nervous horse, making it run toward the open barn doors dragging the wagon with Matthew on its bench out into the smoky night air, rousing Maria from her trance.

She looked up and watched the wagon come to rest a short distance from the barn, near the old roadway. Matthew was slumped over on the front bench. Seeing him there thrust her back into the horrific reality surrounding her. Maria ran into the barn to release the other animals, and then out through the double doors just as flames consumed the old barn.

"MATTHEW!" she yelled, jumping into the back of the wagon to get to Matthew. Maria lifted his head and face towards her to confirm he was still breathing. She held him under his arms and pulled his body off the seat so he could lie on the wagon's floor. He was alive. She hurried onto the front seat and through swollen eyes she glanced back at the house that was once her safe haven. She felt so empty inside. As she flicked the reins that would take her back to a life that she thought she would never see again, Maria was determined to save the one person who was always there for her.

After a mile, Maria halted the horse, anxious to tend to Matthew. The smell of smoke still permeated the air. She lifted her skirts and swung her legs over the bench to join him.

He was conscious and trying to sit up. "Maria, where are we?"

"I'm not sure—only a short distance away. How do you feel?"

"I've been better." He sat with his legs stretched out before him. "What about you?"

"I have some things in my chest that I could use to secure your leg." She reached to uncover what lay in the rear of the wagon.

At first Maria didn't notice the absence of Sam's chest but as she looked further under the blanket she soon realized that it was missing. Frantic, she shoved things around then screamed, "Where is it? Where's the other chest?"

"Maria? What's wrong? What are you looking for?"

"The chest! Sam's chest! Flailing her arms in search of the riches she yelled, "It can't be gone. It must be here somewhere."

Matthew took hold of her shoulders. "Stop, Maria! Stop!" He made her look into his eyes. "You must trust me. There's nothing here but your travel bag and this small chest."

Shocked, Maria sat against the side of the wagon and whispered, "Why would Sam take the treasure? Where is it?"

Matthew took his place in the driver's seat. "We have to get far from Abigail's house. No one must know that we were ever near it." He held the reins and warned her, "Stay low. It's almost dawn. Hide yourself."

Maria stared, unresponsive, into the night as the wagon rumbled along the roadway. She feared for the next event in her life and how it would harm her. Why was she being punished? What caused the fire? Did she forget something in the kitchen? Everything she touched, died! Her stomach hurt; her chest ached. She could hardly breathe. "My life is over, I want to die. My life is over...." Maria laid her head against the wooden floor, closed her eyes and wished for death.

As the miles rolled by, fate looked mercifully upon Maria and eased her into a small respite of sleep. The wagon slowed its approach to the outskirts of Eastham just before dawn. The silence of its clattering wheels woke her.

"Whoa!" Matthew ordered the horse as he pulled on the reins to stop the wagon. There was something up ahead in the road.

Maria sat up and could see another wagon blocking their way; a horse was lying on the ground to the side. The writhing animal whinnied in pain, trying to stand. An older woman knelt over a small child. A man stood next to her.

"Hello, do you need help?" Matthew called out.

The man ran over to Matthew with terror in his eyes. "Yes, my son is hurt!" He spoke in short sentences. "We've had an accident...not sure what happened...something frightened the horse...the wagon wheel...." His voice trailed off as he looked to his son in the dirt. He ran back to the woman who was dressed in black. "Mother, we have help."

As soon as the old woman stood, Maria recognized her as the Widow Baker.

"Matthew Ellis! Is that you?" The widow called out.

"Yes, ma'am."

She squinted her eyes and asked, "Who is that with you?" Unable to see who was in front of her, she changed her tone and pleaded, "Please, we need your help."

Embarrassed at his helplessness, Matthew answered, "My leg is injured. I don't know how much I can help."

He turned to Maria, looking for her assistance.

Maria didn't move.

Matthew quickly understood her hesitation. She was facing exposure. The disregard to laws that had been placed upon her now jeopardized her safety. He started to climb out of the wagon, but Maria stopped him.

When the widow saw Maria coming to their aid she growled with pursed lips, "Maria Hallett!" Then she screamed and took a protective position between Maria and the little boy. "I don't want that witch coming near my grandson."

Jonathan Baker chastised her, "Mother, please! Stop!" Looking at Maria, he begged, "Can you help him?"

Little Isaac Baker, not more than six years old, lay screaming in a pool of blood, his hand crushed.

Jonathan Baker knelt by his son. Tearfully he sobbed to Maria. "I tried to grab him. He fell to the other side of the wagon when the horse reared."

Maria could see the intense pain in the small boy's face and quickly ran to retrieve Minda's healing herbs from her chest. The widow and her son watched as she took a small bottle of the special brewed tea that eases pain from a leather pouch. Holding the boy's head up, Maria poured the bitter drink through his lips. Then she tied a piece from her woven cloths around the boy's wrist to stop the bleeding. Because of his size, the boy responded to the calming effect of the tea within minutes.

"I have stopped the bleeding, and he seems calmer. You'll have time to get him safely to the midwife, but you must hurry." Maria stood and handed the small bottle to Jonathan. "When he wakes, give him sips of this to ease his pain. Move him to our wagon. You'll have to come back for yours. And the horse?" she asked.

"I'm afraid I can't do any more than put it out of its misery," he said.

He cradled his son with loving arms as he placed the little boy behind Matthew in the wagon. The Widow Baker climbed in next to Matthew in the front on the bench, and Maria sat near the boy in the back.

Jonathan Baker walked over to his wagon to fetch his rifle. Patting his horse goodbye, he stood and released a bullet into its head.

54

May 4, 1717
EASTHAM – CAPE COD

WHILE THE MOON WAS STILL IN ITS WANE, the sun rose in the opposite end of the sky as they entered Eastham. Maria lay on the floor next to Isaac. Jonathan Baker sat to the side.

Matthew looked over to the Widow Baker. "I pray I don't need to worry about your silence regarding Maria's presence here today?" He hoped that she would understand the necessity of secrecy.

The widow shifted in her seat. "I fully appreciate the fact that she has given aid without malice to me and my family." Looking straight ahead, she added, "Rest assured I will remain quiet."

Jonathan responded from the rear, "I will do the same."

* * *

The midwife, Lucinda McNeely, opened her door upon hearing the wagon.

Widow Baker called out, "Lucy, we've had a terrible accident. My little Isaac is hurt bad!"

Jonathan jumped out and scooped the boy into his arms. He carried him past Lucy and into the house as Maria hid herself under a blanket. The widow scrambled out of the wagon and followed behind her son.

Lucy called to Matthew, "Is that you, Matthew Ellis?" Wasting no time with further conversation, she shooed everyone into her house without approaching the wagon where Maria hid.

Matthew flicked the reins to leave. The Widow Baker watched him drive away from behind the half open door of the midwife's house.

*　*　*

Over the next hour, Matthew's wagon passed through the more populated areas of Eastham. He was trying to figure out what he should do next while Maria lay hidden from anyone's sight. As individual houses came into view, he sensed the beginnings of the day in each household. Fires in open hearths, biscuits baking, and sounds of family life all filtered through the chilled morning air. The newness of the spring season filled his senses with hope. Would Maria come away with him? He imagined the two of them married, loving and enjoying each other as they went about their days.

Maria slowly lifted the edge of her covering to see how far they were on their journey. "Matthew, is it safe for me to come out?"

"Yes, we'll soon be at your house."

She threw back the blanket, knelt down and rested her forearms on the bench next to him. She watched the road go by under the horse's feet.

"How are you feeling?" he asked her, hoping that she would be agreeable to his wishes of coming with him.

"My heart is so heavy. I don't know what to feel."

He placed his hand on hers.

Maria pulled it away, turned her back to him and sat down on the floor of the wagon. She rubbed her face and slumped forward.

His heart sank. He didn't know what to say to her.

Matthew pulled the horse to a stop in front of the McKeon house. It looked uninviting and desolate, just as before—neither one of them moved.

Still unsure of the fate of his leg, Matthew cautiously stepped from the wagon. As he put his weight on it, he discovered that most of the pain had subsided, and it was thankfully not broken. He took this as a good sign. He unloaded Maria's chest and travel bag into the house, then limped back to Maria, who was still sitting in the back of the wagon. I can't leave her in this awful place, he thought.

He held his hand out to her, and she took it, her face showing no emotion. With Matthew's help, she climbed out of the wagon. He placed his arm around her waist. "Maria, you don't have to stay here. Come with me."

As they walked together to the door, he felt her body next to his. He didn't want to let go of her. He waited for her to speak her answer, but she said nothing. Dejected, he turned to leave.

"Matthew, wait!"

His heart jumped. She came close to him and placed her hand on his scarred face. "I'm sorry that Sam did this to you. I'm sorry for everything. You never deserved this." She pushed a lock of his hair behind his ear and studied his face for a moment. "I know that you love me and it's possible that I'm in love with you, too." She moved her hand over his cheek. "But I can't destroy anyone else's life with whatever plagues me."

She looked up at his face one more time, then kissed him on his cheek. "Go now, Matthew. Find your way without me."

She ran into the house and secured the door behind her. With her back against the closed door, she swallowed her cries as tears streamed down her cheeks.

Matthew ran after her.

She felt his fist as he pounded on the door. "MARIA! Listen to me! You can't shut me out of your life again."

He waited for her to answer. He hit the door again and called out, "MARIA! Can you hear me?" Matthew laid his open hand on the door and tried to feel her presence. Then he whispered through his tears, "I will return for you." No response came from within. He turned away, climbed into his wagon and drove away.

Maria threw herself down on her bed. She remembered hearing Sam repeat the same words, 'I will return for you.' Her head ached with dizzying thoughts of Sam and Matthew. The horrible fire flashed across her mind. She thought of poor Abigail and could see Matthew's bloodied face. She beat her hands on the pillow and pulled at her hair, trying to rid herself of the pain and sadness in her head.

After tossing and turning over and over in her bed, she finally stopped, exhausted. Now she felt empty of all feelings. Her eyes burned from the salty tears and the fire's smoke. She could still hardly breathe.

Maria blew away the mucous that blocked her air passages with the bottom of her skirt, then lay back on the bed. Taking a deep breath, she closed her eyes and fell asleep.

Maria's cathartic purge helped her sleep so deeply that she stayed asleep through the next day and into the following morning. When she finally woke, she lay still, moving only her eyes. She could see the rough-cut ceiling over her head, spider webs dancing in the air, blown by the drafts coming from holes and openings in the old house. Her eyes traced the familiar log walls and their thick, bumpy mortar. They seemed to hypnotize her as she followed the white lines joining the logs together around and around her room. Everything was the same; it was as if nothing had happened. She was in her house just as before, still bound by a punishing law that forced her to be ostracized from the community.

The sun shone into the one window, making a long rectangular mark on the dirty floorboards. Particles of dust floated through its sunbeam. The air was heavy and humid. Forcing herself to sit up, she stood to look out the window and wondered what time of day was it?

Her skin felt sticky, and her arms were spotted with black smudges. The bottom of her outer skirt was matted into a ball, and her inner skirt was ripped across the bottom. In the silence, she heard the faint bleating of her little goat out in the back near the shed. No need for anything else to suffer on my account. She grabbed a pail as she walked past the hearth.

The small black goat was happy to see Maria and stamped its feet in the hay as she came near. When she returned to the house with the full pail of milk that was warm and smelled sweet, she tried to kindle the fire with a piece of flint. She questioned herself about the need of a fire when she had no food but kept striking the flint until it caught its spark. Thirsty, she walked around the chest and travel bag still sitting in the middle of the kitchen and went outside to the well.

As Maria carried the heavy pails that dangled on the ends of a piece of wood across her shoulders, the cool water splashed about her body. It seemed to refresh her, but it also reminded her of her dirty laundry, a depleted woodpile, and the untilled garden beds. She breathed a heavy sigh. Almost to the house, she spotted something that looked out of place. She'd never noticed the large basket on the bench near the open door. She lowered each pail to the ground and stood the wooden pole against the other side of the doorframe. She scanned the surrounding area but saw no sign of another person. Within seconds her curiosity bettered her caution and she began to inspect what was inside.

A bag of oats and flour were the largest of the items, and nestled between them was a covered jar of 'starter' for dough that needed leavening. On the other side of the basket was a pillar of salt wrapped in paper and a jar of cider. In the middle of it all, three large biscuits lay wrapped in a cloth and a letter addressed to Maria Hallett.

To Maria Hallett,
My sincere gratitude to you upon your much-needed assistance in the untimely accident of my son, Isaac. Please accept these items as my thank you.
Jonathan Baker

Maria smiled at this simple gift and felt a small twinge of warmth in her heart. She unpacked her travel bag, washed herself and changed her clothes. Sam's gifts of china pieces from her small chest were placed on the table. She returned the pouch of herbs and medicine to its same spot on the shelf and pushed her keepsake box back under her bed. The bag of coins and gold pieces that were set aside to use on their journey sat next to the china.

As the sun began to set on this, the second day of Maria's return, she began her evening meal with a bite from a soft biscuit that rested on a blue flowered china plate. Her cider filled the delicate cup resting on its matching saucer. It tasted good to her.

She stacked gold coins in piles of ten in front of her, smiling at how considerate Sam was when he'd asked her to put them in her small chest instead of his. Picking up the last morsel of her tasty treat with her fingertip, she licked it clean.

The sun cast a warm red glow across the evening sky as Maria gazed out the window. She needed to think about many things. And Matthew was one of them.

55

Present Day
BREWSTER

TWO MEN SAT IN A PICKUP TRUCK parked in the Caldwell's driveway. For a few minutes neither said a word. When they decided that no one in the Caldwell house had noticed the truck, the driver, Neil Hallett, said, "Lucky for us, that lightning made a great distraction." He looked over to Jack Hennessey. "Now remember, you've got to be quick. Secure the woman and signal me when it's done."

"Got it," his cohort said.

"Take that stupid mustache off. You look ridiculous," growled Hallett.

Hennessey pulled the stylish handlebar from his upper lip. "I may just grow one of these. I like it."

Hallett continued, "I've got everything we need in the back: lights, generator, rain gear and shovels. It shouldn't take more than an hour, tops!"

Hennessey adjusted the ski mask over his head, zippered up his black jacket and pulled rubber gloves over his hands.

"You got the bottle and the rag?"

Hennessey put his hand in his left pocket. "Check."

"Duct tape?"

He touched his other pocket. "Check."

"Now get going!" Hallett ordered.

"Okay, Boss." Hennessey began to repeat Hallett's advice under his breath.

Hallett caught Hennessey's arm. "Don't forget to keep the stuff away from your own face."

As Hennessey walked up the walkway, his eyes skirted between the glow of the TV in the front parlor's windows to the one light in the back. He quietly stepped towards the middle of the house to the kitchen window. Slowly, he cut the screen away from the single window, pushed the glassed panes up and climbed in.

Hallett watched his accomplice enter the house while he anxiously waited for a signal. He whispered, "I hope the chloroform from that old fisherman works. Hennessey is not the brightest tool in the shed." He stuffed tobacco chew into his mouth and remembered all the people who had speculated about where Bellamy's lost treasure was buried, and even if there were any. They'd always searched in Eastham or Wellfleet, never near Brewster. The vellum pieces with the letters and the date, plus the gold coins, all fueled his theories, telling him that he was on the right track. Hallett sneered. In a few hours he would be a rich man.

* * *

Familiar with the layout of the house from his previous visit, Hennessey crept towards the front parlor. Nancy, his target, sat watching the TV with her back to him. He unscrewed the cap to the chloroform and poured a small amount onto a cotton square. Quickly recapping the small brown bottle, he put it back into his pocket and moved closer.

* * *

I laughed as the little kid named 'Chunk' enjoyed a special moment with the lovable monster 'Sloth' over a Babe Ruth candy bar. Within seconds, a piece of material was thrust over my mouth. It smelled like the hospital. The room spun around me and I felt like vomiting. I could hardly hold my head up. I tried to scream but couldn't move my lips. Paul... Where are you? I need you. As my eyes closed, I could feel myself falling over to the side.

*   *   *

Hennessey poked at his victim to make sure she was out. He bound the Caldwell woman's ankles and hands with duct tape and sat her back into an upright position on the couch facing the TV. He stuffed a rag in her mouth and taped it shut. With a sigh of relief, he pulled off his ski mask, adjusted his jacket, and straightened the Hawaiian shirt that peeked out beneath the bottom of his black leather coat. He headed towards the foyer door by the kitchen where he'd broken in.

Unlocking the door, he peered into the dark night. Hallett's truck was visible in the driveway. After fumbling to find the right switch, Hennessey flicked the outdoor light on and off a few times, giving Hallett the all-clear signal.

He hurried back into the kitchen and picked up the Caldwell's main house phone, pressed TALK and placed it on the table, blocking all incoming and outgoing calls. Under his breath he went over the checklist from Hallett, then left the house through the back porch to meet his boss by the cellar.

*   *   *

Hallett shifted into low gear and drove his truck closer to the back of the garage. It rolled quietly over the gravel. When the equipment was unloaded, Hennessey set up spotlights around the edge of the cellar and flipped the switch on the generator.

Hallett stood next to the spotlights on the grass. "It shouldn't be too far down. They already found some coins near the surface." He watched Hennessey climb down into the hole to begin shoveling more dirt out of its bottom.

56

Present Day
BOSTON

PAUL DECIDED TO GIVE NANCY ONE MORE CALL to say goodnight. He asked the kids to turn the TV down in the hotel room as he pressed the button on the keypad for HOME. No answer. He'd call again in a minute.

Paul sat on the edge of one of the queen-sized beds. After five minutes, he redialed, but still no answer. His hands began to perspire as he called her cell phone. Nothing! He paced from the bathroom to the bed and back again, then tried one more time. Under his breath he whispered, "Come on! Come on! God damn it! Pick up the phone!" He called Jim's cell as he stood by the curtained window that overlooked the parking lot.

Molly glanced over at her daddy as she colored on the bed. She thought he looked angry.

There was no answer from Jim. "Jim, this is Dad…call me as soon as you can. It's important." He flipped his phone shut and went back to his pacing.

"What's wrong, Dad?" asked Brian.

"It's your Mom—she's not answering…." Paul's words were cut short by his cell ringing. He answered in a flash. "Hello!"

"What's going on, Dad?" Jim asked on the other end.

"Where are you, at the restaurant?"

"Yeah, why?"

"Do you think you could check on Mom? She's not answering her cell or the home phone, and I'm worried."

"Let me see if I can leave."

Paul could hear the sound of dishes clattering in the restaurant and people laughing in the background as he waited impatiently for Jim to return.

"Yeah, I can go and check it out."

"Thanks…and Jim…be careful. If I don't hear from you in twenty minutes, I'm calling the police."

"Okay, Dad, I'll get back to you as soon as I can."

57

Present Day
BREWSTER

JIM'S SIZE FIFTEEN SNEAKERS floored the gas pedal as he barreled out of the restaurant's parking lot. He thought that his dad was overreacting, but he wasn't going to take any chances. It would take him only a few minutes to check on his mom. He wondered why his dad would call the police. He strained to see through the foggy darkness as the wipers cleaned a light drizzle of rain from the windshield. If there's something wrong, I need a plan, he thought. Recalling all the mystery and adventure movies he'd seen, he tried to remember some of the moves the good guy did that made him a hero.

He cut the headlights and drove slowly up the berm and onto the driveway so as not to disturb the gravel. He could see that the TV was on in the front parlor. Turning off the engine, he let the car coast the rest of the way in.

He stopped the car facing the back yard instead of pulling to the side. As his eyes adjusted to the dark, the rear end of a black truck near the edge of the garage came into his view. He whispered, "Something's up. Whose truck is that?"

Jim told himself to be calm, and remembered that Dad would contact the police after twenty minutes. He checked his cell phone for the time but couldn't remember when he'd received the call. It didn't matter, he thought, as he stepped out of the car. He kept the door ajar, so there would be no closing noise. Spotting his baseball bat in the back seat, he grabbed it. Jim looked again to make sure the dome light in the car was off. It was.

He walked silently towards the entryway of the foyer. His eyes scanned the area from side to side and into the dark shadows that blanketed his peripheral vision. He stepped quickly but was careful not to slip on the wet decking.

The first thing he saw was that the screen had been cut on the kitchen window. His adrenalin went into overdrive. He fumbled for his key only to find the door already open. His heart pumped even faster. Mustering all his courage, he crept inside, still gripping the bat in his hand. He heard the sound of a generator to his right, and then spotted a circle of bright lights in the backyard. He wished he had a gun.

Jim stepped softly across the foyer and into the old kitchen. He remembered the fake gun Molly had found in the root cellar. Where was it? The green numbers on the clock radio's screen lit his way over to the counter. The toy gun looked real in the semi-darkness. Tightening his grip on the bat, Jim put his keys into one pocket and picked up the gun. He turned and headed towards the front of the house to find his mom.

A HOTEL IN NEW YORK

Paul thought about the weird guy from the museum. He dialed 411 to get the museum's number. As he dialed, he tried to recall the man's name. He knew it began with a K...Kearney? Kennedy? Kennedy, that's it! He scribbled the phone number on the hotel notepad as fast as he could and then punched it into his phone.

"The *Whydah* Museum," a man answered. "I'm sorry, we're closed."

Paul pleaded with the man. "I just need to ask you a question."

"Okay."

"Do you have an employee by the name of Kennedy working for you?"

"Nope."

"Thanks." Paul hung up.

He turned to the kids. "Pack your things. We're leaving. Right now! I'll explain everything later. Brian, you'll have to drive if I get sleepy."

As the kids packed their backpacks, Paul keyed in 911 to alert the Brewster Police. He wasn't waiting for Jim's call.

BREWSTER

I could open my eyes but not my mouth. There was something in it, and tape over it. I saw tape on my hands and feet. Thank God, I was alive. I tried to stand, but couldn't move. I bent my body over to pull myself up to stand, but couldn't get my balance. I looked over to the TV, where my cell phone was vibrating on top of it. If only I could reach it! It was probably Paul.

I twisted my shoulders back and forth; a sharp pain shot up my side. I thought of the baby and sat back against the couch. I prayed in my heart: Oh dear God, please don't let anyone come back and hurt the baby or me.

There was a horror movie playing on the TV now. What was going on? I felt disoriented. It was pitch black outside. Terrible thoughts crept into my head: Was someone still in the house with me? Were we being robbed? Was I going to be raped? My knees shook, and my heart raced. Be strong, I told myself. Stay calm. Remember the baby.

There was no other noise except for the TV. I turned my head, but couldn't see anyone behind me. Maybe they'd left already? I prayed again: Please, let whoever did this to me be gone by now.

I wiggled my hands and feet, thinking the duct tape might break loose. It didn't. I tried lifting my feet up and down in a march, hoping to free them. Nothing. I started to gag from whatever was in my mouth. I forced myself to relax. My throat hurt each time I tensed up; my mouth was so dry.

Breathe in. Breathe out. Damn it! I needed to stand up. Carefully: I didn't want to fall and injure the baby. I leaned forward to try to stand again. With all my strength, I pushed my body up, only to be shoved back down by a large hand that grabbed my shoulder. I let out a muffled scream as someone moved in front of me. I looked up to see...my beautiful son, Jim. I burst into tears.

Jim held his finger up to his lips, "Shhhhhh." I anxiously watched him unwrap the tape from my hands and then my feet. Once freed, I quickly clawed at the tape across my mouth and pulled out the wad of material. Saliva wet the inside of my mouth with a sweet moistness. It felt good to be able to swallow again.

Jim stood for a few seconds watching me. I looked up at him. He spoke in a whisper, "Are you okay, Mom?"

I rubbed my face, as if to erase the memory of how I got into this predicament. "I think so, but I don't know what's going on."

He knelt down in front of me to check that I was all right. My whole body was shaking; my knees bouncing up and down. He looked me straight in the face. "Somebody's in the backyard with big lights on that old cellar."

He stood up and stepped back to give me room to stand. I just sat there and started to cry again, but I stopped myself, looked up to Jim and asked, "How did you know I was in trouble?" I didn't wait for him to answer. I stood up and flung my arms around him, still holding the crumpled duct tape and wadded cloth. "I'm so glad you're my son." He hugged me back.

Our roles of parent and child had become reversed; he was protecting me now. Then common sense returned, and I blurted out, "Oh my God, whoever it is must think that there's still treasure down in the cellar. That's got to be it!" I pulled back from our hug. "There's no other reason somebody would be digging in our backyard." I grabbed his arm. "Your father was right. He had his suspicions about all the publicity in the paper from that stupid reporter."

Jim breathed a sigh of relief. "I'm just glad you're okay, Mom."

I rubbed my wrists, trying to get the circulation back into them. "I can't believe this is really happening to us."

"Mom, Dad's been trying to call you. He got worried when you didn't answer your phone, so he called me."

"I knew it was him. I've been watching my phone light up since I opened my eyes."

"It's a good thing I got here."

"Thank you, honey. You came just in time." Jim still looked worried, and so was I. "Now what do we do?"

Jim showed me the bat. He reached into his pocket and took out the gun. "Don't laugh, I needed another weapon, so I grabbed that old toy gun Molly found. What do you think?"

I almost did laugh, but caught myself, because it did look real. "It looks real enough for me."

I grabbed the gun from him and held it as if I could do some serious damage with it. I moved it up and down in the air to feel its weight. "It feels like a real gun." I turned to leave. "Okay. We should go through the studio and into the garage for something else, maybe a shovel?"

Jim nodded.

"First I'm calling 911, and then your Dad!

"Let's go," he said, "but we gotta be quiet."

I grabbed my cell phone and turned off the ringtone so it wouldn't make a sound if Paul called back. I punched in 911 as we walked through the dark house. I clutched the gun in a tight squeeze. By the time we passed the porch door, on our way to the garage, I was whispering into the phone, "Hello, this is Nancy Caldwell. There's a burglar in my house...."

Once we reached the garage, the rain began to come down harder. I saw a man in a rain slicker standing with his back to us; he was watching someone else shoveling dirt out of the old cellar.

Jim handed the bat to me and grabbed a big shovel. We started for the outhouse door that led out of the gallery and into the backyard.

"Jim!" I handed him the gun. "Here...show it...but only if necessary." He took the toy gun and stuffed in his back pocket.

"Okay. Stay here, Mom, and wait for the police. I'll be fine."

"Jim," I whispered again and reached for his arm to hold him back. I couldn't bear the thought of my son getting hurt, or worse.

"Mom, I'll be all right. Stay put!"

He was right. I stood my ground and held the bat ready, just in case I was needed.

Jim was no weakling. He'd won a gold medal for shot put in his last year at high school. I wondered if he'd ever been in a fight. I watched him walk out the tiny door and step closer to the dark form in front of him. The downpour covered any noise from his movements. He raised the shovel up in the air and crept closer and closer to the edge of the cellar.

Jim brought the shovel down with a loud whack against the rain-soaked back of his target. I got caught up in the moment and cheered him on in a whisper. "Now that's what I'm talking about. Good for you!"

The shadowy figure arched his back, lost his balance and fell into the hole on top of the other intruder. Jim stood above them, clutching the shovel.

I could see the second guy in the cellar was scrambling to get his buddy off of him. Jim ran over to the other side by the steps. Hurry up, I prayed. As the other man started to climb out of the cellar, I screamed into the dark. "Look out, Jim!"

Jim saw him and lifted the shovel once more. He walloped the second guy on the head and knocked him back into the cellar, on top of the first casualty.

I finally got up enough courage to approach the cellar with the bat in a firm grip, ready to spring into action if needed.

I was relieved to see the two men lying on top of each other at the bottom of the cellar. I looked over to Jim, who caught my stare. We both knew what the other was thinking. It was over.

Seconds later, two police officers ran from the back of the garage with flashlights and guns drawn. Both officers pointed their revolvers down into the root cellar. "This is the police. Put your hands up and slowly get out of the hole."

No one moved, including Jim and I.

The first officer repeated the command, only louder.

It was Officer Gomes. Boy, was I happy to see a friendly face.

When the police were sure there would be no resistance from the intruders, Officer Gomes went down the steps while his partner held a gun pointed toward the two men in the cellar.

I walked over to Jim, who still held the shovel in his hands. "Are you okay?"

He looked at me and lowered the shovel, but maintained his grip around its handle. He looked visibly shaken, but said, "Yeah, I'm fine. Can't believe I did that."

"You did a great job. I love you."

He saw me clutching my wooden weapon. "Mom, I think you can let go of the bat now."

I looked at the bat and loosened my grip.

Officer Gomes roused one of the men and pushed him up the steps as his partner's gun followed from above.

"It's Kennedy," I whispered to Jim. "The guy from the *Whydah* Museum."

"What guy?" Jim asked.

"Never mind. I'll explain later."

Before Gomes went back for the second man, he handcuffed the first intruder and sat him on the ground. When I saw the other man's face as he came out of the cellar, I yelled out in surprise, "It's Neil Hallett!"

"You know him?" Gomes asked.

"Yes, I do. He was over here earlier when we first discovered this whole thing. He must have thought there was more treasure in the cellar. It's hard to believe he was so certain about the legend that he would risk jail time."

"Crime never pays," Officer Gomes said in a serious tone as he handcuffed Neil Hallett.

Officer Gomes's partner pushed Hallett's accomplice towards the front of the house. "You at it again, Hennessey? You never learn, do you?"

Another police car approached with its siren echoing through the foggy night. Lights flashed blue, white, and yellow in the driveway as Hennessey, alias Kennedy, and Hallett were loaded into the back of the cruisers. Jim and I walked around the garage, behind the police, but ducked into the house as rain began to pour again.

Collapsing into one of the kitchen chairs, I noticed it was almost 10 p.m. "I'd better call Dad and tell him what's going on."

Jim kept watching outside through the kitchen windows until the police cruiser holding Hallett and Hennessey left.

"Paul?"

"Nancy!" he yelled. "What's happening?"

"Everything's fine. The police are here and...." I couldn't talk. I started to tear up.

"The police? What's going on?" Paul sounded frantic.

"It's okay...here...talk to Jim. He's my hero. Officer Gomes is coming in to ask me some questions." Before I released my grip from the phone I added, "Paul, I love you. I can't wait to feel your arms around me again."

"I love you, too. We're on Interstate 95. We'll be home soon. Now where's Jim?"

I handed the phone to our son with a sigh of relief.

58

Spring 1718
BARNSTABLE – CAPE COD

THE SUN'S DAPPLED LIGHT crossed the wood-planked floor of the print shop. It looked like it would be a pleasant day ahead, but Matthew's left calf ached. Over a year had passed since Sam Bellamy had hit his shin with the handle of a pitchfork, leaving him with a throbbing leg each time a storm was approaching. He rubbed his leg and thought of Maria's sweet face and smile. It always eased his pain.

His apprenticeship with Mr. Johnson had proved a success, and he had learned the skills of printing and bookbinding well. He took to his craft in earnest and quickly became proficient—competent enough that, when the health of Mr. Johnson began to fail, Matthew offered to buy the little shop with the money he'd saved from the sale of his family property. This agreement had brought the best result to both men.

Today was the day he'd been planning since he'd left Eastham and moved to Barnstable. It was the second of June, and he was returning for his Maria with hope in his heart that she would accept his proposal of marriage.

Starting this morning, Matthew's young apprentice would take over the shop while he was gone. Feeling a sense of personal pride for his new stature as a businessman, Matthew looked sternly at his new hire as he was about to leave. "James, I trust you will be able to handle things in my absence?"

"Yes, sir." James wiped his hands across his ink-stained apron.

Matthew tried to hide his excitement, but as he hurried out the door of the print shop, he fell on the hard packed dirt road and dropped his baggage and ticket for the packet ship. Embarrassed, he pulled himself up, brushed the dirt off his waistcoat and looked up the road to see if anyone had seen him fall.

"Don't forget to finish the handbills for the court," he barked at James.

"Yes, sir." James looked up from the letter cabinet and dashed over to the doorway to help Matthew gather his papers.

Matthew softened his tone. "Farewell, James." A broad smile brightened his face as he spoke his parting words. "See you in a few weeks."

"Yes, sir." Matthew's new apprentice grinned as he thought of what his employer was about to do. He whispered under his breath, "Good luck."

It would take Matthew several days to reach Eastham. His plan was to stop at Paine's Creek Landing after sailing on the packet *Marie* from Barnstable. Once there, he'd see about purchasing a wagon and horse so that he could accommodate Maria's belongings on the long ride home.

He hoped she would say yes.

That night a strong nor'easter pummeled Cape Cod. Matthew sat in the local tavern, cursing the unfortunate weather. His anticipation for his beautiful Maria grew stronger with each passing hour.

EASTHAM 1718

Maria stood close to the hearth and reached into its warmth for the blackened kettle of steaming water. As she turned away from its heat, she glanced at the delicate blue flowered cup and saucer that rested on a small table. The beautiful china contrasted with her dreary surroundings. She brewed herself a cup of tea, her only comfort through the stormy night. She could barely bring herself to think about him without crying. Bowing her head, she covered her eyes and tried to hide the images of so many lonely nights that she had waited for his return. Always hopeful, she kept her daily watch no matter the weather, or how she felt. Ever faithful to her task, like the tides of the sea, her duty of watching never wavered.

Maria stood to straighten her back, then returned the kettle to its hook above the fire. A chill slid down her spine. She shivered and pulled her woolen shawl closer around her shoulders. She hated the musty smell of damp wool. A strong gust of wind rattled the broken shingles on the old McKeon house. Maria slumped into her chair beside the table while wind continued to howl and blow heavy rain against the door.

She tried to reassure herself that no harm would come to her from the storm that swirled outside. She sat taller in her chair, but could not dismiss the memories of so many other frightful nights. She prayed in the candle-lit room: "Please, Lord, if You are there, stop this eternal wind."

Maria rubbed her arms and shook her body like a stray animal against the cold. Returning to the table, she caressed the dainty teacup for its warmth, but it was already chilled. She found her gloves in a basket hanging by the side of the hearth. They slowly soothed her numb fingers. There would be no more work at her spinning wheel tonight; the air was too cold, and her hands ached. The wind blew harder and shook the door. Her thoughts turned to the safety of her bed, and she persuaded herself to retire early.

Making sure the door was latched tight, Maria added the last logs for the night to the fire and pushed them to the back of the hearth. She blew all the candles out but one, which she carried to her bed. Crawling under her bedcovers, she closed her eyes and could see his handsome face. He was not like other men; he was kind and he possessed a strength that protected and comforted her. She knew he loved her, and once more she felt a small flicker of desire for Matthew deep inside her. It warmed her and made her smile as she drifted into sweet sleep.

* * *

Maria woke to the aftermath of the same untimely storm that had delayed Matthew. Remnants of sea grass that had been blown up onto the bluffs lay scattered over the scrub by her house. Her broom and other tools were strewn across the dirt. Several pieces of linen, which had been drying on a tree, lay atop the marsh grasses. Large tree limbs blocked the path leading to her house. She took her time to fetch water from the well as she began her day, not sensing any urgency to clear away the debris. No one ever visited her. She thought Minda might come, but surely the storm's fury would have made it difficult for the old woman to travel. There was time to clean up and move the large branches later.

Maria stoked the hearth embers from the previous day's fire to heat the kettle for her morning drink. After such a cold and frightening night it would taste good. Sam's gift of china had become a pleasant habit for Maria to use with her daily meals, and today was no different.

She sipped her tea outside, where the air was cool but smelled fresh and clean. Glancing toward the grasses and wild flowers that grew across the dunes, she knew winter would soon be over.

On the horizon Maria saw her friend, the old *Poh Wah*, climbing over the fallen branches on the path ahead. As she approached, Maria called out, "Minda, you're an early riser. You surprise me today."

Minda took her seat next to Maria on the bench. "Just anxious to visit you," the old *Poh Wah* told her young friend. "I hope you fare well?"

"Yes, I do," Maria answered. "May I interest you in some tea?"

Observing Sam's fine china in Maria's hand, Minda replied, "Yes, but a simple cup, if you please."

Minda had made a habit of visiting Maria throughout the past year. On this occasion, it was to be a quick visit. She was needed among her people. With the death of Reverend Treat, last March, the Nauset Indians had been worried about his replacement and how his passing would affect their relationship with a new reverend and the people of Eastham. Her counsel was important to the Nausets.

Minda felt the warmth of the sun as she sat on the bench and let her thoughts ramble. Maria had survived well. The settlers now came to her for help in the dark of night, hiding their clandestine visits from the elders, seeking relief from their aching bones, or other mysterious illnesses that no one but Maria could understand. Minda was pleased that they wanted Maria's herbs and medicines. In return, the villagers left food or extra supplies in payment. Minda grinned. The whispers from old Widow Baker about the banished girl and her supposed witchcraft practices only brought success to Maria and never scorn upon her reputation. Minda had taught the girl well.

Maria was pleased that there was enough honey to sweeten their peppermint tea. Mr. Leach, who'd been worried about his wife when she was with child, had come to Maria for a loadstone amulet to strengthen the infant within her and to prevent a miscarriage. He'd looked very happy when Maria had wrapped the small stone in linen and laced it with a piece of thin leather for his wife to hang above her navel. Satisfied with his child's healthy birth, he had left two jars of honey on Maria's stoop in exchange for payment.

The two friends drank their sweet tea and looked out over the newly grown green marshes.

Minda asked, "Do you still hurt in your heart for Sam?"

Maria shook her head. "No, the hurt grows smaller each day."

Minda reached over and held her hand. "That is good. When your sorrow is small, the hole in your heart is easier to mend."

Maria sipped her tea.

"Do you think of Matthew?"

"Yes, almost every day." Maria sighed. "I watch for him now as I watched for Sam."

Silence fell between them except for a bird's serenading song.

Minda looked up at the swaying trees and listened to the pines whispering in the spring breeze. "I have heard that some people call you a witch."

"I'm aware of that gossip, but I pay it no mind." Maria traced the delicate lines of the flowers on the china cup with her finger. "As long as they treat me with respect, even if it's only for my strange ways, I can benefit from it."

Minda's heart was content at the thought that this young girl had grown into a smart and resourceful woman. Maria's mother would have been proud.

*　*　*

Matthew was able to leave near high noon. It was going to be a warmer ride than expected, leaving so late in the day, but it didn't matter, because he was happy.

The narrow rutted cart-way, soon to be dedicated as the King's Highway, took him away from Stony Brook Village toward the Doane homestead, where the memory of that fateful night and horrible fire reminded him even more that he needed to take his Maria away to a safer place.

Matthew stopped the wagon and noted traces of charred grasses where the Doane house once stood. The large oak tree had survived the intense heat of the fire, but the side closest to Abigail's house was blackened and bare, while the other side grew green. It was as if it was telling Matthew to travel that way to Maria. She was all he cared about, all he thought about. He rubbed the pain in his leg, flicked the reins and drove the wagon toward the direction of the growing leaves.

It was dusk and on the verge of total blackness when Matthew drew near to the McKeon house. He stopped a short distance away and sat to contemplate what he was about to do. He repeated in his head: I love her; I'm certain of that. Does she love me enough to come with me now?

The soft glow of candlelight flickered in the window of the small house. He could see the outline of a woman by the hearth. After the horse and wagon were tied to a tree, he walked towards the door.

Matthew straightened his waistcoat and stood tall with his hand poised to knock.

* * *

Maria and Minda sat at the table eating their evening meal of rabbit stew, courtesy of Mr. Jackson's constant bouts of indigestion. A knock at the door stopped their spoons in mid-air.

"Another visitor from Eastham?" Minda asked.

"I don't know who that could be." Maria beckoned to her friend. "Please hide in the shed out back so you aren't found with me." Minda obliged her, but held the back door ajar so that she could see who was visiting. She stood quietly in the darkness and waited.

Maria placed her hand on the latch. "Who's at my door?"

The voice spoke, "Maria? It's Matthew."

The sound of Matthew's name startled her at first, and then her heart leapt with joy. She threw open the door, put her arms around his neck, and would not let go. He twirled her across the threshold and into the house.

"Matthew, Matthew, it's so good to see you," she said, looking into his wide eyes and laughing. A wellspring of youth surged within her, and she felt as if they were children again.

Matthew gently let Maria go, but he couldn't take his eyes off her.

"What brings you here tonight, Matthew?"

"Something I have thought about for a long time." He gazed at how her brown hair fell loose around her shoulders. His heart raced; his body surged with passion at the sight of her, and he remembered why he loved her so deeply. "I can't hold my tongue any longer; I'm bursting with love for you, Maria."

Maria stood still. Matthew's touch surprised her and pleased her all at once. She looked at him with a great affection in her heart. He stood before her now: a strong, handsome man she could live with and love for the rest of her life.

He reached out, held her close to his body and stroked her cheek. With tears in his eyes he asked, "Maria, will you be my wife?"

"Yes."

Matthew needed no more words. He pulled her even closer and kissed her over and over, sealing their pact.

Minda opened the back door and entered the room, singing a loud 'whoop' signifying her joy.

But Matthew and Maria paid no attention, lost in the beginning of their new world.

*   *   *

That night, as Matthew loaded Maria's things into the wagon, she sat at the table in the kitchen and placed the last of the blue china in the small chest on the floor. She closed its lid and remembered back to her once-passionate love for Sam. Although it was now a distant memory, she still kept a piece of him in the corner of her heart, not for love, but for compassion and sympathy for the man who'd loved her and had simply wanted a life better than the one he'd been dealt.

Sam Bellamy was her first love, but not her last. He was a good and true prince of pirates. He'd given his life trying to save Abigail.

The spinner took precedence over all and stood tallest in the wagon. Matthew made sure it was secure. It was surrounded by Maria's special keepsake box, yarns, threads, weaving supplies, the small chest filled with the blue dishes and whatever coins were left from Sam, and of course, the herbs and medicines that Maria was so adept at dispensing.

Minda felt proud as she watched the two lovers work as partners readying for their journey together. She beamed as if she were Maria's mother, pleased to see a daughter who had found love and security at last.

The supplies were covered with a large blanket. There was just enough room for Matthew and his new bride-to-be to sit on the bench.

By early dawn, they were prepared to leave.

"Maria, we must go now."

"Coming, my love."

The old McKeon house sat empty in the early pre-dawn hours except for the table, chair, and bed that had been there when she first met Sam. One final hug and words of goodbye were exchanged between the two old friends. Maria knew she would never see Minda again. The only thing that she would miss of her past life was the old *Pow Wah*.

Minda held the nanny goat that would return with her to the Nausets as she watched Maria begin a journey to the next stage of her life. She sang a blessing for them as they made their way through the first cluster of houses near the village, then to its center, and finally onto the open road. No one would notice them in the early morning light, and if someone did, it did not matter; Maria Hallett was leaving Eastham.

Maria held Matthew's knee as the wagon rumbled along the cartway. "I cannot remember a time when I was not watching or waiting for someone or something. My life has been like the shoreline, with tides forever washing away parts of my life while also cleansing it for something new to begin."

She kissed him on the cheek and looked straight ahead, comforted by Minda's sweet goodbye song.

59

Present Day
BREWSTER – CAPE COD

LITTLE DANIEL, A HEALTHY BABY BOY, was born in February. By the time he was five months old, I was still carrying most of my extra weight from his pregnancy, but remained steadfast at getting those pounds off.

It was June, and I felt hopeful for the coming season. Tourists once again filled the grocery stores, and there was the hustle and bustle of businesses opening their doors across the main streets of Cape Cod. It was music to my ears. I could hardly wait for potential buyers to walk into our little gallery. Money was tight. Danny's birth was only partially covered by our insurance, so we were still paying off the debt. But my family was happy.

Paul had been productive through early winter and had helped me in the first three months of the year with baby Daniel. He'd painted every day, creating art pieces that rivaled anything else he had ever done. The natural light of the Cape glistened across his new paintings with masterful brushstrokes. It looked like it was going to be a good season.

Jim was in the West Indies for his first year in the Peace Corps and was already accomplishing great things. Brian had been elected president of his junior class and was finally happy about our move to the Cape. Casey had made a lot of friends and was enjoying her new school. Molly was her usual precocious self, making us all laugh.

When I wasn't taking care of Daniel, I explored our two acres of land and promised myself that I'd make paths throughout the woods as soon as the ground was a little drier. Such a simple thing to do, but the wooded trails would provide adventure for the whole family, and all the friends and relations who would visit in the coming summer days.

Half of our land was a tangle of wild roses, grapevines, blackberries, and hardwoods mixed in with a lot of scrub. Clearing the pathways could be fun and would provide no-cost exercise for me.

One crisp morning, my strategy was planned as I enjoyed a warm cup of coffee. I bounced Daniel in his baby seat near me on the kitchen floor.

"Paul, as soon as I put Daniel down for his morning nap, I'm going to start my paths."

Paul poured his last cup of coffee from the thermos. "No problem, I'll take the baby monitor into the studio."

I picked Daniel up. "Okay. I figure I have a couple of hours before Molly comes home on the bus from kindergarten."

By 10 a.m. Daniel was asleep. I went into the barn to gather some tools and grabbed a garden rake or 'whacker' for prickly vines, some hand clippers, and the heavy artillery: a big shovel for pushing away the really tough thorns and vines.

As I walked around the perimeter of the woods, I tried to find a natural entrance. On the ground, near the edge of the woods, I noticed some deer droppings. Looking up ahead I could see a subtle path. I hit the brambles a few times with my shovel and stepped into the thicket. I'm in, I thought to myself. Out came the hand clippers from my pocket to cut away the wild rose vines that were sticking to my clothes and arms as I ventured deeper in.

After five minutes of cutting, I looked up and spotted another opening between two trees. An hour passed before I reached the straight trunks of my targets. When I turned around, I saw a twenty-foot path behind me. Tired but happy, I leaned on my shovel, a strong sense of accomplishment coming over me.

I heard the sound of traffic stopping in front of the house and stood taller above the brambles to hear it clearer. It was the school bus dropping Molly off from kindergarten. I held the shovel up to mark my position for her and called out, "Molly, I'm in the woods, over here."

"Mommy, Mommy," she yelled out as she ran down the driveway.

It didn't take her long to find the rustic entrance I'd made so she could enter the woods. She kept her eye on me as she ran down the new path. My gray hair bobbed up and down as I continued to whack and cut my way deeper into the prickly scrub. When she finally reached me, Molly dropped her little backpack and asked, "Whatcha doing?" and gave me a big hug and kiss.

"Whacking!" I said as I brought the rake down hard onto the unruly brambles.

"Can I try?"

"Sure, but be careful."

Molly took hold of the big rake and smacked the ground, almost falling forward with its force.

"Whoa. Be careful." I caught her by the shoulders before she fell over. "Go and change your clothes if you want to help me."

"That's okay. I'm hungry and my show is on soon. I'm gonna go in."

"Daddy's in the studio. I'll be right there. I have to put away my tools."

I bent over to pick up the rake and shovel. "I love you."

"I love you too." Molly's tiny voice trailed off, singing a little tune from Sesame Street.

*   *   *

The following two days were filled with rain, which gave me no opportunity to continue my paths. Disappointed, I sat at the kitchen table and opened the mail. "Nothing but bills," I said to Paul.

"So what else is new?"

I unfolded the local paper. "Hey, look at this. It says here in the court records that Jack Hennessey was convicted of assault and battery with attempted robbery. They gave him six years."

Paul sat next to me. "What about Neil Hallett?"

Running my finger down the column, I spotted his name. "Neil Hallett was convicted of breaking and entering with attempted robbery. They gave him two years and fined him $1,000.00."

The thought of someone breaking into our house made me upset again. Neil Hallett should not have been so greedy and sneaky. "God, I'm glad that's over," I whispered.

Paul began filling the dishwasher with the dirty dishes.

I tapped my finger on the newspaper's words and rehashed the whole scenario in my head. I'd always felt there was a thread that intertwined Maria Hallett, Sam Bellamy, and our property even though my theory was never officially recognized by the *Whydah* Museum in Provincetown. I glanced at the two pieces of vellum from the old cellar that Paul had framed in a shadow box in the kitchen. "I was thinking, if you don't mind, I'm going to work on my paths. It looks like it's stopped raining."

Paul smiled at me. "Sure, go ahead. I'll listen for Daniel. Pretend all those prickers are Hallett and Hennessey, and whack 'em good!"

"Will do!"

Paul gave me a big hug. "Nancy? Please don't go finding anymore root cellars."

I kissed him on his bearded cheek. "Thanks for filling it in and planting grass over it."

"Anything for you."

The grass wet my hiking boots after only a few steps, but they were waterproof, so I didn't care. Following my new path into the woods, I saw a large ivy-covered mound up ahead, ten feet beyond where I had stopped whacking the other day. I zeroed in on it as a marker, representing the goal for the day's clearing. I smiled to myself and thought that when I finished, these paths would be so neat for the kids to play on. I could hardly wait to take everyone on a tour.

Deep in the woods, I continued cutting and trimming everything that stood in my way. Leaves and clippings were thrown off the path with my raking.

I finally stood next to the huge mound that was my goal. It was almost as tall as I was. I noticed a tick crawling up my pants, so I quickly leaned one hand against the thick ivy that covered the mound to pick off the tick.

The damp ivy felt unusually sturdy under my palm. Curious, I pulled some of the green vines away and exposed the gray of a huge rock underneath. I grabbed the clippers and started cutting into the dense ivy. As I pulled the long spindly strands of the invasive plant up and out of the ground, dirt sprinkled across my boots. The more I pulled and cut, the larger the exposed surface of the boulder grew. I stood back a few feet to see exactly how big this behemoth was. My eyes followed the curve of the huge stone, tracing its outline from top to bottom. Then something shiny caught my attention at its base.

I ripped off my garden gloves and lunged towards it. I pulled out a round yellow disc from the freshly scattered, loose dirt and recognized it immediately. It was just like the three gold coins that had been found in the old root cellar. My stomach did flip-flops. I knelt down and frantically started to dig with my bare hands in the hope that there were more coins. I only had to go down a few inches to see the remnants of a rotted wooden lid.

I felt a little dizzy as my fingers scratched at the black dirt around its outside, exposing a rectangular shape. I sat against the back of my calves, staring at what I had uncovered. I couldn't believe my eyes, and pushed my hair back so I could see it better. I brushed as much dirt as I could away from what lay before me. My hands were filthy—I wiped them on my pants—then reached deeper into the rotting lid and down into layers of gold coins, red rubies, and gold necklaces.

I picked up a pendant with an emerald-green stone embedded in its center and then dropped it back into the jumbled mess. It was happening again—only this time it really was the answer to my prayers. I felt the flush of euphoria rise into my neck and face. A fortune like this was something beyond my wildest dreams! I thought discovering the old cellar and the three small gold coins was the closest thing that I would ever get to real treasure. I thought of Neil Hallett and laughed out loud. He was right after all; he was just in the wrong spot. My heart raced. I felt vindicated.

I looked down at the gold pieces, and for a second, thought of Maria Hallett. I didn't know why she and Sam were in Brewster and not Eastham, but I did know that I'd just found the missing treasure of the pirate Sam Bellamy, the legendary booty that everyone had been after for almost 300 years.

I wiped my face, streaking my cheeks with dirt, just the way Molly did when she played outside in the gardens; only I wasn't playing. A handful of gold coins sifted through my fingertips. The next ones were cradled in the front of my shirt close to my waist. I could hardly get off my knees, but managed to push my way up to a standing position with my free hand.

Fearful of stumbling over exposed roots because my legs were shaking, I forced myself to slow down and walk the new path with care. I started to yell as loudly as I could, "Paul! Paul!"

As I came closer to the edge of the woods, I couldn't contain myself anymore. I screamed Paul's name and ran towards the house while clutching the treasure in a rolled-up ball against my stomach. "Paul! Paul! You're not going to believe this. Look what I found!"

The End

INCORPORATIONS

PLYMOUTH	1633	CHATHAM	1712
SANDWICH	1639	EASTHAM	1651
FALMOUTH	1686	ORLEANS	1797
BARNSTABLE	1639	WELLFLEET	1763
YARMOUTH	1639	TRURO	1709
DENNIS	1793	PROVINCETOWN	1727
HARWICH	1694		
BREWSTER	1803		

'THIS MAP IS FOR GENERAL REFERENCE ONLY.

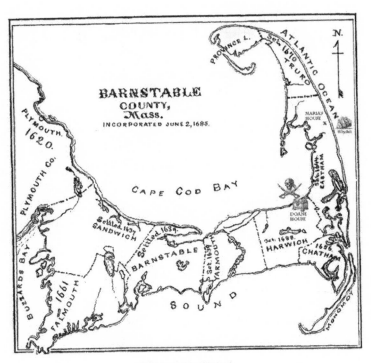

SETTLEMENTS

PLYMOUTH	1620	CHATHAM	1656
SANDWICH	1637	EASTHAM	1644
FALMOUTH	1661	ORLEANS	
BARNSTABLE	1639	(PART OF EASTHAM)	
YARMOUTH	1639	WELLFLEET	
DENNIS		(PART OF EASTHAM)	
(PART OF YARMOUTH)		TRURO	1670
HARWICH	1688	PROVINCETOWN	
BREWSTER		(PART OF PROVINCE LANDS)	
(PART OF HARWICH)			1717

*THIS MAP IS FOR GENERAL REFERENCE ONLY.

Acknowledgments

On my 11th birthday, I received my first diary. Recording my daily activities and thoughts became a labor of love for me and still continues to this day. Throughout those many decades, my passion for writing and telling a good story grew stronger as did my enjoyment of the process. But bringing a novel to a published book was a task that took me by surprise. It was a lot of work.

So, I would like to thank first and foremost my patient, attentive, and loving husband Tim, who encouraged me to never give up and who provided one of his beautiful watercolors to grace the cover of my book. Thanks also to my children and their spouses: Scott, Carly, Tim, Jen, Heather, Annie, Eric, and Michael, who hovered behind me when it was close to dinner or humored me on the phone as I worked through my plots and premises.

Of course, I could not forget my two writing groups who were there when no one else wanted to listen to the same words that I had written over and over, but only slightly different in arrangement or meaning:

The Monday, Tuesday Group That Meets on Friday: Anita, Joan, Barbara#1, Yvonne, Jerri, Pat, Nikole, Marie, Iris, and Carol.

Writers In Common: Dona, Marsha, Katrina, Jason, Debbie, Susan, and Barbara K.

Thank you to my early readers who caught the little details that I missed, like giving the same name to two of my minor characters. They are Heather, Sara, Charlotte, Barbara#1, Pat M., Ezra H. and Maryanne.

Last but not least, Nicola Burnell, who was my first mentor in writing and became my editor for *The Old Cape House*.

Thank you all for being there when I needed you.

ALSO BY BARBARA EPPICH STRUNA

The Old Cape Teapot (Historical Fiction) Nancy Caldwell returns in this second novel in a series of adventures. When she finds an old map on Antigua, it leads her on a journey across Cape Cod filled with danger and lost treasure.

Made in USA - Crawfordsville, IN
51415_9780997656602
04.06.2022 1820